When danger
Liane and Neille
they can trust,

BODYGUARDS

Keeping watch—day and night

Although born in England, **Sandra Field** has lived most of her life inCanada; she says the silence and emptiness of the north speaks to her particularly. While she enjoys travelling, and passing on her sense of a new place, she often chooses to write about the city which is now her home. She has been writing for Mills & Boon® since 1974 and has currently sold over fifteen million copies of her books, translated into more than 15 foreign languages. Sandra says, 'I write out of my experience; I have learned that love with its joys and its pains is all-important. I hope this knowledge enriches my writing, and touches a chord in you, the reader.'

"Sandra Field pens a phenomenal love story."
—*Romantic Times*

Elizabeth Oldfield's writing career started as a teenage hobby, when she had articles published. However, on her marriage the creative instinct was diverted into the production of a daughter and son. A decade later, when her husband's job took them to Singapore, she resumed writing and had her first romance accepted by Mills & Boon in 1982. She has written over 35 books and has currently sold nearly 15 million copies worldwide. Now hooked on the genre, she produces an average of three books a year. They live in London, and Elizabeth travels widely to authenticate the background of her books.

"Ms Oldfield dazzles her lucky readers."
—*Romantic Times*

TAKEN BY STORM
by
SANDRA FIELD

BODYCHECK
by
ELIZABETH OLDFIELD

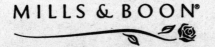
MILLS & BOON®

*MILLS & BOON and MILLS & BOON with the Rose Device
are registered trademarks of the publisher.*
Harlequin Mills & Boon Limited,
Eton House, 18-24 Paradise Road, Richmond, Surrey, TW9 1SR

Taken By Storm and *Bodycheck* were first published in
separate, single volumes by Mills & Boon Limited.
Taken By Storm in 1992 and *Bodycheck* in 1986

Taken By Storm © Sandra Field 1992
Bodycheck © Elizabeth Oldfield 1986

ISBN 0 263 80476 3

05-9707

*Printed and bound in Great Britain by
Caledonian International Book Manufacturing Ltd, Glasgow*

TAKEN BY STORM

by

SANDRA FIELD

For Dodie With Love

CHAPTER ONE

MONEY can do anything, Liane. Money can do anything at all.

Liane Daley leaned forward in the car seat, peering through the windscreen where the wipers swished back and forth, back and forth, in a rhythm that should have been soothing and was not. For it was not rain that the wiper-blades were clearing from her vision. It was snow. Small, thick, purposeful flakes of snow.

The snow had started falling that afternoon while she and her father had been talking in the formal living-room of his big house by the sea. Liane turned the heater-fan up another notch, her mouth twisting, for talk was a totally inadequate word to describe what had passed between her and Murray Hutchins behind doors carefully closed so that none of the servants would hear. Arguing would be a more accurate term. Although even arguing could not carry the full weight of that disastrous conversation that had ended with her father choleric and herself white-faced and terrified.

The word she used to describe that conversation did not really matter. By the time she had left Halifax two and a half hours ago it had been snowing heavily, and in ordinary circumstances she would never have set off on a journey that on the best of days could take five or six hours. But circumstances were not ordinary; no power on earth could have made her stay in that house.

So here she was a hundred miles from Halifax in the middle of the Wentworth Valley. She had skied here in her younger days on the slopes a few miles up the road.

It was a beautiful valley, with its rounded hills and its beech and maple groves. It was also an area notorious for heavy snowfalls and high winds, and right now Liane would have given everything she owned to be on the straight stretch of highway beyond the valley, heading for the border between Nova Scotia and New Brunswick. Heading for the ferry that would take her back to Prince Edward Island and home. Home, where Patrick was.

Her hands tightened unconsciously on the wheel. She could not afford to think about Patrick. Not now, when keeping the car on the road required every ounce of her concentration and skill.

The snow, which was dense and settling fast, had been rutted and grooved by the traffic, and her car was a small and venerable Volkswagen; if she got into the deep stuff, she would be in trouble. A big grey Chevrolet was ahead of her, and a nondescript dark blue car behind. She had been between these two vehicles for at least an hour, and had come to think of them as friends. Ahead of the Chevrolet was a four-wheel-drive wagon in a cheerful cherry-red. If she were driving that, she thought enviously, she wouldn't have a worry in the world.

The road had not been ploughed for at least an hour. The ruts were getting deeper by the minute, and, worse, the tracks worn by the tyres were greasy with ice. A salt-truck, Liane thought longingly. A big green salt-truck. Or a nice yellow snow-plough with its orange lights flashing. Either one would do. She wasn't fussy.

The back end of the Chevrolet swung wildly from side to side. Liane eased her foot off the accelerator. As the Chevrolet straightened, she saw a small beige car halfway in the ditch, its driver shovelling the mounds of snow from under the back wheels. The beige car was the size of hers; she bit her lip and increased her speed fractionally.

Even though she had directed all the heat on to the windscreen, the wipers were getting caked with ice, making smears in the glass. Tension banding her forehead, Liane hunched a little further over the wheel. Her feet were cold. But her feet would have to wait.

The digital clock on the dash flicked from six fifty-nine to seven o'clock. She was at least eighty miles from the ferry, and it was already getting dark. But at least it wasn't windy. The ferries would be running, and the flow of traffic from the ferry would carry her safely as far as the city of Charlottetown. She lived not far from there; she could surely manage the last few miles on her own.

The highway curved gently to the right, a high cliff looming on the far side. Then through the blurred white of the snow Liane saw the flash of yellow lights, and her heart lifted. The plough. Something being done to improve the atrocious condition of the road. Wonderful!

As quickly as they had risen, her spirits plummeted. The yellow lights were on two tow-trucks clustered around a transport truck that had jack-knifed into the ditch on the far side of the road, its cab leaning drunkenly against the granite face of the cliff. If a truck that size ever skidded towards her, she wouldn't stand a chance.

Nothing was going to happen, she told herself stoutly. As long as she followed the cherry-red wagon and the grey Chevrolet, she would be all right.

Her tyres whined on a patch of ice. The brake-lights gleamed on the red wagon, and the Chevrolet followed suit. Liane shifted to second gear, then down to first, as the cars ahead of her slowed to a virtual crawl. Ten kilometres an hour, she thought despairingly. She'd never get home at this rate. Oh, Patrick...

Money can do anything, Liane. Money can do anything at all.

The worst thing about her present situation was that she herself had instigated this second visit with her father. Of her own free will. From the best of motives. Two weeks ago, when she had read of her brother Howard's death in the newspapers, she had gone to the funeral, taking Patrick with her. Howard and she had never been close—eleven years older and a replica of her father, Howard had always kept his sister at arm's length—so she had gone to the funeral more for her father's sake than for her brother's. This visit today, which she had undertaken alone, had been motivated by compassion for the small, shrunken man her father had become, for the bewilderment she had glimpsed beneath his pathetic composure at the funeral service, for the shakiness of old limbs under the immaculately tailored black suit. She had expected to give comfort today, and had hoped to give love; the reality, however, had not turned out that way at all.

Abruptly she came back to the present. There were more lights ahead of her, flashing through the shifting curtain of snow—red and blue lights this time. Police cars had red and blue lights.

An accident?

Her stomach tightened. That would explain why the traffic had slowed so suddenly a few minutes ago. Praying no one had been hurt, she inched forward.

The brake-lights ahead of her snapped on again. The red wagon stopped. The Chevrolet pulled up behind it. Liane, gritting her teeth in mingled frustration and fear, also came to a halt.

Without the churning of packed snow between her wheels, the interior of the car seemed very quiet. The motor hummed away and the wipers swished across the glass. Then the driver of the Chevrolet got out of his car and walked towards the flashing lights of the police car. Liane sat still, paralysed by indecision. If there was an accident, there would be a delay, a prolonged delay; if not, then why were they stopped?

Pulling on her gloves, she left the engine running and got out of the car. The snowflakes brushed her face, catching on her lashes and melting on her forehead as she trudged through the snow towards the red wagon. She was wearing very impractical knee-high leather boots, bought three winters ago on sale and cherished ever since, and a hip-length wool jacket in rose-pink, also bought on sale; her entire outfit had been chosen to give her courage for the visit with her father rather than to protect her from the elements. Avoiding the deepest snow, feeling the cold air bite through her thin leather gloves, she passed the Chevrolet and saw a police officer in a bright orange coat standing in front of the red wagon. The driver of the wagon had rolled his window down to hear what the policeman was saying. The man from the Chevrolet was listening as well, his hands thrust in his pockets. To her infinite relief there did not appear to be any signs of an accident.

And then she heard what the police officer was saying. 'Road closed, sir. We've arranged temporary accommodation at a school just up the road. If you'd return to your vehicle, my colleague up ahead will direct you. Thank you, sir.'

'Damned nuisance,' the Chevrolet driver blustered. 'I've got an important meeting in Moncton.'

'The highway's closed between the border and Moncton, too,' the policeman said soothingly.

The man was not mollified. 'A school? What kind of accommodation's that?'

'Best we can do in the circumstances, sir. Some of the local women are organising a supper for you; you'll find it much more comfortable to stay there overnight than in your——'

Liane said blankly, *'Overnight?'*

'That's right, ma'am. The latest forecast is for the snow to continue until well past midnight, and we don't have enough ploughs to keep the road operable.'

'But I can't stay overnight!'

'I'm afraid there's no other choice.'

Patrick ...

'I can't! It's impossible.' Liane heard the edge of hysteria in her voice, and fought it down, the snow on her face and the chill in the air both forgotten in this greater peril. 'I have to get back to Prince Edward Island tonight——'

'Ferries aren't operating, ma'am. If you'd please return to your vehicle so we can keep the traffic moving here...'

Liane could see his face in the alternating flashes of red and blue light: a young man with blond hair doing his job in very difficult circumstances. 'Is there a telephone I can use?' she asked desperately. 'I have to get a message through; it's extremely important!'

'At the school, ma'am. Providing the lines are still in operation.'

From the red wagon behind Liane a clipped voice said, 'Young lady, would you kindly return to your car so the rest of us can get inside in the warm?'

Liane turned in her tracks, the intensity of her anger in direct proportion to the intensity of her fear. 'Would you kindly mind your own business?' she snapped.

'When you're holding up a whole line of traffic in a snowstorm, it is my business.'

In the blue light his hair was black, in the red light auburn. In either light he was the most attractive man she had ever seen, and she disliked him on sight. Her cheeks pink from more than the cold, she opened her mouth to retaliate, and heard the man from the Chevrolet bluster, 'Now that's no way to speak to a lady——'

The policeman said loudly, 'Please return to your vehicles immediately. Sir——' this to the driver of the wagon '—would you follow the other car, please?'

The driver of the wagon, not bothering to give Liane a second glance, rolled up his window and began edging towards the second police car, which was parked a little further along the road. Had Liane been wearing her old hiking boots, she might well have stamped her foot; as it was, she gave the red wagon a dirty look and marched back to her car, slamming the door hard after she had got in. Insufferable man! He'd had no right to speak to her like that, no right at all.

In a clash of gears she surged up the slope, her mouth set mutinously. Of course she had complained when she was suddenly told she was not allowed to proceed to her destination; it had been a perfectly natural reaction... And here her temper died, smothered by a flood of fear so strong that she forgot everything else: the interminable snowfall, the polite policeman, and the rude owner of the wagon. She would not get home tonight. She would, instead, be spending the night with a group of strangers in a country schoolhouse in the middle of a blizzard being fed soup and sandwiches by the local ladies. If her need to be at home were not so compelling, the situation would almost be funny.

The police car, lights still swirling in the gathering dusk, turned down a side-road which had been ploughed fairly recently, and which was flanked by spruce trees weighed down with snow, and by gaunt maples whose limbs touched fingers overhead. The road soon opened into a yard, in the middle of which was a one-storey white-shingled school. Its windows were decorated, rather optimistically, with paper cut-outs of scarlet tulips and yellow daffodils.

Liane parked beside the grey Chevrolet and shut off the ignition. A telephone, she thought numbly. I have

to get to a telephone. She reached in the back seat for
the small kit bag that she had used in the motel last night,
looped her handbag over her shoulder, and got out of
the Volkswagen just as the dark blue car parked beside
her. Its driver was one of those undistinguished men one
could pass in a crowd and never notice.

The second police officer, who looked even younger
than the first one, waited until a dozen or so cars had
trailed into the yard, then said matter-of-factly, 'Would
you follow me, please, ladies and gentlemen?'

Of the motley group huddled in the snow there were
only two other women, both attached to men who looked
like husbands; Liane was the only woman on her own.
She was glad in one way, for the last thing she felt like
was company and small talk, and most certainly she
could not share her fear with anyone. Yet, as she followed four or five of the others into the front door of
the school, she felt very much alone.

The school was warm, and smelled as schools always
did, of chalk and damp rubber boots and floor wax.
The policeman led them into an auditorium with a tiled
floor and a stage, flipped on the lights, waited until they
were all gathered there, then said, 'A farmer just up the
road should be along shortly with something hot to
eat... if you could see your way to pay him a small
amount, I'm sure it would be appreciated. There are bed-
rolls in the furthest classroom down the hall, and
blankets in the closet there. And we ask you not to smoke
inside, please.'

'Sounds like this has happened before,' said the more
jovial-looking husband.

'Every year, sir, at least once,' said the policeman with
a grin. 'This is a bad stretch of highway. No one else
will be joining you, because we also closed off the road
behind you a few miles back. You should be able to get
on your way by daylight tomorrow, say seven or so...one

of us will be here to advise you.' He paused enquiringly. 'Any questions?'

Trying to keep her voice level, Liane asked, 'Is there a telephone I can use?'

'There's a pay-phone down the hall, ma'am. Oh, and the toilets are to the right. Anything else?' He waited a moment, then saluted them with a cheery smile and left the auditorium, his boots clicking on the tiles.

The jovial man took charge. 'Why don't we go round the group with first names,' he suggested, 'seeing as how we're going to spend the night together? I'm Joe and this is my wife, Mabel.'

Mabel smiled self-consciously, plucking at the buttons on her plain wool coat. Liane said her name in turn. The driver of the Chevrolet, who had his eye on her already and would have to be handled firmly, was called Henry, while the undistinguished man who had parked next to her mumbled something that sounded like Chester. The owner of the red wagon, who proved to be just as attractive under fluorescent light as outdoors, and who did not look as though he wanted to be within ten feet of her, was named Jake.

Jake. The name suited him, she decided caustically. A very masculine name, brief and uncompromising.

Not that it mattered to her what his name was.

She excused herself and found the telephone, fumbling for a coin in her wallet. The phone was in working order; with a silent prayer of gratitude, she dialled the number, and waited for someone to answer.

'Hello?'

'Megan? It's Liane.'

'I'm *so* glad to hear from you; I was worried about you. We've got a foot of snow already, and more to come; why is it that the storms that aren't forecast are always the worst ones—are you all right?'

Pauses when Megan stopped for breath always had to be seized. 'I'm spending the night in a school in the Wentworth Valley,' Liane said. 'Megan——'

'How romantic! Any tall, dark strangers?'

'No,' said Liane, remembering how Jake's hair had shone black as a raven's wing under the fluorescent lights. 'Megan, will you keep a close eye on Patrick for me? Don't let him——'

'What a worrywort you are,' Megan interrupted fondly. 'I always keep an eye on him, you know that; we're playing checkers right now, and as usual he's beating me. He says he gets his brains from his mother, which hardly seems fair when you're so beautiful as well... What did you say?'

'I said may I speak to him?' Liane put in, feeling her lips curve in a smile. It was hard to feel terrified when talking to Megan.

'Of course you can... Patrick, it's your mother.'

The receiver changed hands. 'I've got four crowns already,' said Patrick. 'Megan's only got one.'

Liane swallowed hard, suddenly overcome by the sound of his voice, so well-known, so well-loved. Patrick was her vulnerable point, the chink in her armour; and how shrewdly her father had divined that.

'You there, Mum?'

'Yes, darling, I'm here... Patrick, I won't be home until tomorrow; I'm stuck in a schoolhouse because of the storm——'

'We got the afternoon off school, and me and Clancy made a launching pad in the snow for our rocket.'

Patrick's present career plan was to be an astronaut. Liane said carefully, 'Patrick, don't speak to any strangers, will you? Or take a ride from anyone you don't know.'

'You've told me all that stuff trillions of times, Mum.'

'Well, I'm telling you again,' she said, and heard the unaccustomed sharpness in her voice.

Patrick heard it, too. 'OK,' he agreed, sounding subdued.

'It's important, Patrick,' she insisted. 'I'll explain when I get home. What are you having for supper?'

'Tacos with jalapeno peppers,' he said enthusiastically, and began to describe the cookies Megan had made that afternoon.

Someone had carved a set of initials in the doorframe by the telephone; Liane traced them with her fingernail, not noticing the man who had come out of the auditorium to stand in the hallway only a few feet away from her. 'Darling,' she said finally, 'I've got to go; someone else might want the phone. Take care of yourself, won't you? And remember what I said... I love you, Patrick.'

'Me too,' replied Patrick, his standard reply ever since he had stopped being one of the little kids at primary school.

Liane rang off, and for a moment rested her forehead on the cold blue metal of the telephone. He would be all right until she got home. Of course he would be. Her father didn't know where she and Patrick lived. She had to hold on to that fact, and stop panicking.

'I'd like to use the telephone, if you don't mind.'

Liane jumped, knocking the receiver off the hook so that it banged against the wall; she had thought she was alone. Knowing who she was going to see, because she had recognised the voice, she slowly put the receiver back, trying to calm the inner trembling that had been with her ever since her father's ultimatum. Only when she thought she had herself under control did she turn.

Jake was standing not twenty feet from her. The hall was brightly lit, and she saw no reason to amend her initial impression that he was the most attractive man she had ever seen. Yet, despite the bright lights, she thought of him instantly as a man of darkness. Thoughtfully she let her eyes rove over him. Was it the jet-black hair, a little too long for current fashion? The deep-set eyes, so dark as to seem black as well? Or the faint stubble of beard, black against his tanned skin? Even his tan was too dark for a Canadian winter.

It was none of those things, she decided. It had more to do with his stillness as he waited—the stillness of the hunter waiting for its prey, and with the guardedness of his eyes—eyes that could keep any number of secrets, and keep them well. His height, the breadth of his shoulders, she saw and dismissed. It was the paradoxical blend of looseness and tension in his body that held her attention. He was, she was quite sure, in superb condition.

'The telephone,' he repeated with rather overdone patience.

Liane flushed, aware that she had been staring at him in a way she never ordinarily stared at a man. But if she had been staring at him, so had he at her. He would have seen her rose-pink jacket, she thought, and the matching angora sweater, its neckline hugging her throat, her pencil-slim grey skirt and polished brown boots, the soft fall of her blonde hair over her collar. These were obvious to any observer. But would he have discerned the wariness in her blue eyes, the withholding that so often characterised her dealings with the opposite sex? And would he pick up the anxiety that was shivering along every nerve in her body?

She said, holding his gaze with her own, and not allowing even a trace of sarcasm to show in her voice, 'Thank you for waiting.'

He took a couple of paces towards her. 'You get under my skin, you know that?'

'You make it fairly obvious.'

'I'm not usually so lacking in subtlety.'

'I'm sure you're not,' she retorted drily.

'It's not just that you're beautiful,' he said in a voice without a trace of emotion. 'Lots of men must have told you that, and I never did like being one of the crowd.' He paused, scrutinising her as if she were a specimen on a tray. 'You look so goddamn fragile with those big blue eyes of yours...you've got that air of helpless, appealing femininity down to a fine art, haven't you? Most men fall for it, of course—I'm sure it's a very valuable commodity.'

Her eyes sparking with fury, Liane snapped, 'Are you implying that I'm trying to attract *your* attention?'

'Not necessarily mine.'

'Oh, so any man will do?' She gave a sudden snort of laughter. 'I hate to ruin your theory, but you're way off base.' Then she paused, raising her brows with gentle irony. 'For someone who was in a hurry for the phone, you're spending rather a lot of time talking to a woman it's clear you detest. Are you sure you're not trying to attract *my* attention?'

'Who's Patrick?' Jake said abruptly.

Liane paled, her voice like a whiplash. 'How do you know about Patrick?'

The dark eyes gleamed at her quizzically. 'You told him you loved him not two minutes ago.'

'Oh...of course.' Liane rubbed her forehead with fingers that were unsteady, realising once again how deeply off balance she was. She said flatly, 'Patrick is not, and never will be, any concern of yours.'

'That's quite an act—the trembling fingers, the pale cheeks...very clever.'

With total honesty, and with the flood of energy that such honesty usually brought, Liane said, 'I don't like you! I don't like you at all.'

'So perhaps we'd better agree on mutual dislike, and stay out of each other's way for the next twelve hours?'

'That seems like a fine idea to me,' Liane agreed vigorously. 'The smartest thing you've said so far.'

Jake took another few steps towards her, close enough for her to see that his hair was shiningly clean, curling around his ears. Well-shaped ears, Liane thought, she who never normally noticed a man's ears. 'So you don't think I'm very smart?' he said smoothly.

Suddenly wishing Mabel or Chester or even Henry would appear, Liane replied, 'You've stereotyped me from the first minute you saw me—admit it! The helpless little woman, the typical dumb blonde.'

He favoured her with a wolfish grin. 'Not quite typical, my dear.'

She didn't know which infuriated her more—his smile or his endearment. She did realise that her hands were no longer trembling and that her nerves seemed to have settled down. So unwittingly he was doing her a favour, this black-haired man who hated blondes. And how often, she thought wryly, did one have the chance to be as blatantly rude as she was about to be? She said crisply, 'Let's get a couple of things straight. I was born female with blonde hair and blue eyes, and my genes dictated that I stopped growing at five-foot-five—not much I can do about any of that. So if you have a problem with the way I look, that's *your* problem. Not mine. Secondly, I hope that when you deign to favour a woman with your attention you choose a redhead or a brunette. For her sake, poor thing.' She smiled at him sweetly. 'Now perhaps you'd better make your phone call...you wouldn't want to keep her waiting, would you?'

His grin this time was frankly appreciative. 'Did I say helpless? I take it back. You're as helpless as a barracuda.'

If she had thought him attractive before, his smile made him nigh on irresistible. Which, Liane thought crossly, he no doubt knew. It was time—past time—she got out of here. She said coldly, 'We're descending to the level of childish insult,' and stalked past him.

Or at least that was her plan. But Jake, in a gesture so swift that she didn't even see it, grabbed her by the sleeve of her jacket and said, 'Trading insults is rather exhilarating, wouldn't you agree? If we'd met at a cocktail party we'd be making civilised small talk, and we'd both be bored to tears.'

Liane was not sure it would be possible to be bored in the same room with this man, although she was not about to tell him that. 'Trading insults would pall just as quickly,' she asserted, and reached down to pluck his hand from her sleeve.

His fingers were warm and lean and very strong, gripping her jacket tenaciously. Her own looked slim and—yes—very feminine resting over his. She said sharply, 'Please let go.'

'When I'm ready.'

Any pleasure in the exchange was gone. Drawing on every ounce of her self-control, Liane told him evenly, 'You have two choices. You can let go, or I'll scream my head off, which will bring Joe, Chester and the rest to the rescue, and surely cause you at least minimal embarrassment.'

Jake dropped her arm immediately, his eyes trained on her face. 'Three choices,' he said. 'I could have prevented you from screaming.'

Liane felt a shudder of animal fear course along her nerves. Jake could have prevented her, she was sure of it. Her mind flinching from the means he might have used, she stepped back and said with as much dignity as she could muster, 'I don't want anything more to do with you—so kindly stay away from me.'

'My pleasure,' he responded with another of those predatory smiles.

Wishing she could have had the last word, Liane turned on her heel and hurried back towards the auditorium. The girls' toilet was just beyond it; she went inside, hearing the door swing shut behind her, and thankfully found herself alone. The mirror over one of the institutional white sinks showed her blue eyes that were undoubtedly big, and a bone-structure undeniably fragile. She also looked exhausted.

After seven o'clock tomorrow morning she would never need see Jake again. Drawing several deep breaths, something she always found calming, she washed her hands with the strong-smelling liquid green soap and dried them on a paper towel. Then she went back to the auditorium.

In her absence Joe and two of the other men had set up long tables along the wall, and through the door at the far end a couple of men were carrying large aluminium saucepans. Liane went to help, and was sent to the staffroom for bowls and cutlery. The activity was soothing, and, when they all gathered several minutes later around one of the tables for soup and sandwiches, there was definitely the air of a picnic. The soup—chicken and vegetable—was delicious, Jake was sitting at the far end of the table from Liane, and she had not eaten since breakfast. She tucked in, chatting to Mabel on one side and being careful not to be too friendly to Henry on her other.

Her enjoyment was augmented when she heard Jake mention that all the airports in Nova Scotia and Prince Edward Island were closed. So her father's hands were tied; he could do nothing while the storm lasted. Patrick was, for now, safe. The other thing she learned during the meal was that Jake was on his way back to Ottawa, having been visiting friends in Halifax. Ottawa was hundreds of miles from the little village of Hilldale in

Prince Edward Island. Just as well, she thought, and accepted another helping of soup.

After the meal, in which they demolished mounds of sandwiches as well as three raisin pies, Liane helped clean up the dishes while the men dragged in bed-rolls and arranged them on the floor. An impromptu card game then started. Liane joined in; she had an excellent memory and a mathematical sense of the odds of playing a certain card, both of which she had bequeathed to her son. The contest started mildly enough with hearts, then moved to poker. As the pile of pennies accumulated in front of her, Liane was aware of Jake watching her, his expression inscrutable.

That would show him, she thought wickedly. Dumb blonde, indeed!

By eleven o'clock everyone was settling down for the night, sharing what blankets they had. Liane had elected to stay in her clothes, because she had not brought a housecoat and her nightgown was made of pale blue satin, which did not seem very appropriate for the floor of an auditorium. Not to mention Henry, who had already made several heavy-handed and suggestive remarks in the course of the card game.

She used her jacket as a pillow, and wrapped the rather musty blanket that Joe had found in one of the cupboards around her legs. The only light came from the tall poles outside the school. Closing her eyes, and blanking her father, Patrick, and Jake from her mind, Liane fell asleep.

CHAPTER TWO

IT WAS dark when Liane woke. Her legs were cold, and her neck cramped by the bulk of her jacket; Joe, on her right side, was snoring energetically. She lay still, remembering all that had happened the day before, wondering if it was still snowing, already worrying whether the ferries would be running.

They had to be, she thought. She had to get home.

Money can do anything, Liane. Money can do anything at all.

Clenching her fingers into fists, she closed her eyes again, desperate for the oblivion that sleep brought. But she could not shut out her father's voice any more than she could control the black thoughts that the middle of the night could foster so easily.

Her father wanted Patrick.

Her father was a rich man, used to getting his own way, used to buying people as easily as if they were the possessions with which he surrounded himself. He would not allow his daughter, his only remaining child, to thwart him. Sooner or later he would find out that she and Patrick lived by the Hillsborough River on an estate that belonged to Alma and George Forster. And then what would he do?

He would take Patrick. She knew he would. He had as much as said he would.

What in God's name could she do?

She spread her jacket over her feet and rested her cheek on her arm, staring into the darkness, feeling more alone than she ever had in her life. She had to fight. With every weapon at her command she had to try to outwit Murray Hutchins. Because Patrick deserved better than the kind of upbringing she had had.

But her father had money. He could hire lawyers to blacken her character, make her seem an unfit mother for a young boy—that was one of the threats he had hurled at her yesterday after he had lost his temper with her. He had a great deal of money, and the power that money brought. She had neither.

Liane turned over on her other side, pulling the blanket to her chin. Resolutely she closed her eyes, determined to sleep, for she would need all her strength for the day ahead. But her shoulders began to itch in the angora sweater, while her toes, despite her jacket, remained ice-cold. And she was thirsty.

Against her will, her thoughts marched on. The worst thing about yesterday's visit was not that she had insti-gated it herself, but that she had been reduced to the status of a child again. She was twenty-seven years old, and in the eight years since she had fled her father's house she had borne a son and made a way in the world for the two of them. Yet three-quarters of an hour with Murray Hutchins had pushed those years aside. She had felt like a five-year-old, his fierce blue eyes and gravelly voice awakening memories of long-ago rages for mis-demeanours she had since forgotten.

She had hated feeling like that terrified little girl.

Liane curled her toes into the warmth of her jacket. For ten more interminable minutes she wooed sleep, during which time Joe stopped snoring, Henry started, and a snow-plough rattled past the school, turned around and rattled back again. She waited two or three more minutes to see if anyone else had woken up, then very quietly got out of bed. Padding on her stockinged feet out of the auditorium, she went to the toilet, where she splashed cold water on her face and drank deeply from the tap.

She was wide awake. Leaving the toilet, she crept down the hallway to the furthest classroom, which was decorated with coloured cut-outs of snowmen and skiers, and whose desks obviously belonged to very small children. Obscurely comforted by the clutter, which reminded her of Patrick's bedroom in the loft at home, Liane perched herself on top of the desk nearest the window, rested her elbows on her knees, and gazed out into the darkness.

A few tiny snowflakes were drifting past the rectangular panes. The radiators gurgled and groaned. Otherwise the world was silent, and she alone in it. Alone, and not knowing what to do.

She tried to think, to assess her options logically. She could stay in the house she and Patrick had shared for the last three years, and assume her father would not have the nerve to kidnap his only grandchild. She could hire a lawyer, lay the whole story in front of him and count on the law to protect her. Or she could leave the house and go into hiding...but where, and how? Patrick had to go to school and she had to work, so how could she hide? Besides which Patrick loved living in their wing of the big brick house, and needed the stability of the life Liane had been able to build for him. For Patrick had no father of his own...

There was very little she could do, Liane thought, feeling panic nibble at her control. Her father held all the high cards; her hand was virtually worthless.

But if she did nothing her father would take Patrick. He had always taken what he wanted.

Round and round her thoughts chased each other. She could move to Toronto and lose herself among the crowds; but she could not afford to live in Toronto. She could move in with Megan, Fitz, and the boys, but she could not stay there forever, and her father could afford to wait. She could get a very large dog and leave it loose to wander the grounds.

That seemed the best idea yet. Greatly cheered by a mental image of her father being chased by a slavering Great Dane, she gazed out of the window, and in the reflection she saw someone move into the doorway behind her.

Stifling a shriek of alarm, Liane swivelled on the desk and saw that it was Henry. Not Jake. Not sure whether she was relieved or disappointed, and not wanting to dwell on either of these responses, she pulled her skirt down over her knees and said, 'The snow-plough woke me—but I was just about to go back to bed.'

Henry was somewhat overweight, and rolled from side to side like a dory on a swell as he navigated the aisle between the desks, ending up too close to Liane for her own comfort. He said breezily, 'You look as though you've got the cares of the world on your shoulders—a pretty little thing like you... what's the trouble—hubby pulling a fast one on you?'

Were life so simple... Liane thought ironically. A wandering husband she could cope with. She said coldly, 'I don't have a husband,' and slid down from the desk.

It was a tactical error. Henry loomed over her. 'No husband, eh?' he said with a laugh that was meant to be convivial and sounded merely coarse. 'Then I can fix what's ailing you.' He reached for her with a hand like a bear's paw.

Liane was young and agile. She ducked, slid between two desks and, with her knee, shoved one of them in Henry's way. 'I do not need fixing, as you so crudely phrase it,' she seethed. 'Neither do I need a husband, thank you very much. And if you so much as put a hand on me I'll smash this desk over your head!'

In an injured voice Henry said, 'Now that's no way——'

From the doorway someone laughed, a deep belly-laugh of genuine appreciation. 'I think she means it, Henry,' Jake said. 'If I were you, I'd go back to bed.'

Laughter still lingered on his words. Nevertheless, Henry, after muttering something very rude under his breath, made a bee-line for the door. Jake stood aside with a mocking grin, and watched Henry's no doubt rapid progress down the hall. Then he said to Liane, 'A midnight tryst? Did you think the better of it when the time came to deliver?'

Liane replied trenchantly, 'I wouldn't have expected *you* to interpret that charming little scene in any other way—it would have to be me who lured him in here with my big blue eyes, wouldn't it? It couldn't possibly be the man who was at fault.'

Jake sauntered into the room, his hands in the pockets of his well-cut trousers, his bulky wool sweater making his shoulders look broader than they were. 'Henry's a wealthy man, and recently widowed. He surely shared that little snippet of information with you?'

'I didn't give him time,' Liane replied pithily. 'And, believe me, wealth would not recommend him to me.' She put her head to one side, fluttered her lashes, which were long and thick and one of her better points, and discovered to her surprise that she was enjoying herself. 'So, besides being a helpless clinging vine, I'm also a ruthless gold-digger? Quite a combination.'

'Money is a very useful commodity.'

'Indeed it is. But not so useful that I would contemplate even for a moment allowing the likes of Henry to maul me.'

'Bigger game in mind?' asked Jake.

He was standing with one row of desks between her and him. Plenty close, thought Liane, watching the shadows slant across his face. 'The only game I play is poker,' she said.

'And that extremely well.' He stepped over the desks so that he was between her and the door. 'A poker-face is a bit of a cliché, isn't it? Yet you've obviously trained yourself to keep your thoughts hidden...I wonder why?'

Struggling very hard to maintain the inscrutability he was describing, Liane suggested pleasantly, 'To keep men as inquisitive as you guessing, perhaps?'

He gave a reluctant smile. 'You have an answer for everything, don't you? So if you didn't entice Henry in here with dalliance in mind, why *are* you gazing out of the window at a view that's less than inspiring at——' he checked his watch '—three in the morning? Anyone with a clear conscience would surely be asleep.'

'So what's on your conscience, Jake?'

This time he laughed outright. 'I left myself wide open for that one, didn't I? I saw you leave the auditorium, and then a few minutes later I saw Henry go after you... Put it down to simple curiosity.'

'I don't think anything's simple with you,' Liane said, and wondered where that knowledge came from.

Jake said very softly, 'You're a witch, do you know that?'

She took a deep breath, not sure she could trust herself to speak. If she was a witch he was the demon king, she thought fancifully, with his black hair and his black eyes and the sheer power of his presence. For she was aware of him through every pore in her body, in a way she did not care for at all. In a way that was both unique and frightening. She said steadily, feeling the edge of the desk press against the back of her thighs, 'I'm neither witch nor gold-digger, nor clinging vine, Jake. Just an ordinary woman. That's all.'

His eyes trained on her face, he observed, 'An ordinary woman who happens to be scared out of her wits—what are you so afraid of, Liane?'

'I'm not!' Involuntarily she moved back; the legs of
the desk scraped on the floor.

'Yes, you are. You have been ever since you talked to
the police officer who was directing the traffic yesterday.
What have you done to make you so afraid?'

'Oh, it would have to be something I've done, wouldn't
it?' she said bitterly. 'That's the way your mind works.'

'That's right...so who are you running from? Why
don't you tell me? Maybe I can help.'

For a wild moment she was tempted to pour out all
her troubles, to see if indeed there was some way he could
help; for she needed help—she knew that. She could not
fight her father alone; she had never been able to.
Swallowing hard, she told him in a stony voice, 'Your
imagination's working overtime. I was upset because the
roads were so bad; I've always hated driving in snow.'

Jake said calmly, 'You're lying.'

Quite suddenly Liane lost her temper. In an exhilarating flood of energy she snapped, 'Yes, I'm lying. Very
clever of you, Jake, congratulations! What do you do
for an encore?'

'This,' he said, then took her in his arms, and kissed
her.

It was a hard kiss, fuelled by anger; it was also brief
to the point of insult. Frozen by surprise, Liane stood
stock still as he released her, and said the first thing that
came into her mind. 'You use the same aftershave as my
father.'

'But not the same as Patrick?'

'Oh, no,' she said, 'not the same as Patrick.'

She scowled at him, remembering the bite of his fingers
through her sweater and the rasp of his beard on her
chin. 'You and Henry are birds of a feather—I'm not
the slightest bit flattered by the attentions of either one
of you.'

She had known Jake would not like being bracketed with Henry; nor did he. She also knew a scathing retort was on the tip of his tongue, and braced herself. But instead he kept silent, regarding her unsmilingly, his mouth a forbidding line in a face carved to stillness. When she was sure she could not stand the silence a moment longer, he said in a voice from which any emotion had been removed, 'I apologise for kissing you. I had no right to do that.'

Liane's jaw dropped. 'I have never in my life met anyone as disconcerting as you!' she exclaimed. 'And that's the plain truth.'

He gave her a crooked smile. 'I believe you. So is my apology accepted?'

'Would it matter to you either way?'

'Enough that I'm asking.'

She said slowly, 'Yes, it's accepted.'

'Good. Why were you so scared yesterday, Liane?'

In her stockinged feet Liane was considerably shorter than he. She gazed up at him, again visited by the urge to share the terror lurking in her heart like a coiled snake, yet at the same time knowing how impossible it was that she tell her story to a complete stranger. 'I can't tell you, Jake,' she said honestly. 'I can't . . . I'm sorry.'

In the dim light of the classroom her eyes were clear and candid. The man made a gesture of frustration that he halted in mid-air. 'You don't trust me.'

'How could I? I don't know you. And you've made it very clear you don't like me.'

'Yeah . . .' For a minute he hesitated, as though considering what to do next. Then he said, clipping off the words, 'You'd better go back to bed. I have a feeling the police are going to arrive at daybreak to hustle us out of here before school starts.'

Liane felt a strange, and very strong, pang of loss. Tomorrow this dark-browed stranger would go his way

and she would go hers, and they would never meet again.
She was quite sure he didn't like her, equally sure he had
meant his offer of help. Perplexed, she murmured, 'I
guess you're right . . . do you realise I don't even know
your last name?'

'Brande. Jacob Brande. Spelled with an "e".'

Seven years ago, when Patrick was born, Liane had
legally changed her surname to her mother's maiden
name. 'Liane Daley,' she replied formally.

'Miss?' he asked.

For Patrick's sake she went by Ms, which left open
the question of her marital status. 'I've never been
married,' she said.

'You must have been asked. Didn't any of them have
enough money?'

She replied inelegantly, 'Stuff it, Jake—we women
aren't all gold-diggers.'

'Bed, Miss Daley.'

She could have argued; she could have prolonged this
peculiar conversation in the middle of the night in a
country schoolhouse. But what was the point? Despite
the emotion that crackled between them, an emotion as
strong as it was negative, she and Jake had nothing to
say to each other. No shared past and no possible future.
Only a present, as inconclusive as it had been, oddly
enough, enlivening.

'Goodnight,' she said, and found herself holding out
her hand.

Jake took it in his, pressed it firmly, and released it.
'Goodnight, Liane.'

She had liked the strength of his grip, the smoothness
of his palm against hers. Unaware of how her features
were revealing her inner confusion, she turned away from
him and hurried down the aisle, her feet whispering on
the tiled floor.

The auditorium contained the same array of humped bodies, Henry with his back ostentatiously turned to her. Joe was snoring again. Liane lay down, fully intending to analyse what had transpired between her and Jake Brande, and woke to hear Mabel calling her name. 'Time to get up, dear; the road's open and the storm's over... Did you have a good rest?'

Liane sat up, rubbing her eyes. She had been dreaming, one of those horrible dreams where you knew you could never run fast enough to escape your pursuer; she felt exactly like someone who had had five hours' sleep, and the prospect of the day ahead made her want to bury her head in her jacket and pretend the rest of the world did not exist. 'Fine,' she croaked.

'That's good,' said Jake.

Liane winced. He was standing not ten feet from her, eyeing her sardonically. She blushed, wondering if he had been watching her sleep, wondering if the way he had kissed her was as fresh in his mind as it was in hers. She scrambled to her feet, showing rather a lot of leg as she did so, and pushed her hair back from her face, knowing from long experience that there would be blue shadows under her eyes, for her skin was too fair to hide the marks of a sleepless night. He, of course, looked fit and wide awake, newly shaven, his hair gleaming under the lights. Not even a cut on his chin, she thought sourly. The man was inhuman.

She bent to get her toothbrush out of her overnight bag, and heard him say softly, for her ears alone, 'A witch, a gold-digger, and a grump in the mornings.'

Aware that she was being thoroughly bitchy, and not in the least repentant, Liane retorted, 'I hope you've never married, Jake Brande—think of the poor woman who'd have the gargantuan task of living up to you. Perfection is so difficult to emulate.'

'So your tongue's just as sharp first thing in the morning,' he observed amiably. 'Why don't you go and wash your face? You'll both feel and look better.'

There was a gleam of amusement in the black eyes. Liane fought back a smile, glad that her son was not here to listen to this undignified exchange—an exchange for which she would have chided him, and said ingenuously, 'I could hardly feel worse—I've never been a morning person; I don't start to wake up for another two hours.' Then, wondering what had possessed her to share this piece of rather personal information with a man who disliked her, she hurried to the toilets.

Hot water, a liberal application of make-up and a hairbrush made her look a great deal better. And Jake *had* called her beautiful. Wishing she could deal as easily with the knot of tension in her stomach as she could with her face, Liane went back to gather up her things. The bed-rolls had been stashed away, and only a few of her fellow travellers were left.

Jake was nowhere to be seen.

Neither, on the plus side, was Henry.

Mabel bade her a hasty farewell. 'Joe's in a hurry to get his first coffee of the day... fun, wasn't it, dear? Stay between the ditches, now.' And she laughed heartily at her own wit.

Liane pulled on her jacket and zipped up her bag. Her car keys in her hand, she left the auditorium and headed outside. The cherry-red wagon was gone.

He had not even said goodbye.

Her shoulders slumped, she unlocked her car. Before she could move she had to shovel behind the back wheels and clear off the front and back windscreens; her thin leather gloves and her boots were not improved by either task. Nor was her temper. He could at least have said goodbye. Or did he make a habit of kissing women at three in the morning—women he didn't even like? But, if he didn't like her, why was she so upset that he had left without bothering to speak to her?

He'd be adding feminine illogicality to her list of bad traits, she thought petulantly, slamming her door with unnecessary force.

Her own stormy blue eyes glared back at her in the rear-view mirror. If Jake didn't like women, it was equally true that she didn't like men. She certainly didn't trust them. So what was all the fuss about?

It was an unanswerable question. Dimly aware that the inoffensive Chester was scraping the ice from his window a few feet away, she waved goodbye and backed out of her parking space. The sooner she got on the road and forgot about Jake Brande the better.

It was a beautiful day—the kind popularised by calendars and postcards. The sun was rising pale gold in a clear blue sky. The trees cast long purple shadows on the snow, where each branch was etched with the clarity of an Oriental print. The snow itself lay deep and smooth, simplifying the blinding whiteness of the landscape to a series of rounded curves.

Liane pulled on to the highway between tall banks of snow that the plough had left. Mabel and Joe were already out of sight. She moved up a gear, getting the feel of the road, which had been salted as well as ploughed, and trying at the same time to settle her mind for the day ahead. She'd stop at a restaurant and get some coffee and toast, then she'd drive as fast as she could for the ferry.

The first restaurant she came to had a car she recognised as Joe's parked outside, but no red wagon. Liane kept going. The second restaurant, attached to a petrol station, boasted a half-ton truck and a Cadillac. She could not—would not—pursue Jake any further. Her mouth set, Liane pulled in between the two vehicles and got out of her car. From the front seat of the Cadillac a primped little poodle wearing a pink satin bow on its collar barked at her hysterically. She pulled a horrible face at it and went inside.

Coffee and two very good home-made doughnuts made Liane feel much better. Half an hour later she was on her way again. She had to drive carefully because there were big patches of slush on the road, and she continually had to be washing the salt from her windscreen; but the miles slowly accumulated, and by ten past nine she had left Nova Scotia and was taking the turn-off to the ferry. The countryside was now level and open, with farmhouses scattered here and there. The sun was convincingly warm through the car windows, and soon she would be home. Even the thought of her own four walls gave Liane confidence. She would figure out a way to deal with her father. Maybe she would have to alert all the neighbours, get a lawyer, and buy the Great Dane— all three strategies at once. Certainly she would have to tell Patrick what had transpired in his grandfather's house.

The miles ticked by. The road was flat and very straight, and her terror of the night before began to seem an exaggeration, exactly the kind of reaction her father had counted on. This time she wouldn't play, she thought fiercely. This time he had the wrong woman.

A bus roared towards her, slopping wet snow across the glass in front of her eyes. She blinked, turning on the wipers and watching the bus recede in her rear-view mirror. Then her hands suddenly tightened on the wheel and the car swerved. There was a small red dot on the far horizon, following her.

Jake?

You're imagining things, Liane, she scolded herself. There are lots of red cars, any number of which could be heading for the ferry. A red vehicle does not have to belong to Jake. Anyway, Jake left ahead of you. Jake's probably halfway to Montreal by now.

The red dot was far enough behind that she could not distinguish whether it was a car or a wagon. Biting her lip, angry with herself that she could even care whether Jake was following her, she slackened her speed. She was climbing a long, gradual incline; once she was on the other side, and out of sight of the red vehicle, she'd slow right down and let it catch up.

Why, Liane? Why do you have to know whether it's Jake? What's Jake to you?

I'm interested, that's all. He's a very attractive man with whom—in one sense—I spent the night.

He didn't bother to say goodbye, though.

Scowling ferociously, Liane reached the top of the slope and started down the other side, and in a few moments the road behind her dropped out of sight. She then slipped back to third gear and coasted down the hill, feeling her heartbeat quicken in her breast and her knuckles whiten on the wheel.

With excruciating slowness the digital clock on her dashboard counted off the seconds. Then, in her rear-view mirror, she saw a cherry-red wagon come over the hill. She would have recognised it anywhere. It was Jake's.

She speeded up again, and wondered if it was her imagination that the wagon had braked at the crest of the hill when the driver had seen her. And why was Jake coming to Prince Edward Island? In the summer, attracted by its miles of beaches, visitors inundated the island. But not in the winter. And last night he had told everyone he was on his way back to Ottawa.

He wants to see you again, Liane. That's why he didn't say goodbye.

Don't be silly! I outgrew Cinderella years ago.

She accelerated gradually. The wagon made no effort to catch up with her, maintaining the same distance between them. Realising that she was smiling to herself, an idiotic smile she would have found difficult to erase or explain, Liane turned on the radio and began to sing along with Anne Murray's latest release.

The Northumberland Strait came into sight, its steel-blue water patched with drift ice. When she reached Cape Tormentine, the red wagon pulled in at a petrol station and parked by the pumps. Liane kept going, for where else would Jake be headed but for the ferry? She stopped at the toll booth, paid her ten dollars, and proceeded to the row of parked vehicles. Three other cars drove in behind her before the red wagon came into sight in her mirror and took its place in the line.

There was a twenty-minute wait for the next crossing. Liane stayed in her car, wondering what Jake would do.

He did nothing.

Ten minutes later the loudspeaker announced the boarding of the ferry, and the first vehicles started off for the loading-ramps. Keeping her place in the line, Liane accelerated up the slope, then heard the hum of metal beneath her tyres as she drove on to the upper deck of the boat. Obeying the traffic director, she parked in the inner lane. From experience she knew that drivers were not permitted to remain in their cars for the crossing; Jake would have to make a move. Checking her make-up in the mirror and smoothing on fresh lipstick, she wondered what he would say to her.

A dark blue car passed her, starting a new line of vehicles to her left. She instantly recognised the driver, for he too had spent the night in the school. Chester. A man as nondescript as his car.

With a pang of sheer terror Liane suddenly grabbed at the steering-wheel, and the tube of lipstick fell into her lap. Jake behind her. Chester ahead of her. It could not be coincidence.

Either or both had been following her ever since she had left her father's yesterday afternoon. Either or both must be in her father's pay.

What a fool she had been! It was totally logical that her father would have her followed. It was the obvious thing for him to do, because it was by far the easiest way for him to find out where she was living. Keep a safe distance behind her and let her lead them to the place she called home. Let her betray her own whereabouts—her father would like that. And also, of course, the whereabouts of Patrick, the place he too called home.

She had almost fallen into the trap.

Either or both, she thought numbly. Jake in her father's pay? Or Chester? Or both? How could she know?

She couldn't.

She couldn't trust either one.

CHAPTER THREE

CHESTER was getting out of his car, hunching his neck into the collar of his coat against the wind that was whistling across the open deck. Or was that his motive? Liane wondered, watching him with wide eyes. Maybe he was hunching down to hide from her. The traffic warden had inadvertently made him park in a place she could scarcely fail to see him, so now he was doing his best to be unobtrusive.

Was that why Jake had made no effort to catch up with her, or to talk to her in the ferry car park? He didn't need to. He had her in his sights, he knew where she would be for the next hour. He therefore had no need to talk to her.

For much the same reasons he had not needed to say goodbye to her at the school this morning.

To the tension lying like a lump of stone in her belly she now added pain. For she and Jake had connected. Something—an emotional charge, an attraction neither had been willing to acknowledge, let alone act upon— had happened between them. Something real. And now she was faced with the very strong possibility that Jake was in her father's pay.

As her thoughts carried her inexorably forward, Liane slumped down further in her seat, wondering if she could get away with disobeying the injunction to leave her car. Jake seemed a much more likely suspect than Chester. For Jake was dangerous—she had recognised that immediately. Far more dangerous than the inoffensive Chester. Had Jake not wanted her to scream last night, she would not have screamed; and he would not have been fussy about his methods.

The traffic director tapped on her window, his bright orange jacket flapping in the wind. 'We ask the passengers not to stay in their vehicles, please, miss,' he said.

He looked large and solid and safe. She wondered what he would say were she to tell him why she wanted to stay in her car. He'd probably have her committed for paranoid delusions, she thought wryly, and smiled up at him. 'I'll be right out,' she said.

She picked up her lipstick, put it back in her handbag, pulled on her gloves, and got out of the car. Although the wind was bitingly cold, keen with the knife-sharp tang of the sea, she walked over to the railing and stood there for a moment, watching the slush of ice particles undulate on the swell, the lamenting of the grey and white gulls like a dirge in her ears. What was she going to do? She could not possibly drive straight home, leading Chester and Jake to the place where she lived. Leading them to Patrick.

The engines began to rumble and the deck shook as if it had the ague, as, in a swirl of foam, the ferry edged away from the dock. Gulls rose, screeching, from the breakwater. The wind sliced through Liane's jacket and reddened her cheeks. What she could not do, she decided ruefully, was stay on deck for the next forty-five minutes.

She went downstairs and joined the queue at the canteen, ordering a muffin, an egg and coffee. When she had paid for the food, she picked up her tray. Jake was sitting at a window table. He raised a hand in casual salute, and indicated the empty seat across from him.

It was his very casualness that angered Liane the most. She shot him a fulminating glance, and carried the tray to a booth on the opposite side of the room. Chester was nowhere in sight.

The window was streaked with salt; through it she watched the shoreline recede as she munched on her muffin.

An all-too-familiar voice remarked, 'It's past ten o'clock—or are you a grump until noon?' Then, without asking her permission, Jake sat down opposite her.

Although his voice had had a trace of amusement in it, his eyes had none. His eyes, which had seemed black in the middle of the night, were actually a very dark brown, the peat-brown of a bog, full of unknown depths and hidden dangers. Liane said evenly, 'Jake, I don't want to sit with you. Will you please leave?'

'What's happened between three in the morning and now?' he asked. 'You weren't in any hurry to get rid of me then.'

She looked at him in silence, seeing other details that had escaped her in the half-light. His lashes were as long as hers, and as black as his hair; there was a small white scar over one cheekbone. She had thought him honest, she realised painfully. Honest in his dislike of her, honest in the sparring they had indulged in. But it had not been honest at all. He was her father's henchman. And as if to emphasise the distance between them, to her nostrils drifted the scent of his aftershave.

'Say something, Liane—because you're still running scared, I can tell.'

That he should openly allude to a fear whose cause he knew very well, and was contributing to, filled her with ice-cold rage. Yet could she afford to let him know that she had guessed why he was following her? That she was wise to his game? Poker-face, she warned herself. Better to lie low rather than alert him that she would be using every ounce of her intelligence to evade him once they were off the ferry. With an almost superhuman effort she swallowed her rage and said with cool precision, 'I thought you were very rude to leave the school without saying goodbye. I place a high premium on good manners.'

Jake leaned back in his seat. 'I knew I'd be seeing you again.'

Every sense alert, Liane regarded him through narrowed eyes. Was he about to throw his hand openly on the table? 'And how did you know that?'

His smile was lazy, full of assurance. 'You need help. I've got some spare time—I don't have to be back in Ottawa right away. So I followed you.'

'You weren't behind me when I stopped for coffee,' she flashed.

'You've got a PEI licence plate, and you told the police officer last night you had to get back to the island. I didn't have to be Sherlock Holmes to figure out where you were headed.'

'I don't want your help,' she said.

'I know you don't. But I don't like seeing people frightened to the extent you——'

'Chivalry went out several centuries ago,' she interrupted, allowing some of her fury to surface. 'As did knights in shining armour. I can look after my own life, Jake. I don't need a man to do it for me.'

'Why is it,' he remarked, 'that every time I come within ten feet of you I want to kiss you?'

Across the room a child started to cry; with a loud clatter someone dropped a plate at the food counter. Liane remembered that brief kiss of the night before, the unexpected warmth of his lips, the shock and heat that had chased each other through her body, and said in a choked voice, 'Unless you want half a fried egg dumped on your head, don't even contemplate kissing me again.'

'I didn't say I was going to kiss you, I only said I wanted to. And I'll fantasise if I please. What I'd really like to know is why *you're* the one to set me off... I don't even like blondes.'

'You don't like women!'

'You have a point there,' Jake drawled. 'So why you?'

Because my father is a very rich man? The words were on the tip of Liane's tongue; she bit them back, gave him a leisurely survey, and said, 'You're not bad-looking, Jake, and despite the feminist movement there are a lot of women around who seem to think a man will solve all their problems—perhaps you're just not used to females who don't fall flat on their backs at the first glance from you... I, however, will admit to finding your techniques a trifle heavy-handed.'

She smiled at him placidly and took the last bite of muffin. He had not liked her little speech, she could tell; in fact, if looks could kill, she would be slithering to the floor of the canteen right now. But when she thought of Patrick she could not dredge up even a twinge of repentance.

'Given the opportunity,' Jake said silkily, 'I'm sure I could change your mind as to my—er—technique.'

'I'm not going to waste any chips on that particular hand.'

'I can see that there was too much talk last night and not enough action.' He pushed himself up from the bench, so that momentarily he towered over her, and she was forced to crane her neck back to meet his eyes. He was, she saw, extremely angry. 'I won't make the same mistake again.'

'Not with me you won't,' she answered cordially. Then she directed her most dazzling smile at him, for she had just thought of how she would get rid of both him and Chester on the way to Charlottetown. It was a very simple plan, and, as with most simple plans, she was almost sure it would work.

'You haven't seen the last of me, Liane,' Jake said levelly, then turned on his heel and left the canteen. He was wearing a very expensive leather jacket over his sweater. Her father must pay well, she thought bitterly, and took a gulp of coffee. It was lukewarm. She pulled a face, and tried to forget the undeniable menace in Jake's parting statement by concentrating on her plan. All she had to do was find a pay-phone once she was off the ferry, and pray that her friend Percy was home.

She finished her coffee, wandered through the lounge, where Chester was curled up in a corner seat with his eyes closed, and Jake was reading a magazine, and went out on deck. The wind was still ice-cold. But it was clean and it was honest, thought Liane, taking a deep breath as it whipped her hair around her ears. Chester on one side of the lounge, and Jake on the other—how she loathed them for their duplicity and their greed!

She found a corner near the bridge where she was sheltered from the wind and where the white-painted bulwarks reflected the sun, and leaned back, closing her eyes. If her plan with Percy worked, she would be as safe as it was possible for her to be, because she was not in the phone book and she could not be traced through her licence-plate numbers. She would have bought time. Time to come up with a strategy to outwit her father.

The sun was warm on her face and the engines grumbled in a comforting rhythm. When next she opened her eyes, the red cliffs of the island she had called home since before Patrick was born were close to the boat. Red cliffs capped with white snow under an achingly blue sky—another postcard scene, she thought, and went below to sit in her car because she did not want to talk to Jake again.

In her car she kept the windows rolled up, and locked her doors, staring straight ahead as Chester walked past her. The ferry bumped against the dock, and the ramp creaked down on its pulleys. The first cars drove off. Liane followed, watching for a pay-phone as she drove into the little town of Borden. When she saw one at a petrol station, she pulled out of the line of traffic, parked in front of the phone, and inserted her money in the slot with fingers that felt clumsy with nervousness. Willing Percy to be home, she rang his number.

'Hello there,' Percy bellowed.

Percy, who had perfect hearing, operated on the principle that the rest of the world was deaf. 'It's Liane,' she answered in a moderate voice. 'Percy, will you do me a favour?'

'Was thinking about you yesterday... Rosie had twins and I figured your Patrick might like to see 'em.'

Rosie was a very large Holstein. 'I'm sure he would,' Liane said, and from the corner of her eye saw Jake draw up at the opposite end of the tarmac and park, making no attempt to disguise his presence. 'Percy, I need a favour and I can't explain what it's all about right now. I've just got off the ferry—in about twenty minutes I'll be driving past your place, and I'm being followed by a bright red wagon and a small dark blue car—I think it's a Honda... Will you let me pass and then drive your manure-spreader across the road and pretend it's broken down? The longer you can delay them, the better.'

Percy gave an astonished snort of laughter. 'You've been watching too much TV, girl! Sure I'll do it—be a change from workin' in the barn. If you get ten minutes or so, that be enough?'

'More than enough. Bless you, Percy... I'll explain in a couple of days.'

'You do that—and bring your boy with you.' Percy gave another uncouth snort. 'I got some real ripe pig manure; that'll fix 'em.'

Chester's blue car slowed fractionally as it passed the petrol station, then kept going. 'I've got to go,' Liane said, her mouth suddenly dry. 'Thanks a million, Percy. Bye.'

She got back in her car and edged into the line of traffic again. Two blocks further on she saw the dark blue Honda tucked into the car park of a bank; had she not been looking for it, she would have missed it. So it was the two of them, she thought, and swallowed hard. Jake alone was a formidable opponent, without adding Chester as well.

As she left the town and headed inland the traffic gradually thinned, until Jake was four cars back and Chester three behind him. Very carefully Liane tried to increase the gap without being too obvious about it, grateful that the highway had been so well ploughed. Although one of the cars between her and Jake pulled off at a restaurant, and a few minutes later another took the turn-off to Victoria, Jake seemed content at the distance between them, making no effort to close it. And Chester, of course, would follow Jake.

Aware that under all her other concerns she was burningly angry with her father for subjecting her to this ridiculous chase, Liane drove on. The gentle hills and snow-filled valleys, the tidy farms with their dark green woodlots passed her one by one, all familiar, all somehow increasing her rage at her father—and therefore at Jake and Chester—that her home, her place of sanctuary, was no longer inviolate.

She checked her watch, knowing that in five minutes she would reach the sprawling acreage on both sides of the road that had been in Percy's family for over two hundred years. On the next straight stretch the black car between her and Jake passed her, leaving only a small truck in sight apart from her two pursuers. Mentally apologising to the driver of the truck for the delay she would be causing him, she drove up the last hill before Percy's, her fingers tense on the wheel.

As soon as she came in sight, a green tractor pulling a long red manure-spreader lurched on to the road. It was Percy's largest tractor. Liane put her foot to the floor, surged past him and waved her gloved hand, grinning widely. Percy waved back, crossed her lane with the tractor, and stopped. The tractor was nearly in the ditch, while the spreader, which indeed smelled very ripe, had its back end in the driveway. The road was completely blocked. Liane waved again, and speeded up. This was her chance. She must take full advantage of it.

She kept on the same road at the first set of cross-roads, but at the second, having first checked in her mirror that she was not being followed, she turned left. Then she took a series of right and left turns, staying both north and west of the city of Charlottetown, glancing nervously in her mirror at every turn. Although for a few miles a battered old jeep followed her, then a shiny green sedan, there was no sign of either a red wagon or a small dark blue car.

She had won. With Percy's help she had duped Jake and Chester, and had, at least temporarily, defeated her father as well.

Beginning to relax, Liane went north again, and only when she was well away from the city did she turn back towards the river. It was the most circuitous route she had ever taken to get home. But it had worked. She would not be seeing Jake or Chester again.

Chester she could not have cared less about. Jake she did.

Scowling to herself, she topped a hill and saw below her the wide valley of the Hillsborough River, a river that nearly divided the province in two. She would soon be home.

Eight years ago, three months pregnant, Liane had run from Murray Hutchins and from all that he represented, settling in a new province that had a wide stretch of water between her and him. Supporting herself with the money her mother had left her, she had given birth to her son, and had begun to make new friends.

When Patrick turned two, she had started taking courses in landscape design, and when her mother's money had run out she'd worked in the summers for nurseries and in the winters at the local library. Three years ago, through her friends Megan and Fitz Donleavy, she had met the Forsters, an elderly couple who summered on the island and spent the rest of the year in Florida; they were looking for someone to care for their gardens in summer and the greenhouse and conservatory in the winters. For Liane the job could not have been better, for she could live in one wing of the house with her son, work on the premises all summer, and still keep her position at the library.

The Forsters were away at the moment. She and Patrick were alone in the big house on the banks of the river, a fact that until yesterday had never worried her at all. Megan and Fitz lived a mile away in the village of Hilldale; a mile was not far, she told herself firmly, and took the turn-off to the estate.

The Forsters owned the better part of three hundred acres, with formal gardens around the gracious brick house, merging into carefully tended woods which in the spring were a blaze of colour from azaleas and rhododendrons, and which opened out into a field of wildflowers that led down to the river. Liane had loved the property from the first moment she had seen it, had felt her spirits expand and her soul heal as she worked on the grounds, and had soon seen how much happier Patrick was here than in the city.

I won't leave here, she vowed, parking in the small garage that adjoined the east wing, and climbing out of her car. I won't let Father tear my life apart again.

She locked the garage door and went into the house, turning the furnace up to take the chill from the air, and then going straight to the phone. A quick call first to Patrick's school, to alert him to get off the bus at his own house rather than Megan's, and then a call to Megan.

'You're back!' Megan exclaimed. 'How was the driving, and was it fun at the school?'

'It was certainly interesting.'

'Oh? You'll have to tell me all about it. And your father, how did that go?'

'That was interesting, too,' Liane said, realising she could not possibly describe the events of the past twenty-four hours on the telephone. How melodramatic they would sound! Tycoon Claims Grandson as Heir, Mother Flees into Storm. No, the story would have to wait. 'I'll tell you everything that happened the next time we get together, Megan. Thanks so much for keeping Patrick for me—I called the school, and he'll get off the bus here.'

'It was a very humbling evening—having wiped me off the board at checkers, he then proceeded to bankrupt Fitz and me at poker. He'll go far, that boy.'

'Mars is the present plan. He's saving all my tin cans to build a rocket.'

'There's an awful lot you're not saying,' Megan remarked. 'You wouldn't just whet my appetite?'

'Not right now. I promise I'll give you every grimy detail when I see you.'

'I'll hold you to it.' Sounding quite violent, red-haired Megan added, 'You don't have to do what your father says just because he's got lots of money.'

She might not be given the choice. 'I know,' Liane said.

'Don't you forget it, then,' Megan ordered. 'Tomorrow's our day in Charlottetown...want anything?'

'Fitz is getting me the lumber for the bottom three steps in the basement—the wood was rotten, so they had to be taken out, remember? But I don't think I need anything else, thanks. I'd better go, Megan; I have to take something out of the freezer for supper...talk to you soon.'

She put a pan of homemade lasagne out on the counter to thaw, then took her keys and went through the connecting door into the main house, with its luxurious carpets and eighteenth-century oil paintings. Letting herself into the conservatory, she inhaled the familiar damp warmth, scented with orchids and freesias, a miniature haven of tropical colour against the backdrop of snow-blanketed woods. She felt very much at home in this room, for she loved caring for all the plants, nurturing them to bloom in the long months of winter. She felt at home; and she felt totally safe. Even now, with the threat of Jake and Chester in the background, she still felt safe.

Shying away from the thought that Jake, for money, had done his best to despoil this safety, Liane noticed a number of small tasks that needed attention. She set to work, and by the time she left the conservatory an hour later she had decided that tomorrow evening she would lay the whole story in front of Megan and Fitz and ask their advice. Fitz, who made rather ugly pots that the tourists seemed to love, concealed a strong streak of practicality under a somewhat Bohemian exterior. Fitz would know what to do.

Fitz would protect her from Jake.

CHAPTER FOUR

Two hours later the yellow school bus stopped by the road and Patrick got out. Liane watched him race down the driveway, his jacket unzipped, his boots unlaced, and felt her heart contract with a long-familiar blend of love and vulnerability. If the lush gardens here at 'Riversedge' had helped heal the arid desert of her own childhood, Patrick had preserved her from more adult resentments. For Patrick's father had laughed in her face when she had assumed he would marry her, and her own father had demanded an abortion for the sake of something he called the family honour. Liane had fled from both of them, and, when the red-faced, squalling bundle who was her son had first been placed in her arms, had found out why.

Patrick burst in the door, shucked off his boots on the mat, and cried, 'Kim and Clancy are going tobogganning on Mason's Hill—can I go?'

Under his thatch of auburn hair, a legacy from his father, grey eyes that were totally his own looked up at her. She bent to hug him, sensing that today he would be safe from Chester and Jake, wondering how in the future she would deal with situations like this. 'I wish you'd tie your boots, Patrick,' she said. 'I'm always scared you'll trip on the laces.'

'Takes too long to take them off if they're done up. Can I, Mum?'

'Yes, you may. Want a glass of milk before you go? How was school today?'

'I got a hundred in maths.'

51

'And English?' Liane asked, head to one side.

'Fifty-seven. It was a stupid test.'

'If you're going to be an astronaut you have to be able to write reports. After supper we'll go over the test together. Change into your ski-suit, and there are dry mitts on the radiator.'

Ten minutes later Patrick was hauling the long wooden toboggan up the hill, waving at his two friends on the road. Liane smoothed out the despised English test, which was a thicket of red marks, and went into the kitchen to make a salad. As the shadows lengthened on the snow and a medley of old Broadway tunes came over the radio, she felt her nerves settle more deeply into the comfort and peace of her home. Jake and Chester would not find her here. She and Patrick were safe.

She carried this conviction through the evening, and because it was so strong she did not tell Patrick about his grandfather's demands; she woke up after a good night's sleep with the same sense of safety. After waving goodbye to Patrick, as he trudged up the hill for the bus, she changed from her housecoat into her oldest jeans and a T-shirt that had shrunk and was consequently no longer wearable in public, and tied her hair in a knot on top of her head. It was time to start some seedlings in the workroom, and when better to do it than this cold, overcast February day?

The workroom was in the opposite wing to her own, a spacious room with a cement floor, banks of fluorescent lighting, and wide windows that overlooked the trees and the distant river, now heaped with ice. Liane turned the radio on to catch the latest news, and began opening the boxes of supplies she had ordered a month ago, piling the green plastic trays on the table and sorting through the packets of seeds, humming as she worked. She grew all the annuals from seed, and a good many of the perennials; it was work she enjoyed, for the tiny green seedlings thrusting up towards the light always inspired in her a kind of tenderness for the forcefulness and fragility of life.

She was almost ready to break for coffee when a movement through the window caught her eye. She glanced up, a big bag of potting soil in her arms. A man was standing outside in the snow, looking in at her through the window, a tall man in a leather jacket. He had black hair and eyes that looked black against the grey sky.

Jake.

For a moment Liane could neither breathe nor move. Imagination, she thought wildly. It's my imagination. But when she blinked he was still there, still staring in at her. A man of darkness against the snow.

Jake. Come to get Patrick. In the one place she had thought she was safe.

With a terror-stricken whimper Liane dropped the bag of soil. It burst, scattering peat moss and vermiculite all over her shoes. Then Jake gesticulated, pointing to the front of the house.

He had rung the doorbell, she thought numbly. He, on the most clandestine of errands, had rung her door as if he were an ordinary visitor on ordinary business. Swallowing a spurt of hysterical laughter, she knew she could not bear to have him staring at her a moment longer. Pivoting, she ran through the door, slamming and locking it behind her, leaning against it as she fought to slow the pounding of her heart.

She had no idea what to do next. The safety she had cocooned herself in for the last twenty-four hours had been an illusion, a dangerous falsity. For the fox had found its prey.

How, she could not imagine. How did not really matter, she thought, drawing a ragged breath. What mattered was what she did next.

No point in phoning Megan or Fitz; they'd gone into the city and wouldn't be back until their two children got home from school. Percy, willing though he might be, was too far away. The police?

She thought of the explanations this would entail, and her spirit quailed. But one thing she could do—must do—was phone the school and make sure Patrick got off the bus at Megan's.

A concrete plan, no matter how small, enabled her to push herself away from the door, to leave her mud-stained shoes on the mat, and to scurry through the Forsters' hallways to the door that led to her wing. She picked up the telephone, spoke in a normal voice to the secretary, and left her message. She then replaced the receiver.

The doorbell chimed.

Her heart gave an exaggerated leap. She crossed the hall to the door, and through the letter-box shouted, 'Go away, Jake! Or I'll phone the police.'

'I'm not going anywhere until you and I have a talk. So you might as well let me in.'

She remembered that tone of voice all too well. She said viciously, 'Go back to my father and tell him I don't want anything to do with him, now or ever. Patrick is *my* son. Not——'

'I am not working for your father! Chester is, but I'm not. Let me in—or I'll break in.'

'You and Chester are both in his pay!' she cried. 'I don't know which of you I despise more. Because I will not let Father get his hands on Patrick, do you hear?'

'You've got it all wrong,' Jake said tightly. 'I'm not here to take Patrick from you, and I've never met your father——'

'Oh, sure, Jake. You've got the wrong woman—I don't believe in fairy-stories any more.'

There was a charged silence. Then Jake said, 'I'm going to count to ten, Liane. If you haven't opened the door by then, I'm coming in anyway.'

The door was oak, with a dead-bolt. Like a mouse pinioned by the yellow gaze of a cat, Liane stood very still, and part of her brain was screaming at her to call the police and the other part told her he could not possibly mean what he said. Then she heard a series of small scraping sounds from the other side of the door, and to her horror the door-knob began to turn.

She whirled and saw straight ahead of her the entrance to the basement. There was a door to the back garden in the rear wall of the basement. If she could only get outside she might have a chance to escape, for she knew the terrain like the back of her hand—every tree, every shrub, every hummock in the ground.

The front door swung open. With a choked cry Liane pitched herself down the stairs into the darkness of the cellar, and it was only when she was halfway down that she remembered with a surge of hope that the bottom three steps were missing; after the wood had rotted, Fitz had removed them altogether, claiming they were no longer safe. She knew the steps were missing. Jake did not.

She jumped to the ground, kicked a loose board across the path and ran for the back door, and, with the acute hearing of extreme fear, heard Jake plunge down the steps behind her. As she seized the door-handle, Jake suddenly grunted in mingled surprise and alarm, his feet scuffling for a purchase. The loose board banged against the stairwell. Then he gave a bitten-off cry, and through the gloom she saw him fall sideways, saw his frantic clutch at thin air, heard the horrible thud as his head struck the upright beam supporting the ceiling. His body slid to the floor.

In the ominous silence the harsh sound of her own breathing smote her ears. Although she had felt terror when she had taken the stairs two by two, it was nothing like the terror she felt now. She had killed him, she thought, staring fixedly at the dark outline of Jake's body crumpled against the post. She, Liane Daley, who had never committed a violent act in her life, was responsible for a man's death.

Dragging her feet, she approached him, and it never occurred to her that he might be faking. Kneeling on the concrete floor, she took his flaccid wrist in her fingers and felt for the pulse.

It was beating. Strong and sure beneath her fingertips, she felt the pulse of Jake's blood in his veins.

With an incoherent sob Liane scrambled to her feet. She had to call the police now; this had gone too far for her to deal with alone.

The officer on the phone sounded very calm, as though women called up every day to report an unconscious man on their basement floor. He assured her that a patrol car and an ambulance would be there within ten minutes, and rang off. She switched on the basement light and slowly went back down the stairs.

Jake had not moved. She knelt beside him again, her eyes travelling over his face as though she could thereby understand him, and the only conclusion she could reach was that he did not look like a man who would kidnap a child for money. Even with the dark eyes closed, there was the imprint of intelligence and will on Jake's features: the mouth was uncompromising, the profile proud.

She brushed a lock of hair back from his forehead, and saw the wet darkness of blood from his scalp. His hair was soft, and very clean; to touch it filled her with a confusing mixture of panic and, unquestionably, desire.

She had not felt desire since Patrick had been conceived. She had not allowed herself to feel it.

Of their own volition her hands pushed aside the heavy folds of his leather jacket, finding the pulse at the base of his throat, bared by his open-necked shirt. This pulse, too, throbbed against his skin, vital and alive.

Liane sat back on her heels, wishing he would stir, wishing the police would arrive, anything to deliver her from the grip of emotions she thought she had subdued forever. And what a crazy twist of fate that a man she loathed, a man who had, moreover, shown every sign of disliking her, should be the one to arouse these emotions.

Upstairs the bell rang. She clambered up the stairs and went to open the door. A blue and white police car was parked outside and an ambulance was following it down the hill. Two young men in regulation uniform were standing on her step.

She ushered them in, introduced herself, and said baldly, 'He's downstairs—the bottom steps are missing, and he fell. He broke in the front door.'

One of the officers looked at the lock, then said briefly, 'Professional job. Let's take a look.'

'You go ahead, I'll take the medics in.'

So once more Liane went down to the basement, where Jake was still lying exactly where she had left him. Swiftly the policeman went through Jake's pockets, extracting a leather wallet, and flipping through the assortment of cards it contained. Then, with a small whistle of consternation, his hands stilled. 'Well, ma'am,' he said, 'you caught yourself a good one.'

'W-what do you mean?' she faltered. Was Jake a known criminal? Did he have a record? Not Jake, she thought painfully. Please, not Jake.

'This guy's a top-ranking officer in the international force.'

Liane's jaw dropped. 'You mean he's a *policeman*?'

'He sure is.' The young man looked at her through narrowed eyes. 'Just why was he breaking into your house?'

'To kidnap my son,' she said faintly, and to her infinite relief saw a paramedic come down the stairs with a collapsible stretcher. If Jake was a policeman, he couldn't be in her father's pay...could he?

She rubbed at her forehead, wondering if any minute she would wake up under the blue duvet in her own bed and find this had all been a bizarre nightmare. As the medic checked Jake over, she asked even more faintly, 'How is he?'

'Concussion—shouldn't be anything serious,' the medic replied with a cheerfulness that grated on Liane's nerves. 'An X-ray'll be in order, though. Do you want to come with us in the ambulance, miss?'

'I'll bring her,' the policeman said. 'Once she's answered a few questions.'

With professional speed the two medics strapped Jake's body to the stretcher. Then, with the help of one of the policemen, the stretcher was carried up the stairs and out of the door, a process during which Liane discovered how strongly she did want to go with Jake in the ambulance. In the kitchen she patiently went over the events of the last couple of days, rather heartened by the flicker of amusement in the officer's eyes as she described the intervention of the manure-spreader. She had no idea whether he believed a word she had said; she was not sure she would, were she him. When she had finished, he closed his notebook, and said stolidly, 'We'll check Mr Brande's credentials and get back to you, Miss Daley. Shall I drive you to the hospital?'

'Please,' answered Liane, and grabbed her pink jacket from the cupboard.

At the hospital she was kept waiting until Jake was settled in a room. 'He's only in for observation,' the daunting, grey-haired matron said. 'But you mustn't stay too long.'

Liane thought there was a distinct possibility that Jake, if conscious, would instantly show her the door. 'I won't,' she promised, and crept into the room.

Jake was lying flat on the bed, his face almost as pale as the sheets, his eyes closed. She tiptoed closer, wondering if he had been drugged, knowing that no matter what he had done she was deeply grateful that he was alive. There was a neat white patch over the wound on his head; she reached out a hand to brush his hair back from his face, and knew that what she really wanted to do was cradle his head to her breast and hold him there.

For a moment her hand was arrested in mid-air. She hated him. She feared him. She despised him. Yet she wanted to hold him in her arms and comfort him . . .

As if she were under a spell, watching another woman altogether, she followed the drift of her fingers as they very gently touched his cheek and moved towards his hair.

Jake's eyes flew open, staring straight into her eyes that were so close to his and so bemused. In a blur of movement he circled her wrist with fingers as cold as a handcuff. 'What the devil do you think you're doing?'

'I—I don't know,' Liane stammered, and knew her words for the literal truth.

'Trying to finish me off? Since the clever little trick with the missing steps didn't work?'

'Of course not! I was terrified that I'd killed you.'

'Yeah?' With his other hand he flicked at the loose tendrils of blonde hair curving around her cheeks. 'I rue the day I ever associated the word dumb with you . . . you're about as dumb as a rattlesnake. And just as deadly.'

Liane had been quite prepared to apologise for what she had done. But she was not prepared to let him walk all over her. 'Try looking at it my way, Jake Brande,' she fumed. 'A man twice my size who's been following me for two days jimmies the lock on my front door, and breaks into my house—you think I should have smiled at you sweetly and made you a nice cup of tea and then handed over my son?' She glowered at him, her mouth a mutinous line. 'Not likely.'

'I do not want your son!' Jake roared. 'Will you get that through your thick head?'

'Then what the hell *do* you want?' she yelled back.

In a crackle of starched skirts the matron marched in the door and impaled Liane with a glare like a gimlet. 'I shall have to ask you to leave!' she announced. 'The patient must not get over-excited.'

Jake directed a smile at the matron that would have melted a glacier, and said pacifically, 'It was all my fault...will you let her stay just a few more minutes if I promise it won't happen again?'

Something approaching a smile creaked across the matron's face. 'Very well,' she agreed, 'five minutes more.' She swept out of the room without deigning to look at Liane again.

'Boy,' said Liane, 'you sure know how to turn on the charm, don't you? Why haven't you ever tried that little gambit on me?'

Jake loosened his hold on her wrist, smoothing the skin with his fingers in a way she tried futilely to ignore, and remarked, 'Your cheeks are the same colour as your shirt. Is it your son's shirt? It certainly doesn't look as though it was made to fit an adult.'

Liane flushed an even brighter pink. 'With you bleeding on the concrete floor and looking as though you were dead, and with policemen and ambulances all over the place, it didn't occur to me to change my shirt,' she hissed.

Jake's gaze wandered in a leisurely fashion from her face to her breasts, outlined faithfully by the clinging pink fabric. 'I'm very glad it didn't.'

She yanked her wrist free, hugged her jacket around her body, and said the first thing that came into her mind. 'Are you really a policeman?' she demanded. '"A top-ranking officer in the international force", quote, unquote?'

'Yeah . . . I've been overseas for the last four years. Up in Ottawa they haven't figured out what they're going to do with me yet—that's why I've got time off.'

Her father had money and power; but not even her father could have subverted the entire police force. Liane said flatly, 'So you're not in my father's pay?'

'No. Chester is, though. As I believe I might have mentioned in our discussion through the letter-box.'

'I thought both of you were,' Liane admitted, frowning at him, and by no means ready to forgive him yet. 'Hence the manure-spreader.'

'Ah, yes, my introduction to farming at its most elemental level . . . I will admit that the manure-spreader was one of the reasons I turned up on your doorstep this morning.' Very gingerly Jake patted the bandage in his hair. 'I deserve to be fired for falling—literally—for your little trick with the basement stairs, though.'

Subduing an emotion that was unquestionably guilt, Liane asked coldly, 'So what were the other reasons you broke into my house, Jake?'

'Haven't you guessed?' In another of those lightning-swift moves, he seized her by the elbows, pulled her off balance so that she fell across his chest, and kissed her full on the mouth.

Although Liane was twenty-seven years old and the mother of a son, she was not overly experienced in the art of lovemaking; however, she knew enough to recognise when a kiss began in anger and ended in something else altogether. For the first few moments, moments when she was frozen with surprise, Jake's lips were hard and unyielding, fuelled by an emotion as far from tenderness as it could be. But, as she collected her wits and tried to pull away from him, he murmured something deep in his throat, his hands kneading her flesh through her jacket, his kiss gentling seemingly in spite of himself, seeking rather than demanding.

His demands she could have repulsed. His gentleness, a gentleness that seemed entirely out of character, disarmed her. She relaxed. And as she did so she felt desire uncurl within her, licking like flame through her limbs, softening her lips, blanking out everything but the insistence of the present.

'Really!' cried the matron. 'This is quite outrageous!'

Jake raised his head and let go of Liane, who scrambled to her feet beside the bed with less than her usual grace. If her cheeks had been pink earlier, she thought, they must be as red as geraniums now. Quelling an absurd urge to burst out laughing, she said meekly, 'I'm truly sorry, Matron; he was only kissing me goodbye. Because we won't be seeing each other again.'

'Humph,' said Matron. 'Mr Brande has suffered a concussion. *That* is my concern, and my only concern.' With a militant gleam in her eye she advanced on Jake and took his pulse. 'As I suspected,' she said triumphantly, 'much too fast. No more visitors today, Mr Brande.' As he opened his mouth to protest, she neatly popped a thermometer in it.

Liane, who had not had as much fun in many months, said limpidly, 'Goodbye, Jake; it's been most instructive knowing you. Next time, may I suggest you look before you leap?'

She winked at him, slipped out of the door, and drove home.

CHAPTER FIVE

DESPITE having so sanguinely said goodbye to Jake, Liane was almost sure she had not seen the last of him. In fact, she realised, as she stepped inside, she would be very upset if she thought she would never see him again. And explain that, Liane, she said to herself.

Ahead of her was the door, now closed, to the basement. She gazed at it, lost in thought. He made her feel fully alive, was that it? For, whatever the reason, when she was with him all her emotions were keyed to their highest pitch, be they anger, fear, or—and this was the most difficult one for her to accept—desire.

In the year of Patrick's conception and birth Liane had been so at the mercy of a whirlpool of emotions that afterwards she had deliberately set out to make a life for herself where she was protected from such turmoil. Her emotions towards Patrick, of course, she felt to the fullest, and she had been close friends with both Megan and Fitz—she was not afraid of that kind of intimacy. But she dated only rarely, she had had nothing that could be constructed even remotely as an affair, and after two or three rebuffs right after Patrick was born she had learned to stay away from her father.

Jake, whom she now knew she had met by chance rather than from any design of her father's, could change all that. He had been rude to her, he had pursued her across three provinces, and he had scared her out of her wits; yet when he had kissed her he had broken through all her defences. She had not put up even a token struggle.

She hung up her coat and wandered into the kitchen, where through the window the snow and the sky were the same leaden grey. The changes were in her, thought Liane, and felt a *frisson* of fear course along her spine.

She began to make a meat loaf together with baked potatoes, and the simple task calmed her. She would not see Jake today—the matron would see to that. And after supper she would ask Megan and Fitz for advice. It wouldn't matter if Patrick was late getting to bed, because it was Friday.

So at six-thirty that evening she was being ushered in the door at Megan's, the two dogs barking at her heels. Both Megan and Fitz were a little larger than life, for Megan was statuesque and full-breasted with a mop of tangled red curls, while Fitz boasted a beard of Old Testament proportions and a booming voice worthy of any prophet. As always, the pots he made for the tourists were scattered throughout the house; only a few people, Liane among them, knew of the very different pieces he kept tucked away in his storeroom, and of the lack of confidence that kept him from displaying them publicly. According to Megan, he was near a breakthrough. Liane, who liked him very much, hoped Megan was right.

Clancy and Kim had already taken Patrick down to the games room to play computer games. Bouncer, a large and endearingly clumsy mongrel, flopped down near the stove, while Trojan the dachshund headed single-mindedly for the food dish. The three adults settled in the untidy, comfortable living-room with its wood-stove and thick shag carpet. Fitz had made mulled wine; curving her hands around the warm glass, Liane began to describe the events of the last three days, leaving out nothing but Jake's two kisses.

She could not possibly have complained about her audience, because her two friends were plainly enraptured by her story. When she finished, Megan breathed, 'How romantic...'

'Hard to see a manure-spreader as romantic,' Fitz commented. 'Did he make a pass at you, Liane?'

She should have remembered that Fitz was not noted for his tact. She took a gulp of wine, and said primly, 'He's scarcely had the opportunity.'

'Doesn't sound to me like the kind of guy who'd let that stop him. You figure he's going to turn up on your doorstep tomorrow?'

'Maybe.'

'If your father's halfway serious, you'd better let him in. Your father's big problem is that too many people are afraid of him—you included.'

'I'm right to be afraid of him, Fitz,' she retorted. 'I know him better than you do.'

Fitz was unabashed. 'You're twenty-seven now, not nineteen. Time you took him on.' He tugged at his beard, his amber eyes laughing at her. 'Hire this Jake as a bodyguard. That'll give him lots of opportunities.'

'You're not being very helpful,' Liane said crossly.

'OK, OK—get a pencil and paper, Megan, and let's see what we can do here.'

When Liane left two hours later she was carrying a neatly written and very helpful list of suggestions. The one to which Fitz had given priority was that she should tell Patrick everything that had happened. Tomorrow, she thought. Tomorrow's Saturday, I'll tell him then.

She turned off the road down the long slope of the driveway to the Forsters' house. In front of the house, parked with no attempt at concealment, was a cherry-red wagon.

The glare of her headlights illuminated the man sitting behind the wheel. It was, of course, Jake.

As strong as it was unexpected, Liane felt an uprush of an emotion she could only call joy. He had come back.

He had not accepted her goodbye as final at all. She said to Patrick with careful truth, 'That's a man I met when I stayed at the school; his name is Jake, and he's a policeman. Let's go and see what he wants.'

She knew one thing he wanted; keeping her mind firmly away from that, she walked across to the wagon. Jake opened the door and climbed out. 'I've been waiting for over an hour,' he complained.

Liane had left three outdoor lights on, so it was not difficult to see that he was still frighteningly pale. Nor did she think his tiny stagger when his feet hit the ground was in any way assumed. 'You'd better come in,' she said formally. 'This is my son, Patrick.'

Patrick held out his hand, eyeing the white patch on Jake's forehead. 'What happened to your head?'

'I fell down some stairs,' Jake replied, and shook Patrick's hand as briefly as good manners would allow.

'We've got three stairs that are being fixed,' Patrick said, not seeming to notice the brevity of Jake's hand-shake, and favouring him with an angelic, gap-toothed grin. 'You'd better watch out.'

'I had indeed,' agreed Jake, directing an enigmatic glance at Patrick's mother.

Liane, who had noticed the brevity of the handshake, returned look for look, and said calmly, 'I'm sorry you had to wait. But then I didn't know you were coming, did I?'

'You might have guessed that after six hours of Matron I was in serious danger of a relapse.'

In spite of herself her lips quirked. She turned to unlock the front door, switched on the lights, and said to Patrick, 'Upstairs and clean your teeth, hon; I'll be up in a minute to say goodnight.'

For a moment Patrick held his ground, staring up at the tall man standing inside the door. 'Did you help my mum when she got stuck in the snow?' he asked. ''Cause you're a policeman?'

For a moment Jake looked nonplussed. Liane said quickly, 'Yes, he did. Off you go, Patrick.'

'You can come up to my room with her and see my rocket models,' Patrick offered, 'if you want.'

Liane knew this was an invitation not extended to many adults. She held her breath, and heard Jake say, after the smallest of hesitations, 'Thank you, I'd like that.'

Jake did not want to go up to Patrick's room—she knew that intuitively; yet equally he had not wanted to hurt a small boy's feelings. Suddenly liking him very much, she gave him her most generous smile.

Patrick had taken the stairs to the loft two by two. Jake said roughly, 'I've spent a great deal of my career assessing people, with my life often depending on how accurate I was. But you, Liane—I don't have a clue what you're all about. All my training and experience fly out the window when I'm within fifty feet of you.'

He did not look friendly. Liane's smile faded. She indicated the door into the living-room and said, 'You'd better sit down before you fall down—as a policeman, you should have known better than to drive in your condition.'

He walked ahead of her into the room, saying impatiently, 'I'm fine.'

'Sit,' Liane ordered.

As Jake sank rather abruptly into the nearest chair, she further hardened her heart. 'I assume you're booked into a motel?'

'No.' With a ghost of a smile he said, 'I'm here to protect you.'

How pleased Fitz would be with this turn of events, Liane thought sardonically. 'So you're planning to move in? Were you thinking of asking permission, or isn't that on your agenda?'

He said flatly, 'I know fear when I see it—and you're a frightened woman. I don't like what you're doing to your father, but I didn't like Chester very much, either. So you're stuck with me for now, until I figure out what's going on.'

She clenched her fists. 'What do you mean, what *I'm* doing to my——?'

Patrick's voice wafted down from the loft, 'Mum, I'm ready.'

'I haven't told Patrick anything about Chester or my father yet,' Liane announced, glaring at Jake. 'I don't want you saying anything.'

Jake got to his feet, standing only six inches from her. 'I'm sure you don't,' he replied with equal anger.

She had no idea what he meant. Tossing her head, she marched out of the room and up the stairs, Jake following her, and it took an actual physical effort for her to say pleasantly, at the top of the stairs, 'The Forsters very kindly remodelled the attic into a room for Patrick...it's nice, isn't it?'

'The Forsters?'

'The people who own the house.'

'*You* don't?'

Liane gave him an astounded look. 'Are you kidding? I'm lucky to be able to afford the rent.'

'The Forsters live in Florida all winter,' Patrick explained. 'Mum's their gardener. My models are over here.'

He was wearing an old tracksuit emblazoned with the insignia of the Edmonton Oilers, and his hair was standing up in spikes all over his head. Liane glanced over at Jake, who was still standing in the doorway, and felt his reluctance to enter as palpably as if it had been her own. She had never felt so at loss with anyone before, so lacking in understanding; she said lightly, 'Watch your head, Jake; this room wasn't built for men over six feet.'

He crossed the room and bent to the models. Liane did a little perfunctory tidying, listening to the two voices, Patrick's so familiar and well-loved, Jake's deeper one making all the right responses, yet somehow dead. She threw five dirty socks in the hamper, wondering where the sixth one was and why mittens and socks never got lost in pairs. Then she straightened, gazing sightlessly out of the window into the darkness that lay over the river. Patrick loved his room. If Jake's presence enabled her to keep both Chester and her father at bay so that she and Patrick could stay here, then Jake must stay. For as long as necessary. Or for as long as he was willing.

Jake had said goodnight. Liane crossed the room, hugged Patrick close, and whispered the ritual words. 'Sleep well. I love you.'

'Love you too, Mum. G'night.'

She left the night-light on, and followed Jake down the stairs and into the living-room. As he turned to face her, she went on the attack. 'I have one question—how did you find out where I live?'

'Your licence plate—I pulled rank and got access to the files.'

'Oh. Can Chester do that?'

'No. But he'll find you sooner or later; it's almost impossible in a place as small as this for you to stay hidden.'

She looked straight at him. 'I do need your help, Jake. My father wants Patrick, and he won't be scrupulous about his methods... Can I hire you, even if it's only for a few days, to keep an eye on Patrick?'

There was not a trace of expression on Jake's face. 'I've got a month's leave—you don't have to pay me.'

'I'd prefer to. This is a business deal.'

'For you, maybe,' he said. 'Yes, I'll stay—although not necessarily for the reasons you might think.'

'I don't want to know what your reasons are!'

His eyes narrowed as he stepped closer. 'Oh, don't you?' he grated. Then he grabbed her by the shoulders and bent his head to kiss her.

Liane could have avoided him or pushed him away, for he did not look as though he wanted to kiss her. Rather, he looked like a man driven to do so, and strongly resenting his own compulsions. Instead she stood still, achingly aware of the warmth and weight of his hands, of the fierce demand of his lips, of her own wild and wayward response, so undeniable and so immediate. She could not hide it; she did not want to. She swayed towards him, her body moulding itself to his, and opened willingly to the first dart of his tongue.

Time vanished. Thought vanished. She was drowning in sweetness, in the throb of her blood and the hot, red insistence of desire, too long subdued. Jake's hands were roaming the curve of her spine, straining her to him, even as her fingers traced the breadth of his shoulders and then buried themselves in his hair. She had forgotten about the wound in his scalp. Inadvertently she touched the dressing, and felt the flinch of pain travel the length of his body.

She pulled free, saying in distress, 'Jake, I'm sorry...'

He was breathing hard, his eyes dark-shadowed and full of turmoil. He asked harshly, 'Are you always that willing?'

Feeling as though he had slapped her, Liane said, 'I was that willing once before. Patrick is the result.' And then, because she was essentially a truthful woman, she added with a puzzled frown, 'Although in all honesty I don't remember ever wanting Noel as much as I just wanted you.'

For a moment Jake looked visibly disconcerted. Then, almost as though another man had taken over, he sneered, 'You expect me to believe that?'

'I'd like you to,' she said evenly. 'Because it happens to be true.'

He ran a finger down the side of her face, and she knew in her bones that he did not mean it as a caress. 'So Noel is Patrick's father.'

'That's right.'

'Why didn't you marry him? Wasn't he rich like your father?'

She struck his hand away, suddenly furious. 'I don't have to take this, Jake! If you like so little of me, why do you keep on kissing me as though I'm the last woman on earth, and why the *hell* did you bother tracking me down all the way from the Wentworth Valley to here?'

'If I knew the answer to that question, I probably wouldn't be here!'

He looked as angry with himself as with her. Ignoring this, Liane swept on, 'Then let me make something clear—I'm not looking for a father for Patrick—I like my life just the way it is, and if you think you're going to have a cosy little affair with me in return for watching over Patrick you're quite wrong! That's not in the cards. I don't have affairs—the cost's too high. So if that's why you're here, now's your chance to leave.'

She had run out of words and breath at the same time. Fitz would not have approved of her last speech, she thought, trying to calm the racing of her blood in her veins, and wondering what she would do if Jake walked out of the door. Call him back? Slam it behind him? Burst into tears?

'Why didn't you marry Noel, Liane?'

She was too upset for anything but the truth. 'Because he laughed in my face when I suggested it. A good enough reason, wouldn't you say?'

For several long seconds Jake was silent. Then he said, raising one brow, 'Did he now? Perhaps he was afraid of your temper. How often does Patrick see him?'

'Noel made it very clear he did not want at any time to see the baby he was fifty per cent responsible for and that I was foolish enough to want to keep. I got in touch with him when Patrick was born, but he was too busy getting ready to move to Vancouver to visit either one of us.'

Her blue eyes were bleak. Patrick's birth had taught her about vulnerability, and she had been deeply hurt that the man who had fathered her son had not even wanted to see him. Then she shrugged her shoulders. 'It's over now, done with. Are you staying or leaving?'

'Oh, I'm staying. You're more of a mystery than nine-tenths of the cases I've worked on.'

Liane's first emotion was relief that she would not have to face Chester alone, her second, fear that she was letting a man as powerful and inimical as Jake within her four walls. Her third, as she looked up at his drawn white face, was compassion. 'I don't have a spare bedroom,' she said. 'But the couch here is a sofa bed; I'll make it up for you, and get you some towels...do you have a suitcase?'

'In the wagon.'

She started taking the cushions off the couch. 'I'll get it for you—and don't argue.'

'You're a very strong-willed woman.'

She flashed him a wicked grin. 'Whereas you, I would suspect, are quite unaccustomed to taking orders from anyone. Least of all a female.'

As he suddenly smiled back, a smile that transformed his face, Liane dropped a cushion. 'Your suspicions are entirely correct,' he said.

She scurried from the room to find sheets and towels. When she came back, Jake had disappeared into the bathroom. She made up the bed, drew the curtains, and put a glass of water on the table by the bed. Then she went outside to get his case.

The clouds had cleared a little, so that patches of stars were intermingled with larger patches of blackness; it was very quiet. Her footsteps crunching on the ice, she pulled his case from the floor of the wagon, and saw that the tattered flight tickets still attached to the handle were from Hong Kong, Bangkok, and Vancouver. It seemed very strange that this tall, dark-haired man who was such an enigma to her should have ended up on the shores of a river thousands of miles from any of those places. Even stranger that he would be sleeping only a few feet away from her.

She eased the tension from her shoulders, not liking the direction her thoughts were taking her, and shut the door of the wagon. Then she lugged the case, which was very heavy, into the house and across the hall. Jake was still in the bathroom. After heaving the case on to the old pine blanket-box by the wall, she turned to leave the living-room.

Jake was blocking the doorway; she had not heard even a whisper of his steps. She said disagreeably, 'I wish you wouldn't sneak up on me like that.'

'You'd better get used to it—one of the hazards of living with a policeman.'

His smile had not reached his eyes. He stayed where he was, leaning against the doorframe as he let his gaze wander around the room, with its unpretentious furniture and its inexpensive framed prints. 'This must be a far cry from your father's living-room,' he said, a wealth of innuendo in his voice.

'Thank goodness,' retorted Liane, her chin tilting defiantly.

She knew it was not the answer he had been looking for. He snapped, 'You don't have to play games with me, Liane. I'm in your pay—it's far better that you be honest.'

'Jake,' she said forcefully, 'I'm tired, and you look as though the only thing keeping you upright is the doorpost. I have a very busy day tomorrow, but I promise that once Patrick is in bed you and I will sit down in here and you can unburden your soul of the multifarious suspicions you're harbouring towards me. But we will not do that tonight, thank you very much!'

'When you get angry, your vocabulary goes haywire,' he remarked. 'Tomorrow night—it's a date.'

'It is not a date,' Liane retorted, her cheeks still flushed, 'it's a business arrangement.'

Jake straightened with the lazy grace that she already recognised as characteristic of him. 'Besides being a mystery, you're also extremely argumentative. Out, Liane. Unless you want me, despite my present decrepitude, to take you to bed.'

Hovering at the back of her mind had been just that possibility, she realised, appalled that she could even consider it. Schooling her face to what she hoped was a non-committal smile, she said, 'Not what the matron would recommend after a concussion...goodnight, Jake.'

'I don't think the matron would recommend it at any time,' was the dry response. 'Detrimental to the blood-pressure and bad for the heart. Not to mention the morals.'

Liane choked back a laugh and left the room, closing the door behind her. She had invited far more than a bodyguard for Patrick into her house, she thought, crossing the hall to her own room. But she was not nineteen any more; she was a mature woman who was quite capable of keeping Jake Brande in his place. In his own room. In his own bed.

And she in hers.

CHAPTER SIX

WHEN Liane got up about nine the next morning and went to the bathroom for a leisurely shower, the scent of Jake's aftershave was the first impression to penetrate her sleep-fogged brain. So when she went into the kitchen half an hour later, she was not surprised to find him sitting by the window with his feet propped up, reading the paper.

He looked very much at home. Too much so.

Patrick was at the table, surrounded by a litter of corn-flake crumbs, reading the comics. With his mouth full he mumbled, 'Hi, Mum. Garfield's neat; you gotta read it.'

Jake looked up. Liane was wearing tailored trousers with a mohair sweater she had knitted last winter, in varying shades of blue. She had pulled her hair on top of her head in a loose knot, and her face was innocent of make-up. 'Morning,' he said. 'Coffee's made.' And he went back to the paper.

Liane, who preferred to be ignored first thing in the morning, found herself resenting both Patrick and Jake for ignoring her now. Don't be such a grump, she chided herself, and buried her nose in her coffee-mug. The coffee was delicious. A man of many talents, she thought uncharitably, and grabbed the middle section of the newspaper.

Her edginess seemed to accumulate as the day went by, as the three of them bought groceries, got Patrick's hockey skates sharpened, and did several errands in town. She could not blame it on Jake, for he was polite without being intrusive, and she could not have faulted the inconspicuous way he kept an eye on her son. Neither was it Patrick's fault; Patrick had an easygoing disposition that every morning she envied. The fault was hers, she thought unhappily, starting to put the groceries away as Patrick raced into the living-room to watch his favourite television programme, and wishing Jake could be equally interested in the exploits of the starship *Enterprise*.

Jake said softly, 'Relax, Liane.'

She shoved the bin-bags under the sink, and said with at least partial truth, 'I'm not used to having anyone else around all the time. Except for Patrick.'

'If I'm going to be here for a month, you'd better get used to it.'

A month sounded like forever. A life sentence. Aware with every nerve in her body of him standing only two feet away from her, hating herself for this awareness, Liane said desperately, 'Do you want broccoli or peas with roast beef?'

'Broccoli. Shall I peel the potatoes?'

'You're behaving more like a husband than a bodyguard,' she cried, and then could have bitten off her tongue.

'In my day I've been both,' Jake answered. 'Your vegetable knife needs sharpening.'

Her fingers gripping the broccoli as tightly as if it were about to run away, she said, 'There's a whetstone in the drawer by the stove. Are you still married?'

'Divorced. Five years ago. Have you got some oil?'

She put the broccoli down very carefully, reached into one of the lower cupboards, and held the can out to him. 'Didn't she like you being a policeman?'

Jake grabbed the oil from her. 'Don't pry.'

But she had seen the tightening of his jaw, the barricading of his eyes against her. 'You brought the subject up... is she the reason you hate women?'

'You're making several very facile assumptions right now,' he said tautly. 'And I have no intention of starting a fight when Patrick's in the next room.'

She had forgotten about Patrick. Jake had been here less than twenty-four hours and already she knew her house was too small for three people when one of the three was a large and highly disturbing male. Wishing she could banish him to the Forsters' part of the house, knowing that was impossible, Liane busied herself with the roast and tried to maintain a dignified silence.

But Jake would not let her. He wanted to know how much broccoli, he couldn't find the saucepans, he then decided to sharpen her carving knife, and before she knew it they were comparing likes and dislikes among everything from vegetables to popular music. It was all so domesticated, Liane concluded later in mixed exasperation and pleasure as Jake carved the roast, a task she always hated. *Was* this how husbands behaved?

Fitz loved cooking, his speciality being curries hot enough to necessitate the consumption of quantities of beer. Liane stared into the green florets of the broccoli, knowing she had often marvelled at the laughter, the stormy fights, and the deep companionship of Fitz and Megan's marriage. Marvelled, yet never expected that she herself could have such a marriage.

Her mother, to the best of her knowledge, had never raised her voice to her father. But then, her mother had died when Liane was only seven, so what did she know about it?

'The meat's getting cold, Liane.'

Liane gaped up at Jake as though she had never seen him before, and blurted, 'I think that for a marriage to work the couple has to be able to fight. What do you think?'

For a moment he looked truly amused. 'There's one thing about you—I never know what you're going to say next; I was expecting a profundity on the nature of green vegetables, not on marriage. I'm not the one to ask—my wife left me.'

As he took the saucepan from her and drained it in the sink, a cloud of steam fogged up the window. 'And I bet you've never told anyone how you feel about *that*!' Liane asserted.

'You'd better call Patrick, hadn't you?' Jake suggested pleasantly. 'Supper's ready.'

Baffled, knowing she would get no more confidences from him, Liane did as he suggested. The meal was delicious. After the dishes were done, they all played cards around the kitchen table, and, because Jake was every bit as quick-witted as she and Patrick, there was a great deal of laughter and bantering. When she glanced up at the clock, Liane exclaimed, 'Goodness, it's nine-thirty, Patrick—bedtime!'

'One more hand, Mum—he's ahead of me.'

'Just one, then.'

Patrick, scowling in concentration, eventually laid down four of a kind, thereby defeating Jake. Jake laughed, reached out to ruffle Patrick's hair, and then suddenly stopped, his hand frozen in mid-air, his face a rictus of agony. Patrick did not notice, being absorbed in gathering the cards and shuffling them. Liane, who had noticed, found herself instinctively glancing away, for whatever the source of Jake's emotion she was sure it was intensely private.

Jake has a son, she thought, knew her words for the truth, and said matter-of-factly, 'Clean your teeth, Patrick; I'll be up in a minute.'

Patrick grinned at Jake. 'Will you be here tomorrow night? Can we play again?'

Jake had himself fully in control. 'I guess so,' he said.

It was enough for Patrick, who ran upstairs to get ready for bed. Liane put away the cards. Jake stared out of the window.

Fifteen minutes later, after Liane had said goodnight to her son, she and Jake went into the living-room. Liane sat down in the wing chair, and Jake on the chesterfield across from her. The interrogation can begin, thought Liane, who was feeling very nervous, and equally determined not to show it.

Jake took the initiative. 'I've decided that if you still want to hire me I'll take whatever salary you think you can afford—that way we'll be on a business footing.'

Liane had expected to have to fight for this. Deflated, she named an amount. Jake nodded in agreement. Then he said, 'Why don't you tell me your version of events— why were you so frightened at the schoolhouse?'

'I'll tell you the truth,' Liane rejoined crisply, and proceeded to do so, beginning with the day nearly three weeks ago when she had read about her brother's death in the paper. 'I went to the funeral, of course, even though my brother and I had never been close. My father scarcely seemed to know what was going on; he was in shock, I suppose. I felt sorry for him, so two weeks later—last Wednesday, the day we met—I went to see him again.' Scarcely aware of her audience, she grimaced. 'Big mistake. He'd had the time to think, and he presented me with an ultimatum. Because of my brother's death he'd lost his heir. He wants Patrick to be his new heir, to live with him in his house, to be groomed to take over the family business...I could move back into the family home, but Patrick would be sent to private school in the winters and to camp every summer.'

Unable to sit still, she prowled over to the window and gazed out into the darkness. 'I refused. He threatened me with any number of dire consequences. I left. Whereupon, as you know, Chester followed me and I eventually got home.'

'What sort of threats?'

'To kidnap Patrick. And then, if I tried to get him back, to take me to court and sue for custody. He would, he said, produce witnesses to say I'd been a drug user, had had casual affairs, was not a fit mother...oh, on and on.' Keeping her voice level with an immense effort, she finished, 'They're ridiculous accusations. But it's entirely possible he would succeed. Money will make people swear black is white if need be.'

Jake said calmly, 'I would have thought there would have been many advantages for Patrick, living with his grandfather. The best education money can buy, opportunities to travel...'

She turned to face him. 'I happen to disagree.'

'Why, Liane?' Jake asked, his eyes as impenetrable as the night beyond the window.

'Because I will not force upon him the kind of upbringing I had!'

'Ah...now we're getting to it. You hate your father, don't you?'

She said with scrupulous accuracy, 'I thoroughly dislike some aspects of his behaviour. Nor does he love Patrick.'

'You've never given him the chance to.'

His voice had the bite of steel. Hearing her blood thrum in her ears, Liane asked, 'What are you getting at, Jake?'

'Let's try a slightly different version, shall we? From motives of revenge you've kept Patrick from his grandfather ever since he was born. Now, with your brother's death, you're suddenly in an excellent bargaining position. If your father wants to see Patrick he has to go through you; and he's going to have to pay through the nose. *That's* why you were so terrified at the school—you were afraid your father was having you followed and would find out where Patrick lives. Blow your cover. Because if your father can turn up on your doorstep to see Patrick any time he likes, you won't make a cent, will you? So of course you want to keep your son out of sight.'

Jake's voice had not altered in pitch; his eyes were trained on her face. Liane took a deep breath. 'You don't really believe that,' she stated.

'Your father's a very rich man. And it's pretty obvious you don't have much in the way of worldly goods.'

Feeling as though an abyss had just opened in front of her, Liane replied with a steadiness of which, dimly, she was proud, 'I have a great deal. I have a son who loves me and whom I love more than anyone else in the world. I have good friends. I have work that I enjoy, and I'm lucky enough to live in a place I find very beautiful... These are the things that matter to me. Not my father's money.'

Jake got up and walked over to her, his eyes never leaving her. 'How very pure-minded of you. Are you saying you've never hankered after even a fraction of your father's fortune?'

'No, I'm not saying that! There have been times when I've been desperate for money. But I won't jump to his tune—not for anything will I do that, and if he said that I would then he's wrong.'

'I've never met your father,' Jake retorted, 'I keep telling you that. Chester is the one who told me the game you're playing.'

'At the manure-spreader,' Liane said slowly, and gave a rather wild giggle. 'How very symbolic. And you chose to believe a hired thug instead of me?'

'I believed the version that made sense of the facts.'

Her eyes glittering, she struck. 'So why did you follow me, if I'm nothing but an unprincipled, manipulative money-grabber?'

He seized her by the arm. 'In the five years since my wife left you're the only woman I've met who's got under my skin—and make sense of that if you can,' he challenged furiously.

'I sure don't understand how you can be attracted to a woman you despise,' she retaliated, and then winced as the words replayed themselves mockingly in her ears. She was attracted to Jake. Even now, when he was glaring at her in hatred and frustration, and when he had just finished tearing her character into shreds, she felt the pull of her body to his, the joined throbbing of their blood.

Fighting against it, yet knowing it to be deeper than herself, stronger than rationality, she added shrewishly, 'You can't be much of a policeman if you allow your hormones to lead you around the countryside.'

He snarled, 'Oh, you're not the only reason I'm here. There's another player involved, or have you forgotten him? Patrick. I'm here for Patrick's sake.'

'Then why aren't you ushering Patrick's grandfather up the front path?' she cried.

His grip tightened unconsciously. 'I'm not a fool, Liane. Murray Hutchins has built a commercial empire for himself, and you don't do that by being a nice guy. I'm prepared to admit your father could be ruthless in the pursuit of something he wants—and that's where I come in. I won't have Patrick being made a pawn between you. Played one against the other like a wild card. That's why I'm here. To protect Patrick from both of you.'

Her eyes blazing, Liane spat, 'You'd be better employed looking after your own son!'

The colour drained from Jake's face, and his fingers loosened their hold. 'How do you know about my son?' he whispered.

If ever she had seen raw pain in a man's face, Liane saw it now, and she had been the cause of it. 'I—I'm sorry,' she faltered, 'I shouldn't have said that.' Her voice gathered strength. 'But *my* son isn't your business, Jake—I've looked after him for seven years on my own, and I don't want the help of someone who hates me. If I can hire you, I can also fire you—and that's what I'm doing right now. I want you gone from here tomorrow. You can say goodbye to Patrick in the morning and then leave.'

'No.'

She shook her arm free. 'You'll do as I say! This is *my* home and I'm the one to decide who comes in that door and who stays.'

He was fully in command of himself again. 'Not in this case, Liane. I'm here and I'm staying.'

Beside herself with fury, Liane said incoherently, 'I'll *make* you leave!'

'How?' he queried gently. 'You can't call the police. Anyway, if you really are afraid that Patrick might be kidnapped, I would have thought you'd be begging me to stay.'

Her nails were digging into the palms of her hands; she had never felt such a turmoil of frustration and rage. Because, of course, Jake was right. She *was* afraid that Patrick would be kidnapped. And Jake, for all his one-sided view of her motives, would not allow anyone to take her son against his will.

She bit her lip, trying to still the racing of her heart, striving to calm herself. 'Promise me something, then,' she said, looking straight up at him. 'Swear you won't take Patrick to his grandfather's or get in touch with Chester.'

'For a period of one month I swear I won't do either one. Beyond that, I won't swear to anything.'

Liane's shoulders sagged. She had won a month's grace. For a month Patrick would be safe. 'Thank you,' she said quietly.

'Do you know what drives me crazy about you?' he exploded. 'It's as though you've got two faces. The one is so goddamned beautiful—the curve of your cheekbone, your skin smooth as the petal of a flower, the blue depths of your eyes—yet you'd cheat an old man out of seeing his only grandson. And how in hell do I reconcile that with the rest of you?'

Liane suddenly wanted to weep, for it had been a long time—too long—since a man had looked on her with the eyes of wonderment and desire; and now it was a man who thought her soul was as tawdry as outwardly he found her beautiful. She said with the courage of desperation, 'I can only be myself, Jake. Sometimes I don't think you're seeing me at all—you're seeing other women, stereotyping me. I don't know who they are or what they did to you... but you're judging me as if I were one of them.'

For a long moment Jake was silent, his face shadowed and withholding. Then he moved his shoulders restlessly and stepped back from her. 'It can't be that simple,' he muttered.

Liane stayed where she was, aware that at some level she was as exhausted as if she'd scrubbed down the greenhouse or dug up the perennial bed. Her shoulders ached and her legs were weak. She said, trying to keep her voice from shaking, 'I'll see you in the morning. Patrick has a hockey game at eight at the rink in Centreville, so we'll have to be up early.'

Jake shot her a quick glance. 'I can take him.'

'I always go.' Her grin was self-deprecating. 'One-woman cheering section.'

'OK. I'll be up.'

He gave her a curt nod. She slipped past him, and went to her own room and closed the door. Standing at the window, she stared down at the river, where the faint gleam of a new moon silvered the water. In the last few minutes it had become quite clear to her what she wanted in the next month. She wanted Jake to believe in her. To see her as she really was.

The alarm startled Liane out of a confusing dream in which she and Chester were chasing a polar bear down by the river, and the bear when it turned at bay had the face of her father. She sat bolt upright, jammed her finger on the switch to stop the beeping, and put her feet to the floor, knowing from experience that it was fatal to lie down again. Scarcely awake, she stumbled to the bathroom.

Jake was just coming out of there. Liane blinked, and clutched the semi-transparent folds of her nightgown to her chest. 'Oh—I'd forgotten about you.'

It was obvious that she was speaking the truth, and that seduction was the last thing on her mind. Jake's eyes raked her from head to toe, missing not one detail from her tumbled curls to the pale jut of her hip-bone under the thin blue nylon. 'I wish I could say the same,' he rasped.

An angry Jake at seven a.m. was more than Liane could handle. 'Make yourself useful, Jake,' she sputtered, 'and go put the coffee on. I can't face the rink without at least one cup.'

Uncannily he echoed her perceptions of the day before. 'You know what's driving me crazy? This is all so domesticated—sharing the bathroom, cooking dinner, playing cards at the kitchen table. But we're not married, are we, Liane?' Very deliberately he ran one finger from her throat to the curve of her collar-bone, and, as he did so, his wrist brushed her breast.

She could not have prevented her tiny indrawn breath, for in his touch was all the magic of spring and the heat of summer. But he hated her, she thought frantically. And it was not summer. It was winter. She backed into the bathroom, praying he would not try to stop her. 'I won't be long,' she muttered, and closed the door in his face.

She squinted at her dishevelled hair and sleep-warm lips in the mirror. A month of living with Jake? It would drive her crazy, too. To start with, she must get in the habit of wearing a housecoat. And the first time she went into the city she was going to buy him a different brand of aftershave.

Fifteen minutes later, while Patrick told Jake in exhaustive detail about the exploits of his team, the Hilldale Tigers, Liane sat down to drink a mug of coffee and eat a piece of toast. Jake then warmed up the wagon, scraped the ice from the windscreen, and helped Patrick haul the big canvas bag of gear outdoors. Liane said, still not fully awake as Jake held the passenger door open for her, 'Life's certainly a lot easier with a man around.'

'So anyone would do—just as long as he's male? Thanks a lot.'

'Jake, you're as grumpy as I am in the mornings,' she observed roundly. 'Besides, I never said you were just anyone.'

Something flared in Jake's eyes. Hurriedly Liane clambered into her seat, and allowed Patrick to chatter all the way to the rink. The car park was already crowded with vehicles and small boys. Patrick disappeared into the dressing-room, and Liane led Jake up into the bleaches, where several other parents were already sitting, huddled in blankets against the early morning cold. Quickly she went down the row of names. 'Margot and

Sean, Danny, Brian, Jean, Bill and Lindy...this is Jake, a friend who's staying for a few days.'

'Hi there, Jake,' Bill said, moving over a little to make room for him. 'Where do you hail from?'

Feeling a little as though she had cast Jake to the lions, Liane chatted to Lindy and listened with one ear to Jake fielding questions with a skill that amused her. The boys came out on the ice and warmed up. Then the game started.

Liane had long ago decided that, if she was going to drag herself out of bed before dawn in the middle of winter, she was going to enjoy the games when she got there. So she yelled and clapped and booed, groaning as Patrick missed a shot on goal, laughing as five boys tumbled one over the other in front of the net. The final score was a tie. She grinned over at Jake. 'That was fun, wasn't it?'

She was wearing a bright pink ski-suit with white fur mittens, her cheeks as pink as her suit, her eyes sparkling. Bill was stretching his legs, explaining the referee's last call to his wife; Jake said softly, 'I'd like to be carrying you off to bed right now.'

Liane's heart leaped in her breast. Caught by his eyes, black as night, she was pulled to him as magnets were pulled: by lines of force invisible to the beholder. He was not touching her. He had no need to, she thought wildly, for he was surrounding her, holding her in a way that had nothing to do with either words or touch. His power was immense; she would have gone with him anywhere he asked.

Then Bill leaned over, holding out a gloved hand. 'Nice to have met you, Jake,' he said bluffly. 'See you around. See you, Liane. Our boys did a good job, didn't they? But they sure gotta work on their defence.'

The spell was broken. Liane stood up, her eyes downcast, and followed the others to the dressing-room.

Patrick rehashed the game on the way home; she made a big breakfast of omelettes and muffins, and then disappeared to her room to read while Patrick did his homework.

After a late lunch, she and Patrick walked down to the river to watch the ducks circling in the open water where currents kept the ice from forming. As the two of them tramped across the frozen marsh grass, Liane said, knowing she had to do this but hating every minute of it, 'Patrick, there's something I need to talk to you about.'

'I studied English for a whole half-hour,' he said.

'It's not that—it's about your grandfather.' Choosing her words with care, she explained what had happened on her last visit, and described Chester to him. 'So I don't want you talking to any strangers, or getting in anyone's car, OK? And Jake's here to keep an eye on you, too.'

Patrick's eyes grew round. 'Like a security man when you get to be prime minister? Has he got a gun?'

'I sincerely hope not!'

'I'm going to ask him. Wow, that's neat!'

'But you mustn't tell anyone at school.'

His face fell. 'Not even Clancy?'

'Not even him. Jake is just a friend who's visiting us for a while.'

'Oh... I thought perhaps he was your boyfriend, and that maybe you and him'd get married,' Patrick said, slanting a look up at her through lashes as long as her own.

'No, darling,' Liane replied, and for once did not correct his grammar.

Golden-eye ducks, neatly patterned in black and white, were swimming in the channel in the middle of the river. She and Patrick watched them for a while then wandered back to the house. Jake had parked his wagon in the garage, and was fiddling with the engine; Patrick went to join him, and Liane heard him say, 'Mum told me you're my bodyguard, like the pope or the president. You got a gun?'

Not waiting to hear the answer, Liane went indoors. Patrick had never before raised the possibility that she might get married, or that he in any way craved the kind of home life that most of his friends took for granted. She felt a surge of anger against her father, that because of him Jake's presence was such a necessity. For Jake, just by being here, would bring change. Of that she was sure.

CHAPTER SEVEN

THAT evening the three of them were invited to Megan's for dinner. Liane had brought a cyclamen from the greenhouse, the plant a mass of showy pink blooms. Holding it out of Bouncer's reach, she gave it to Megan once they were in the door. Megan buried her face in it, laughing at her own enthusiasm. 'I love winter,' she said. 'It just goes on too long, so that by March I'm craving colours and flowers and leaves on the trees. Thanks, Liane, you're a darling. And you——' she looked up at Liane's companion '—must be Jake. Well…Liane didn't tell me you're a knock-out. How do you do?'

'Behave yourself, Megs,' her husband said amiably, and shook Jake's hand. 'Fitz Donleavy. Pleased to meet you; come on in and I'll make you a drink.' He took Liane's coat and kissed her on the cheek. 'As gorgeous as ever,' he told her.

Liane grinned at Jake. 'Discount at least half of what he says. And treat his curry with great respect.'

Jake, who looked extremely handsome in tailored trousers and a bulky sweater over an immaculate white shirt, smiled back. His smile hurt something in Liane, something she was not sure she could have defined. Although he was self-possessed and outwardly at ease, she wondered how often in the five years since his wife had left he had indulged in the kind of banter that was an integral part of the Donleavy household. Not often, she'd be willing to bet. Impulsively she tucked her arm in his as they went into the kitchen, where the wood-stove sent off a comfortable heat and the air was redolent with spices. 'Despite what I said, Megan and Fitz are my best friends,' she added. 'I met them in Charlottetown when Patrick was only a baby, and it was Fitz who found me the job with the Forsters. For which I remain everlastingly grateful.'

Jake's wrist was tense under her fingers. Perhaps, Liane thought in a spurt of annoyance, he distrusted her motives in bringing him here. And perhaps he was right. Had she not hoped that if he met her friends he would be less judgemental of her? More ready to accept her at face value?

She moved away from him, lifting the lids of the saucepans on the stove and inhaling cautiously, determined not to let Jake ruin her evening. Giving one of the pots a stir, she laughed over at him. 'I trust you're going to drive home... I have a feeling I may have to wash this down with a fair bit of wine.'

'Just as long as I don't have to carry you into the house,' Jake replied blandly.

She would like that, Liane thought, and said decorously, 'In all the years I've known Fitz and Megan, I only once had to spend the night on the couch.'

'That was when I made cranberry wine from my grandmother's recipe,' Fitz chuckled. 'You weren't the only one in trouble that night. My grandmother was a strict teetotaller, Jake—the wine was for medicinal purposes only, of course. To prevent the croup.'

'I could have cleaned the drains with that wine,' Megan said feelingly. 'I hope you like curry, Jake.'

'I spent the last four years in the Far East, during which I learned two things—to eat curry hot enough to peel the skin from the roof of your mouth, and not to enquire too closely as to what particular animal had ended up in the pot.'

Fitz laughed. 'Had I known that, I would have been more adventurous. Megan never lets me get too carried

away when it's someone we haven't met before...
Whereabouts were you, Jake?'

Jake related some of his experiences in Thailand and
Malaysia, after which Megan described a hair-raising
adventure from her hitch-hiking days in Turkey. The
second bottle of wine was opened, the children were fed,
and the adults settled around the old oak table in the
dining-room. Liane was very happy. Jake fitted in
beautifully with her friends, and was giving every appearance of enjoying himself; and how could he not?
she thought, for it was one of those evenings when
everyone seemed a little wittier than usual, when good
fellowship flowed easily and laughter echoed around the
table. Because she was happy, she flirted outrageously
with Jake, edged on by Fitz, and none of it, she knew,
was due to the wine.

The children were put to bed at eight-thirty, because
there was school the next day. At one, the adults regretfully called it a night. 'Patrick can stay if you like,
Liane,' Megan offered artlessly. 'I'll get him off to school
in the morning.'

Liane would then be alone with Jake in the house.
Very strenuously avoiding looking at him, she said, 'He
didn't bring his homework, and if he doesn't hand in
his English assignment tomorrow he's going to be in deep
trouble.'

'Another time, then,' said Megan. 'You can carry
Patrick, can you, Jake?'

'Sure,' Jake replied with one of those fractional hesitations that Liane had noticed before. 'I'll go and turn
on the heaters in the wagon first.'

When he came back in, blowing on his fingers to warm
them, Liane led the way upstairs to Clancy's room.
Patrick was sprawled on the old couch under the window,
wearing his Edmonton Oilers tracksuit, fast asleep. 'We'll
wrap the blanket around him,' she whispered.

Jake bent to gather the child into his arms while Liane adjusted the woollen folds of the blanket around Patrick's dangling limbs. Patrick muttered something fretfully, then burrowed his head into Jake's chest. For a split second the man looked as though someone had just skewered him with a knife; Liane's breath caught in her throat, but before she could say anything Jake's face had settled back into impassivity.

They went downstairs and said their goodbyes, then walked out into the cold, starlit night, the snow creaking under their boots. Liane climbed into her seat, and took Patrick from Jake, cuddling the boy to her chest, her chin resting on his auburn curls. They drove home in silence. Jake parked by the door, then walked round to take Patrick from her. 'I'll carry him upstairs,' he said briefly.

Patrick's homework occupied one half of the bed, his collection of hockey cards the other. 'I wonder how much English did get done?' Liane murmured, clearing the stuff away and pulling the bedspread back. Jake laid the boy on the mattress, and Liane covered him up. Patrick opened his eyes, said distinctly, 'The ref said it was for high-sticking,' and closed his eyes again.

Although a half-smile tugged at Jake's lips, his eyes were full of pain. Liane had drunk a considerable quantity of wine that night, and it was very late. Moving away from the bed, she said, 'You must miss your son.'

Jake's reaction, had she stopped to think, was entirely predictable. His fingers biting through her jacket, he took her by the elbow, hustled her down the stairs and yanked her round to face him in the hall. 'How many times do I have to tell you to keep out of my private life?' he snarled.

Just so had her father looked when she had told him, eight years ago, that she was pregnant. But Jake was not her father. Liane planted her feet firmly on the carpet and drew herself to her full height. 'Private life, be darned! What you're afraid of is being a human being. With feelings and regrets and pain. You're the typical macho male, the kind that Hollywood adores, all stiff upper lip and suffering in noble silence. You're not a man at all, Jake Brande—you're a robot!'

There was an instant's dead silence, while her words echoed in her ears and she had the time to be horrified that she had actually spoken them. 'Oh, am I?' said Jake, hauling her closer. 'We'll see about that.'

Liane knew instantly what he was going to do, and knew too how wrong it would be. There had been enough angry kisses between her and Jake. Too many. With the-atrical eloquence she let her eyes roll back in their sockets, her head flop forward, and her whole body go as limp as Patrick's.

She was a small woman; but she was also a dead weight. Jake staggered a little, cursing under his breath as he lowered her, more or less gently, to the floor. With what she felt privately was great artistry, Liane lay very still, feeling his knee dig into her spine and hearing against her cheek the steady beat of his heart.

He said drily, 'It's OK, Liane—you've accomplished your purpose. You can come to now.'

She sneaked a look at him through her lashes. 'You mean you weren't taken in?' she asked in an injured tone.

'Most police officers get so they can recognise a genuine faint when they see one.'

She sat up, pushing her hair back from her face. 'I got second prize for acting at the finishing school I went to in Switzerland.'

'I believe every word of it. I'll drop my so-called macho image long enough to tell you that I wish to God I could tell when you're acting and when you're not.'

'You think I'm acting all the time.' Her forehead wrinkling in thought, speaking more to herself than to him, she went on, 'I haven't needed to act since I left my father's house. I've learned to be myself instead...funny, I hadn't realised that before.'

His voice like a whiplash, Jake demanded, 'So are you implying I'm like your father?'

Her leg was lying half across his as they crouched on the carpet, his face not six inches away from hers. It was, she decided, a very odd conversation to be having on the floor in the middle of the night. 'No, you're not,' she said thoughtfully. 'The only emotion I ever get from my father is anger. I get anger from you, too. But I also see pain and laughter and gentleness.' Her eyes suddenly danced. 'But they're all rusty from disuse—that's it! You've put them all in cold storage, and now you're having a hard time making them work again.'

'You're mixing your metaphors.'

She had no idea what he was thinking, or whether every word she had said was nonsense. Unprompted, she rested her palm on his cheek, feeling the roughness of his beard and the heat of his skin. 'I'm glad you're here,' she said.

He took her uplifted hand in his own, staring at it as if he had never seen a woman's hand before, tracing the lines in her palm with one fingertip, then stroking the thin, capable fingers, bare of rings. Liane held her breath, the contact spreading from her hand through her whole body in waves as warm and full of colour as a tropical sea. This was what she had wanted, she thought. This. Not a kiss fuelled by anger.

Jake looked up, and the emotion in his eyes made the blood race in her veins. With exquisite gentleness he cupped her face in his hands and lowered his face to hers, his mouth drifting from her cheekbone down the smooth slide of her cheek to find her lips.

Liane forgot about the carpet and the lateness of the hour. She felt as though she were swaying on a raft on the tropical sea, and the sea was beckoning her, beckoning her to slide into the silken warmth of depths that were unknown to her yet charged with fascination. She felt languorous and boneless; she also felt infinitely generous.

Their tongues met and played, a cave-dance under the sea. Then Jake's hands slid beneath her jacket, finding the curve of her breast through her sweater, taking its fullness into his palm and caressing it. As sensation lapped at her, a rising tide impossible to hold back, Liane moaned with pleasure, and his kiss deepened.

Through his shirt she explored the taut, rounded muscles, probing with her fingers to learn what he felt like, this man who had come into her life so violently and so inevitably. But it was not enough. She hungered for the slide of flesh on flesh, for the removal of clothes that were in the way, barring her from truly knowing him.

As though he had read her mind, Jake raised his head, his eyes like smouldering coals. She saw him struggle to find a normal voice, and heard the hoarseness underlying it when he spoke. 'You want me as much as I want you, don't you, Liane?'

'Did you ever doubt that?' she asked with a wobbly smile.

'I doubted it.' He suddenly grinned at her, as carefree as a youth. 'You seem to spend most of your time yelling at me.'

'Sublimation.'

'Ah...' Jake kissed her again, his lips brushing hers with an open sensuality that made her sway towards him. 'We shouldn't be doing this. We have a business arrangement—you hired me, remember?'

'As a bodyguard,' Liane said, twin devils of laughter sparking her eyes.

He said with all the intensity she could have wished for, 'I don't want to guard your body—I want to possess it and put my mark on it and learn every inch of it.'

It was exactly the way she felt about him. And perhaps because her face mirrored her thoughts, Jake said roughly, 'Come to bed with me.'

She wanted to. Oh, God, how she wanted to. But eight years ago life had taught Liane a hard lesson, and that lesson was still part of her. She said in a small voice, 'I can't—I'm not protected against a pregnancy, Jake,' and watched shock and surprise chase themselves across his face.

'I thought all women were nowadays.'

'Not this one. I haven't had a lover since the man who fathered Patrick.'

'*Eight years*?'

'That's right.'

Jake eased his knee out from under her and flexed his thigh. 'So why me?' he asked bluntly.

She spoke the literal truth. 'I don't know.'

'After eight years I should think anyone would do.'

Liane's chin snapped up. 'I've had the occasional date in those eight years. I have never once felt impelled to rip the man's clothing off and drag him to the nearest bed.'

He gave a short laugh. 'I'm flattered.'

'You've gone away, Jake,' she whispered. 'What happened?'

'I don't know where I am with you,' he said violently. 'I just think I'm getting you figured out and you throw me for a loop again. *Eight years . . .*'

'I had a child to raise and a roof to put over our heads and money to earn—I didn't have the time or the energy to go chasing after everything in trousers! Anyway, the only men I've really known have been my father, who I'm not sure has ever loved anyone, my brother, who

was a carbon copy of Father, and Noel—who abandoned his own child without a thought. Why should I
go chasing after another man? They're not that great!'

Liane scrambled to her feet, cold under her jacket,
wishing once again that she had kept her mouth shut.
Jake stood up with a lean grace that, upset as she was,
still did funny things to her insides. 'I don't like women
and you don't like men,' he said. 'So why are we making
love on the hall carpet at two a.m.?'

'You tell me,' Liane answered irritably.

He chucked her under the chin. 'Go to bed, Liane.
Or you'll be even grumpier in the morning than you
usually are.'

'Don't patronise me!'

'What a little wildcat you are under that china-doll
exterior. Goodnight...pleasant dreams.'

He was openly laughing at her. Her body an ache of
sexual frustration, her emotions churning like waves on
a reef, Liane went to bed.

Monday morning. Monday mornings should never have
been invented, Liane thought, tempted to throw the
alarm clock at the wall as her feet hit the floor with a
thud. She hauled her nightgown over her head, pulled
on a tracksuit, and headed for the bathroom.

The living-room door was open. The sofa bed was
neatly back in place, and Jake was on the floor doing
push-ups. One right after the other, his back a long,
straight line, the muscles in his arms flexing in a way
that privately fascinated her. She said sharply, 'You're
a masochist, Jacob Brande.'

He glanced at her over his shoulder, not missing a
beat. His T-shirt, wet with sweat, clung to his spine, and
his forehead was slick with sweat. 'Dressed already?' he
panted.

'Now that you've moved in I'll have to buy a housecoat.'

'I thought a housecoat was part of every woman's wardrobe... twenty-eight, twenty-nine, thirty. Phew!' He stood up, bouncing on his bare feet and swiping at his forehead with the back of his arm, his grin infectious. 'It's a lovely day, Liane; the sun's shining and the sky's blue. Why don't you own a housecoat? Not that you don't look very charming as you are.'

She had made the mistake of wearing this particular outfit to the greenhouse once, and the stains had never come out. 'All the housecoats I can afford are boring,' she said obligingly. 'Terry-cloth and seersucker and insipid pink satin. I want something exotic. An embroidered caftan or a silk sarong.'

'You mean a caftan would make you spring out of bed in the mornings full of *joie de vivre*?'

'I wouldn't guarantee that.' Although right now she was certainly full of sexual energy, which, while not quite the same as *joie de vivre*, was for her most definitely a new phenomenon. And one Jake was quite astute enough to discern. She gave an exaggerated yawn, not realising how this made her breasts rise and fall under the loose top. 'Monday morning is the worst time of the week.'

He advanced on her, his eyes dancing. 'Perhaps we could improve upon it.'

His hair was clinging to his scalp, and something in Liane that had been repressed for far too long leaped up in response to the mischief in his face. 'Just what would you suggest?'

Glancing down at his damp T-shirt, he said, 'How about a little long-distance intimacy? Stand still, Liane.'

Liane was not sure she could have done otherwise. Jake leaned forward and, as the laughter in his eyes flared into another emotion altogether, he found her mouth with his own.

He kept his hands at his sides, and made no move to close the gap between them, leaving all that he wanted to say to a kiss so sensual that Liane was lost in a haze of delight. She parted her lips to the gentle urgings of his tongue, to an exploration as intimate as any she had ever known; and she longed to disobey him, to step closer and wrap her arms around him and feel the hardness of his body press into the softness of hers.

Then he eased away from her. She opened eyes dazed with pleasure, unconsciously leaning towards him in an arc of hunger, and heard him say, 'Does that improve the prospects of a Monday morning?'

'Immeasurably,' Liane whispered, and was amazed that she could produce a sound at all, let alone a word of more than one syllable.

His gaze lingered on her flushed cheeks and tangled hair. 'You don't look the slightest bit grumpy.'

She said gravely, 'Oh, I feel very grumpy. Because instead of doing what I want to do right now, I'm going to get Patrick up and go to work.'

'I shall take that as a compliment.'

'Certainly I withdraw any complaints I might once have made about your technique.'

He flexed his muscles. 'You ain't seen nothin' yet, babe.'

Liane laughed, a light-hearted peal of laughter that Fitz would have approved of. 'A whole new perspective on the first day of the week, and all before breakfast,' she said, and took herself off to the bathroom.

She worked at the library all day, and that evening helped Patrick wrestle with a one-paragraph composition about dinosaurs. There was no recurrence of the kiss in the hallway. The next day she worked in the greenhouse. Jake was gone all day, returning only when Patrick got out of school; she did not enquire where he had been. But after an early supper she said to Patrick,

'Would you like to go to Percy's this evening? Rosie had twins.'

Despite his attachment to the vast reaches of the universe, Patrick also loved the clutter and the rich odours of Percy's farm. 'Yeah!' he said. 'Right now?'

'I'll give him a call to make sure he'll be home.'

Percy's voice reverberated into the room; he would indeed be home. Liane looked across at Jake, who was still sitting at the table; he had treated her like a piece of furniture the last two days. 'Percy is the owner of the manure-spreader,' she told him repressively. 'You probably wouldn't want to come.'

He raised an expressive brow. 'I'll drive you in the wagon.'

'Let's go, then,' she said, rather ungraciously, and made sure she sat in the back seat on the way. But in the warm, hay-scented barn, where the cows shuffled in their stanchions and where Percy was so patently pleased to see them, Liane couldn't stay cross for long. The knobbly-kneed calves were as fascinated with Patrick as he was with them, there was a new crop of kittens in the feed-room, and three dozen chicks peeping under an infra-red bulb in one of the stalls. Their feathers were the soft yellow of marguerites.

Right behind her Percy boomed, 'Glad to see you've made up with Jake—took to him right away last week.' He gave her a wink that distorted his whole face. 'You need a man. All women do.'

This, even for Percy, was somewhat heavy-handed. 'Nonsense,' Liane replied. 'You men aren't nearly as indispensable as you like to think you are.'

'Not right, you bringing up a boy on your own.'

Liane flinched, for this was a direct hit. Jake interjected smoothly, 'She's doing a great job, Percy. Tell me, what's your monthly milk yield?'

Another heavy-handed intervention, but it worked. Percy loved his dairy cows, and would discourse on butterfat and milk quotas for as long as he had an audience. Half an hour later they went to the farmhouse for tea, and then they drove home, Patrick chattering excitedly to Jake the whole way. Jake buried his nose in a book for the rest of the evening.

Liane worked in the library four more days that week because she needed the money, both to pay Jake and to add to the fund she had been saving for Patrick's March break; she had reserved a chalet in the Laurentians so that they could ski. As February blustered its way into March, and the days slowly lengthened, she sometimes wondered whether she had dreamed the encounter between her and Jake on the carpet in the middle of the night, or the salutary Monday-morning kiss in the hallway. Although he was pleasant and unfailingly polite to her, he was also as remote as the far shore of the river; the channel that had opened so briefly between them had frozen over.

She kept busy, determined that he not see that she was hurt. Gradually it became clear to her that she was acting again, playing the role of a cool, self-contained mother when she felt like someone quite different.

Certainly she was a mother; she had no problem with that. But cool? Self-contained? Whenever Jake walked in the room she breathed him in through every pore in her skin, and felt his physical presence pierce every nerve-ending, as though her fingertips had been thrust into the blue heart of a flame. But his eyes were like doors shut tight against her, like stones unmoved by either her presence or her absence.

He had come close. He had retreated. She could understand neither the intimacy nor the separation. She could only ache with the loss of the closeness and yearn for its rebirth. And, because she was too proud to show her true feelings, she acted. She did not like this. But she did not know what else to do.

Midway through Jake's second week, Liane was standing at the kitchen counter one morning making Patrick's sandwiches for his school lunch when Patrick said, through a mouthful of cereal, 'Is it OK if Jake takes me to hockey practice this evening, Mum?'

Wondering if she would have enough lettuce, she replied absently, 'He always does.'

'I mean just him and me. Not you.'

Suddenly Patrick had her full attention. She flicked a glance at Jake, sipping his coffee and reading the paper, and saw this had not originated with him. 'Why?' she asked blankly.

Patrick wriggled in his seat. 'The other guys' dads take them,' he said.

But Jake's not your father, she almost blurted out. Choosing her words, Liane said, 'You'd like a man to take you?'

'Yeah. Just for today. Bobbie Graves, his dad always takes him, and he was teasing me 'cause I haven't got one.'

She stared down at the bright green lettuce leaves, which she had grown herself. 'Sure, that would be fine.'

Patrick was not insensitive. 'You don't mind, do you, Mum?'

It took every ounce of her fortitude to smile at him and say easily, 'It's a great idea—I'll put my feet up and read for an hour... You'd better go and clean your teeth, Patrick; the bus will be here soon.'

Patrick ran for the stairs, Jake rustled the newspaper, and through a sheen of tears Liane neatly wrapped the sandwiches in waxed paper. Patrick had never before told her that the boys teased him because he only had a mother, and she had always assumed he was quite happy that she was the one to take him to hockey. A tear plopped on the cookie tin as she lifted it out of the cupboard.

Jake's chair scraped on the floor. Dropping his hand on her shoulder, he said, 'It had to happen sooner or later, Liane.'

She jumped, and a cookie fell to the floor, chocolate chips shooting under the cupboard. Twisting to face him, her blue eyes anguished, she cried, 'I've failed him—by not giving him a father.'

'Don't be——' Patrick's steps thudded on the stairs. Jake added urgently, 'Wipe your eyes, kiss him goodbye, and once I've seen he's safely on the bus we'll continue this.'

She scrubbed at her eyes, sniffing hard. 'I have to be at the library at nine.'

'You'll be five minutes late.'

Liane quickly put an apple and the cookies in Patrick's lunch-box, and bent to hug him. He and Jake left the kitchen. She knelt to clean up the cookie crumbs, and suddenly found herself leaning her forehead against the cupboard door and weeping, a great flood of tears she could not have stemmed for—for all her father's money, she thought dimly, and wept the harder.

She did not hear Jake come back in the room. She felt him take her by the shoulders, and with a sob buried her face in his chest, clutching him convulsively.

She cried for a long time. But eventually her tears ran out, as tears did, and she heard Jake say, 'Here, blow your nose.'

He put a box of tissues in her hand. She blew her nose, cleared her throat, and said, 'I'm going to be more than five minutes late.'

'I phoned them,' he told her. 'I told her you weren't feeling well but that you'd probably be in after lunch.'

She looked at him through lashes stuck together in wet little clumps. 'I can't go taking time off like that. I don't get sick leave because I'm only part-time, and I need the money—you're expensive.'

'You don't have to pay me for this morning. Because you're going to put on a jacket and boots, and we're going to walk down to the river—both of us off-duty.'

There had been fresh snow in the night, the sun was streaming through the window, and Jake had just held her in his arms. 'All right,' Liane said.

'Docility—I don't believe it.'

'I told you I was a good actress.'

He reached out a hand to pull her to her feet. 'So you did. Then tell me something—why do we always have these scenes at floor level?'

His fingers were warm as they curled around hers, and all the magic of his touch flowered instantly to life. Liane snatched her hand back. 'Not that. Not right now.'

'It's always there, though, isn't it?' Jake said slowly. 'Every minute I'm in this house I'm aware of you.'

'But you never touch me,' she said with painful truth. 'You haven't for days.'

'I'm afraid to—didn't you guess that?' He grinned mirthlessly. 'I can face a gang of drug bandits in the jungles of Thailand, but a woman who's five-feet-five has me on the run.'

She eyed him warily, scrambling to her feet. 'We're going for a walk,' she reminded him. 'Outdoors. After I wash my face.'

Her face, in the bathroom mirror, looked exactly like that of a woman who had just cried her eyes out. Liane splashed cold water on it, and made no attempt to repair the ravages of too much emotion; let Jake see her as she was, she thought. The real woman. She was tired of acting. She pulled on her pink ski-suit, which matched her pink nose, and went to join him at the back door.

CHAPTER EIGHT

IT WAS a beautiful day, the sun sparkling like flung jewels on the white carpet of snow, the sky as blue as Liane's eyes. She took a deep breath of the clean, cold air and was glad she wasn't buried in the stacks at the library, and even more glad that she was with Jake.

Truly with him. Jake, who was a man who kept his emotions tightly under wraps, had just admitted he was afraid of her. She needed time to think about that.

While they wandered down to the river she described what the gardens looked like in summer, her hands gesticulating, her face vivid with enthusiasm. The rhododendrons and azaleas, sheltered by tall pines, stood sturdily in the snow, their branches laced with long necklaces of crystals that sparkled more brightly than diamonds. The buds were tightly folded against the cold. 'This one's called Snow in Summer,' Liane said. 'Pure white petals with just a touch of scarlet in the centre.'

'You know a lot about gardening.'

'When Patrick gets a little older I'd like to take more courses on horticulture and landscape design . . . I love it.'

They were emerging from the trees. Jake suddenly put a hand on her arm and whispered, 'Look . . . to your left by the alders.'

A red fox, his bushy tail brushing the snow, was loping across the field. As if he had sensed their presence, he stopped, testing the air with black nostrils, his ears pricked. Then with a great bound he headed for the tangle of shrubs, and disappeared.

'Wasn't he beautiful?' Liane breathed. 'So wild and free...'

Jake said harshly, 'Freedom's an illusion, Liane.'

His words touched a chord she had secretly known was there, a raw place where resentment lingered. 'That's easy for you to say. You've got a month's holiday, and you can decide to spend it here, there or anywhere. I love Patrick, but that love costs me my freedom. I'm not free—not like you!'

'You think I wouldn't trade what you've got for what I've got?'

'I would have thought you'd have spent your month off nearer your son,' she said, and knew she had put into words the one facet of Jake's character she could not deal with.

The lines were scored deep into Jake's face. 'I can't,' he told her. 'He's dead.'

Into the silence a crow cawed somewhere over their heads, and from the riverbank another answered. '*Dead*?' Liane whispered.

'For four years.'

She felt his pain as if it were her own, for how would she survive if something happened to Patrick? Jake was standing under a pine tree, his face in shadow; she closed the distance between them, stepping into the shadow to join him, and instinctively put her arms around him. But Jake struck her away. 'Don't!' he said violently.

Keep your distance. Stay away. Without a trace of the emotion that was churning within her, Liane said, 'Your wife left you five years ago...was your son living with you, Jake?'

He replied in the flat voice of one who had recited these facts before and had not allowed them to touch him. 'No. I left him with her; I thought it was better that way—she was his mother. She re-married almost immediately, a decent enough guy, a lawyer with a nice,

steady nine-to-five job. Five months later, after giving
Daniel time to settle in, they went for a delayed
honeymoon. I was going to take him for three weeks,
but I had a case to tie up beforehand, so we'd arranged
that he go to camp for a week... He fell out of a tree
his fourth day there, and was dead by the time the other
boys got to him.'

'And you've been blaming yourself ever since.'

'Wouldn't you?'

'Probably,' she said honestly.

'My wife blamed me, too—or rather my job. She's
had two children since then, both boys.'

'Whereas you left the country.'

'I applied for an overseas posting, and when I got it
I did my level best to get killed in the line of duty.' Jake
kicked at the snow with his boot. 'As you see, it didn't
work. But, because I took every risk there was to take,
I turned up drug cartels under every bush, and got myself
promoted into the bargain. Two months ago head office
pulled me out of there; it was getting a little too hot even
for me, and that was when I realised I no longer wanted
to end up six feet under the ground in the rain forest.'
He pushed away from the tree. 'I guess you could call
that a cure of a kind.'

He was not cured at all, Liane thought, vaguely aware
of how cold it was in the shade of the tree. 'I'm truly
sorry I said that about freedom, Jake.'

'Loving Daniel was the closest I ever came to freedom,'
he revealed with painful exactitude. 'My wife and I fell
out of love almost immediately. She'd married the glamorous police officer in the red serge uniform, and soon
found out that there was precious little glamour in my
job. I'd married a woman I'd thought was independent,
and found her clinging to me night and day. But I loved
Daniel. To use your words, I loved him more than anyone
else in the world.'

Blinking back tears, Liane said, 'I understand now why ever since you arrived you've been keeping your distance from Patrick.'

Finally Jake reached out and touched her, his hand in its leather glove resting briefly on her pink sleeve. 'If I find myself getting too fond of Patrick, I'll have to leave,' he told her.

Feeling as though he had just punched her in the stomach, Liane said sharply, 'And let him be kidnapped?'

'I don't think that's going to happen, Liane. Your father wouldn't court that kind of publicity—taking a child from its mother. Not in the circles he moves in.'

The cold was penetrating to her very bones. 'He knows what you seem to be blind to—that he has the power and I have none. No money, no influential friends. Only the vulnerability that comes from loving my son.'

'I've been here nearly two weeks. Not a move. No sign of Chester—who could certainly have found you by now had he wanted to. I think you were exaggerating.' Jake's voice gentled. 'I understand why. But I don't believe Patrick's in jeopardy.'

'Do you still think I'm trying to con my father?'

'I'm not quite so ready to believe that, either.'

She should have been pleased by this admission; and she too had had moments of doubt about her father, for he was a man who moved fast when he wanted something, and as far as Patrick was concerned he had not moved at all. But she was neither pleased nor relieved. She moved back from Jake, not wanting him to see that she was shivering, and took refuge in anger. 'Then if, according to you, Patrick's in no danger, maybe you're right and you should leave, Jake—before you risk loving someone again. Patrick. Or me. It doesn't really make any difference who, does it?'

His mouth a thin line, Jake snapped, 'I said I'd stay for a month.'

'I absolve you from that—you can leave any time you like. The sooner the better.'

'I'll leave when I'm good and ready!'

'And what if Patrick gets attached to *you*? Have you thought of that? You saw what happened this morning— he could get hurt too, especially if he starts seeing you as a father-figure.'

Jake said tightly, 'Yes, I'd thought of that.'

He too had stepped into the sunlight. His eyes looked almost black to Liane, like the plumage of the crows cawing by the river. Seven crows a secret. Not stopping to think, because if she did she wouldn't say it, she went on, 'I'm at risk, too. I'm in danger of falling in love with you, and I don't want to do that. So why don't you go home and pack your bags before anyone gets hurt— you or Patrick or me?'

He said flatly, 'You have this gift for taking me by surprise—what do you mean, you're in danger of falling in love with me? It's called lust, Liane. Not love.'

Liane retorted, grappling with a truth she had only just acknowledged, 'I'll call it what I like. And love is the word I used.'

'You don't like men—you said so.'

With a faint smile she responded, 'You're not men, Jake—I thought I'd made that clear to you. You're one particular man who affects me in a way I've never been affected before. I don't know if this is what falling in love feels like. I do know that it would be better for all of us if you left.'

His eyes were like storm clouds at dusk, gathering in the blackness of the sky. 'If we went to bed together, you'd understand what I mean when I talk about lust and love.'

'Make love just to prove you right? No!'

'Make love for pleasure. For fun and laughter and sharing. But not for love.'

To her dismay her whole body sprang to life. Almost inaudibly she said, 'And then you'll get dressed and pack your bags and head off into the sunset? No, Jake, I won't do that.'

'I'm not Noel!'

She glared at him across the snow. 'I don't know who you are!'

She looked away, unable to bear the intensity of his gaze, and from the corner of her eye caught sight of the fox tracks, the paw-prints close together where it had been trotting along, then abruptly separated by stretches of unmarked snow where it had bounded for the safety of the shrubs. It had known when to run, she thought, it was smarter than she was, and heard Jake say, 'We talk too much, you and I. Let's go back to the house.'

'We argue too much,' she corrected. 'We came out for a walk, and here we are fighting again.'

'We wouldn't fight in bed,' he said.

She bit her lip. She had no difficulty at all picturing herself and Jake lying naked side by side in her bed, his dark head cushioned on her breast, his strong thighs holding her close. She said frantically, 'Stop it—I can't stand it!'

He ordered her pitilessly, 'Go back to the house by yourself, then—and in the interests of compromise I'll stay until next week, when you and Patrick leave for the Laurentians.'

Five more days. Pain constricted Liane's chest and tightened her throat. 'Making love means just that,' she asserted stubbornly. 'Making *love*.'

Deliberately ignoring her, Jake said, 'You'll be working at the library until six tonight, won't you? I'll get Patrick's supper.'

Five days. Then he would be gone, and she would never know if making love to him would have been different from the nights she had spent in Noel's cramped and not very clean apartment down by the waterfront. She was almost sure it would be different. Almost.

Inexorably her thoughts carried her forward. She had used the word risk a few moments ago; but how long since she had actually taken a risk?

Eight years ago, she thought. That was when she had come back from the protected environment of a very strict finishing school to go to university in Halifax. Drunk with freedom, she had gravitated to the art school crowd, fascinated by their repudiation of all the rules that had governed her life, enthralled by Noel, their flame-haired ringleader. Patrick had been the almost inevitable result.

Since then her whole lifestyle had mitigated against risk, especially where the opposite sex was concerned. Instead she had opted for non-involvement. For safety. Risk she had banished along with all the untidy emotions that it could bring.

She took a deep breath and said steadily, 'I've got a better idea, Jake. Let's go back to the house together and I'll show you what making love means to me.'

Her words seemed to hang, frozen, in the crisp winter air; yet she had said them. Unquestionably she had said them. Dredging up all her self-reliance, she told herself that at least this way she would have memories when Jake was gone. Memories, and the satisfaction of knowing she had broken out of the shell she had built around herself so long ago.

Jake's whole body had gone very still. 'Liane, do you mean that?'

She raised her chin. 'Yes, I mean it.'

'I'll protect you from pregnancy,' he said.

She did not want talk of pregnancies; she wanted talk of love. And wondered if she was a fool to take this particular risk with this particular man, she who was not at all sure she knew what love between man and woman meant.

Then Jake said softly, 'I've never faulted your courage.'

Swinging her up into his arms, he began jogging through the pines, past the leather-leaved rhododendrons and out into the open space of the garden. Liane hung on, bouncing against his chest, feeling the strength of his arms and hearing his breath rasp in his throat. He took the back steps two at a time, and then he was pushing through the back door and locking it behind him, kicking off his boots as he did so.

Still holding her in his arms, he carried her to the door of her room. There he put her down. 'I'll be back in a minute,' he said. 'Don't go away.'

She knew where he was going: to get the protection he had mentioned. I'm crazy, she thought shakily. I'm doing exactly what I said I wouldn't do—having an affair with a man who's made it quite clear he doesn't love me now and won't hang around long enough to find out if he could love me in the future. This isn't risk. It's madness.

She was still standing rooted to the spot when Jake came back. He had shed his outer garments and was barefoot. Again he caught her up in his embrace, lifting her over the threshold and putting her down on the bed. Then he yanked off her boots and unzipped her snow-suit, all with a businesslike air that terrified her. 'Jake——' she gasped. 'Jake, I don't——'

He dropped the snow-suit to the floor, and lay down beside her on the bed, gathering her into his arms. 'Don't look so worried, sweetheart,' he said. 'Maybe what you call making love and I call sharing is the same thing.

Maybe we should just forget all the words and all the other people—Noel, and my wife and my son and yours—and do what seems the most natural thing in the world whenever we're together...'

Sweetheart, he had called her, he who was not a man to use endearments lightly. And the light in his eyes as he pushed her hair back from her face with hands that were not quite steady could very easily be construed as tenderness. Jake, I love you, Liane thought experimentally, and let the simple little words echo in her heart. Jake, I love you...

She had no idea whether she meant them or not; she did know she was glad to be where she was, lying beside him on the bed, that it was where she had wanted to be for what seemed like a very long time. She smiled into his eyes. 'I think you've got the right idea. No talk...'

'No arguments,' he added, laughter-lines fanning from the corners of his eyes.

'No past or future,' she went on seriously. 'Just the present.'

'Here and now, you and me. Show me how you'd make love to me, Liane.'

His voice had a note she had not heard before, and his face was unguarded, gentle in a way that was new to her. Perhaps here in her bed she would learn more about Jake than about herself, she thought, taking his face between her palms and kissing him. The first touch of her lips was shy, tentative, poised for flight, because she was, at some level, still afraid. But his mouth was warm and familiar to her, and very much desired, so that she found nothing to frighten her and everything to encourage her. As he threw his thigh over her legs, just as she had imagined he would, she dropped her hands and started undoing the buttons of his shirt one by one.

He leaned up on one elbow, watching her, his eyes intent on her face. She glanced up, her lips a warm curve, her face open to him and without guile. When he kissed her, a slow, sensual kiss, she lost track of the buttons and instead ran her fingers through the dark hair that covered his chest, and then clasped his ribcage, exulting in the hard curve of bone and the heat of his skin. With a tiny ripping sound the last button gave way.

Against her mouth Jake said, 'You did once mention tearing my clothes off, didn't you?'

She chuckled. 'I hadn't realised I was so literal-minded.'

And then she said nothing for quite a while, as Jake lifted her shirt over her head and unclasped her bra, tossing the garments to the floor and taking the fullness of her breasts in his hands. A few minutes later his shirt joined hers, and then two pairs of jeans and two sets of underwear.

They were facing each other on the bed, the clear winter sun falling impartially on them both as Jake's hands ran the length of her body from her shoulders down the pale slope of her breasts to the slim, neat waist and the stretch marks on her belly. He said huskily, 'Every night since I've met you I've lain awake in the middle of the night and tried to picture your body... I never imagined it could be this beautiful.' His face was suddenly full of doubt. 'I'm afraid I'll hurt you, you're so small and delicately made...'

Intuitively Liane knew that it was his wife, the woman who had never accepted Jake as he was, who was responsible for his doubts. Fiercely she said, 'I'm tough, Jake. I've borne a child, remember? And I want you so much I don't see how you could possibly hurt me.' She reached out a hand, wrapping it round all the hardness that was his need for her, and saw his face convulse with longing.

He said jaggedly, 'It's been so long...oh, God, come here, Liane.'

She met him more than halfway, and their first coupling was fast and primitive and strong, over almost before it had begun. But even as Jake lay across her, panting, his hand was smoothing the length of her thigh and the rise of her hip, and without haste he started kissing her again, slow kisses of exploration and burgeoning desire. And again Liane met him more than halfway, letting him see her own hungers, guiding him to touch her where she was most sensitive, finding what pleased him and giving with measureless generosity and obvious pleasure.

The second time was like the gradual opening of a summer flower to the sun, and, as the golden heat enveloped her and the flames pulsed within her, Liane clutched Jake to her with all her strength, hiding from him neither the broken cries coming from deep in her throat nor her passion-dazed eyes. She saw his face clench, felt his own throbbing as if it were her own, and buried her face in the hollow of his shoulder, loving him with all her heart.

He collapsed beside her on the bed, his chest heaving, holding her as if he never meant to let her go. Feeling utterly safe, a safety she was not sure she had known since the long-ago days when her mother had held her, Liane said, 'Do you know what?'

Jake raised his head, his eyes suddenly full of laughter. 'I couldn't begin to guess.'

She ran her fingertip along the entrancing dip of his collar-bone. 'This all felt so natural,' she murmured. 'As though we've been doing it together for years...do you know what I mean?'

He nodded. 'Is that new for you?'

'Oh, yes.' Her forehead wrinkled. 'I was paralysingly shy with Noel, and it was always awkward, jumpy, full of fits and starts. And in the end I never quite felt the way I thought I should—I was often disappointed, and yet the fault had to be in me; Noel seemed to think everything was fine.'

In a carefully non-committal voice Jake asked, 'And today was different?'

Liane's smile was lilting. 'You're fishing for compliments, Jake Brande! You know darn well it was different. I never knew I could be so—so swept up, so completely taken over.' She gave a sigh of repletion, nuzzling at his throat. 'It was wonderful.'

He hesitated, and she felt the tension in the arm lying across her. 'It was different for me, too. You gave me more than I've ever been given. Freely. Because you wanted to.'

His wife had not been like that; Liane knew she had not. She said simply, 'I didn't even think about giving— I just did what felt right, and loved every minute of it.'

She had used the word love. And could use it again, she thought slowly. Could say to him, Jake, I love you, and know the words for the truth. She scanned his face, letting her eyes dwell on every detail, so well-known to her, so dearly loved, and heard him say harshly, 'When you look at me like that, I—hell, I don't know what I'm saying. It hurts, Liane. Hurts something so deep that I scarcely know it's there.'

She held her breath. 'Tell me about it.'

He shook his head, running his fingers through his hair. 'It's nothing; I'm being a fool...' With an effort she could actually see, he banished the shadows from his face. 'If you're going to work this afternoon, you'd better get moving, lady. It's eleven forty-five.'

She sat up, gaping at the clock by the bed. 'It can't be! Already?'

'That's what happens when you're having fun,' Jake said, leering at her as he buried his face between her breasts.

She giggled, pushing him away. 'Stop that! How am I going to face Miss Mablethorpe at the library after doing what we've just done? It must be written all over me.'

Jake scanned her flushed cheeks. 'Tell her you've got a fever,' he suggested. 'Maybe she'll send you home to recuperate.'

'Maybe she'll send me down to the basement to unpack books,' Liane countered. 'I won't even have time for lunch.'

Jake's grin was frankly lascivious. 'I thought I'd already given you lunch...but, if you insist, I'll make you a sandwich.'

Liane pulled a face at him, bounced out of bed and started grabbing clothes from her closet. 'Peanut butter and cheese spread,' she said promptly.

Jake raised an expressive eyebrow. 'You'd prefer *that* to me?'

Liane turned, a skirt and blouse draped over her arm, and fluttered her lashes coyly. 'Oh, I wouldn't go that far.'

'How about some black olives on the cheese spread?' he asked, getting out of bed and stretching with a muscular grace that made her wish Miss Mablethorpe on the other side of the continent.

'I wouldn't go that far, either,' she replied, and fled to the shower.

She got to work with two minutes to spare, two minutes that Jake spent very comprehensively kissing her goodbye, and sneaked in the side-door of the library. Miss Mablethorpe was undoubtedly related to the matron in her moral standards if not by ties of blood, and would be genuinely scandalised were she to suspect just how Liane had spent the morning.

Fortunately Miss Mablethorpe was still on her lunch-break. Liane settled herself with a pile of new orders and began cataloguing them, although she did have a tendency every little while to gaze off into space with a tiny smile on her lips. Jake had been wonderful—the kind of lover that subconsciously she had always dreamed of, and now that they had crossed the bridge into true intimacy she did not think there would be any more talk of his leaving. Only when she remembered the pain that had surfaced in his eyes, a pain he had refused to talk about, would a frown cloud her face.

The afternoon seemed to last forever. At five to six Liane put the pile of cards on her boss's desk, and said goodnight. Miss Mablethorpe, who had probably never told a lie in her life, smiled at her trustingly. 'Goodnight, Ms Daley. I'm glad you're feeling better.'

Liane fought down a blush and escaped to the outdoors. The red wagon was parked on the street, Jake at the wheel, Patrick and all his hockey gear in the back. Jake said casually, 'I'll drop you off at home, Liane, and we'll go on to the practice.'

She had forgotten about the hockey practice; yet that was what had started everything. Jake drove off, his attention on the road, his ungloved hands resting lightly on the wheel. She thought of some of the things those hands had done to her, shivered with secret pleasure, and turned in the seat so that she could see Patrick. 'How was your day?' she asked, and was surprised to hear that her voice sounded quite normal.

He gave her a gleeful grin, his red hair sticking out like the halo of an unruly saint. 'I made a hundred in maths and thirty-three less in English,' he said.

Liane did some quick calculations in her head based on the last test. 'Thirty-three is better than forty-three.'

'That's what I thought...Bobbie'll be surprised to see me at hockey with Jake. Jake's gonna referee the game—the coach asked him to.'

'I used to play Junior A hockey,' Jake interjected, turning down the driveway.

He had yet to look her in the eye. Suddenly frightened out of all proportion, feeling exiled from far more than a hockey practice, Liane reached for the door-handle. 'Have fun, Patrick,' she said with a lightness she was far from feeling.

Jake briefly touched her on the shoulder. When her eyes flew to meet his she was rewarded with a smile of singular sweetness that made her long to throw her arms around him and never let him go. 'See you later,' he said.

It was not often that Liane wished Patrick a thousand miles away, but right now she did. 'OK,' she replied, and slid to the ground. The wagon drove away. She went in the house.

In the kitchen a hearty stew was bubbling on the stove, the vegetables were prepared, and on the table in an exquisite crystal vase that she had never seen before was a single deep red rose. The base of the vase was resting on a small envelope. Liane opened it. In a decisive and very masculine scrawl Jake had written, 'Thank you for this morning. You more than proved your point. Jake.'

Liane sat down in the nearest chair, inhaled the elusive scent of the rose, and wondered why, when she was so happy, she should feel like crying.

CHAPTER NINE

WHEN Jake and Patrick returned, Liane had the kitchen cleaned up and was sitting in the living-room knitting, having discovered she could not concentrate on a book. Patrick dashed in the room and flung his jacket on the nearest chair, his hair plastered to his forehead where he had perspired under his helmet. 'We had a practice game and the coach put me on forward and I got two goals,' he announced. 'Bobbie got three penalties, didn't he, Jake?'

'Two for icing, one for roughing.'

'It was fun,' Patrick said with immense satisfaction. 'Will you take me again next week, Jake?'

'You'll be on your school break next week,' Jake replied evasively.

'Oh, yeah ... are you coming with us? Is he, Mum?'

Liane opened her mouth with no idea what she was going to say. Jake put in smoothly, 'No, I can't come, Patrick.'

Patrick's face fell. 'We're going skiing in the Laurentians—I bet you're a good skier. Why can't you come?'

Quickly Liane said, 'Jake's reasons could be private, Patrick; you mustn't pry.'

Staring at Jake, Patrick said rebelliously, 'But you'll be here when we get back, won't you?'

Jake knelt beside him, clasping the boy by the shoulders. 'I don't know. Your mother hired me to keep an eye on you because of the threats that your grandfather made. But it's beginning to look as though he didn't mean them, and I can't stay too much longer—I have a job to go to up in Ottawa.'

Patrick's lower lip quivered ominously. 'Why don't you marry my mum, and then we could all stay together?' he blurted.

One of Liane's knitting-needles slid to the floor and she dropped six stitches. She had been afraid that her son would get too fond of Jake, and she had been right. Jake said soberly, 'I understand how much you'd like that, Patrick, but your mother and I can't make that kind of commitment just because you want us to.'

'Don't you like her?' Patrick demanded, glowering at the man hunkered down in front of him.

'Of course I do. But there's more to marriage than liking someone.'

Patrick's grey eyes flooded with tears that spilled over and began to stream down his cheeks. 'I don't want you to go!' he wailed, and threw himself into Jake's arms. Jake staggered under the weight, bracing himself as he hugged the boy to his chest, his mouth set and his eyes grim. Liane said nothing, her stomach curdling with fear. What was it Jake had said? If I find myself getting too fond of Patrick, I'll have to leave...

Although Patrick cried only rarely, he did a thorough job when he did cry. Jake's jacket was blotched with tears when the boy finally pushed himself away, his nose red and his eyes still watery. 'I'm going upstairs,' he muttered, and ran from the room.

Unable to bear the look on Jake's face, for the last boy he would have held like that must have been his own son, Liane bent and picked up the needle and then got to her feet. 'I'll go and see if he's all right,' she said.

'Leave him, Liane.'

Jake had levered himself upright, and was picking Patrick's coat up from the chair. 'He's upset,' she told him unnecessarily.

'And you can't make it better. So don't try.'

In a voice she strove to make casual, Liane asked, 'Won't you be back after the break?'

'After what just happened, you should be begging me to stay away,' he said grimly.

In the same even voice she heard herself ask, 'You wouldn't give any thought to marrying me?' and as soon as the words were out wished them unsaid, for the look on Jake's face gave her her answer.

'You're the one who said no past and no future, only the present.'

He was right, of course. She had. Abruptly she headed for the door, giving him a wide berth. She need not have bothered; he made no attempt to stop her.

Patrick was curled up in a ball on his bed. Liane sat down beside him, inwardly praying for wisdom. 'Why don't you get into bed and I'll bring you up some cookies and milk?'

'Not hungry.'

'I'll leave them by your bed, then, in case you want a midnight snack.'

Patrick lifted his face; because he was fair-skinned, there were blue shadows under his eyes. 'I bet if you asked him to marry you, he would,' he burst out. 'It's OK for girls to ask—our social studies teacher said so.'

The social studies teacher was an ardent feminist. Wishing she could find this funny, Liane said, 'I'm afraid you're wrong, Patrick. To Jake we're just part of a job he took on. And now he doesn't think the job needs doing any more. So he'll be leaving very soon.' Maybe if she said this often enough she'd begin to believe it herself.

'I hate him!' Patrick cried, tears spurting over his lashes again.

Knowing better than to debate this, Liane said firmly, 'That's enough, love. Hop into bed and I'll bring you up the cookies.'

When she went downstairs there was a note on the hall table in handwriting she now recognised. 'Gone for a walk. J.' Risk, she thought bitterly, smoothing the scrap of paper in her hands. After today, she would never take another risk in her life.

Patrick had calmed down by the time she went upstairs with the cookies and milk; she read to him until she saw his lashes drift to his cheek and his head fall sideways on the pillow. Then she switched out the light and went back downstairs.

There was no sign of Jake. Liane soaked in a tub filled to the brim with hot water, picked up the dropped stitches and knitted several rows on her sweater, and went to bed, closing the door behind her. An hour later she was still wide awake, staring into the darkness, when she heard the soft opening and closing of the front door and then the squeal of the hinges as Jake pulled out the sofa bed. He went to the bathroom. The bedsprings creaked as he lay down. And eventually she must have gone to sleep.

Liane woke at one and at two-thirty and at twenty to four, and each time she lay with burning eyes praying for sleep so that this interminable night would be over. Normally she hated mornings. But tonight she found herself longing for the arrival of dawn, which couldn't possibly be worse than the agonising slowness of these hours of darkness.

When she saw her bedroom door open and heard a voice whisper her name, she almost thought it was part of a dream; certainly it did not occur to her to be frightened. She half sat up, pushing her hair back from her face. 'Jake? Is that you?'

Jake came through the door, then closed it behind him. He was wearing a pair of jeans, the hair on his chest a dark blur. Leaning against the door, he said in a voice gravelly with exhaustion, 'I couldn't sleep. You were awake, too.'

She hugged her knees under the covers, almost dizzy with happiness that he was here in her room. She nodded, not trusting herself to speak.

'I should stay away from you,' he rasped. 'Stay away and get the hell out of here in the morning.'

'Don't talk that way!' she cried. 'I hate it when you do.'

He said, speaking so low she had to strain to hear him, 'I want you so badly I don't know myself any more—don't know why I'm here or what I'm doing or where I am...you're the only reality. The perfume of your body. Your incredible generosity. Your——' he hesitated, searching for the words '—beauty of soul.'

Liane said quietly, for those last three words were the kind of words she had wanted from him for what seemed like forever, 'Come here, Jake.'

He was still standing by the door, his eyes like black holes in his face. She reached down, pulled her nightgown over her head and tossed it to the floor, then held her arms out to him, her breasts a pale gleam in the darkness. With a muffled groan Jake crossed the distance between them, like an arrow flying to the gold. He fell on top of her, wrapping his arms around her with crushing strength, holding her as if he never meant to let her go. Her nostrils were filled with the scent of his body, her nipples rasped by the mat of hair on his chest, and again she felt that dizzying surge of happiness. 'I want you too,' she whispered. 'Oh, Jake, I want you so much...'

The words were almost banal, but not the intensity with which she spoke. Jake raised his head and kissed her, an impassioned kiss full of desperation and hunger, and somehow she caught the mood from him. They made love in silence, claiming each other with a raw honesty and pride that made a mockery of both modesty and inhibition, and that allowed no barriers between them. He rode her like a wild stallion, and frantically she gathered him in, arching her back, her own rhythms galloping through her body, carrying her to the very brink of the cliff and the long plunge into an oblivion that was balanced on the knife-edge between pleasure and pain.

Jake collapsed beside her, and they lay still, their limbs entangled and hearts racing, and Liane could not have separated her own panting breath from his. She did not want to, she thought muzzily. She didn't ever want to be separated from him.

As if someone had pulled a black curtain over her eyes, she fell asleep.

Liane woke to the pallor of a winter dawn and to Jake's hand edging itself from under her breast. Rubbing at her eyes, feeling once again how natural it was to wake and find him there, she wrapped her arms around his ribs and said contentedly, 'Good morning. I didn't dream you after all.'

With a thread of laughter in his voice Jake replied, 'For dreams like that you could be arrested.'

She smoothed her palm over the crest of his hip-bone to his thigh. 'You feel so nice,' she murmured. 'Did we really do some of the things that I remember us doing?'

'And more,' assured Jake.

'Well,' said Liane.

He kissed the tip of her nose. 'It's five to seven and I'd better get out of here before Patrick wakes up.'

She groaned. 'You mean I have to get up and make his lunch and go to work? Maybe that's why I'm such a grump in the mornings . . . because I'd rather be in bed with you.' And, her eyes brimming with mischief, she did something very suggestive with her free hand.

The response raced across Jake's face. 'You're a temptress. A siren. I'm going to put the coffee-pot on.'

But for a moment he stayed where he was, resting on his elbow, drinking in the pale beauty of her body. Liane said shakily, 'When you look at me like that I can hardly breathe.'

'I know the feeling.' He smiled at her, a smile that made her heart turn over with love. 'You look like the cat that ate the canary . . . a rather tired cat, at that.'

'A substantial canary,' Liane added demurely.

He laughed. 'Wipe the grin off your face—Miss Mablethorpe will know exactly what you've been up to.'

He climbed out of bed, and Liane watched as he pulled on his jeans, admiring the long line of his spine and the smooth play of muscles in his back, already feeling the emptiness in her arms where she had been holding him. From the bedside table the alarm began to beep.

Her feet hit the floor. '*That* takes the grin off,' she announced, and yawned, stretching her arms over her head, her naked body silvered by the pale morning light.

Jake had been standing by the door, his hand on the knob. He said in a voice raw with feeling, 'I can never get enough of you . . . right now I'd give everything I own to be able to spend the morning in bed with you.'

Fear brushed her like the wings of a moth that dwelt in the dark, for the emotion in his voice had not been pleasure but a kind of baffled resentment. She picked up her nightgown and pulled it over her head. 'I've got to have a shower, Jake.'

'Yeah . . .' He was looking at her almost as if she were an enemy; she scurried past him and locked herself in the bathroom. Her eyes, like Patrick's last night, were blue-shadowed. Scowling at her reflection, she reached

for her toothbrush and tried to submerge her confusion
in the routine of an ordinary weekday morning.

Patrick looked tired, and at the breakfast table spoke
to Jake as little as possible. Liane kissed him goodbye,
and watched him trudge up the hill to catch the school
bus, his boots scuffing in the snow. How had Jake so
swiftly found his way through their defences? she wondered helplessly.

Because Patrick wants a father. And because I was
ready to fall in love.

The big yellow bus pulled up at the top of the hill,
and Patrick climbed aboard. Although Liane was sure
he wasn't watching, she waved anyway. Then she went
indoors to make her own lunch, after which Jake drove
her to the library. 'Patrick and I will pick you up at six,'
he said. 'Don't shelve the As under Z, will you?'

'Jake, I——' She stopped, frustrated, wondering if all
love-affairs were so difficult, so fraught with undercur-
rents, knowing in a way that she was glad to have a few
hours away from him. 'I won't,' she told him, and despite herself leaned over to kiss him goodbye. Their lips
met and fused as if the wild coupling in the night had
never happened. She pulled back and said unhappily, 'I
wish I knew what was going on.'

'I'll do my best not to hurt you—I swear that. And I
promise I'll be here tonight.'

Tonight, yes. But what about tomorrow and the next
day and the next?

At four o'clock Miss Mablethorpe beckoned Liane to
the telephone, her lips pursed. 'A personal call, Ms
Daley,' she said, passing the receiver across her desk.
Personal calls were frowned upon in the county library.

'Hello?' said Liane.

'It's Megan. Patrick got off the bus here, says he wants
to stay the night. Is that OK with you? It's fine with us.'

Liane knew instantly why Patrick wanted to be at Megan's: so he wouldn't have to deal with Jake. Her heart sank, for how could she blame him? Horribly aware that her boss was listening to every word, she said, 'Jake says he's leaving on Monday... that's the problem.'

'I rather thought so. Fitz says there are ways you could change his mind.'

'Tell Fitz to get lost.'

'Jake *can't* leave, Liane—he's perfect for you!'

Liane was in complete agreement. Perhaps her silence spoke for itself; Megan added, 'He could go with you to the Laurentians, couldn't he?'

'Patrick already asked him—he doesn't want to.'

Megan said something very pungent that Liane hoped Miss Mablethorpe had not overheard. 'Do you want me to speak to him? Jake, I mean.'

'No! Megan, I've got to go. Tell Patrick to let Jake know where he is. And phone me if Patrick changes his mind this evening and wants to come home.'

'Will do. Good luck—he's such a *fool*!' And Megan rang off.

She had not been referring to Patrick. Liane replaced the receiver, gave Miss Mablethorpe a vague, unhappy smile, and went back to the stacks. She would have approximately fourteen hours alone with Jake in the house. Fourteen hours to change his mind.

But how?

Jake's opening words as Liane climbed in the wagon were, 'Patrick's staying at Megan's.'

'I know. She phoned me.'

'You don't think he should be home on a school night?'

She raised her chin in deliberate challenge. 'Tomorrow's the last day of school before the break.

And if you're still planning to leave on Monday, what's the point of him seeing more of you than he has to?'

'Patrick's the crux of the matter, isn't he?' Jake banged his clenched fist on the wheel in frustration. 'Liane, if this were just a question of you and I, two adults, I'd probably stay. But it isn't. There's a seven-year-old boy involved, a boy who's crying out for a father and who's incapable of hiding his feelings. If you and I got involved and it didn't work out—sure, we'd get hurt, but we could handle it. But I can't risk that with Patrick! I won't!'

She could see the tension bunched in his fists, taut in his jawline. 'Because your own son's dead,' she said.

Staring straight ahead of him through the windscreen, Jake said tightly, 'I wasn't always a perfect parent—who is? And now that Daniel's dead I can't make amends... but what I can do is not mess up Patrick's life.'

When she touched Jake on the arm she could feel the tremors running through his body. Acting on instinct, she took him by the shoulders, saw the tears blurring his eyes, and drew him close, her heart aching for him.

His head sagged on to her shoulder and she felt a hard, dry sob shake him, the pent-up emotion of a man who had never given himself permission to cry. Holding him close, Liane let her cheek drop on to his hair, so thick and clean and soft.

The library door opened and Miss Mablethorpe came out, carefully locking it behind her; she never trusted anyone else with this task. Then she walked down the path towards the wagon. From her perspective she would have seen a furtive embrace in the front seat of a car on the premises of her beloved library. Liane, glaring at her over Jake's head, dared her to do anything about it.

Head in the air, Miss Mablethorpe scurried past the wagon, got in her little brown two-door, and drove off with an unladylike clash of gears. Greatly heartened by this small victory, Liane rubbed her cheek in Jake's hair and murmured, 'If men could cry more and women could yell more, we'd all be a lot better off.'

Slowly he freed himself, making no effort to hide the tears streaking his face. 'But real men don't cry...'

'And nice girls don't get angry.'

'It does seem kind of ridiculous, doesn't it? Maybe if I'd let out some of the emotion clogged up inside me after Daniel died, I wouldn't have tried so damn hard to walk in front of a stray bullet out in Thailand.'

Liane said forcefully, 'I'm very glad you didn't succeed.'

'So, right now, am I. Who walked past a moment ago?'

She should have known he wouldn't have missed that. 'My boss. She undoubtedly thinks that by now we're fornicating on the floor of the wagon.'

'Between the brake pedal and the clutch...it would have the charm of novelty, Liane.'

She loved it when he smiled like that. 'I'm ten years too old,' she insisted.

'Somehow I doubt that.' He brushed her lips with his. 'Thanks,' he said. 'Shall we go home?'

When she walked in the door there was a stack of mail on the hall table, including a large flat box neatly wrapped in brown paper, the return address a street in Ottawa she had never heard of. Jake said with unusual awkwardness, 'It's from me—something I had at home that I asked the housekeeper to send here.'

She gave the box a little shake. 'You mean it's a present?' Jake nodded. Her face lit up, almost as Patrick's would have. 'What is it?' she asked, starting to tear at the paper as impatiently as a child.

'It's not—well, you'll see.'

The parcel had been thoroughly taped. Liane ripped at it, lifted the lid of the box and pushed aside the tissue paper. A length of raw silk lay in the box, gleaming dully, its shade somewhere between turquoise and blue. She shook it out, holding it against her in front of the hall mirror. 'It matches my eyes,' she marvelled. 'Is it from Thailand?'

'Yes...I bought it because I loved the colour.' He hesitated. 'It's almost as though I knew I'd meet you.'

'I could make a housecoat out of it—a caftan.' She shook out the rest of the fabric, swatching herself in it and admiring her reflection. 'Jake, it's beautiful—thank you so much.'

Her eyes were brilliant, her cheeks flushed with pleasure. Jake said hoarsely, 'Come to bed with me, Liane. Now.'

She clutched the fabric to her breast and met his eyes. 'It's where I've wanted to be all day,' she told him.

He led her into the room, tossed the material on the bed, and began undressing her, his face intent, his movements deliberate, as if he had all the time in the world. When she was naked, he lifted her on the bed, so that she lay in a tangle of blue silk, her skin like ivory, her irises catching all the hidden fire of the fabric. 'I'd like a painting of you like that,' he said huskily, unbuttoning his shirt and throwing it over the chair. Liane lay still, her limbs heavy with desire, and watched him take off his clothes, wondering if she would ever have enough of him, this dark-eyed man so well-known to her yet still so much a stranger.

They made love with the same deliberate intensity with which Jake had undressed her, in utter silence, as though they could trust their bodies to say all that needed to be said. Afterwards Liane drifted into a light sleep, waking to find that Jake had switched on the lamp by the bed and had been watching her sleeping face. She smiled at him drowsily, admiring the play of light and shadow on his face. 'You look very serious,' she said.

'Trying to figure you out,' he replied with a lightness that did not quite ring true.

She answered with the same lightness, 'What you see is what you get.'

'You're an enigma to me,' he burst out. 'A mystery.'

Unconsciously her muscles tensed. He was lying just far enough away from her so that she lacked the courage to touch him. 'No mystery, Jake. I'm an ordinary woman who had an illegitimate child and who's been trying ever since to cope as best she can.'

She was not sure he even heard her. 'Since I was just a kid I thought I had women taped,' he said in a stony voice. 'They were the leavers and the takers. My mother left my father when I was four. She'd fallen in love with an Italian count who didn't like children, so she left me behind and never once visited me. For the next twelve years, which is when I left home, my father had a series of mistresses. He'd lavish expensive gifts on each one until she bored him, then out she'd go, and along would come the next one. Grasping women, greedy women, out for all they could get, women who would either sneer at the word love or who would look at you with total incomprehension, so far was it from their experience. My father, you understand, is a very rich man. Richer than yours.'

Jake drew a ragged breath, and his eyes, lost in the past, slowly took note of the woman lying beside him on the bed. 'I never meant to tell you this,' he said irritably. 'I don't know why I am.'

The aura of safety in which Liane had fallen asleep was gone, for Jake's face was the face he had shown her in the schoolhouse when they had first met: closed, angry, and guarded. She propped herself up on her elbow and said strongly, ticking off her points one by one, 'I'm not like your mother—I'd never leave Patrick! Neither am I one of your father's mistresses. I don't want your money, or my father's. You're a highly intelligent man— intelligent enough to know that all women aren't like them.'

His eyes were like flecks of obsidian. 'My wife, who I thought was different, was like them. Once she figured out life as a police officer's wife wasn't the bed of roses she'd expected, she left me, got the biggest settlement she could out of the courts, and then blamed me when Daniel was killed.'

'I'm not her, either,' Liane blazed. She sat up, searching vainly for something to cover herself other than the crushed length of silk. 'I'm tired of feeling as if I'm on trial for crimes I've never committed. For heaven's *sake*, where's my nightgown?'

'You're not on trial! I'm trying my damnedest to trust you.'

'It's called risk, Jake,' she said tempestuously. 'You can take the risk of trusting me, or you can drive off to Ottawa on Monday morning congratulating yourself on what a narrow escape you had. But you can't play it both ways. Because it hurts too much.'

Her voice had cracked. Furious with herself, she got out of bed and began gathering up her clothes, pulling them on any which way. She was buttoning her blouse on the wrong buttons when Jake's hand fell on her wrist. 'I'm learning to trust you, Liane—I swear I am. It's just—this has all happened so fast. It's not even three weeks since we met each other, and I never in my life expected to be affected by a woman the way you affect me.' He managed a smile. 'I'm still reeling from the shock.'

She had had some of the same feelings herself. In a small voice she conceded, 'I guess I shouldn't have lost my temper.'

'It cleared the air,' he said wryly. 'Here; your blouse is crooked.'

His fingers brushed her breasts as he fumbled with the tiny buttons. His attention on them rather than on her, he said, 'I need to go to Ottawa next week—there's some business I have to deal with, and I have to see my boss at headquarters. But if you like, I could come back.'

She swallowed. 'Yes, I'd like that.'

He glanced up. 'Sweetheart, don't cry...'

'It's b-because I'm happy.'

He put his arms around her, holding her wordlessly, and in the warmth of his embrace Liane indeed felt happiness well up within her, golden as the sun. He would come back. He trusted her, and he would come back. He had promised he would. So she did not need to tell him that she loved him; there would be time for that.

Time, she thought, dizzy with joy, wondering if there had ever been a more beautiful word in the whole language. Time for trust to build. Time for love...

CHAPTER TEN

LIANE had no idea how long she and Jake stayed locked together in the middle of the room. Her face was radiant when she finally looked up, although her words were prosaic. 'We haven't had any supper,' she said.

'Put on your best dress and I'll take you out.'

'I could wrap myself in blue silk.'

'I wouldn't be able to keep my hands off you. Mind you, I may not be able to anyway.'

The expression on his face made her heart skip a beat. 'It's our first proper date.'

He looked over at the tumbled sheets. 'Past due, I'd say.'

An hour later, in the formal dining-room of one of the city's hotels, they were sipping wine and eating mussels broiled in garlic butter. Liane was wearing her favourite colour—a rose-pink dress made of the finest wool, and her face glowed with happiness. Jake, in smart trousers and a blazer, looked subtly different from the man she was used to in blue jeans; but the expression in his eyes was well known to her, and made her heart sing. She ate salad and medallions of pork and fresh California strawberries, and all the while at the back of her mind was the thought that she and Jake could spend the night together—a whole night in her bed, in an intimacy that did not preclude sex but that somehow went beyond it.

They lingered over coffee and liqueurs, and when they finally left the dining-room Liane gave it a last glance over her shoulder, knowing she would always remember how happy she had been this evening, certain that this was the first of many such evenings to be spent with Jake.

When they got home, Liane unlocked the front door, and the warmth and silence of the empty house enfolded them. Jake tossed her fur mittens on the hall table, inadvertently knocking the pile of letters to the floor as he did so, and took her in his arms, kissing her very tenderly. 'We could go to bed,' he said. 'We might even go right to sleep.'

She laughed, for she knew what he meant. The sense of urgency, of desperation, was gone; they had time, he and she, time to discover and to build. 'What are the odds on that, do you think?' she asked, her eyes twinkling as she took off her coat.

'I love it when you smile like that...perhaps sleep could be delayed,' he drawled.

As he hung up her coat, Liane knelt to pick up the mail that had fallen on the carpet. A VISA bill and the telephone bill, her monthly bank statement, a package of free coupons, and a letter. She stared at the envelope, a very expensive vellum envelope with her name and address printed in a precise, cramped hand that had not changed in twenty years, and said in a voice from which all the laughter had vanished, 'This is from my father. He never writes to me.'

She was holding the letter in the very tips of her fingers, staring at it as if it were a poisonous snake that might lash out and bite her at any minute. Jake said, 'Open it and see what it says.'

She stood up, reluctance in every move of her body. 'I could leave it until the morning.'

Jake commented slowly, 'You're really afraid of him, aren't you—even now, eight years after you left home?'

She nodded, for it was useless to deny it. 'I've always been afraid of him.'

'You're a grown woman who's made her own way in the world and is managing just fine—you don't need to be afraid of him.'

In a flash of temper she retorted, 'That's easy for you to say.' If Jake hadn't knocked the pile of envelopes to the floor, she thought wretchedly, the letter would have stayed where it was until morning, and she and Jake would have been in her bedroom by now. 'I'll read it tomorrow,' she said.

'Read it now, Liane.'

Although it was on the tip of her tongue to argue with him, she knew he was right. The letter had already come between them. Better to read it and be done with it. She tugged at the flap, extracted the single, closely written sheet of paper, and began to read.

A frown furrowed her forehead. She read the letter once, then again, striving to make sense of it, wishing the cold, sinking sensation in the pit of her stomach would go away. 'I don't have a clue what he's talking about,' she said finally. 'He's saying how glad he is that I've accepted the money, and he wants me to get in touch with him to make the arrangements we agreed upon about Patrick.' She looked over at Jake, anxiety and puzzlement warring in her face. 'What money? What arrangements?'

Jake said with a careful lack of emotion that frightened her as much as the letter had, 'May I see it?'

She passed it to him with patent unwillingness, her eyes glued to his face while he read it. He too was frowning; he looked every inch a policeman. 'Have you taken money from him?' he rapped.

'No—of course not. I don't understand what he means.'

'He seems very sure that you have.'

She said in a thin voice she scarcely recognised as her own, 'Am I on trial again, Jake?'

He was looking over at the pile of mail on the table. 'Wasn't there a bank statement in with those letters? Why don't you check it out?'

He didn't believe her. In a flood of primitive terror she cried, 'Jake, I have not taken money from my father!'

'I'm not saying you have. But I'd like to get to the bottom of this—just see what the statement says.'

Feeling as though she had been backed against a wall with a knife at her throat, Liane picked up the bulky envelope from the table. She did most of her business by cheque, and every month the cheques were returned to her, along with a statement of credits and debits. Her fingers were cold, so cold she had trouble tearing the envelope open; but she had nothing to fear, she thought stoutly. She had not taken any money from her father. So the statement held no threat for her.

She put the pile of cheques on the table and spread open the balance sheet. Then her throat closed with the same terror she had felt only moments ago. For the final balance, which should have been in the vicinity of a thousand dollars, was fifty-one thousand dollars.

She had never in her life had that much money.

Her eyes flew up the sheet. Nearly a week ago a deposit of fifty thousand dollars had been made into her account. With a trembling hand she pushed her hair back from her face, and wondered if this was really happening.

The hallway was as it had always been, and the table, when Liane reached out a hand to steady herself, had the same dent in its edge where Patrick had banged against it with one of his skates. And Jake was standing in front of her, indisputably real, although his face was a mask and his body had somehow withdrawn from her. She said numbly, 'I didn't make that deposit.'

He plucked the statement from her hand and scanned it rapidly. 'A week ago,' he said matter-of-factly. 'Almost a week after I arrived here.'

Clutching at straws, Liane said, 'I have a bank card—someone else could have made the deposit.'

'They'd have to know your code, and you're the only one to know that.'

'There's an outside slot for deposits,' she pointed out stubbornly. 'To use that, all someone would have to know is my account number. Maybe Chester snooped in my handbag at the school.'

'Maybe,' said Jake.

'You don't believe me, do you?'

He replied heavily, 'It's the scenario Chester outlined. The daughter holding out for money before she lets her father see his grandson.'

The pain that ripped through Liane had nothing to do with her father and everything to do with Jake. Liane said, the words falling like shards of broken glass, 'And now the money's arrived.'

'It sure would explain why we haven't seen hide nor hair of Chester. Or why the kidnapping scheme that you were apparently so afraid of hasn't materialised.'

'Apparently?' Liane repeated in a dead voice, wondering how one word could destroy so much.

When Jake suddenly hit the statement with his fingertips, the paper snapped with a crack like a gun-shot. 'The money's here!' he thundered. 'That's a fact. Your father has given you fifty thousand dollars and now expects to see his grandson—that's also a fact. I deal in facts, Liane.'

'Yes, you do, don't you?' she blazed. 'That's all you know, Jake. You're drowning in facts, smothered in facts, buried alive in them! And you've lost touch with everything else. Real emotion. Sharing and trust and——'

'Facts don't lie!'

'But women do,' she stated with immense bitterness. 'Don't you think I'd have held out for more than a paltry fifty thousand? My father, like yours, is a very rich man.'

'Fifty thousand must seem like a lot to you right now.' He raked his fingers through his hair. 'I can't read your mind; how should I know?'

Abruptly Liane was swamped by a fatigue so deep as to seem like death. She sagged against the wall, her face as white as the papers Jake was still clutching, and said tonelessly, 'If you believe me capable of taking money from my father, of using Patrick as a pawn, then we're finished, you and I. It's over. Over almost before it's begun.'

'We never should have started.'

The words were a death knell. Far beyond tears, and certainly beyond pleading, Liane watched Jake put the letter and the statement back on the table on top of the envelope of free coupons. Nothing's free, she thought distantly. You pay for everything—and knew that at some time in the future she would pay for the happiness she had felt this evening in a pain beyond anything she had ever known. Dimly grateful for the anaesthesia that at present seemed to be keeping that pain at bay, she heard Jake say, 'I'll pack up my stuff and get out of here.'

Turning on his heel, he went into the living-room, and a few moments later Liane heard the slide of the zip on his suitcase and the small sounds of clothing being stuffed into a bag. It was better that he go. She could not bear for him to spend the night in her house when they were so deeply estranged from each other.

In a few minutes he came back into the hall, carrying his suitcase and his leather jacket. Liane said in a brittle voice, 'What shall I tell Patrick?'

'I'll come back for a few minutes after school tomorrow to say goodbye to him.'

'I'm working at the library tomorrow, so he'll be going to Megan's until six.'

'Then I'll go to Megan's.'

The words, she knew, were a cover for all that she and Jake were not saying. His eyes impaled her to the wall, eyes that were a turmoil of suppressed emotion. The silence between them seemed to scream in her ears; her heart was slamming against her ribs, her breathing so shallow that she felt light-headed. It seemed a strange combination of physical symptoms to usher in a broken heart, she thought, and wished he would go so that she could be alone.

'Anything I can think of saying sounds stupid and banal,' Jake muttered. 'I won't see you tomorrow... so I'll say goodbye now.'

'Why say anything?' Liane asked, and, because that word goodbye had touched a nerve, flicking her with agony, her voice sounded cold and detached. 'Just go.'

He took a step towards her, as if he meant to touch her. Liane shrank back against the wall, knowing that if he did so she would begin to cry, and that she would die rather than cry in front of him. He halted immediately, his mouth a tight line. Then he said with a formality that to her ears sounded callous, 'I hope that you can reconcile with your father, Liane. You don't need to be afraid of him—not now... and I'll try and make Patrick understand tomorrow why I have to leave. As for you, I—damn it, there aren't any words, are there? All I know is that I'll never forget you any more than I've ever understood you.'

He did not say goodbye. He gave her a curt nod and crossed the hall in three swift strides. The door closed behind him, and seconds later she felt the draught of cold air against her legs. Then the engine of the wagon roared into life. The tyres crunched on the snow and the engine retreated up the hill.

Her mind a blank, Liane checked the lock on the front door and switched off the hall light. In the darkness the walls slowly took form. Feeling her way, she went into her bedroom, the room where she had known delight beyond any imagining. She pulled her dress over her head and got a clean nightgown out of the drawer—a nightgown Jake had never seen. When she had put it on, she decided that next she should clean her teeth. However, as she rounded the end of the bed her bare foot stubbed against a box lying on the floor, the box in which she had so meticulously folded the length of blue silk that Jake had bought in Thailand. As if she couldn't help herself, she stooped, opened the box, and ran her fingers over the slight roughness of the fabric, hearing it rustle like the far-away sighing of wind in tall trees. What had he said? 'It was almost as though I knew I'd meet you...'

With a tiny mewling sound of distress she ran into the hall and up the stairs to Patrick's room, where she threw herself across his bed, her nails digging into the spread. She couldn't sleep in her room tonight. She couldn't.

Because Jake had gone. And he would not be back.

At five-past six the next day Liane pulled up outside Fitz and Megan's old farmhouse. There was no sign of Jake's wagon. Not that she had expected there would be. Jake, by now, would be on the ferry, glad no doubt that the expanse of water was ever widening between him and the woman he could not bring himself to trust.

She had got through the day by rigorously avoiding even the thought of his name; she did not think she would be allowed this luxury at Megan's. Mentally steeling herself, she got out of the car. Trojan and Bouncer gambolled up to meet her. Patting them half-heartedly, she headed for the house.

Megan and Fitz were sitting by themselves at the kitchen table. The air smelled pleasantly of roast chicken and apple pie, and the wood was crackling cheerfully in the stove. Liane said brightly, 'Is Patrick ready to go?'

'The three of them are upstairs having their supper,' Megan announced.

'What's going on between you and Jake?' Fitz asked bluntly.

Liane had been afraid of this. 'I really don't want to talk about it,' she said, and cursed herself for the tell-tale quiver in her voice.

'Pour each of us a glass of wine, Fitz,' Megan ordered, 'and I'll serve the dinner. Then we're going to get to the bottom of this. Quite apart from the fact that you look like a grey day in winter, Liane Daley, your son was extremely upset this afternoon. The big glasses, Fitz—we need them.'

Liane said loudly, 'I'm not——'

Fitz neatly divested her of her coat, and pushed her down into the nearest chair. 'Yes, you are. No point in arguing with Megs when she uses that tone of voice; I learned that years ago.'

His lips were smiling at her through the tangle of his beard; his eyes were as light as Jake's were dark. Liane said, 'Just because you're my best friends doesn't mean you can push me around,' and burst into tears.

Her storm of weeping was as short-lived as it was violent. When she surfaced, Fitz had put a large pottery goblet of wine within reach and Megan was proffering a box of tissues. Liane blew her nose, took a big gulp of wine and said defiantly, 'Jake thinks I'm a liar and an extortioner. As you would have known had you asked him. Now can we talk about the weather? Or about anything else other than him?'

'I did ask him,' Megan said. 'And was told in no uncertain terms to mind my own business. I told him you
were my business. Whereupon he suggested, more or less
politely, that I ask you.' She grinned at her husband.
'Then Fitz got in the act and said that if Jake thought
you were dishonest in any way it was time he retired
from the police force and became a human being instead... oh, it was quite exciting for a while. Not that
we got anywhere.'

'He doesn't listen,' said Liane.

'We noticed that. So what's the story?' Fitz demanded.

To her own surprise Liane began pouring out all the
events of the last two weeks, the words tumbling from
her tongue as though by hearing them herself she might
gain understanding. When she finished with a summary
of her father's letter and the disastrous evidence of the
bank statement, Megan drew a fascinated breath. 'The
money has to have come from your father.'

'It's a set-up,' Fitz said thoughtfully, tugging at his
beard as he always did when perplexed. 'And what it
accomplished was to get Jake out of the house... you're
still convinced your father means to kidnap Patrick?'

Liane nodded unhappily. 'When he threatens to do
something, he's a man of his word.'

'Well, the coast's certainly clear now, isn't it? No
policeman living on the premises, standing in his way.'

His musings had a horrible logic; Liane gaped at him.
Megan put in excitedly, 'And who was the first one to
plant the story in Jake's mind that you were out for
money? Chester! It didn't work right away... Jake went
and stayed with you anyway. So what do they do next?
Deposit money in your account with a nice little ex-
planatory letter from your father. And this time it works.
Jake leaves, and you and Patrick are alone again.' With
a smug smile she added, 'Maybe *we* should apply for
the police force, Fitz.'

'Jake sure hasn't been using his brains,' her husband commented.

'Well, he's in love,' Megan said dismissively, as though the two states were mutually exclusive.

'He's not!' Liane snapped.

Fitz's amber eyes and Megan's green ones swerved round to Liane's face. 'Of course he is,' said Megan.

'Not a doubt,' Fitz corroborated.

More tears welled up in Liane's eyes and streamed down her face. 'He hates me,' she wailed.

'Dearest Liane,' Megan said forcefully, 'hate is the opposite side of love, and if I ever saw a man in the grip of strong emotion, and fighting it every step of the way, it was Jake. Fitz, you've got his phone number, haven't you? All we have to do is call him and tell him all this, and he'll come back, I know he will.'

Liane sat up straight in her chair, her tears forgotten. 'Oh, no,' she said, 'you're not going to do that—not a chance!'

'Why ever not?' Megan asked. 'Look at you; you're a wreck. Of course you want him back.'

'The only way I want him back is if he makes up his own mind to come back,' Liane insisted, her chin jutting. 'He's got to trust me. Anything else is useless.' She gave Fitz an unfriendly look. 'And how did you get his phone number? *I* don't have it.'

'I insisted he leave it with me,' Fitz said blandly.

Unexpectedly Liane chuckled. 'I'd like to have heard that little interchange.'

Fitz leaned forward. 'Wouldn't it be better if I spoke to him, Liane? It would save you a lot of heartache.'

'No.'

Megan poured herself more wine, her red hair more than usually tangled. 'You're very stubborn,' she said, her tone not complimentary.

'He believed my *father*, Megan. My father, rather than me. Yet I'm supposed to get down on my knees and beg him to come back?'

Fitz replenished his own glass. 'You're in love with him,' he stated.

'Oh, yes. More fool me.'

'Hmm...why don't we eat?' Fitz suggested. 'Maybe your admirable dinner will change her mind, Megan.'

'Don't badger me, Fitz,' Liane retorted. 'I'm not going to change my mind.'

Nor did she accept the offer they made later that evening for her and Patrick to stay in the old farmhouse for the weekend. 'Our theories about Chester are all very clever,' said Fitz, 'but, if they're true, then Patrick could be at risk again.'

Liane had already thought of that. 'I can't stay; you know that—the Forsters expect me to be in the house, and the only way I can leave on Monday is to have Percy's cousin come in to take my place. What I will do is accept the loan of one of the dogs each night, though.'

So at nine o'clock she and Patrick drove home with Bouncer breathing heavily in the back seat. The dog's presence, she soon saw, had the very desirable side-effect of cheering her son up. She agreed that Bouncer could sleep on the floor in Patrick's room, and was not at all surprised when she went upstairs an hour later to find both boy and dog sprawled fast asleep on the bed.

She had to sleep in her own room that night—no choice. She put the box of silk in the very back of her wardrobe, changed the sheets on the bed, and lay down, thinking determinedly about all the work she had to do in the greenhouse before she and Patrick went skiing for the week. She did sleep; and over the weekend, by working very hard at the library, in the greenhouse, and at home getting ready for their trip, she managed to keep the worst of her emotions at bay.

Fitz took Patrick to his hockey game, and Megan invited the two of them for dinner both nights; not for the first time, Liane gave thanks for her friends. Patrick never mentioned Jake's name, and when Liane tried to talk about him the little boy listened politely and changed the subject as soon as he could.

The day after Jake left, Liane wrote a cheque to her father for fifty thousand dollars, and sent it to him recorded delivery. She did not get any response. There was no sign of Chester.

Liane enjoyed the week in the Laurentians far more than she had expected to. She was an ardent and daring skier who had passed along her enthusiasm to her son, and the days spent high on the slopes in the cold, crisp air were good for both of them. When she went to bed in the chalet set among the spruce trees she fell asleep instantly, and the daily physical exercise made her passionate longing for Jake less acute. She had colour in her cheeks when she and Patrick got home, and Megan's heartfelt, 'You look wonderful!' was, if not totally true, at least considerably more accurate than it would have been the week before.

When she actually entered the house again after being away for seven days, Liane was glad of Bouncer's antics and Patrick's chatter, for the memories of Jake hit her like a blow as soon as she stepped across the threshold. He had stood in that doorway, he had propped his feet on that chair, he had kissed her in the hall and made love to her in the bed in her room. His presence surrounded her, his absence mocked and flagellated her, and the week she had been gone might never have happened.

That night, after Patrick and Bouncer had gone to bed, she hauled the box from the back corner of her cupboard and pulled out the length of silk. Stripping off her clothes, she wrapped it around her body and looked at herself in the mirror, dispassionately observing the vivid blue of her eyes, the pale gleam of her skin, and the way the fabric clung to the curves of her body. Just so must Jake have seen her, she thought, and wondered if she was a fool not to write to him at the address on the corner of the box, or phone him at the number that Fitz had given her.

But Jake had not believed in her. He had not trusted her. So what was the point of getting in touch with him?

CHAPTER ELEVEN

LIANE cried herself to sleep that night for the first time since Jake had left. But the next Saturday, out of some stubborn need to assert her independence, she went into Charlottetown with Patrick and bought a pattern and thread to make a caftan out of the length of silk, and that night she cut it out.

Bouncer continued to spend his nights on Patrick's bed, although the threat of Chester had receded for Liane; with the passage of each day she was more inclined to believe that she had exaggerated her fears, as Jake had so often suggested. Her father, who had never been a patient man, would have acted long before now. So when on Thursday, her day off from the library, she went to the school to pick Patrick up at three-thirty, she was not particularly worried when he didn't appear right away. He was probably trading his hockey cards, she thought indulgently, waving at a couple of his team-mates as they ran for the bus.

The first two buses pulled out of the yard. Clancy dashed down the steps, his lunch-box banging against his knee, and slid across the new-fallen snow, yelling to a couple of his friends. Liane rolled down her window. 'Clancy! Have you seen Patrick?'

Clancy skidded to a halt and jogged over to the car, staring at her in bewilderment. 'You picked him up at noon—for the dentist.'

Liane's smile faded from her lips. 'No, I didn't,' she said blankly. 'Wasn't he in school this afternoon?'

'Nope. The teacher had a note about the dentist, and after lunch your car was outside on the street, and Patrick left.'

'*My* car? I've been home all day, Clancy.'

Clancy's freckled forehead puckered in thought. 'Well, it looked like your car—it was a Volkswagen, and kind of old.' His face brightened. 'He's probably gone on the early bus. P'raps he's at my place.'

Liane did not think he was. 'I'll go and see the teacher about the note,' she said, keeping her voice level with an effort. 'Thanks, Clancy; I'll see you later.'

Forcing herself to keep panic at bay, she walked across the school yard and up the steps. As she swung open the door, the smell of the air reminded her sharply of another school, in a valley miles away; tightening her lips, she almost ran down the hall. Patrick's teacher, an energetic brunette fresh out of university, rummaged through the waste-paper basket and came up with the note. 'I didn't think much of it,' she said, worried. 'We get notes like that all the time—I hope I haven't done anything wrong.'

The note asked for Patrick to be excused at twelve forty-five for a dental appointment, and was signed 'Liane Daley'. The handwriting was not hers or her father's. Liane replied quietly, feeling her veins turn to ice, 'No, you did nothing wrong. Thank you.'

She hurried out to her car and drove home. Patrick was not in the house, nor did his regular bus halt at the top of the hill to let him out. She then drove to Megan's. Her heart was throbbing like that of a terrified bird, and her eyes were wide in her face when she burst in the back door. Megan was rolling out pastry, her fingers coated in flour. 'Liane! What's——?'

'Is Patrick here?' Liane demanded, biting her lower lip as she waited for the answer.

'No...should he be?'

Liane collapsed in the nearest chair. 'I think my father's taken him,' she said in a voice drained of emotion.

Abandoning her pie crust, Megan called Fitz, who came out of the studio wiping his hands. With a kind of nerveless precision Liane recited what had happened. 'I'd stopped worrying,' she said helplessly. 'Oh, Megan, what have they done to him? How did they get him in the car? He wouldn't have gone willingly, I know he wouldn't. Maybe they hurt him...he'll be so frightened.'

'We'd better call the police right away,' Fitz rapped. 'Your father won't get away with this.'

'He'll take me to court for custody,' Liane said, her terror-filled eyes a stark blue. 'He'll prove I'm not a fit mother.'

Fitz's expletive was not one she had ever heard him use before. 'We'll stand up in court and contradict him. You think you haven't made an impression on the community in the last couple of years, Liane? You think people haven't noticed how you take Patrick to hockey twice a week, and skiing on his breaks, and camping in the summer? Your father might have money on his side, but he doesn't have truth.'

Despite his green-checked shirt Fitz could have been a prophet of old, railing against corruption among the elders; Liane felt strength flow back into her limbs, and with it the beginnings of anger. 'I've always been so afraid of him,' she confessed. 'Ever since I was little. When he'd yell and rant and roar, I used to hide in the broom cupboard so he couldn't find me... Twice I saw him hit my mother.'

She shivered, remembering the frightened little girl cowering in the darkness of the cupboard, her father's rages as awesome as thunder and as unpredictable as lightning. 'But that's a long time ago, isn't it?' she went on, more to herself than to Megan or Fitz. Sitting up straight in her chair, recognising this simple act as symbolic of a far more significant shift, she heard her voice gather force. 'He shouldn't have taken my son; that's a terrible thing to have done. I'm going to phone him right now and tell him I want Patrick back.'

When Murray Hutchins came to the phone, his voice was fainter than Liane recalled, but insidiously all the old fear crept into her limbs when he spoke. 'Ah, yes,' he said, 'I've been expecting you to get in touch. Patrick should be arriving from the airport shortly. I won't keep you from him totally—that would be foolish; but don't try and get him back, will you?'

She thought of what Fitz had said, and how Jake had urged her to outgrow the reactions of a much younger Liane, and she remembered her own anger of a few moments ago. 'Of course I'll get him back,' she said, her knuckles white where she was holding the receiver. 'I'm his mother and he——'

'I understand that a man you met on the road spent several nights in your bed, my dear... not the kind of behaviour to which a seven-year-old should be exposed. As I'm sure any court in the land would agree. Don't push me too far, Liane—I want Patrick and I'll fight for him.'

Her knees were trembling. Despising herself for her weakness, Liane retorted, 'And I'll fight back! You're not going to get away with this—kidnapping's a serious offence. I'll phone later to speak to Patrick.' Without saying goodbye, she replaced the receiver, and noticed with icy detachment that her hands were trembling as well.

Fitz had been listening unashamedly. 'Good for you! Now we'd better call the police——'

Megan interjected, 'I've got a better idea—why don't we call Jake instead?'

'Megs, you're a genius,' her husband said warmly. 'We wrote the number in the back of the book, didn't we?'

'You are not to call Jake,' Liane said through gritted teeth.

'We'll start with him,' Fitz insisted, interposing his big body between her and the phone as he began to dial. And Liane, standing to one side, could not have said if she was praying for Jake to be out or praying for him to pick up the phone.

'Jake?' Fitz boomed. 'Fitz Donleavy here. Liane's father kidnapped Patrick this afternoon; how can we go about getting him back?'

There were five seconds of dead silence. Then Liane heard the faint crackle of Jake's voice, punctuated by grunts from Fitz. 'Sounds good,' Fitz said finally. 'Here she is.'

He passed the receiver to Liane. 'He wants to talk to you.'

Gingerly she took the receiver. 'Hello,' she mumbled, and, her breathing suspended, waited to hear what he would say.

'I'll get Patrick back for you,' Jake said forcefully. 'You're not to worry, do you hear? You'll have him back by nightfall.'

The timbre of his voice cut through all her fears for her son; it was as if Jake were standing in the room with her, so close did he sound. She tried to think of a reply that would make sense, failed utterly, and heard him rap, 'Liane—are you still there?'

'Yes,' she whispered. 'He'll be frightened...I'm so afraid they'll have hurt him.'

'If they have, they'll have me to answer to,' he said so savagely that Liane flinched. 'Liane, please stop

worrying! Patrick knows me; he won't be afraid to leave
with me. I'll fly from here to Halifax, leaving in about
half an hour, and once I've got him we'll flip over to
the island. He'll be home by bedtime—much as he might
prefer it to be midnight.'

Unable to laugh at this smallest of jokes, Liane knew
she had to warn Jake of what he might expect to hear.
'My father knows about you and me—that we had an
affair. He's threatened to use that, Jake.' It was the first
time she had used his name; it sounded foreign on her
tongue.

'He won't dare to, not with me,' Jake said forbid-
dingly. 'I'm more than a match for your father. You be
at the airport by nine tonight, and Patrick and I will be
there.' Then his voice changed, softening so that she felt
clothed in a powerful mingling of warmth and pain, and
almost tangibly reminded of the strength of his arms
around her. 'Don't be frightened, Liane. I've fouled up
just about everything in your life since I met you, but I
swear I won't foul this one up. Get Fitz to drive you to
Charlottetown, and I'll drive you home. Chin up.'

The receiver clicked in her ear and she was left with
the steady hum of a broken connection. She put the
phone back in its cradle, and heard his voice echo in her
ears. 'I've fouled up just about everything in your life...'

Fitz said with immense approval, 'A man of action.
Private jets and the whole works.'

Liane gave him a blank look. 'Private jets?'

'Didn't he tell you? His first cousin owns a fleet of
corporate jets—Jake's going to commandeer one of
them.' Fitz chuckled. 'He'll probably get to Halifax
before Patrick does.'

'Fitz, this isn't a laughing matter!'

Fitz's face fell much as Patrick's tended to when Liane chided him. Megan patted her husband on the arm. 'Talking to Jake has upset her.'

Talking to Jake had set every nerve in her body on edge, Liane thought miserably. 'Sorry, Fitz,' she said with a shamefaced smile. 'Here I am being a grump at five in the afternoon.'

Fitz gave her one of his bear-hugs. 'Time we got the wine out,' he decided. 'This love-affair of yours is going to turn us all into alcoholics.'

'Just as long as you're sober enough to drive me to the airport by nine.'

Fitz's reply was unquestionably sincere. 'I wouldn't miss it for anything.'

Megan finished her pie, and set Liane to work making a salad, and within the hour they were all seated around the table eating. The meat pie was excellent. Liane discovered she was hungry, for talking to Jake had relieved some of the terrible burden of fear she had been carrying ever since she had read the note about the fake dental appointment. Jake was the best person to try and get Patrick back. She had no idea how he would do it, and perhaps that was just as well. But she would not want to be Chester right now. Or her father.

She chewed mechanically, focusing all the love she felt for Patrick in an unspoken message of encouragement and comfort. Jake's coming, Patrick...Jake will get you out of there. Patrick, she thought drily, would probably be delighted to be rescued by Jake. But what would happen if, once they were home, Jake left them on the doorstep?

Megan touched her on the arm, smiling at her. 'I've asked you twice if you'd like more salad.'

'Oh, no, thanks...Patrick *will* be all right, won't he?'

'I have every faith in Jake,' Megan replied, patting Liane's arm for emphasis.

Liane had faith in Jake the policeman; but her faith in Jake the man had been sorely tried. And which one would she be meeting in Charlottetown at nine o'clock tonight?

Fitz and Liane were standing in the arrivals area of the airport by eight-thirty. Liane had insisted they get there early, partly because once the dinner dishes were washed and put away she couldn't stand doing nothing, and partly because she couldn't bear the thought of not being there to greet Patrick if he should arrive early.

He was not early. Nine o'clock came, then five-past, ten-past, twenty-past—by which time Liane had left uncertainty behind and was in an agony of fear. Something had gone wrong. Jake had not been allowed entry to her father's house. He had been arrested for illegal entry. Patrick had been taken somewhere other than the big brick mansion near the sea. Jake had been hurt. Patrick was not fit to travel.

Round and round her brain went, frantic as an animal in a cage as it circled these same possibilities again and again, yet too frightened to encompass any worse scenarios. She looked at the big round clock-face once again. Nine twenty-two. It had moved exactly two minutes since the last time she had looked.

'There they are!' Fitz exclaimed.

Liane whirled. 'Where?' she said stupidly.

Then she saw them. Hand in hand, Jake and Patrick were coming through the sliding doors. Under the fluorescent lights Patrick looked pale, his eyes shadowed as they always were when he was tired. As soon as he saw his mother he dropped Jake's hand and ran towards her.

Liane ran as well, stooping as he catapulted into her arms, his weight almost knocking her backwards. 'Patrick!' she gasped. 'Oh, darling, are you all right?'

He was holding her with a feverish strength that said more than words how glad he was to see her. She eased her head back, searching his face. There was a small bruise on his cheekbone and his hair was tousled, but no more than if he had been playing hockey. 'Did they hurt you?' she asked. 'Patrick, I've been so worried! I'm *so* glad you're safe.'

'They put something over my face, just like the time I had the appendix operation,' Patrick said, grimacing. 'I didn't like that very much, 'cause I thought it was you in the car...then when I woke up I was at Gramps's house.' He added with some satisfaction, 'I threw up all over the carpet.'

A man had walked up to them. Liane's eyes travelled the length of his body from his mountain boots and navy cords to his down-filled jacket, coming to rest on his face with its familiar dark eyes and black hair. 'Jake,' she said. One of the things she had worried about from eight-thirty to five to nine was what on earth she would find to say to him; now that he was in front of her the problem solved itself. She got to her feet, keeping her arms tightly wrapped around her son, and said simply, 'I can't thank you enough for what you've done. To have Patrick safe...' Her eyes flooded with tears. She blinked them back, and added very naturally, 'Shall we go home? We can talk on the way.'

His smile was stiff. 'I ordered a rental car; I just have to pick it up...hello, Fitz.'

'Good work!' Fitz said, pumping Jake's hand as energetically as if it were the handle of the old water-pump in the barn. 'James Bond had better look to his laurels.'

Jake gave a reluctant grin. 'Hardly... I did very little, actually. Excuse me for a minute, will you?' And he strode off in the direction of the car-rental counters.

'Close-mouthed so-and-so,' Fitz commented. 'You've got your work cut out for you, Liane.' He hunkered down by the little boy. 'Quite an adventure you've had. Clancy'll be waiting to hear every detail. You hungry?'

'We had something to eat on the plane. It's a private jet, Mum, you should see it—with a kitchen and a bar and two bathrooms, one with a shower, and I was in the cockpit with the pilot—he's a friend of Jake's. It was neat!'

'Neat' was Patrick's highest word of commendation. Liane smoothed his hair, again feeling the tightness in her throat and the surge of tears; the other worry, that she had so assiduously refused to consider as the hands of the clock had crept around its face, was that Patrick, like Daniel, might be dead.

She could admit it now that he was safely in her arms. And she could admit also that in the deep recesses of her mind she had feared for Jake's safety.

Through a mist of tears she saw Jake come striding towards them. His jacket was slung over a Scandinavian sweater patterned in greys and blues—casual clothes, with no obvious signs of a gun, yet she would not want to have him as her enemy. He said brusquely, dangling a set of keys in his hand, 'No problem; the car's outside in the car park. Shall we go?'

The four of them went out into the cold, star-etched night. Fitz said heartily, 'Come and see us, Jake—glad to have you any time. And I'll add my thanks to Liane's—a good job; I'll look forward to all the details. Including——' he ruffled Patrick's hair '—who cleaned up the carpet.' He kissed Liane's cheek, and ambled off between the double row of cars, a giant of a man who did not look as though he had a creative bone in his body.

Jake stopped by a gleaming sedan. Wanting to break the silence, Liane remarked, 'What a gorgeous car, Jake—it's huge.'

Jake said gruffly, 'Thought you and Patrick might want to sit together in the front.'

There were three sets of seatbelts across the front seat. Liane said, 'That was sweet of you—dammit, why do I keep on wanting to cry?'

Patrick said, grinning up at her, 'I cried a little bit, when I came to and didn't know what was happening.'

At seven-going-on-eight he was not as ready to admit to tears as he had been at five. Liane smiled back and replied feelingly, 'I bet you did.'

Jake opened the door, Patrick sat between them, and they drove off. About to ask her son for all the details, Liane heard him ask, 'When can we go and visit Gramps, Mum? A proper visit.'

Her jaw dropped. She had been quite prepared for Patrick to hate his grandfather after the day's events. 'You'd want to?' she asked, feeling her way.

'Yeah...he used to collect baseball cards when he was a kid; he said he'd show 'em to me.'

'Yes, not "yeah",' Liane corrected automatically, thinking fast. 'I didn't expect you to like him very much after what he did today, Patrick.'

'After I got sick, it was OK—up till then I didn't feel so hot.' Patrick snuggled into her pink jacket, the one she had been wearing the first time she had met Jake. 'Mrs Petrie gave me some ice-cream, and then he sort of stood around looking at me, like he didn't know what to do next. So I told him all about my hockey team and how you take me to the games, and then he showed me his house. All those rooms just for him.'

Mrs Petrie was the housekeeper, a woman of fearsome efficiency, and the only person Liane had ever known who could order her father around. 'What kind of ice-cream?'

'Swiss chocolate almond,' Patrick said with gusto. 'I showed her how to add pop and make a float. That was after she cleaned the carpet. She said the float tasted really good, but Gramps said champagne and straw-berries were more to his liking.'

This was obviously a direct quote. Liane smothered a smile; it sounded as though Patrick, in less than an hour, had disrupted the routine of the brick house quite com-mendably. She said cautiously, 'Did your grandfather want you to visit?'

'After Jake came, and when me and Jake were ready to leave, he said he'd be honoured if I would come again and bring my hockey card collection with me. You can come too, Mum; he said so.' Patrick paused, trying to smother a yawn. 'You know old Mrs Hatchett, who lives up the road all by herself, and likes to have the school kids go in for a visit? He reminded me of her. Sort of lonesome.'

Of all the words Liane might have chosen to describe her father, that would not have been one of them. She said, even more cautiously, 'I expect we could go for a visit, Patrick. Some time.'

'That's good,' Patrick replied sleepily, his eyelids be-ginning to droop. 'Can I go see Clancy tonight?'

'Tomorrow,' his mother said.

The boy did not argue, for he had fallen asleep. Liane pressed a kiss on the top of his head, her heart over-flowing with gratitude for his safety.

She glanced over at Jake. He was staring straight ahead at the road, his profile a series of angular lines that did not encourage communication. She said prosaically,

'He's tired out.' Jake nodded and flicked on his high beams.

She couldn't be angry with Jake, not when she owed him so much...could she? She added with rather overdone politeness, 'Did you run into any trouble?'

'None whatsoever.' A wintry smile crossed Jake's face. 'The housekeeper was in the middle of scrubbing what looked like a genuine Aubusson when I rang the front door. I suggested baking soda.'

'You don't mean to tell me they just let you walk in the door and then ten minutes later walk out with Patrick?'

'Well, no, it wasn't quite that simple. Chester, who does not improve upon acquaintance, was prepared to get nasty until I showed him the error of his ways. Then your father tried to throw his weight around—metaphorically speaking—so he and I had a little talk. Whereupon any urge he might have had to take you to court and blacken your name deserted him.'

'Jake,' said Liane in exasperation, 'what did you *do*?'

'Nothing very subtle. Your father is a big fish in a small pond. Mine is a big fish in a big pond. Mine could ruin yours with two or three carefully placed phone calls—I just thought I should point that out to him.'

'Oh,' said Liane, adding naïvely, 'Your father must be *very* rich.'

'Very.'

'So my father will never try to kidnap Patrick again?'

'Never.'

'You don't look like the son of a very rich man,' she commented, glancing over at his unpretentious clothes.

'I always wanted to make my own way in life. Not hang on to his coat-tails.'

There was a dismissive note in Jake's voice. End of conversation, thought Liane, and said calmly, 'That's right; you told me you left home at sixteen. So how do you get along with your father now that you're older?'

'For two men whose value systems are almost totally opposed, and who share a somewhat stormy past, we get along remarkably well,' Jake said wryly. 'As I would suspect Patrick and your father would get along, given half a chance.'

Direct hit. 'If my father's lonesome it's his own fault,' Liane asserted hotly.

Jake glanced at her over Patrick's head; he had made very little eye contact since they had left the airport. 'There's something I want you to do,' he said.

'Oh?' Her tone was not encouraging.

'I want you to go and see your father. On your own. It's time you laid that particular ghost to rest.'

'He's no ghost!'

Jake said patiently, 'He's an elderly man who's lost a son and thereby lost his grip on the future. He did a great wrong to try and seize the future in the form of Patrick—I'm not excusing or condoning that. But if you went to see him—and I mean really *see* him, Liane—you'd find pitifully little to be afraid of. For Patrick's sake, if for no other reason, I'd like you to go.'

She stared straight ahead at the black ribbon of road edged by dirty banks of snow. Refusing to commit herself, she answered, 'Perhaps I will.'

'Good. I'll stay with Patrick tomorrow, and I'll phone Miss what's-her-name at the library and tell her you were called away on urgent family business.'

'Tomorrow?' Liane repeated, feeling her temper rise. 'What do you mean, tomorrow?'

'The jet's at the airport; you can fly to Halifax—a car will be there for your use, and you can fly home all in the same day. Simple.'

'How nice of you to arrange my life for me!'

'I will not try and arrange it in any other way, I swear,' Jake said tightly. 'Seriously, Liane, it's a good time for you to go, while your father's still feeling chastened and while Patrick's visit is fresh in his mind. And it won't cost you a cent.'

Underlying anger at Jake's cavalier methods and trepidation at the thought of facing her father was another emotion: hope. If she went to Halifax tomorrow, Jake would still be here when she got back. And in all honesty she suspected Jake was right, that it was time she confronted her father as an adult and attempted to build a new relationship with him, however tenuous that might be. A relationship, moreover, that included Patrick.

'Very well,' she said stiffly. 'I'll go.'

'Good. You should make a fairly early start...I'll give Joe—he's the pilot—a call tonight to arrange it.'

Feeling as though she had been picked up by a whirlwind and set down in a place where everything had subtly shifted, Liane said nothing. A mile further on Jake took the side-road to Hilldale, and then swung down the Forsters' driveway. The house was in darkness because she had never thought to turn on any lights when she had run through the rooms at four o'clock this afternoon calling for Patrick. It seemed a lifetime ago.

Jake turned off the engine. 'I'll carry Patrick up to his room,' he said, and unbuckled the boy's seatbelt.

Liane climbed out of the car. Her limbs felt stiff and she was aware at some level of a deep emotional exhaustion. But she could not afford to give in to that, because somehow she had to break through Jake's reserve. She wanted him in her bed tonight, wanted his naked body next to hers, wanted to fall asleep beside him and wake up enfolded in his arms.

He had not touched her once since they had met at the airport.

He was gathering Patrick's limp body into his arms. She remembered how he and her son had walked hand in hand from the plane, and felt a pang of what could only be jealousy. Horrified with herself, she found her key and led the way into the hall, switching on the light. After Patrick had stumbled into the bathroom and stumbled out again, Jake carried him upstairs, Liane undressed him, and they both got him into bed. The room was dark and the task intimate; Liane felt her nerves stretch to the breaking-point as she kissed her son goodnight. She then walked downstairs, knowing that Patrick had fallen asleep again even before she had left the room, achingly aware of Jake following her.

In the hall she turned to face him, standing between him and the door, the overhead light shining on the vulnerable curve of her mouth and on her anxious blue eyes. The pink of her jacket emphasised the pallor of her face as she rested her hand on the sleeve of his sweater and said tentatively, 'Jake?'

'Let me use your phone to call Joe, will you?'

She let her hand fall to her side. 'You know where it is.'

He went into the kitchen, and Liane heard the low murmur of his voice. Then she heard him dial a second number. She stayed where she was, huddling her jacket around her because she was cold and only Jake could warm her, and watched as he came back into the hall. He said, 'The weather reports are good for the next twenty-four hours, so he'd like to leave by ten...that OK with you? It'll give you time to get Patrick off to school before you go.'

She nodded, realising she would have agreed to five in the morning or nine at night, for what difference did it make? 'Fine,' she said.

'Joe'll be waiting for you in the departures area—short guy, balding, in a blue uniform. He'll let you know how long you can be with your father, too—he wants to be back in Charlottetown by evening. And I let your father know you'd be coming.'

'I'm not getting out of this, am I?' said Liane, wondering if she was being fanciful to think that Jake's eyes were like black pits, swallowing her in darkness.

He said harshly, 'Well, I'd better be going. Have a safe journey tomorrow.'

Her heart gave an uncomfortable jolt in her breast. 'Going?' she repeated in a voice that seemed to come from a long way away. 'Aren't you staying here?'

He shook his head. 'No need . . . you'll be quite safe now.'

'It wasn't my safety I was thinking of, Jake.'

'I made arrangements this morning to stay in a motel near the airport.'

His face gave nothing away, while his voice held as little emotion as if he were talking to a stranger and not to the woman he had made love to in the bed not twenty feet away. Liane told him doggedly, forgetting pride— for what did pride have to do with the way she felt about Jake?—'I want you to stay here. Please, Jake.' In magnificent understatement she added, 'I've missed you.'

Something flickered across his face, so rapidly that she might have imagined it. His eyes dropped as he did up the zip on his jacket, and he said with a cold formality far more devastating than anger, 'Then you're a fool, Liane.'

As he took the car keys out of his pocket, she stood her ground, sick at heart, his words thrumming dully in her tired brain. A fool, a fool, a fool... Then he elbowed past her, the contact shuddering through her body. She watched him go, her throat muscles paralysed, her emotions a tangle of anger, pain and exhaustion. He closed the door with a decisive snap.

Like a figure captured by the snap of a camera, Liane stood still. She had told him what she wanted. But he had not heard her. Because, quite clearly, he did not want what she wanted.

CHAPTER TWELVE

AT ELEVEN-FIFTY the next morning Liane was ringing the doorbell of her father's house. The pines that flanked the long curve of the driveway were swaying in the wind that blew cold from the Atlantic and she heard the distant rattle of waves on the rocky shore. Mrs Petrie opened the door, and nodded with more politeness than warmth. 'Good morning, Miss Hutchins. We were expecting you.'

Liane did not like being called Miss Hutchins. Sitting in the plush seat of the private jet as it winged across the strip of water between Prince Edward Island and Nova Scotia, she had decided that today was to be a day of changes. Jake was first on the list. When she got home tonight she would not meekly allow him to walk past her into the darkness as she had last night; she would fight for him, even if that meant telling him she loved him. And in her father's house, to the best of her ability, she was going to act from her strengths as a mother and a provider rather than from her weaknesses as a frightened, subservient daughter. On her last visit she had run from her father's anger. She was not going to run from him today.

So she said, handing over her pink jacket with a pleasant smile, 'I use my mother's maiden name now, Mrs Petrie—Daley.' Bending to change from her boots to her best shoes, she added, 'I do hope the carpet has recovered from my son's visit yesterday.'

'A most unfortunate accident,' said Mrs Petrie. 'However, there should be no lasting damage. Mr Brande was very helpful.'

Liane's smile did not waver. 'An accident that was scarcely Patrick's fault.'

Mrs Petrie inclined her head, for if she was a cold woman she was also a fair one. 'That is certainly true,' she agreed. 'Mr Hutchins is in the drawing-room.'

Liane straightened her spine, kept her smile firmly in place, and opened the tall panelled door into the drawing-room. 'Good morning, Father,' she said.

Her father put down the magazine he had been reading, and got to his feet. 'Liane,' he said. 'Would you like coffee after your journey?'

She walked across the room, her heels tapping on the inlaid oak floor, and kissed him on the cheek, noticing with a touch of amusement that she had taken him by surprise. 'No, thanks, I had some on the plane.' She sank gracefully into a velvet wing chair. 'I gather you enjoyed Patrick's visit yesterday?'

Murray Hutchins sat down opposite her, wincing a little as he crossed his legs. She added quickly, 'Is your arthritis bothering you?'

'This confounded winter weather,' he replied.

He looked shrunk in the big wing chair, wizened like a gnome. 'You should be heading south and lying in the sun.'

'I'm a busy man, Liane.'

She ignored this undoubted red herring, and said with gentle persistence, 'You didn't answer my question.'

Her father frowned at her from beneath bushy white brows. 'He's a young man who believes in speaking his mind.'

'Thank you,' she said serenely. 'I've brought him up that way.'

'Children were seen and not heard in my day.'

'Which is perhaps why your emotions are still locked away inside you. To the detriment of all of us.'

In his wrinkled face his eyes were still as blue as hers; they did not falter. 'Let me offer you a sherry,' he said.

'That would be lovely.'

She watched as he tottered across the room, and did not offer to help when he had difficulty wresting the stopper from the crystal decanter. Had he always been so unsteady? Or had she never, as Jake had suggested, really seen him clearly before?

She did not want to think about Jake—not now when she needed all her wits about her. She took the glass from the ornate silver tray and sipped the pale, dry liquid. 'Despite his outspokenness, would you like to see Patrick again?'

'I would not have expected such an offer after yesterday.'

'Jake said that what happened yesterday will never happen again.'

'It will not.'

He took a gulp of sherry; he had never been a moderate man. Liane asked evenly, 'Are you sorry for what you did?'

His blue eyes bored into hers. 'You want your pound of flesh, don't you?' he said unpleasantly.

Inwardly Liane quailed, as she had always quailed before her father's anger. Outwardly she remained composed, her fingers curved a little too tightly around the stem of her glass, and made no reply.

Impatiently Murray Hutchins admitted, 'I shouldn't have done it. It was wrong of me. Does that satisfy you?'

She nodded, for she knew that for him these were massive admissions. 'I've done wrong, too,' she said steadily. 'I've been afraid of you for as long as I can remember, so I've kept Patrick from——'

'You don't look afraid of me right now!'

He was glaring at her. 'I'm not, actually,' Liane said, unable to repress her smile. 'A lot of things have changed since I saw you last. I'd be happy to see you more often, and to bring Patrick with me—he'd like to visit you, too.'

The glass in her father's gnarled hand shook so badly that the sherry slopped almost to the rim. 'How do you know?'

'He said so.'

A pleased smile passed like the winter sun over her father's face, and was as quickly extinguished. 'He only wants to get his hands on my baseball cards,' he growled.

'He liked you, Dad,' insisted Liane, who in all her twenty-seven years had only rarely used this diminutive.

'Gramps. Dad. What's the world coming to?' Murray grumbled. 'Are you sure he liked me?'

Liane laughed, a delightful laugh of genuine amusement. 'Come on, tell the truth, you're dying to see your grandson again.'

'I wouldn't mind seeing him again, no.'

'You're a hypocrite,' Liane said amiably. 'Aren't you going to offer me another glass of that admirable sherry?'

'Aren't you afraid I'll try and influence your son to take over my business? Because I will, Liane.'

She said, choosing her words with care, 'Patrick is only seven, but he already has fairly definite ideas on what he wants and does not want. At the moment he wants to play hockey and build a rocket to the moon, and he doesn't want to study English. I think you'll find him more than a match for you, Dad. And, who knows, maybe when he's older he will want to take over the business? But only because he wants to, not because you've brainwashed him.'

Murray frowned at her. 'You're being very forthright.'

'Yes,' Liane said in faint surprise, for it had been a great deal easier than she had anticipated, 'I am.'

'So when will you bring him?'

'I'll check my schedule when I get home, and my first free weekend we'll come over—within the next three weeks, I promise.'

He pushed himself out of the chair and took her glass, crossing the glowing crimson patterns of the antique Persian rug on his way to the decanter. His back to her as he poured more sherry into her glass, he said gruffly, 'Thank you.'

He had not actually said he was sorry for kidnapping and for his threats, and he had not been able to look her in the face when he thanked her. But to Liane these were minor concerns. She knew each had travelled a long way today—she probably further than her father; and she was more than content with all she had accomplished.

When Liane got home at seven-thirty that evening, Jake's rented car was nowhere to be seen. She let herself in the front door, knowing instantly that the house was empty, and saw a plain white envelope propped on the hall table, her name printed on it in blue ink. She ripped the envelope open and scanned the single sheet of paper it contained.

'Liane,' it said. 'I hope my returning Patrick to you has in some small way ameliorated my appalling lack of trust in you. Jake.' Beneath this he had scrawled as an afterthought, 'Patrick is at Megan's.'

She turned the paper over, but that was all it said. Not 'Dear Liane'. Not 'Love, Jake'. Nor had he said that she would also find him at Megan's. She ran to the phone and dialled their number. Fitz answered. Forgetting to say who it was, she gasped, 'Fitz, is Jake there?'

'Is that you, Liane? No, he insisted on leaving for the airport half an hour ago. Said he wanted to fly back to Ottawa tonight.'

She and Jake must have passed on the road, Liane thought sickly. In the darkness she would not have seen him. And by now the jet would have taken off for the thousand-mile flight west. She sagged against the wall, all she had achieved that day like dust in her mouth. What good was her decision to make changes in her life if Jake wasn't here? Two people were needed for a relationship to change.

But Jake was gone. He had not waited to see her.

'Liane...you still there?'

'Yes,' she whispered, 'I'm here.'

'I'll run Patrick over. Be there in ten minutes.'

She did not want to see Fitz. She wanted to see Jake.

All her movements automatic, Liane hung up her coat and pulled off her boots. She then went into the bathroom and repaired her make-up, trying to restore some colour to her face. When the doorbell rang, she plastered a smile on her pink lips and opened the door.

'Hi, Mum,' Patrick crowed, waving a sheet of paper at her. 'Look at this!'

It was an English quiz on which he had made the unprecedented mark of seventy-one. Her smile far more genuine, she congratulated him, listened to all the various events of his day, and told him about the proposed visit to his grandfather. While Fitz made himself a cup of tea, she put Patrick to bed and read two more chapters of his latest science fiction book. Then she went downstairs to face Fitz.

Fitz, a man of the moment, had fallen asleep on the couch. Liane shook him awake. He yawned, grinned at her through the tangle of his beard, and said, 'Megs and

I think you should head for Ottawa as soon as you can pack your bags.'

'Why?' asked Liane militantly. 'So Jake can slam the door in my face?'

'So you can talk some sense——'

'He won't listen!'

'Neither will you.'

Abruptly she sat down in the nearest chair. 'I'm tired, Fitz, and not in the mood for an argument.'

'No argument. Jake's a proud and reticent man who knows darn well how greatly he's misjudged you and who cannot get it through his thick skull that just possibly you might forgive him. It's up to you to convince him you do. You do, don't you?'

'So are you suggesting I leave for Ottawa right now?' she said sarcastically. 'Hot on his tail?'

'You could wait until tomorrow. It's the weekend— no school, Megan and I will take Patrick, and I'll keep an eye on the house for you.' He gave his moustache a triumphant swirl.

Liane suddenly dropped all pretence, her face mirroring her misgivings. 'I'm scared to go, Fitz. I'm so vulnerable to him, and if he sent me away again I'm not sure I could bear it.'

Fitz scowled mightily. 'I'm almost sure he won't. But I guess there is that risk.'

Risk. The word she had tossed around so blithely so short a time ago. Had she not sworn she would never take another risk? Liane bowed her head, gazing at her linked hands in her lap, thinking of all that Jake had given her and of all that he had taken away. 'I will go,' she said in a low voice. 'Tomorrow, if I can get a flight.'

She felt nothing. No surge of joy that she would see Jake again, no rush of hope, no flutter of panic. Just a strange, dead sense of waiting.

For the rest would depend on Jake.

The next morning a light snow was falling as Liane left for the airport. When she had made her bookings the night before, the only seats she could get were via Halifax and Montreal with a scheduled arrival in Ottawa mid-afternoon; she had put the ticket on her VISA. It was now up to its limit, because she had also used it on the ski trip to the Laurentians, and the spending money in her wallet had left just enough in her account to cover her bills. I'm going for broke, she thought, glancing at the lead-grey sky as she took the main highway into Charlottetown.

The snowfall was heavier by the time she left her car in the car park. But the first leg of her flight took place without mishap, although the runways and the terminal building of the Halifax airport were blurred by whirling flakes of snow.

She had an hour's wait in Halifax. Trying to ignore how many flights were delayed or cancelled, particularly those from the west, Liane had a coffee in the canteen and wandered round the gift shops. Although her flight was delayed twice, eventually it lifted off.

It was a bumpy flight. Ten minutes out of Dorval the pilot cautioned that they might have to backtrack to Moncton in New Brunswick because of the weather situation. But then, after a further delay, he made an impeccable landing under what must have been very difficult conditions. Montreal was a great deal closer to Ottawa than Moncton; Liane smiled to herself as they taxied to the gate.

A second announcement wiped the smile from her face. The flight was terminating in Dorval, the pilot advised in a soothing voice, due to the snowfall warning and increasing winds. The ongoing passengers would be put up in a nearby hotel and informed as soon as possible of the continuation of their flight. He then thanked them for their patience and co-operation.

Liane, feeling neither patient nor co-operative, filed out of the cabin and was herded into a bus. Now that she was on the ground she was amazed the pilot had been able to land at all. When she got to the hotel she'd find out about taking the train to Ottawa, she decided. She'd rather be at ground level in this.

However, the trains and the buses were all cancelled, the word blizzard bandied about frequently and with varying degrees of excitability. She was stuck. She would have to make the best of it. At least the hotel and her meals were paid for by the airline, she thought, fingering the rather scanty stock of bills in her wallet, and using one of them to buy herself a paperback in the hotel lobby.

The time dragged past. Liane went to bed early, woke up to find that it was still snowing, and was told by the airline that no flights were scheduled until afternoon at the earliest. She could walk to Ottawa faster, she thought glumly, heading for the cafeteria, where she ate far too much breakfast.

By two in the afternoon the snow had all but stopped, the wind had died and the runways had been ploughed. The backlog of aircraft was gradually cleared; at five-past four Liane's flight took off for Ottawa. She took a cab from the airport to Jake's address, a slow trip because of the number of snow-ploughs and heavy-duty trucks on the streets, and paid the cabbie with two more of her precious bills. She stood on the pavement in her leather boots and her pink jacket, looking at his house.

It was a two-storey brick and stucco dwelling set back from the street in a large garden with, she noticed professionally, some beautiful trees. He was renting it, he had told her once, with an option to buy when his career plans were more settled. She walked up the path, which had recently been shovelled, and rang the doorbell. She felt very nervous.

No one came to open the door. There was, she realised with a sinking heart, no red wagon parked in the driveway, which had also been shovelled. She rang the bell again, and, when there was no response, knocked loudly in case the bell was broken. Even if Jake was out, hadn't he mentioned a housekeeper?

Neither Jake nor the housekeeper answered the door. She walked around the side of the house, where a wooden gate led into the back garden past the garage; when she peered into the garage window she saw that it was, except for some garden equipment, empty. No sign of the red wagon. So Jake had to be out.

There was an attractive wooden bench inside the gate, shielded by some evergreens. Liane swiped most of the snow off it and sat down to think.

She had no idea where Jake was, although the shovelling that had been done made her think he would not be long. She counted her money, wondering if she had enough to take another cab into town and stay in a hotel overnight. She rather doubted that she had, unless the hotel was so cheap that she probably wouldn't want to stay in it anyway. She could always sleep on a bench at the airport, she thought sturdily. And she didn't really need any dinner.

Having decided to wait for a couple of hours, she settled herself more comfortably on the bench. Luckily it was not very cold, and the garden was sheltered from the wind. If Jake were not home by nine o'clock, she would go back to the airport and start phoning his number at regular intervals.

She should have told him she was coming. But she had been afraid that he would refuse outright to see her. Turning up on his doorstep had seemed a far better idea.

She read for a while until the light got too bad to see the words on the page. She walked up and down, stamping her feet to warm them, wishing she had worn her less glamorous but much warmer fleece boots. Resolutely she kept her mind away from the subject of food. And still Jake did not return.

Liane had slept very little the last three nights, and she had lived with tension ever since Patrick's kidnapping; eventually she put her small shoulder-bag at one end of the bench, and lay down, pulling her black skirt down over her knees as far as she could. Telling herself she would stay only another thirty minutes, knowing she would never fall asleep because she was too hungry and her feet were too cold, she closed her eyes.

'For God's sake—*Liane*?'

She was beneath a frozen sea, walking through ice caverns that shone pale turquoise, translucent, unearthly. Her leather boots kept slipping on the ice, and her feet were cold...

Someone shook her hard by the shoulder. 'Liane, wake up!' a loud voice said in her ear.

With an incoherent exclamation Liane sat bolt upright, her eyes wide open, and for a horrible moment she had no idea where she was. Then she focused on Jake's face, only inches from hers, felt the unyielding boards of the bench beneath her, and knew exactly where she was. 'You came home,' she said.

'You could have frozen to death,' he said harshly. 'If you hadn't left the gate ajar, I wouldn't have known you were here.'

He did not look pleased to see her. Rather, he looked extremely angry. Liane was so cold she scarcely cared. She let her feet fall to the ground, and gave an involuntary cry of pain at the cramps in her knees. 'For God's *sake*!' Jake exclaimed again, scooped her up in his arms, and tramped through the snow to the front door.

'Put me down,' Liane ordered.

'And have you fall flat on your face on the path? Don't be silly!'

He shoved the door open with his foot, and strode inside, hitting it shut with his elbow. As the warmth of the house enveloped her, Liane realised she was shivering all over, and was quite unable to stop, even her teeth chattering like a distant rattle of snare drums. Jake said, kicking off his boots, 'How long have you been outside?'

'Since about six.'

'Do you know what the time is? Ten-thirty! You're damn lucky I came home as early as I did.'

She sputtered incoherently, 'The way you look I don't think I'm particularly lucky. What was her name?'

He stopped dead at the bottom of the stairs. 'Pete,' he retorted. 'Peter Bennett—my cousin who owns the fleet of jets.'

Pushing her hands under his jacket to find the warmth of his body, Liane said, 'Pete's a nice name.'

Shivering as she was, she could still feel the tension gripping Jake's body. He said hoarsely, not looking at her, 'You're the last person I would have expected to find on my doorstep—what the hell are you doing here?'

Risk. Go for broke. 'I'm here b-because I love you,' Liane stuttered.

Unconsciously his arms tightened their hold. 'I don't believe you. For God's sake don't play games; I can't stand it!'

'I d-do love you,' she wailed. 'Oh, Jake, I'm so cold!'

He stood still. 'How can you possibly love me?' he flared. 'When the chips were down I believed your father's version of events, not yours. I couldn't bring myself to trust you—because you're a woman.'

She scanned his features one by one. He needed a shave and his eye sockets were dark-circled, sunk into his skull. 'You look terrible,' she said.

'Don't change the subject!'

'Look at me, Jake.' With patent reluctance he dragged his gaze down to hers. His eyes were bloodshot. 'What *have* you been doing to yourself?'

'Getting drunk,' he replied economically. 'At Pete's.'

He did not smell of liquor. 'Tonight?'

'Last night.' He put her down so suddenly that she staggered. 'Liane, you can't love me! I believed your *father*—not you.'

'I know you did.' She fought to control the tremors in her limbs, knowing she was battling for her life here. Her life and Jake's. 'You've had lousy role models as far as women are concerned,' she said. 'Your mother, your father's mistresses, your wife—every one of them upped and left you.'

'You're making excuses for me.'

'I'm trying to understand!'

He gripped her shoulders so hard that she could feel the dig of his fingers through her jacket. 'Are you saying that you forgive me?'

Fitz had used the word forgiveness; once again Fitz had known what he was talking about. 'Yes,' Liane said, wriggling her cold toes inside her boots and watching incredulity and hope war in Jake's eyes. 'I forgive you. Why else would I be here?'

He said in a cracked voice, 'I love you, too.'

She had travelled hundreds of miles to hear those words. Yet now that he had said them she felt nothing. Her knees shaking so hard she would have given all the remaining money in her wallet for some of Megan's cranberry wine, far beyond saying anything but the truth, Liane croaked, 'It's funny... you don't know how often I've longed to hear you say those words. But now that you have, I—I'm not sure I believe you. Maybe the only reason you're saying them is because I've forced my way into your house and you're just being polite... I should never have come.'

'Polite?' Jake repeated with an unamused bark of laughter. 'Politeness has absolutely nothing to do with the way I'm feeling right now.' His eyes raked her face, seeing the tension and vulnerability in the curve of her mouth. 'I've loved you since that first moment you appeared out of a snowstorm in the middle of the Wentworth Valley.'

'You have a funny way of showing it.'

He said violently, 'I didn't want to fall in love with you. I didn't want to fall in love with anyone.'

She thrust her hands deep in her pockets. 'Why did you get drunk last night, Jake?'

'Because I couldn't bear the emptiness of my house. Because I missed you so much I thought I'd die for want of you. Because I knew I'd thrown away something utterly precious. Shattered it beyond repair.' His voice was corrosive with self-contempt. 'And all because I was afraid to trust you.'

Aching to smooth the pain from his face, she said, 'I hate to hear you talk that way.'

'Halfway through the bottle of rum, I poured out the whole sorry story to Pete. He told me I didn't deserve you, and that he had a jet going from Ottawa to Halifax this afternoon that could make a detour to Charlottetown, and that I'd damn well better get on it.'

For the first time since she had arrived, Liane smiled. 'Another Fitz.'

'But it snowed all day and the jet was stuck in Toronto. Plus I've got one hell of a hangover.' Jake gave her a crooked smile. 'So the trip was delayed until tomorrow morning.'

'But *you* were coming to see *me*?'

'Yeah. I was ninety-nine per cent sure you'd show me the door. But I had to try.' His eyes, full of strain, met hers. 'Because—and I don't blame you for not believing me—I do love you. More than I can say.'

Liane's body gave a sudden uncontrollable shudder. 'I'm starting to believe you. I think.'

In sudden concern he said, 'You're cold. And you look worn out.' He hesitated. 'Will you stay here tonight? You can sleep in the spare room if——'

'Don't you want to sleep with me any more?'

'Of course I do!'

The intensity with which he spoke made Liane's heart beat faster. 'That's good,' she said. 'Because I don't want to sleep in the spare room, and I can't afford to go anywhere else. I don't normally park myself on garden benches in the aftermath of a blizzard.'

'Do you mean to tell me you don't have any money?' Picking her up again, Jake started to climb the stairs. From the corner of her eye she saw pen and ink drawings on William Morris wallpaper, and heard the mellifluous chiming of a grandfather clock.

'Forty-three dollars.'

'Did you have an alternative plan other than freezing to death on my bench?'

'Sleep at the airport. It's free.'

He said, pushing the bathroom door open, 'You must love me. Explanations later, Liane. I'll start the water and get you something warm to wear...are you hungry?'

Jake was looking more like himself, and less like a man tormented by all the demons in hell. She grinned at him through her lashes. Her teeth were no longer jittering against each other—a distinct improvement—and Jake had twice said that he loved her. 'I ate an open sandwich in Montreal at noon. Courtesy of the airline.'

'I've got some soup in the freezer—I'll heat it up.'

As he passed her a thick wool robe through the door, she added saucily, 'If we're going to spend the night together, I insist you shave.'

'Giving orders already, huh?' The laughter faded from his face. He said quietly, 'I love you so much, Liane. With all my being, I love you.'

Shaken to her soul, Liane felt tears spill from her lashes. 'I love you, too,' she whispered, and knew the simple words for a vow.

'Then we'll be all right, won't we?' He gave her a smile of immense tenderness. 'Take your time. I'll be downstairs.'

Her reflection in the mirror was that of a woman who had been given a gift beautiful beyond belief. Liane bent and turned on the hot tap.

She soaked in the tub, used Jake's Calvin Klein powder liberally all over her body, and wrapped the deep green folds of the robe around her. Then she went downstairs, finding her way to the kitchen, an ultra-modern room adorned with every conceivable appliance. Following her fascinated gaze, Jake said, 'I like gadgets—half the fun of cooking. Here, sit down...are you warmer?'

'Much.' Suddenly shy, aware that under the robe she was naked, Liane bent her attention to the bowl of excellent leek and potato soup and the thick slabs of crusty

French bread. Several minutes later she gave a sigh of repletion. 'That was wonderful; you saved my life.'

'Any time. So when did you leave the island, Liane?'

Briefly she ran through the vicissitudes of her journey, finishing with the bench. 'I never thought I'd go to sleep.'

'Snowstorms seem to follow us around, don't they? Why didn't you phone and let me know you were coming?'

'I thought you'd tell me not to. Would you have, Jake?'

'Friday night I probably would have... I was too ashamed of the way I'd behaved to be anywhere near you. I'd belittled your fear that Patrick might be kidnapped, I'd accused you of trying to get money out of your father, I'd aligned you with all those women who'd been with my father... and on each count I was wrong.'

Like a man mesmerised, he took her hand in his and smoothed the slender length of her fingers. 'Your father did kidnap Patrick, you're absolutely honest about money, and you're brave and responsible and loving. I couldn't have constructed a more false picture of you— how could I ever make amends for that?'

'So you high-tailed it back to Ottawa as fast as you could,' she said, wondering how much longer she would have to wait before he kissed her.

He grimaced. 'I figured you must despise me. Better to get out of your life and out of Patrick's, too. Because apart from falling in love with you, I was also getting far too attached to him. So yeah—I ran away.'

'But on Saturday—thanks to Peter and the rum—you changed your mind?'

'By Saturday night I knew I'd never have a moment's peace if I didn't at least try to repair some of the damage I'd done. I'll never distrust you like that again, Liane; I swear I won't.' Laughter suddenly flashed across his face. 'I'm not saying we won't fight sometimes—I'd be very surprised if we don't. But I promise I won't dump all my past on those fights.'

'I can promise the same thing, Jake...because the visit with my father went really well.' She went on to describe it, and also told him about Patrick's quite astonishing mark in English. And then she ran out of things to say.

There was a short, charged silence. Jake said softly, 'Come to bed with me, Liane? Or shall I propose in the kitchen first?'

She blushed. 'I've been wanting to go to bed with you for the last seventy-two hours. And you can propose anywhere and any time you like.'

'Marry me,' Jake said, his dark eyes caressing her face. 'Please marry me.'

'Oh, yes,' Liane agreed, her features radiant with happiness. 'I'll marry you. For my sake I'll marry you because I love you, and for Patrick's sake I'll welcome you as his father. Just as I'm sure he will.'

For a moment Jake's face clouded. 'My job's probably going to be here in Ottawa—you'd have to move away from Megan and Fitz, and Patrick would have to leave all his friends.'

'He'd be gaining a father, though. And, although I'd miss Megan and Fitz, I'm sure we'd visit back and forth.' She smiled at him. 'Could we live in the country?'

'Of course we could. We'll buy a farm near a hockey rink.'

She said, knowing she had to give voice to the words, 'I understand that Patrick will never take your son's place. But I also know you will love Patrick as if he were your own son.'

Jake cleared his throat, a look on his face that she had never seen before. He said huskily, 'I will—I promise.'

She stood up by her chair, wanting him so badly that her whole body ached with primitive hunger. 'You did mention bed, didn't you?' she asked.

'It's been as much as I can do to keep my hands off you ever since I found you on the bench.'

Liane guided his palm to the swell of her breast under his robe. 'And now you don't have to.'

For a moment he held back. 'You do believe I love you?'

Her answer was instinctive; she walked into his arms, drew his head down, and kissed him full on the mouth. 'Yes,' she whispered. 'I believe you.'

He said exultantly, 'I feel as though I've been let out of prison to be able to say those words to you, and to see the light in your eyes when I do.' Drawing the lapels of the heavy robe apart, he drank in the ivory perfection of her body. 'We'd better go upstairs. Or we'll be making love on the kitchen floor.' Then, lifting one hand to smooth the hair back from her face, he added, 'You've had a rough three days—you're sure you're not too tired?'

Mischief danced in her eyes. 'I'm tired, yes. But I'm sure you can convince me to make love to you, Jake.'

Nor was it at all difficult for him to do so.

BODYCHECK

by
ELIZABETH OLDFIELD

CHAPTER ONE

'Lewis's immediate reaction was to organise personal security.' Mr Trenchard glanced across the dinner table. 'I think that's sensible, don't you?'

Neille paused in licking mango juice from her fingers to grin. 'You mean he's armed himself with a long sharp hatpin? Or has he enrolled for a crash course in karate? Maybe a guard dog would be more his style?' Her grin deepened mischievously as she gouged out another spoonful of ripe golden fruit. 'Maybe not. Lewis would never risk a Dobermann shedding hairs and slobbering all over him.'

'This is a serious matter,' her father demurred. 'The police have been informed and Lewis has requested they launch a full-scale investigation.'

Her grin became a scornful chuckle. 'Isn't that going a bit far? Just because he discovers an obscure little epistle in his in-tray there's no need to——' Neille stopped dead. 'Why didn't he tell me about this yesterday?' she demanded.

'Um.' Suffering a familiar downward plunge of spirits, Mr Trenchard cleared his throat. His daughter's short fuse temper never ceased to alarm him. She could flare up in a moment, and the flash of her blue eyes indicated she might well be ready to flare up now. True, she was restored to her sunny composure with equal speed and never bore a grudge, but in his opinion she was far too headstrong for a young lady, too independent, too self-willed. 'Um,' he prevaricated, 'I suppose Lewis didn't want to spoil your last evening together before he disappeared on his travels.'

'Come clean, Daddy,' she scoffed.

'Um.' Mr Trenchard cleared his throat again. 'Well, he's employed the services of a bodyguard and——'

'A bodyguard!' Neille rocked back with laughter. 'No wonder he kept quiet. I'd never have managed to keep my face straight given that news, and Lewis doesn't exactly appreciate being laughed at.' She giggled, imagining how her amusement would have caused her escort's demeanour to become as bristly as his fair moustache. 'He must be suffering from delusions of grandeur. Who does he think he is—some Getty heir or a pop star?'

'Lewis Mitchell happens to be an important figure in the retail trade,' her father said reproachfully. 'He's managing director of one of the most successful chains in——'

'OK, he's a hot shot,' Neille agreed, intent on stemming the flow. As chief accountant with Mitchells' Department Stores Limited, her father was a company man through and through. For him, the sun rose and set on Mitchells', and never more so than since Lewis had taken control. Mention anything remotely connected with high-street trade, and her father would launch into recitals of past results, present profits, future targets. 'But I still consider he's over-reacting,' she insisted. 'Fancy taking on a bodyguard, that's hilarious!'

'Two bodyguards actually.' Mr Trenchard

gulped in air and continued at a rush, 'One for
him and one for you. Your man, a Mr Rea, will be
joining us in ...' he shot a glance at his
wristwatch, '... five minutes. Lewis tried to fix
him up yesterday, but that was too short notice so
we had no option but to take the chance of
nothing happening in the interim. Thankfully——'

Open-mouthed, she stared at him. 'I beg your
pardon?'

'The note did make a threat against "you and
yours",' her father reminded her, desperate to
utilise this moment of stunned calm to the best
possible advantage. 'And as Lewis doesn't possess
any close family, the "yours" could well apply to
you. Until the police have whoever's responsible
behind bars, it seems wise for you to be—looked
after. Lewis is picking up the tab and I'm very
grateful. These security men don't come cheap. I
understand Jack Rea is one of the best in the
business. Lewis said he'd been highly re-
commended. In his time he's guarded ministers of
state, visiting dignitaries. There's even a rumour
that he once foiled——'

The cornflower-blue eyes sparked. 'He's not
guarding *me*!'

'Now Neille, be reasonable,' Mr Trenchard
implored, wiping a hand across his balding scalp.
His spirits had plunged again. He had known this
volatile only child of his would not take the news
calmly, known he wouldn't be able to cope. He
had never felt properly in charge since she was
knee-high. If only Annette had lived, he thought
wistfully, surely their daughter would have been
far more placid, far more genteel? And surely,
given a mother's guidance, she would never have

chosen to wear such outrageous clothes? He eyed the outsized sherbet-pink T-shirt which persisted in drooping off one tanned shoulder. High fashion, she called it. But that shoulder was too vibrantly naked to be acceptable at a gentleman's dinner table in mid-October. Her tulip-printed trousers dismayed him, too: they appeared to have been scissored at random from a pair of bedroom curtains. Maybe they had. Neille's multifarious talents never ceased to amaze him. 'Lewis thought——' he began, envying his young employer, now safely installed on the far side of the Atlantic and accompanied by his own bodyguard. 'Lewis thought——' Mr Trenchard wished there was someone around to protect *him*. Where tongue lashing was concerned, his daughter could be lethal. 'He thought——'

'I don't give a toss what Lewis thought. How dare he attempt to hobble me to some hulk!' A spoon clattered to a plate. 'And how dare you take his side? Daddy, you're a traitor. You don't expect me to agree to be trailed around by a—a cross between a Russian weightlifter and a gorilla, without so much as a do-you-mind? That note is a load of baloney. What d'you bet Lewis has been lording it over his minions, as he's prone to do, and someone's decided to strike back? He can be incredibly insensitive at times. He's so busy stamping his personality on Mitchells' that he forgets he's stamping on people, too.' Neille yanked at her T-shirt, exposing even more tanned shoulder. 'Of course, you do realise this could just be an excuse to spy on me? There's an element of calculation in all Lewis does, so it's possible he's making a final check to confirm I'm one hundred per cent squeaky-clean and suitable for the lofty position of——'

'You're being unfair. All that concerns Lewis is your safety,' her father soothed. 'And Jack Rea is nothing like a gorilla.'

'You've met this—this yob?' she spluttered.

'Well, yes.' Mr Trenchard felt his cheeks flush. To grow pink with embarrassment was a pathetic trait in a man of fifty-plus, he accepted, yet regrettably a recurring one. Neille rarely flushed. No demure violet she. Not for the first time he found himself wishing he could soak up a portion of her sturdy self-confidence. He'd be grateful for a fifth; even a tenth would do. 'Mr Rea came into the office this afternoon. He—he had to be briefed.'

'About me?' Her father nodded. 'That's a damned nerve!'

'You'll like him.'

'I will *not* like him. And I will *not* have a bodyguard.' Tempestuously she tossed the mane of copper-gold hair from her shoulders, in an action which would have sent photographers all over London lunging for their cameras. 'I can take care of myself, thank you very much!'

'Sweetheart, your life might be in danger.'

'Pull the other one, Daddy. Someone at his office is playing yah-boo with Lewis, that's all. You said yourself the note was vague, probably the work of an amateur. It doesn't demand money or make specific threats, does it?'

'No, but——'

'Then I refuse to be monitored by a barrel-chested thug with a broken nose and cauliflower ears.'

'Do you now?' enquired an alien voice, and Neille shot round in her chair. Beneath the arch which connected the dining area with the living room stood a tall, dark-haired man. 'Jack Rea at your service, ma'am,' he said, dipping his head. 'Nose regrettably unscathed, ears shell-like, chest——'

'How did you get in?' she demanded.

'Through the front door, how else? Someone had neglected to secure the catch. Not a particularly smart omission considering there's a busy street outside, and taking account of present circumstances.' He extended his hand and walked forward. 'Good evening, sir.'

Having admonished Neille—for she had been guilty of forgetting to snap the lock and suspected he had divined as much—the intruder now switched his attention to her father, allowing her time to take stock. The image of a B-movie thicko who communicated by grunts was way off mark. Jack Rea was lean, elegant and composed; the kind of individual who carried his own natural habitat everywhere with him. His grey eyes were pleasant, yet maybe a shade too pale for comfort. He looked—clever. She had no doubt he had already assessed the well-furnished surroundings, her father's anxiety, her rebellion, and stored the information away. Probably slotted it under appropriate headings, too. Suave in a grey city-style suit and pristine white shirt, he was carrying a briefcase. See the man in the street and you'd identify him as the quintessential stockbroker. Kind of a stiff. Clever he might be, but, Neille decided, also deadly dull.

'Couldn't you have rung the doorbell?' she

protested, slicing through the pleasantries which
were being exchanged.

'I did.' He grinned conspiratorially at her father
who had risen to greet him. 'But such a ding-dong
battle was taking place that obviously you didn't
hear.'

'We're just about to have coffee. You'll join us,'
Mr Trenchard urged, a hand on the intruder's
arm. 'Sweetheart,' he said, over his shoulder. 'Mrs
Dawson's left the tray in the kitchen. Be a good
girl and bring it through, will you?' Without a
backward glance her father led the way into the
green and gold living room. He was talking
happily, welcoming the younger man into his
home, making fun of the 'ding-dong' battle. 'My
daughter has a low boiling point,' she heard him
chuckle.

Left alone, Neille stood and fumed. In league
with this Jack Rea, her father would feel the
balance of power had shifted in his favour. Two
against one, she thought caustically. But wasn't it
three against one? Lewis might be wheeling and
dealing in the States just now, and destined to
progress on a fact-finding mission through Japan,
Hong Kong and Australia, but he had initiated
this fiasco. Trust Lewis to barge in without asking
and take it for granted he was calling the shots.
No doubt he fondly imagined he was getting in
training for when she was *Mrs* Mitchell. No way.
A bodyguard—huh!

She collected the tray which the housekeeper
had prepared and stomped through to the living
room. Etiquette demanded Mr Rea be allowed a
cup of coffee, but he would then be advised, most
apologetically, that he must report back to his

superiors with the message that his services were not required.

'Sugar?' Neille rasped, playing hostess with maximum haste, minimum decorum. 'Cream?'

The intruder gave an easy smile. 'Neither, thanks.'

'I believe you used to be in the SAS, Jack?' Mr Trenchard enquired, settling himself down in a comfortable velvety armchair.

Jack! Her father had only met the man that afternoon and already they were buddies. Jack Rea obviously knew how to win friends and influence people, but she was made of sterner stuff. It took more than a smile to dazzle her. Seldom an addict of the softly-softly technique, Neille gave him no chance to reply. If he had been in the SAS, fought lions with one hand tied behind his back, and performed every single stunt in every single James Bond film, good luck to him. But what mattered was getting the man out of the house and out of her hair, pronto.

'There's been an unfortunate misunderstanding,' she announced. 'My father is under the impression I need a bodyguard, but I'm afraid he's mistaken. I lead a busy life and the last thing I require is someone dragging around in my wake. You'd get on my nerves and no doubt I would get on yours.' At this she flung a swift glance defying him to comment, but the grey eyes were dutiful. 'Thank you for your time and trouble, but I shall be remaining a free agent. However, in the unlikely event that I do find myself being pursued by a furtive gent in a trilby and trench-coat, I promise to phone you.' Having curtailed his activities to her satisfaction, Neille decided he should now receive one of her wholesome *ingénue* smiles, smiles which were of inestimable value in the modelling world. 'I have no wish to appear impolite, Mr Rea, and I trust there are no hard feelings, but I'd be grateful if you would kindly hop on your bike and——'

'Aren't you forgetting there's been a threatening letter?' he asked, sipping his coffee. 'I don't think it places too great a strain on the intellect to deduce that someone out there could be gunning for you?'

Neille glowered. If she refused to be impressed by him, it was now apparent he was not impressed by her. So what if she had smiled out from a score of magazine covers and was reputed to be a very pretty girl? She had not knocked the socks off Jack Rea.

'No one's gunning,' she asserted, shaking her head so emphatically that the shining coppery hair swirled around her shoulders like turbulent waves.

'How can you be sure?'

'For the simple reason that the note is a hoax. In any case the "yours" isn't me. Anyone with an ounce of sense must realise "yours" refers to the department stores, or——' She screwed up her face. 'Or—or maybe Lewis's home or possessions.'

Jack Rea exchanged a look with her father. 'At the risk of sounding sexist, couldn't you as his fiancée be deemed to be one of his possessions?' he enquired silkily.

'No, I bloody well could not!'

'Language, sweetheart,' Mr Trenchard rebuked from the sidelines.

'And for your information, I'm not Lewis Mitchell's fiancée.'

'No?' The unwanted guest bent to extract a
sheaf of press cuttings from his briefcase. 'Yet it
says here——'

'Where did you get those?' Neille demanded.

'From a contact on a national newspaper, a
reporter friend. To oblige me he went through
their files and was able to come up with——'

'He came up with nothing but tittle-tattle,' she
pronounced. Jack Rea's reporter friend might have
obliged him, but he most certainly had not obliged
her. The relevant cutting would be recent, but the
majority had to date back two years and more,
and she had no desire to come up slap-bang
against the past. 'You don't believe everything you
read, do you?' she enquired. 'That engagement was
dreamed up by a journalist who had spare column
inches to fill in a hurry. Lewis and I are—quote,
good friends, unquote.' Smug at having got the
better of him, Neille was pert. The war might not
yet be over, but she had won a battle.

Jack Rea shrugged. 'Perhaps whoever sent
your—quote, good friend, unquote—the note isn't
aware of that? The private truth could count for
nothing.' He glanced at her sideways. 'Where
celebrities are concerned, the only truth tends to be
the public one.'

'I am *not* a celebrity, far from it,' she informed
him, the crystal clarity of each word warning he
had touched on a very sore point. 'I'm a model.
One of many. The only reason I ever caught the
eye of the paparazzi was by association.' She
flicked tapered fingers. 'Any froth which gets
reported is without my permission. And ninety per
cent's make-believe.'

'My daughter isn't a member of the jet set,' Mr

Trenchard inserted loyally. 'She takes her career seriously and works hard and long, much harder and much longer than most people.'

'I have no doubt she does, sir, but that doesn't alter anything. The public invariably believes the image which the media presents and——'

'Aren't we side-tracking?' Neille bit out. 'Even if I was the "yours", which I'm not, there's still no risk. Lewis takes life far too seriously. Anyone else would have recognised the note as rubbish and thrown it into the waste-paper basket, but typically he goes for overkill. My guess is that a young sales assistant or a kid in his office happened to watch an episode of Hill Street Blues, or some such series, and decided they'd copy——'

'I don't think so,' Jack Rea objected.

Disposing of the final dregs of his coffee, Mr Trenchard pushed himself up from his chair. 'Um, if you'll excuse me I have figures to check for quarter end,' he said apologetically. Neille was in what he termed her 'terrier' mood, which meant this argument was destined to grind on for a long time. He could see no need for him to sit in on it. Jack Rea was supremely capable of coping alone. Indeed, the confrontation possessed more than an element of immovable object meeting irresistible force. Mr Trenchard edged towards the door. 'Mrs Dawson's made up the bed in the spare room so it's ready when you are, Jack. First left at the top of the stairs. Good night. Sleep well,' he smiled, and disappeared.

Neille stared at the intruder who had leaned forward to pour himself a second cup of coffee.

'Are you supposed to be staying the night?' she demanded.

He set down the jug. 'There's no supposed about it, sunbeam, I am.'

'Good grief! Does nobody consult me about anything?' She swept to her feet and stood before him, hands pushed into the pockets of her voluminous trousers. 'I'm sorry to disappoint you, Mr Rea, but there's been a change of plan. I'm a big girl now, and I don't need my father, or Lewis, or anybody to make my decisions for me. This is nothing personal, I assure you, but I must insist that you leave—*immediately*.'

He looked up and grinned. 'Sorry, I don't take my orders from you.'

'But you can't—you can't guard me against my will,' she spluttered.

'No?'

His cool was such that Neille yearned to stamp on his polished black shoes, or kick the shins beneath the razor-creased grey trousers, or tip the coffee jug over his glossy dark head. Anything to rattle him.

'I shall phone Lewis and instruct him to call you off,' she said, her delicately sculpted chin becoming a blockbuster.

'You could try,' he agreed. He pushed back his sleeve to inspect a gold watch. 'Though the time change could pose a problem. Right now your good friend's airborne, somewhere between Boston and New York. When he lands he goes straight off to a business meeting. Your best bet is to wait until two a.m. London time. He's due to check into the Waldorf Astoria around then.' Jack gestured towards the tray. 'Perhaps you'd care to join me in another cup of coffee while you're waiting?'

Neille narrowed her eyes and glared. 'No thanks,' she muttered.

She was tempted to turn tail and flounce off to bed, but it was barely nine-thirty and why should she be chased away? She belonged here; *he* was the intruder. She dumped herself down in the chair her father had vacated and picked up a fashion magazine, rapidly thumbing through. For once the clothes displayed failed to interest her. All she could think about was the man who sat opposite. There had to be a law against a stranger marching into your home as though it was a garrison and taking up sentry duty. From beneath her lashes she subjected him to an intense scrutiny. If he wasn't El Bruto with shoulders like planks and fists like hams, he did look tremendously fit. On reaching their mid-thirties—his age at a guess—many men added a roll of fat around their middles, but Jack Rea carried no surplus pounds. Also his skin had that sheen of good health. He must take regular exercise; perhaps he worked out in a gym with weights, or had sparring sessions. If an assassin shot through the door this minute, how would he react, she wondered. Throw a punch in a split-second reflex? Kick up a foot? Or would he leap to shield her body with his own? Were bodyguards trained to be aggressive or defensive? She did not know.

'Do I meet with approval?' he enquired, breaking the silence.

'Oh.' Neille realised she had been staring at him. 'I was looking for bulges.'

A droll brow quirked. 'Whatever turns you on.'

'Under your armpit, I mean. A *gun*!' she gulped. Maybe Jack Rea wasn't quite such a stiff, after all.

'It's against the law to carry firearms,' he told her, grinning. 'And a weapon would spoil the cut of my jacket. Mind you, if it's any comfort, I have been known to tote a discreet baton from time to time.' He stretched out his long legs, relaxing. 'Your idea of bodyguards seems sadly outdated. We——'

'Now look here, Mr Rea——'

'Jack,' he insisted graciously. 'And I'll call you Nellie, if I may? We shall be living in close proximity for a while, so it's easier if——'

'Nellie!' she cried in horror.

'Isn't it?' He lifted his sheaf of papers from the briefcase and scanned the top page. 'That's what it says here.'

'My name is Neille,' she blazed. 'Spelt N-e-i-l-l-e.'

'The typist put the "i" in the wrong place, that's all.'

'All! Nellie sounds like an overweight char-woman of uncertain vintage, with plastic hair rollers and a cigarette dangling from her mouth.'

'You don't smoke?' he enquired, dead-pan.

'No, I don't,' she fizzed. She was certain he had known her name was Neille. How could he not know? He had been briefed by her father. He had read those newspaper cuttings. Of course, he had known. By pretending otherwise he had deliberately set out to rile her. He had been demonstrating that he, too, had some weapons in his armoury. Well, such a tactic deserved a counter tactic. 'While we're on the subject of names, isn't Jack rather prosaic?' she asked. 'Shouldn't you be called Champ or Rocky or something similar?'

The rise and fall of his shoulders beneath the

well-cut jacket accepted the put down. 'Like I said, you have totally the wrong idea about personal protection operatives if I may use the jargon. I'm not one to boast but we have ceased to eat peas off our knives, and grey matter is now standard equipment. The bulky philistine who cracked his knuckles in a corner has gone. Minders also keep an extremely low profile, as you'll discover. Half the time you won't know I'm there.' He pursed his lips. 'Earlier I overheard you tell your father how you had no wish to be monitored, but it isn't like that. I give you my assurance here and now that reporting misdemeanours back to Lewis Mitchell is no part of my remit. I keep guard, that's all. I don't snoop. You can rely on my discretion.'

Neille's brows pulled together. 'What misdemeanours?'

'Oh, guys on the side. That kind of thing.'

'I don't have guys on the side,' she said indignantly.

'You don't?' A strand of dark wavy hair had disengaged itself from the neatly brushed crop, and now he pushed it from his brow. 'Then why all the objections to being protected?'

'Because in my judgment the note is sabre-rattling, if that, so protection is unnecessary. And why should I agree to something which is not my choice? I run my life, not Lewis. And I don't require you as a support system, Mr Rea.'

'You don't have any—secrets?' He looked dubious.

'None.' She glanced sourly at his briefcase. 'I'm well aware most of those press cuttings depict me as some skittish filly who's perpetually kicking up her hooves, but if you check closer you'll realise that any cantering—such as it was—came to an end a long time ago.'

'When Simon Gates died?'

Neille lowered her head. 'Yes,' she muttered. She resented a stranger having access to details about her private life, though he knew only as much, and as little, as anyone else who had perused those gossip columns. Or did he? What had her father told him this afternoon? She began to smart. Jack Rea had no right to pry into her background.

'I don't want a bodyguard,' she ground out. 'I don't need a bodyguard, and what's more I refuse to have a bodyguard.'

'Remember the note,' he cautioned.

'I'm taking that with an extremely large pinch of salt.'

He sighed. 'I don't seem to be getting through to you, sunbeam. That note——'

'Is rubbish.'

'I disagree. You are aware of its contents?'

'Not word for word,' Neille admitted, 'but my father told me——'

'Here.' He took a sheet of paper from his briefcase and thrust it forward. 'Rule one in the security game—learn all the facts you can.'

The paper was a photocopy of the original note. Neille saw that the words had been made up of letters cut from a newspaper and pasted on in uneven lines.

This time you have gone too far. Enough is enough.

Trample any more old values underfoot and you and yours will pay the ultimate price.

Goodbye, Mitchell.

'Gobbledygook,' she announced, displaying a lofty disdain. 'Boil it down and what does it mean? Nothing!'

'You can make one or two deductions,' he dissented. 'For instance, I doubt the note was composed by a kid who'd been watching television. Youngsters don't give much thought to old values.'

Neille shrugged. 'So it was written by an adult. So?'

'By an adult who *cares*.'

'About what exactly?'

'The police don't know yet, but they're working on it.'

'I guarantee they never will know,' she pooh-poohed, scanning the photocopy again. 'If this is anything, it's a warning. Trample on any more values and you *will* pay the price—future tense.'

'"This time you have gone too far,"' Jack quoted. 'That doesn't sound like the future. Neither does, "Goodbye, Mitchell".'

'Dramatics,' she rejected. 'A stereotyped and very garbled threat. Whoever composed this was shadow boxing. It's possible Lewis inadvertently stood on someone's toes, and in a fit of pique they decided to cause him some discomfort in return.'

'How would he stand on their toes?'

'Does it matter?' Neille asked impatiently.

'It mattered to whoever wrote the note,' came the swift reply.

'But why should it matter to you?' she demanded. For someone who had walked off the street and into her life less than an hour ago, he was far too curious. 'I understand the police have mounted an inquiry. Why not leave them to ask the questions?'

'Because I need to compile a dossier of my own.' His tone was steadfastly reasonable. 'I liaise with the police but, without a personal awareness of the people involved, the nuances, a possible motive and any other pertinent details which flesh out a situation, how can I decide the area from which danger is most likely to come? I try to climb into the mind of the enemy; doesn't that make sense?' When he saw she was sceptical, he became impatient himself. 'Do you expect me to stand guard knowing damn all? I have far more experience than to do that.'

'But I don't expect you to stand guard!' Neille shot back. 'And there *isn't* any danger.'

Jack gave an exasperated sigh. 'Just tell me how Lewis Mitchell may have stood on toes.'

'Well, he's been making drastic changes in the department stores and in the process gathered more than a few critics.' She spoke with reluctance. The note was flim-flam, concocted by a little person with little peeves, and by being forced to imagine motives she was granting them a degree of substance. 'As you probably know, in his father's time Mitchells' was old-fashioned, prim and proper, but Lewis is keen the stores should appeal to the masses, albeit the middle-class masses. Days after his father's funeral he brought in time and motion experts, architects, shop fitters, consultants of every type, and a streamlining operation began. Over the past eighteen months or so layouts have been updated, departments switched over to self-service, handwritten stock control replaced by an automated system, that kind of thing. In addition,

dead wood has been pruned amongst the staff.
Obviously the redundancies, allied with the
modernisation, have left many people feeling
disgruntled. You've heard about the hoo-ha over
Mitchells' advertising campaign, for example?'

Jack nodded. 'Cartoon figures were used in
television commercials, and the older employees
got up a petition because they felt the image too
low-brow?'

'That's right. Actually Lewis had second
thoughts about the commercials himself. But all
this has nothing whatsoever to do with *me*,' Neille
insisted, a hand starfished against her chest in
emphasis. 'OK, if Lewis feels he needs protection
that's his choice, though I can't see how he's in
any danger now he's gone abroad. And I suppose
a closer eye should be kept on the stores,' she
added grudgingly, 'just in case.'

'A closer eye is being kept. I have guards and
dogs organised on a twenty-four hour watch at
each of the thirty different locations throughout
the country.' He grinned. 'That took some doing
at such short notice, I can tell you.'

'*You* have guards and dogs?' Neille questioned.

He nodded. 'I run Rea Safeguards, a security
company. Our bread and butter work consists of
protecting buildings, payrolls in transit, that line.'

'But if you're the company boss, why——?'

'Why have I deigned to step down from my
pedestal and attach myself to you?' He rubbed his
fingertips together. 'Filthy lucre, sunbeam. I'd
retired from personal surveillance, but Lewis
Mitchell wanted me and I wanted my firm to get
its claws on his security business, so we did a deal.
I agreed to patrol you in return for Rea

Safeguards having a crack at patrolling his stores and warehouses. The regular firm has been stood down for a while, and if our performance is sufficiently impressive maybe they'll be stood down on a permanent basis.'

'In other words, I'm the thin end of the wedge? Thanks for the compliment!'

'You should be pleased your boyfriend cares so much about you,' he replied.

'Well, I'm not.' Neille's original resentment returned to the fore. 'He has a cheek, fixing you up behind my back. I suppose he imagines I'll give in gracefully, but no way.' She shot Jack Rea a look which would have downed a stampeding elephant at fifty yards. 'I'm not being hounded.'

'It won't be that bad. I'm house-trained and quite cute once you get to know me.' His grin faded. 'Why not accept we're stuck with each other and co-operate? Then it'll be easier all round. Hell, chances are I'll only be with you for a month at most.'

'A month!'

He nodded. 'A month is what your good friend requested. I've been asked to stick with you all the time he's abroad. Naturally if the police detain whoever's responsible for the note, I'll make an earlier exit. On the other hand, if more threats have surfaced by the time the situation's reviewed in four weeks' time, I guess my duties could be extended.'

'Over my dead body,' Neille scythed.

Jack Rea gave a slow smile. 'Sunbeam, I'm here to make sure it will never come to that.'

CHAPTER TWO

NEXT morning Neille rose early. Washing as quietly as she could, she pulled on denims and a navy mohair sweater, caught up her hair in a fancy clip, and tiptoed downstairs. The house was dark and silent. Cold, too, for the central heating had yet to click on. Her father's alarm clock wasn't due to ring for another fifty-five minutes and there had been no sound from the spare room. As she devoured a bowl of muesli and her regulation half pint of fresh milk in the kitchen, shivering a little, she polished her plans. It would be the middle of the night in New York, so a phone call to Lewis was out, but in any case contact had now been reserved for later. She needed time in which to nullify the opposition. Today the oh-so-clever Mr Rea was destined to be left stranded. The moment her breakfast was finished, she would be out of the house and away. A series of appointments with the hair salon, photographers, model agency, etc., had been pencilled into her diary, so she would be fleeing around the city at breakneck speed. Jack had small chance of finding her. If, by some fluke, he did manage to make contact at one location, all she had to do was outwit him before she landed at the next.

Neille grinned, visualising the phone call at the end of her day when she would scathingly advise Lewis that his bloodhound had a lousy sense of smell. That would make him stop and think. If she

followed on by stressing her determination to run
her life *her* way, she had no doubt the end result
would be—goodbye, Mr Rea. A night's sleep had
done nothing to shake her conviction that the
threats were not worth the paper on which they
were pasted. Only if, and it was a million to one if,
a second note materialised, would she revise her
views. For now she intended to carry on as normal.

Pushing her arms into her fur jacket, she slung
her tote-bag over one shoulder and, avoiding a
creaky board in the parquet-floored hall, unlocked
the front door. Pale colours of dawn were
streaking a wintry sky.

'Cold for October,' Jack declared, appearing
beside her like a genie from a lamp. He looked
snug in a camel coat. 'Wouldn't even be surprised
if we had snow. Are you a jogging freak or is this a
variation on the moonlight flit?'

Head down, Neille searched in her bag for her
gloves. Damn the man, his appearance was a
deliberate obstruction of her liberty. He must be a
very light sleeper. Light on his feet, too. She
hadn't heard him moving around.

'I have work to do,' she replied saltily.

'So early? I realise modelling can't be the ritzy
life it's cracked up to be, but I never knew it
comprised night shifts.'

'I like to start my day with a brisk walk.' Where
were those gloves? What the hell! She drew her
collar around her ears and plunged feverishly off
along the street. 'The exercise tones me up,' she
said curtly, as he used long fluid strides to keep
pace.

'I'd have thought it'd have worn you down,' he
replied.

Apart from a milk float and a shambling postman, they were the only people on the move, though the occasional light which shone behind upstairs curtains indicated that the rest of the world was beginning to stir. As she walked, shoulders hunched against the icy wind, Neille realised she could be fairly said to have shot herself in the foot. So engrossed had she been in her aim to put space between herself and Jack Rea, she had neglected to line up a bolt hole. Where did she go now? How could she pass the time? Her first port of call was the hair salon, but that didn't open for another hour and a half. And to think she could have been tucked up warmly in bed!

'The catch needs fixing on that small window in the kitchen,' her companion informed her, his breath making white clouds. 'It's a weak spot. And an additional bolt on the front door wouldn't go amiss.'

She came to an abrupt halt. 'You've been snooping,' she accused.

'I've been doing what I'm paid to do, ensuring your safety.'

'Huh!'

Neille resumed her march. It was far too cold to stand and argue. Her nose was nipped and, one by one, her fingers were losing their feeling. Too late she remembered she had left her gloves on the hall table. She cast a glance sideways. Jack had gloves, robust leather ones. They would probably be fur-lined. Damn his gloves! Damn him! Veering right, she tramped with her escort past a small park, then crossed left and left again, bringing them to the neighbourhood's main shopping area.

Dummies smiled incessant smiles in brightly lit windows and neon signs flashed, but interiors remained dark and doors were stubbornly labelled 'closed'. She was a dummy. Why hadn't she waited until a decent hour before eluding Jack Rea?

Neille searched up and down the street for a taxi, but in vain. She heaved a sigh. She would have to use the Underground. Off she headed, Jack in tow, prepared to slog it all the way down the hill to the tube station, when lights suddenly flickered on in a cafeteria.

'I'm having a hamburger,' she announced, swerving towards it. 'Want one?'

He winced. 'At this hour? No thanks. Coffee'll do me.' They made their way through a maze of red and yellow plastic-topped tables to a counter where a yawning chef in grubby whites was attempting to face the day. 'My treat,' Jack said, when, after a lengthy wait, their order was handed over.

'Thanks,' Neille replied automatically, and marched off to find the cleanest of the tables.

'For what?' he asked, joining her. He gazed around, taking note of the smeary windows, the overflowing ashtrays, the packets of sugar which were long-term residents of a stained saucer. 'You didn't exactly bring us to the Savoy Grill.'

'Don't be picky,' she snapped. So calling in at the cafeteria had been a mistake, but it was his fault they were here in the first place. Must he criticise?

Jack took a mouthful of coffee and grimaced, then made doubtful eyes at her plate. 'Should you eat that? It's swimming in grease. Won't it give you spots?'

'I never get spots!'

He cowered back. 'Don't bite my head off. Not only were you up far too early this morning, you also appear to have got out of the wrong side of bed.'

'OK, I'm not all sweetness and light,' Neille retaliated. 'Would you be if someone had lumbered you with a Siamese twin without so much as a by-your-leave?' His rueful smile managed to calm her down a little, and when she next spoke her tone had become reasonable. 'Maybe Lewis thinks that note is for real, but I don't. What's more, I doubt very much if you do either. Be honest, Jack,' she coaxed, using his name as deliberate encouragement, for she also knew a trick or two about winning friends. 'You've had experience of these things. You don't genuinely believe I'm in any danger, do you?' He frowned, but she ploughed on. 'I accept that by nature of his position as a company chief Lewis can't avoid the odd enemy, known or unknown, and that maybe there's a chance, just a slight chance,' she qualified, 'someone might be conducting a vendetta, but my case is different. I don't rearrange people's lives. The influence I wield is zero. I'm just an innocent girl who——'

'Innocent?' He almost choked on his coffee. 'Are you professing to be Rebecca of Sunnybrook Farm? If so, I'm afraid it won't wash.'

'No, I'm not.' Neille pushed the hamburger around her plate. One bite had confirmed her fears. Not only greasy, the hamburger was as tough as old boots. 'But I can't believe I've inspired such impassioned feelings that I've wound up as somebody's target.'

'The world has more than its fair share of crazies. How can any of us know what a twisted mind will decide?'

'You're only saying that because traipsing after me for a month is good news for Rea Safeguards' balance sheet,' she retorted, forcing herself to keep on eating. She wasn't going to back down, not with him watching.

The disobedient strand of hair had once more tumbled on to his brow, and Jack raked it aside. 'I'm saying that because unfortunately it happens to be true. You read the papers, watch television. You know how people can be gunned down by complete strangers.'

'I know that you've played the terrorism game far too long, zonko! I'm not one of your controversial figures.' Neille rammed in another piece of hamburger. 'I'm *ordinary*.'

'Don't speak with your mouth full. Yes, very ordinary. You're a commonplace model who's featured in glossy magazines on a regular basis. You travel the world on assignments, you can earn more in a day than some people earn in a month. And it's on record that you've driven around in fast sports cars with fast young men——'

'Man!' she flashed.

'Man. And danced naked in fountains.'

Neille's blue eyes burned. 'You're as bad as the newspapers, continually harping back to the past,' she complained. 'And that damned fountain incident was a complete misrepresentation of the truth. You don't know the whys and wherefores. You don't know that I'd been forced to go into the water because Simon had——' She brought herself up short. Why was she explaining anything to Jack

Rea? The past was a closed book and better left
that way. There was no need to justify her actions
to a bodyguard, to a man she barely knew. All the
same, she wouldn't want him to think she was
candy-floss. 'The fast cars etc., happened when I
was younger and far less mature. Peace of mind
and sanity are what matter to me now.'

He pulled down his mouth. 'Very sensible. How
old are you—twenty-two going on seventy-five?'

'You've been briefed. You know full well I'm
twenty-four,' Neille replied, thrusting aside her
plate, clear at last.

The grey eyes rolled to the ceiling. 'So old,' Jack
sighed. 'So old.'

Dominic, the hair stylist, had overslept, which
meant that in addition to a freezing fifteen minutes
spent rubbing her arms and stamping her feet in
the doorway—to Jack's ill-concealed amusement—
Neille then suffered a long period in the chair
while the juniors mopped the floor around her.
The image which looked back from the mirror was
uninspiring. Her face had become a red and white
blotch, with shadows the colour of black grapes
beneath her eyes. Make-up would conceal the
worst, but one of her greatest assets was a sparkly
vitality and right now anyone who had crawled
out from a Siberian hedge would have displayed
more sparkle. She should never have persevered
with that hamburger—it lay like a lead weight in
her stomach. If she went down with food
poisoning, she would not be surprised.

Much to her irritation, Jack looked none the
worse for their cold and premature start to the
day. By angling an oblique search through the

mirror, she could see him in the jazzy black, white and purple vestibule. He was chatting to the blonde receptionist. The minute the salon door had been opened, he had shed his coat and made himself at home. Not much later he was installed at the reception desk, using the phone to contact his office and various outposts, while the blonde flitted around providing ballpoint pens and paper, and smiles which represented a criminal offence so early in the morning.

Neille was grateful when Dominic arrived and transferred her to the back-wash bowl, where the reflected figure of Mr Rea and the girl dancing attendance could no longer annoy. Involved in the routine of having her hair shampooed, conditioned and rinsed, she began to thaw out.

'I take it that guy's with you?' Dominic enquired, flexing comb and drier with matadorial finesse.

'Yes, he's——' What did she say? Never 'he's my bodyguard', because a statement like that would have the hair stylist downing tools and demanding to be given full details. A bodyguard was a rarity in anyone's world, and Dominic would be fascinated. Gossip was the staple of life for the satin-waistcoated young man, to be distributed among his clients all day and every day. But the last thing Neille wanted was to be gossiped about. Her days of providing hot news were over. Dead and buried, like Simon. She also baulked at describing Jack as a 'friend'. Dominic's translation was bound to be 'lover', and the gossip would still flow, if along a different channel. '—an admirer,' she settled for. 'But he's a pain and I'm trying to avoid him.'

'Looks a dish to me, ducky,' the stylist protested, sneaking a peek into the vestibule. 'The suit might be straightsville, but don't you have a feeling that beneath it he could be all animal?' Dominic gave a delicious shudder.

'He is all animal—rat.' She crooked a finger to draw him closer. 'When I'm ready to leave, could I use the back door?'

'Whatever you fancy. Mine is not to reason why, mine is just to wash and dry,' Dominic chanted, going off into peals of manic laughter.

Neille settled her bill discreetly and slipped out to the cloakroom at the rear. Knotting a silk square over her head to protect the flamboyant curls and twirls from the tug of the cold wind, she put on her jacket and gathered up her bag. The salon was set mid-centre in a terrace of shops which backed on to a parallel terrace. A narrow alley ran between them and as she emerged on to it, Neille grinned. No sign of Jack. So far, so good. His telephone calls had been completed and she hadn't heard his voice or caught sight of him for ages. No doubt he would be drowsing in the vestibule beneath the receptionist's simpering gaze, or had maybe gone round to the snack bar next door for a decent breakfast. Whatever, when she reached the end of the alley and peeped out, the coast was clear. A woman hurried by pushing a baby buggy, three workmen were digging a hole in the road, other people came and went, but there was no tall, dark-haired man in a camel coat.

Chuckling, she waltzed to the kerb with carefree steps. Her next venue was a studio in Chelsea, and for that she required transport. Conveniently a

black taxi was approaching, its 'For Hire' flag
clearly visible. When the driver stopped in
response to her wave, Neille quoted the address
and reached out for the door handle. A gloved
hand arrived there first.

'Allow me,' said a burnt-toast voice. 'And may I
award you seven out of ten for trying?'

Detective Inspector Brian Gilchrist took a swig of
beer from his glass, wiping the froth from his
mouth with a pudgy fist. 'What is it now, my old
mate—three weeks down and one to go?'

'Almost,' Jack agreed. 'Thank God.'

'Still giving you a hard time, is she?'

'Hard! She's had me on my toes since day one. I
feel like I've aged ten years in the process.'

Grinning, Brian opened out a Sunday colour
supplement magazine and spread it on the bar
table. 'She's beautifully packaged,' he said, voice
hushed with admiration. Under the heading
'Fashion Goes The Way of All Flesh', Neille
frisked, strutted, tantalised in a variety of outfits,
most of which featured a bare midriff and lots of
leg. 'What can you find so bad about guarding a
body like that? I just wish someone'd give us
middle-aged coppers half a chance.'

Jack pulled a face. 'Silent, I agree she's a
knockout. Verbal?' He shuddered. 'I'd fondly
imagined Kay had exhausted the insult supply
prior to our divorce, but Nellie thinks up new ones
every day.'

'Nellie?'

'In-joke. She hates it, so I call her that whenever
she needs cutting down to size. Like every five
minutes.'

'Don't tell me the two of you have yet to become *simpatico*?' the policeman queried, plump cheeks splitting into a smile.

'Ha ha. It's been war ever since she realised Mitchell wasn't going to give me the push.' Jack frowned at the photographs. 'I wonder what he thinks about these? He came over as a most fastidious gent.'

'Stiff and starchy,' Brian agreed. 'I expect he turns a blind eye; what else can he do? It's not as if he's married to the girl and can put his foot down. Though I imagine marriage is on his mind? Who wouldn't fancy snuggling up to that gorgeous little creature every night?'

'Yours truly for a start,' came the prompt reply. 'But I can't imagine them as Mr and Mrs. In fact, it amazes me they're even what Neille calls "good friends". Mitchell's not her type. What the hell can she see in the guy?'

'Never heard of power and wealth, those two supreme aphrodisiacs?' The policeman took a mouthful of beer. 'Is Mitchell still returning home as planned?'

Jack nodded. 'Neille and I hop over to Paris next week for a quick visit, the following Sunday I complete my stint, and he flies into Heathrow late Monday afternoon.'

'You're accompanying your young lady to gay Paree, city of love?' asked Brian, ogling the magazine again.

'Yeah, though she's made it agonisingly clear, in her inimitable way, that she'd far rather do the trip solo. She's landed a modelling job for a fashion house over there, photographs taken by some big noise called André.'

'And you're moseying along?' There was a groan of envy. 'Some blokes have all the luck.'

'Don't you believe it. I've managed to keep one step ahead so far, but how I'll cope over there remains to be seen. I've visited most places in Europe, but oddly enough I've never been to France. Which means I'll be dancing in the dark. Also my French is limited to basic requests, like please pass the butter, and a handful of obscenities. What do y'know but I'll be mouthing those obscenities next week?' Jack unfastened his black leather jacket and spread his legs. 'My guarding Neille has developed into a kind of contest, you see. She has this overwhelming desire to lose me. I know it, and she knows I know it.'

'She's not afraid of being picked off by a hidden marksman if she goes it alone?'

'She's not afraid of anything!' he responded, with a dry laugh. 'Funny thing is, when Derek's on duty, like now, she's good as gold. Then I appear and we're back to cat and mouse.'

The policeman chuckled. 'And mousie's hoping to sneak off down a hole when you're in Paris?'

'She'll try, like she tries here. To be honest, Brian, I've had one or two tricky moments already; not that she knows. Fortunately my working knowledge of London and its back streets means that on the odd occasion when she's gone missing I've managed to pick up her trail pretty quickly. Her hair's distinctive, which is a big help. If I look along a crowded street I can pick her out straight away.' Jack laughed, tugging at an ear lobe. 'Mind you, I once went hurtling after this redhead and it was only when I drew level that I realised the woman I was chasing was fifty if a day, and the colour had come courtesy of a bottle. I was very tempted to tell Neille. She'd have been furious.'

'Vain, is she?'

'Funnily enough, no more so than any other woman. She takes care of her figure and her looks, she wouldn't be a successful model if she didn't, but they're no big thing. She doesn't give a damn about me seeing her with a scrubbed face and hair uncombed first thing in the morning.' He gave Brian a look. 'And you can stop that lascivious mind of yours from working overtime. First thing in the morning means when she emerges from her bedroom and I emerge from mine. Any contact between Miss Trenchard and me is strictly business.'

'No nocturnal solace for the damsel in distress?' The policeman's eyes were twinkling behind his glasses. 'Whatever happened to Jack Rea, super stud?'

'He grew up. Now I drop everything when I'm working, women included.'

'That didn't used to be the case. Women more or less *were* your work, once upon a time.'

'No longer. Now all my energy goes into Rea Safeguards. It's been ages since I've had the time, or the inclination, to pay court.'

'You've lost interest in sex? Come off it, Jack.'

'I've lost interest in casual sex and shack-up deals. When I think how I behaved in the past— Well!' He shook his head in disbelief. 'Don't laugh, but my aim now is to build a nest, a permanent nest, and rear some chicks. The problem is, who with?'

'You're not telling me you're fresh out of beautiful women? My God, you'll have me in tears.'

'No.' He wiped a trickle of condensation from his glass and sucked his finger. 'There's a girl at the model agency. A secretary who's been slipping me Neille's timetable on the sly. Dee's a pretty little thing. Friendly, reliable. I might take her out some time.'

'Big of you,' Brian commented.

He laughed. 'Now you're starting to sound like Neille.'

'She slaps you down?'

'With no paltry skill. She gets so damned frustrated at not being able to shake me off that in retaliation she hurls abuse. I've come in for some pretty heavy flak. If my ego survives this month intact it'll be a miracle.'

'Non-stop aggro?'

'No, not non-stop,' Jack admitted. 'Even Neille couldn't manage that. There are lulls when we share a joke, have a decent conversation. On the odd occasions when she forgets how much she objects to my presence, she's actually good company.' He had a drink of beer. 'She even rescued me once. I was waiting outside this ladies' loo when——'

'Kinky!'

'And how,' he agreed. 'But Neille's developed a fetish for disappearing to powder something or other, which means I get to spend a goodly proportion of my time hovering around outside unsavoury places. It appeals to her sense of fun,' he said wryly. 'However, I'd been hanging around there like a spare part for quite a while when one of your uniformed boys appears. He begins to take an interest and, after dispensing a series of suspicious glances, starts off towards me. I quake. I think, "God! I'm about to be arrested for loitering with intent." Your boy is just about to start up with the "'Allo, 'allo, what 'ave we 'ere then?" when Neille appears. She tumbles to the situation in a flash and leaps on me crying how sorry she is to have kept me waiting, what a pet I am to be so patient etc., etc. Thankfully the constable goes into reverse. It's rare she does me a good turn, but I have to confess she did on that occasion.' When his friend's laughter had subsided, Jack frowned. 'Speaking of your boys, I don't suppose anyone has managed to solve the mystery of Mitchell's nasty letter?'

''Fraid not. We've done the usual enquiries, but drawn blanks all round.'

'There's no one who actively hates his guts?'

Brian scratched his chin. 'No, though the guy possesses a real flair for upsetting folk. He's bursting with bright ideas, but consistently puts them into action without bothering to consult those involved. In consequence, they take the huff. Like your young lady.'

'Except that she's turned taking the huff into an art form! But you're right, I don't think it's me personally she resents so much as Mitchell springing me on her. The way he tries to manipulate is what really gets up her nose.'

'Understandable. For "diplomat" you can read "steamroller" where our store boss is concerned. A prime example is how he dealt with the old guard after his father's death. Most of the directors were doddery old duffers who should've been put out to grass long before, and if Mitchell had employed an ounce of tact I'm sure they'd have been happy to go. Instead he goose-steps in one morning and dishes out dismissal notices. *And* he forgets about golden handshakes or thanking them for past services. Eventually it was smoothed over, but some of the blokes we interviewed went an unhealthy shade of puce when I mentioned his name.'

'So you've not moved any further down the trail?'

'Nope. If we had you'd be the first to know. But we both had a hunch those threats weren't going to amount to anything and now, after three weeks, we've been proved right. You can bet your bottom dollar that whoever wrote the note isn't about to despatch another one. He just wanted to get the bile out of his system.' Brian fixed his glasses more securely on his nose. 'You've never seen anyone acting suspiciously in the vicinity of your young lady?'

'Not a soul.'

'Strange that newspaper photograph of her and Mitchell should've been pinned to the letter. I just wish I could work out its significance.'

'Don't we all? It really terrified her father, though he's managed to calm down a bit now. Old Trenchard lives on his nerves. It amazes me how he ever managed to produce a daughter like his.' Jack took another swig of beer. 'You realise she's still being kept in the dark about the photograph?'

Brian nodded. 'Mr Trenchard insisted she mustn't be distressed.'

'Fat chance.' His lip curled. 'It'd need knives

whistling past her ears before that one'd be distressed.'

'Don't be too hard,' came the appeal. The policeman considered the girl in the colour supplement was a sweetheart, fresh and beguiling. 'If she's a bit of a toughie, perhaps she'd had to be? Who can tell what knocks she's taken?'

'Knocks? She doesn't know the meaning of the word,' Jack derided. 'Believe me, Brian, fairy godmothers were out in force the day Neille Trenchard was born. Not only did they bestow a face and figure which guaranteed a top-notch modelling career, they also provided a father who spoils her rotten, a current boyfriend who's as rich as Croesus, a previous boyfriend who was so damned handsome it makes you want to throw up, a——'

'You mean Simon Gates? That's right,' the policeman grinned when two surprised brows lifted, 'you're not the only one who's done his homework.' His grin widened. 'Actually it was Moira who filled me in. I happened to mention I'd had dealings with Mitchell, and lo and behold my wife knew more about him and your young lady and golden boy Gates than the whole of Scotland Yard put together. A great gal for the gossip columns is Moira.'

'Beats folding doilies all day, I suppose.'

'You male chauvinist, you! And now I'm sounding like your young lady again—right?'

'Right. And my young lady, as you call her, is in for a nasty shock next week. So far I've allowed her a very long length of rope, but the time has come to pull it tight.' Jack's eyes narrowed into a lethal squint. 'One way or another Miss Neille Trenchard will realise she's met her match!'

CHAPTER THREE

FREEZING fog had delayed all flights out of Heathrow. There had been a wait in the lounge before the boarding call came, a wait at the gate, and now on the aircraft little was happening. Stewardesses wafted back and forth wearing fixed smiles, at ten-minute intervals the captain gave apologetic messages of hope, passengers grew restless. Neille peered out at the thick white blanket which comprised the view, and sighed.

'Aren't you sorry you insisted on coming to Paris?' she enquired, turning to her companion who was examining the safety instructions for what had to be the third time.

'I didn't insist, Lewis did.'

'Jack!' she remonstrated. 'You know darned well that if you'd told him there was no danger he'd have been happy to go along with that.'

'Would he?'

'Yes. He listens to you. Grief, *you're* the professional.'

He slung her an amused look. 'Do I hear faint praise?'

'Not a whisper. I'd never praise a man who uses his reputation to get what he wants, with no thought for others.'

'Others being you?'

'Who else? More than three weeks have gone by without me paying the ultimate price of being chopped up into little pieces and fed to the crocodiles, so why can't you admit the note was pure unadulterated——'

'Language, Neille,' he cut in, grinning.

'Beast.' She sat for a moment, then compulsively tried again, even though last minute efforts were futile. 'Look, Jack the Ripper isn't going to follow me to Paris, so why must Jack the Pain-in-the-Neck?'

Realising the Japanese businessman on his other side had begun to take an interest, Jack adopted a woebegone air. 'Oh, sunbeam, you know how fragile I am emotionally and how you wound when you say such things. After these three wonderful weeks, during which we've built up such a——' He placed a hand over his heart. '—meaningful relationship, I had hoped you'd have wanted me close. I don't ask much. Sleeping on a mat outside your door would be enough to keep me content.'

'Sorry to ruin your day, but there's a distinct possibility they don't have mats outside the doors at the George V,' Neille replied. She tossed the Japanese gentleman a throwaway smile, but he continued to listen undaunted.

'That's fine.' Jack stuffed the safety card back into the seat pocket. 'Because we're not staying at the George V.'

'I am,' she said, crisp with conviction. 'The agency arranged the accommodation through the fashion house. A luxury pad happens to be one of the perks.'

'Sorry, but Dee——'

'Dee?' Neille spat out the word. 'What's she got to do with anything? The way that girl drools over you is sickening. Obviously the poor creature's

short-sighted in addition to being just that teeny-
weeny bit cross-eyed. How she ever manages to
type straight is a miracle.'

'Dee has altered the accommodation,' Jack said
heavily. 'At my request.'

'She hasn't?' Neille saw his face. 'She has! My
God, you really are a——'

'Beast?'

'Pachyderm,' she slammed.

A frown from the Japanese interloper indicated
his English had let him down.

'A very large thick-skinned mammal,' Jack
translated, and received a grateful smile.

'You think I'm not smart enough to realise this
cancellation of the George V represents yet
another of your attempts at one-upmanship?'
Neille demanded.

'There you go again, accusing me of base
behaviour,' Jack parried with a grin. 'All the
cancellation represents is safety procedure; you
must have heard of it. Keeping our heads down
makes sense. We're staying in a discreet little hotel
in the fifth *arrondissement*. It might not be as
fashionable as the George V, but Dee assures me
it's clean and comfortable.'

'Dee would.' She ripped the zip of her snowy
white parka higher towards her throat, as if
protecting herself from pollution.

'Sunbeam, why not resign yourself to the fact
that I'm with you until next Sunday?' he appealed.
'That's six days, a meagre six days, that's all.' He
leaned closer, turning his back on their Japanese
audience. The man had seen enough, heard
enough. If he wanted to inspect a pachyderm's
shoulder blades at close quarters, that was up to

him. 'Can't these last few days together be a time of peaceful co-existence? Why not allow *entente cordiale* a chance?'

'What, give up just when I'm warming up?'

'Why not?'

Privately Neille had to admit the idea was tempting. In three weeks of determined effort she had never managed to elude him—not properly—and it seemed doubtful she ever would. But a principle was at stake here. She refused to go soft and bow to his superiority. If she gave up now Jack would win and she would lose, by default. No, she was determined to keep on fighting to assert her independence right until the bitter end.

'What's the matter?' she taunted, giving him an arch look. 'Frightened I might wriggle out of the net once we arrive in Paris?' She glanced at the foggy outdoors. '*If* we arrive in Paris.'

'I'm not frightened of anything,' he vowed. 'I've kept tabs on you in London and I can keep tabs anywhere. I have a highly successful track record; why should Paris be any different?'

'But it is.' Neille raised a slender finger and drew it lightly down the front of his jacket. 'Look at you. We're not even off the ground and already you're different. Gone is the middle-of-the-road stockbroker and here is the—what, macho tourist? Chunky sweater, leather jacket, jeans and sneakers. Myopic Dee would consider you're very . . . sexy.' She pronounced the word as though the letters were eggs, splattering from a great height.

'Leave Dee out of this,' he barked, and she realised he was annoyed.

Strange, for if their time together had taught her anything, it had taught her that Jack Rea

possessed vast reserves of good humour and
control. How he had maintained his calm in the
face of her provocation, she did not know. Neille
would have socked herself one ages ago. Yet he
suppressed any urge to hit back. He had *had* the
urge—often. His grey eyes would narrow, his jaw
clench on receiving a choice custard pie of an
insult, but always he reined in his irritation and sat
tight. She admired his restraint. So why was he
angry now? Because she had maligned Dee?
Because some aspect of the Paris trip worried him?
Because she had mocked his sex appeal? Never
that. Bottle his charm and the man could make a
million. Just a moment ago, when he had been
resorting to friendly persuasion, she had been
uneasily aware of an increase in the tempo of her
heartbeat. And not for the first time, if she was
honest. Neille brushed such thoughts aside. Hadn't
it been pre-ordained that they meet in the role of
antagonists, and thus neutrals?

'You'd like me to keep to heel?' she queried,
keeping her tone light.

'That would be preferable to you persistently
attempting to show me a clean pair of them. Being
civil would also make a welcome change.'

She gave the matter ostentatious thought. 'I
dare say that could be arranged.'

'Don't fool around.' Jack was curt. 'I know you
aren't going to give in that easily.'

'Have you never wondered if you might have
totally the wrong impression about me?' Neille
enquired.

'Never.'

'Oh, Jack.' For the second time she ran her
finger down the front of his jacket, laughing up at

him through inky black lashes. 'You must have realised by now that essentially I'm a girl who's honest and open.' She dug her finger in his ribs. 'As honest and open as you are, zonko.'

Ten minutes later the plane was given clearance to take off and the tension in the cabin began to melt. Once in flight, sandwiches were served and the drinks trolley brought round, and in time the captain reported blue skies at Charles De Gaulle Airport. Jack put aside his brief irritation, and when Neille rummaged in her bag to produce a blood-and-guts thriller, his eyes widened in jokey alarm.

'Don't tell me a sweet young thing like you is an *aficionado*?'

'Guilty,' she grinned. 'Though in defence I should point out I was brainwashed from an early age. Thanks to my cousins, Peter, Paul and Podge, I spent my formative years in mortal fear of doing anything which might remotely be described as feminine.' Neille tapped her fingertips on the paperback. 'I guess something of that's stuck.'

'You were close to your cousins?'

'Very. After all I lived with them in Sussex for thirteen years. It was only after I finished school that I returned to London and my father's house.' She noticed his surprise. 'See, you don't know everything about me,' she said triumphantly.

Jack laughed. 'I know you're not a sissy, that's for sure. So—are you going to fill me in?'

'Provide more facts for that dossier of yours?' she teased.

'If you like.'

Maybe she did like? Even antagonists are allowed to go off-duty sometimes, and fitted into their close-knit weeks had been pleasant patches of relaxation. Jack had proved to be both interesting to listen to, and a good listener.

'My mother died when I was five,' Neille explained, content to leave her book unopened and talk. 'And although I don't remember much about it myself, after her death my father suffered acute depression. Mooie, that's my Aunt Muriel, my mother's sister, arrived one day, decided it was unhealthy for a small child to be cooped up with a brooding man, and whisked me off to stay with her, my Uncle Ken, and their three boys in the country.'

'Didn't you mind?'

'No, I loved it. Throughout her illness my mother had been nursed privately at home, so I was always being warned not to run around, to keep quiet, to be a good little girl. Friends were never allowed in to play. But in Sussex I was free to laugh and shout, and——'

Jack grinned. 'Become a tomboy?'

'Exactly. I was like a puppy let off a leash. Mooie fixed up for me to transfer to the village school and by the time my father was well enough to claim me, I'd become firmly entrenched. I pleaded not to be made to leave, and when he saw the harum-scarum I'd become I suspect the prospect didn't thrill him, either.' Neille laughed. 'He certainly raised no objections when Mooie suggested I become a permanent member of her household, He travelled down to see me at weekends, of course, and we shared holidays together, but Daddy's always found me something of a handful.'

A sardonic brow was raised. 'I wonder why?'

She laughed again. 'I must admit there've been times when I've wondered if I could be a changeling. I'm nothing like my father; nothing like my mother either, so I'm told. She was quiet, demure, shy in company.'

'Did you miss her when she died?'

Neille grew pensive. 'Sad as it sounds, no. She'd been ill for a long time and my only memory is of a pale figure propped up against pillows in a darkened room. She never hugged me or kissed me or swung me round, like Mooie did.' She frowned down at the book, then looked up, teeth worrying her lower lip. 'I was madly jealous of Podge. He's a year younger than me, so we were rivals for a place on Mooie's knee at story time. Whenever we quarrelled Podge always reminded me, with great malicious satisfaction, that she was *his* mother, not mine. It hurt. Funny thing is, it still does.'

Jack was surprised by her disquiet. Surely the girl chewing her lip beside him could not be the same slick miss who was rarely short of an answer? Admissions of vulnerability had not seemed to be Neille's style. Maybe he *did* have the wrong impression about her?

'Your aunt read excerpts from blood-and-guts books?' he enquired, attempting to chase away her melancholy. Neille was tugging strings inside him which hadn't been tugged in a long time, and he found that surprising, too.

'Mooie read boys' stories.' She brightened. 'Biggles *ad nauseam*.'

'Good old Biggles. I had a shelf full.'

'Did you? Do you remember the one about——'

Off they went, swapping memories of childhood books read and re-read over the years. They

discovered they had many favourites in common
and were still deep in discussion when the plane
landed. But conversation had to peter out when,
en masse with their fellow arrivals, they were
directed through the airport's space-age tunnels.

'Suppose I carry the gear while you deal with
the red tape?' Jack suggested, as they joined a
queue which snaked ahead to the immigration
checkpoint. He handed her his passport, and in
return humped her tote-bag on to his shoulder.
'What have you got in here—half a hundredweight
of eye-shadow?' he asked, pretending to sag at the
knees.

'Almost. I thought that as this is my first time in
France I'd better fly all flags, so I've come
prepared.'

'Your first time? Then I presume you aren't
fluent in French?'

'Just the schoolgirl variety,' Neille confessed,
wondering why Jack was smiling. 'Communication
with the celebrated André could present a
problem. If he doesn't speak English it'll need to
be sign language.' Waiting in line, she leafed idly
through Jack's passport. He was thirty-five years
old, six feet two, and well-travelled. 'Identifying
mark, scar on left shoulder,' she read out loud and
grinned. 'What was that, a stray bullet?' He was on
the brink of a reply when Neille gave a trill of
laughter. 'Your name's not Jack, it's Jackson.
Jackson! Oh, I like that.'

'But I don't,' he said, lips thin. 'So we'll stick
with Jack, understand?'

She took no notice. 'Jackson,' she repeated,
rolling the name around her mouth. 'Sounds like a
butler. Fetch me a mint julep, Jackson,' she quoted

plummily, giggling like mad. 'Or a chauffeur. Have the Rolls round at the front portico in two seconds flat and there'll be an extra shilling in your pay packet, Jackson.'

'Bug off.' His eyes were dark and stormy. Vulnerable? He had considered Neille vulnerable? She was as vulnerable as concrete.

'And you.' Her eyes danced. 'Jackson.'

'Nellie.' he retaliated, but the personal high meant she was immune.

'Jackson,' she sang.

'OK, a deal.' He threw down the offer like a hand of bad cards. 'No more Nellie, no more Jackson.'

'We'll see,' she said, as the uniformed *gendarme* in the glass cubicle beckoned them forward. 'We'll see.'

The moment they had been checked and approved, and had moved on, Jack grabbed hold of her arm. 'Yes, we damn well will see,' he hissed. 'You listen to me and you listen good. Make one unilateral move, and you'll suffer. Likewise if you call me Jackson one more time. I've thrown away the kid gloves. From here on in, you get what you deserve. Is that clear?'

'Yes, Jack.'

One other thing shone clear as the sun, now was not the time for a wisecrack. What she had said in the lounge had been true, Jack *was* different and not only in his appearance. He seemed flintier, edgy even. As she made her way beside him across the arrivals hall and out to the taxis, Neille decided there was a streak of tyranny she had never noticed before. But then, he would not be what he was unless he possessed a certain capacity for domination.

'Tell me your plans for the remainder of the day,' he ordered, once the taxi was shooting along the autoroute towards Paris.

Neille checked her watch. 'I had hoped there'd be time for some sightseeing, but now it's too late. I need to prepare myself for tomorrow's photo call.'

'Define "prepare yourself".' His mouth twisted. 'Is that a pseudonym for disappearing off on a jogging jaunt, or do you have an aerobics class fixed in some remote ladies' loo?'

'Neither.' She did her best to sweeten him with one of her wholesome *ingénue* smiles, but Jack remained unmoved. 'I'll be staying in the hotel. Prepare means have a face pack, wax my legs and other sundry tasks. Tomorrow I'm modelling lingerie and one of André's stipulations is that every inch must be smooth and unblemished. Lingerie's a new departure for the fashion house, which makes it vital that these first photographs have an impact. Lingerie's a new departure for me, too,' Neille added, feeling an unwelcome chill of apprehension. 'In my time I've modelled everything from horse blankets to paper dresses, but this is my début into bras and briefs.'

His gaze flickered over her. 'Does Lewis approve?'

'He doesn't know.'

'Shouldn't he?'

'Should he?' she responded, and saw from the abrupt narrowing of his eyes that she had been a shade too defiant. She gave an offhand laugh which was supposed to redress the balance. 'This is the age of topless sunbathing, and girls do appear in night-clubs dotted with little more than six strategically placed sequins. A few shots of me in black lace aren't going to rock anyone back on their heels.'

Jack looked doubtful. 'Not even Lewis?'

'Lewis is just a friend, you know, not my keeper,' she informed him.

'Whatever you call the guy, you have been going out with him for two years,' came the comment, and Neille could not argue with that. 'I agree I only met him for a short time, but it was enough to convince me Lewis Mitchell is a conserative, with a small c.' He paused, choosing his next words with care. 'I'd say he's also acutely conscious of his public image. Don't you think he could get uptight if his girlfriend——'

'Makes like a stripper?' she supplied breezily, hoping to divert him into responding with a quip, but he was stern-faced and intent on making heavy weather.

'Yes. Underwear can be devastatingly see-through these days.' Jack was frowning. 'I presume the photographs will be published in England?'

Neille nodded. 'A week Friday sees the start of a grand advertising campaign in London and simultaneously in other major capitals. This is a rush job, geared to catch the Christmas gift trade. The fashion house has outlets throughout the world, so the exposure will be spread far and wide. It's hard sell.' She neglected to add that she had checked on the timing and range of the campaign before accepting the assignment—or rather, grabbing it with both hands. Prompt and widescale publication of the photographs was of the utmost importance to her. 'Would you become uptight if your girlfriend revealed most, but not all?' she asked, wishing the prospect hadn't suddenly become a screwdriver turning in her stomach.

'That's hypothetical, I'm not Lewis Mitchell,' he replied, showing a stout determination to stay on track. 'I dare say he derives a kick from the media interest generated by his business activities and isn't averse to the odd mention in the gossip columns, as long as it keeps within strict parameters, but you prancing around in next to nothing is ... something else.'

'Is it?' Neille shrugged with studied indifference. 'Well, that's his problem.'

As Jack dissolved into silence, she gave an inward groan. If only she had been able to make this Paris trip on her own, as originally planned. Arriving in tandem was a definite drawback, but no matter how much she had coaxed, pleaded, grumbled, Jack had refused to be deflected. For her own peace of mind she had wanted to play things discreetly, but now she would be observed. She accepted she would be observed by André, dressers, studio staff, etc., and possibly by the great French public at large, depending on locations, but they were strangers. Jack wasn't a stranger. Not any more. The in-pocket living they had shared meant a closeness had evolved, maybe the erratic, temporary closeness of a warden with his prisoner, but a closeness nonetheless. And an annoying offshoot of this closeness meant that Jack's opinion of her had begun to matter. Dare she take him into her confidence and explain—not the entire motivation in accepting the assignment, of course, but maybe a part? If she censored her tale there would be no harm done, and she would feel easier if he understood.

'You owe Lewis a phone call,' he chastised abruptly, and all thought of taking him into her confidence vanished. Explaining anything to a man who was no more, no less than a bodyguard was reckless in the extreme. Jack was no confidant. His single reason for being with her was money, he had made that plain from the start. And who provided the money? Lewis! Jack's allegiance lay with him, she must never lose sight of that. 'The guy's tried to reach you on several occasions, shouldn't you make the effort to get in touch? Why don't I fix for you to speak to him when I report in?'

'No thanks. I'll get in touch when *I* choose to get in touch,' Neille snapped.

Jack's prompting smacked of the hired help overstepping the mark. He wasn't being paid to chivvy, he was being paid to guard, she thought tetchily. And as he spoke to Lewis every two days, it wasn't as though her 'good friend' didn't know what was happening in her life. Good friend! What a brutal misnomer.

'That sounds high-handed,' Jack replied, continuing to show disapproval. 'I'd be obliged if you'd get in touch soon.'

She bared her teeth at him. 'Yes, sir!'

The hotel *was* discreet, so discreet that, although Dee had claimed it was situated in the fifth *arrondissement*, none of the locals had ever heard of the place. The taxi driver stopped—invariably suddenly and invariably in the middle of the road—and leapt out to brandish the card Jack had

provided before passers-by and shopkeepers, but
all he received were shakes of heads and Gallic
shrugs. Up and down the narrow streets they
drove, the taxi driver muttering in despair, until
suddenly Neille cried, 'It's there!'

Discreet to the point of fading into oblivion, the
hotel entrance was a single varnished door tucked
between a *pâtisserie* and a newspaper kiosk. The
lobby made no positive statement, either.
Furnished in a way which guaranteed instant
forgettability, there was an impression of browns—
carpet, walls, sofas.

'We have two rooms booked, adjoining,' Jack
told the matron who sat knitting behind a desk.

She ran her finger down a list to check their
names. *'Ah, oui. Bonjour, monsieur, mais——'* Off
she gabbled into crackerjack French, pushing out
forms to be filled in, handing over keys to rooms
42 and 43, gesticulating to a beetle-browed man
sucking peppermints in a corner, who turned out
to be the porter. 'Dinner is served at eight,' she
said, making a brief foray into English before
returning to her wool and needles.

The porter commandeered their luggage, flung it
inside an ancient and minuscule lift, then indicated
they must squeeze inside. At a snail's pace they rose
skywards, to the accompanying groans of creaking
metalwork. No one said a word. The porter, who
spent the journey undressing Neille with his eyes,
bestirred himself at the fourth floor. Gathering up
their suitcases, he marched along the corridor to
rooms 42 and 43. He unlocked both doors and, for
the first time, directed his attention towards Jack. A
tip was expected. A tip was received. Another optical
tour of Neille, and he departed.

Jack gestured. 'After you.'

One step inside was enough. 'I've seen bigger cupboards!'

'Perhaps the other room'll be better?' he suggested.

It wasn't. Both were identical brown and beige boxes with tiny *en suite* bathrooms. Space was at a premium. A single bed, one chair and a set of open shelves left nowhere to swing the proverbial cat. The wardrobe consisted of a cubby-hole fitted with a rail and three hangers.

'Thoughtful of them to design the bathroom for midgets,' Neille said antiseptically, discovering that wash-basin, shower and lavatory were jammed together like sardines. She needed room in which to prepare herself. Clear surfaces where her potions and lotions could be stored, a decent mirror, a full-sized bath and a shower which boasted proportions a little more generous than this tiled orange-box.

'As you once told me, don't be picky.' Jack completed a swift reconnoitre. 'Though I must admit the accommodation's not what I had in mind.'

'You don't actually agree that on balance the George V may have a little more going for it?'

He ignored her scorn. 'It's not that. The rooms here are on the compact side, but——'

'Compact!'

'But though they adjoin, they aren't connected— at least, not with each other—with the rooms on either side.' Jack rubbed his chin. 'Do you think that's what the receptionist could have been saying?'

'Probably, but does it matter? The ratfink who

left his nasty messages in Lewis's in-tray isn't about to surface here so I don't need you poised behind a door, ready to fling it wide and rescue me in the nick of time.'

'No?'

'*No.*' Neille knew he'd never revitalise the George V booking and she had not the least intention of abandoning their current resting place in order to trail around Paris searching for suitably adjoining rooms. This hotel was bad enough, but others could be worse. 'I'm one hundred per cent safe here,' she said firmly.

Jack walked over to tap the wall between Numbers 42 and 43. 'This seems thin enough. I guess I'd hear if you did get into trouble.'

'I won't!' She crawled across the bed to the window—the only way to reach it—and eased open the catch. She looked out, turning to flash a plastic smile over her shoulder. 'What a wonderful panorama! Do come and share it with me.'

He clambered to join her and together they surveyed the view. Opposite, only a stone's throw away, were office windows where three typists gazed balefully back from behind their typewriters. Look up, to avoid the typists, and you saw grey slate roofs and a small patch of sky. Look down, to avoid the typists, and there was a courtyard where a single tree, at present leafless, struggled for survival. In one corner dustbins spilled more garbage than they held. In another was looped a washing line, naked apart from an ample supply of garish pegs. As their eyes were being drawn magnetically back to meet those of the typists, an invisible clarinettist began to play a doleful lament.

'Paris offers something for everyone,' Neille said, closing the window. 'Eyes across a godforsaken courtyard and all night clarinet concertos.'

'How do you know the clarinet's going to play all night?' Jack asked, as he backed off the bed.

'How do you know it won't?'

'Come on, it's not that bad,' he coaxed. 'Like Dee promised, the hotel's——'

'Clean and comfortable? Didn't she do us proud? Why not drop her a postcard and tell her there are doves on the roof? She'll be thrilled.'

He eyed her with wry tolerance. 'Have you ever considered going into a nunnery? One where the novices take a vow of silence?' He stepped aside to avoid any blows he might have provoked, which meant he was standing by the door. 'I agree this place isn't the George V, but I'm afraid you'll just have to accept it.'

'Why should I?' Neille muttered, as he departed.

Why did she have to accept his decisions? She unlocked her suitcase and fitted what clothes she could on to the three hangers. The remainder had to be crammed on to the shelves with her shoes. Suddenly she tilted her head to one side, and listened. The walls *were* thin, she could hear a shower running in Room 42. She grinned—a wide, triumphant grin. After three long weeks, her time had come. So much for keeping to heel, so much for waxing her legs. She was going out for a walk—alone!

Wary of using the creaky lift, Neille crept down the four flights of stairs, crossed the lobby and exited at speed. Hands in the pockets of her parka, white-trousered legs set apart, booted feet on the pavement, she took a deep breath of fresh French air. She had done it! Freedom at last! Excitement at having got the better of her constant companion bubbled. Now at liberty to do exactly as she pleased, she could thumb her nose at the clever Mr Jack Rea—and at Lewis!

She would explore, though she must be careful not to go too far. A short unaccompanied stroll was one thing, a precipitate rush into the rabbit-warren streets of a foreign city would be another. Neille looked uphill to a crossroads, then downhill to a cobbled square. The square seemed interesting. Unable to detach her grin, she sauntered slowly down. The shops she passed were intriguingly Parisian. A window filled with gold-lacquered antiques first captured her attention, then a quaint booth selling chocolate truffles. She stood for ages outside an art shop where a panoply of oil paintings was displayed. One, an abstract of what appeared to be a hedgehog with a feather, sported a price tag of over fifty thousand francs, expensive in any language. Jack would've had something to say about that!

Reaching the square, Neille sat on a bench to watch the world eddy around her. It was amazing how a short flight, a mere twenty-one miles of intervening ocean, made such a difference. The people were darker, grainier, noisier. The traffic which poured in and out of the square was different, too. Almost every single vehicle sported battle scars, and it was easy to see why. Renaults cut corners, Peugeots charged up kerbs, battered Citroëns performed like crazed rams, banging and barging. And in the midst of it all, on a podium, stood a *gendarme* in a white coat. He was directing the traffic like a lunatic conductor in charge of a homicidal orchestra.

Neille was fascinated, and only the chill of approaching dusk and the increasing frequency of gummy smiles from a gnarled old man who had joined her on the bench, brought an end to her furlough. She tramped back up the hill, thinking how Jack would have enjoyed watching the people and the traffic. What would his comment have been on the hedgehog picture? She must tell him about that. Neille strode across the hotel lobby and into the lift. As she rammed the gate shut, she decided to tell him nothing. She had never intended to keep her excursion a secret, indeed half the fun had been the prospect of being able to gloat, but suddenly it struck her that this itch to tell him was akin to dependency. He was becoming a habit. Would she miss him next week? With irritating honesty, she admitted she would. After all, he had been with her virtually twenty-four hours a day for what was beginning to seem like forever.

She had stepped from the lift at the fourth floor, and was walking along the corridor, when she heard an intake of breath. With a jolt, Neille realised Jack was waiting. Even in the gloom it was plain to see how he bristled with fury, like a predatory beast ready to pounce.

'And where have you been?' he demanded.

'Out.' With a defiant flourish, she unlocked the door to her room. 'I don't live by your rules, Jackson, so I fail to see what——'

'Your lesson for today,' he growled, 'is that my rules are the *only* rules.' One step, and he pressed his hand into the small of her back and thrust her into the room. A backward kick shut the door. Clutching her in a wrestling type hold, he more or less fell with her on to the bed, where he positioned her across his knees. 'Now,' he said, holding her firm. 'How would you like your bottom to be spanked—hard, harder or hardest?'

Winded and face down, Neille needed a moment or two to recover. She twisted her head around to glare, her hair tumbling into her eyes.

'You wouldn't dare.'

'Wouldn't I?' A large hand was ominously raised.

'Arghh!' she shrieked, kicking and struggling for all she was worth. 'Let me go!' It never occurred to her to think what the other guests might make of the noise.

'Like hell. I'm sick and tired of being treated as your stooge. From now on, we do things my way.'

'I wouldn't bet on that, Jackson,' she retaliated.

He was being too Neanderthal for words. How dare he threaten to paddywack her and sling her across his knees like a sack of coal? She had never been so offended, so humiliated. Peter, Paul and Podge may have stuffed worms down her neck, made apple-pie beds, even suspended her head-down over a cow-pat, but then she had been a child. For her, a grown woman, to be on the brink of having her backside paddled represented degradation of the highest degree. But in addition to degradation she was aware of another sneaky feeling—arousal. It was disgusting! The way Jack was manhandling her had set off a raw sexual buzz. Neille was furious with herself. How could she simultaneously feel degraded, yet intimately aware? And suppose he decided to yank down her trousers or even the scrap of white silk she called 'knickers' and administer a full scale thrashing? She would die if he slapped her bare buttocks.

'You louse! You beast! You——' She fought, panting and pawing, but it was no use. One hand pressed down on her spine, Jack used the other to disastrous effect. Thwack! Her posterior tingled. It was unfortunate her blood was tingling, too. 'I'll report you to Lewis,' she cried.

'Is that the best you can come up with?' He laughed grimly. 'Lewis is on my side. He'd agree that this is long overdue. For three damned weeks you've been trying to drive me into a frenzy— well, now you've succeeded. And don't call me Jackson!' His hand was raised. 'Want another one?'

'No, no! Please don't slap me again,' she begged. Neille had just remembered something. 'Tomorrow I'm to be photographed in underwear, so I mustn't be bruised.'

'You don't want to appear technicoloured, black and blue?'

'No way.' Fear of another thwack had her ricocheting from appeals to aggression. 'You wouldn't do this to me if I was a man.'

'Damned right, I wouldn't. I'd probably knock you out cold.'

'But you're supposed to be *protecting* me from violence, not inflicting it,' she yelled, as his hand stiffened in mid-air. 'Jack, I'll behave. I'll never go anywhere without you again,' she gurgled. 'Honest.'

'Honest? You, honest? If I believe that I'll believe anything,' he said, but he relented, shoving her unceremoniously off his knee on to the bed. 'I guess you're right, corporal punishment isn't the answer. And I am here to ensure no one lays a finger on you.' He sighed, wryly shaking his head. 'I consider myself civilised, but somehow you bring out my baser instincts.' He gave a suddenly ferocious glare. '*All* of them.'

Pink-faced, Neille scrambled to her feet. 'I'm sorry. I agree my behaviour hasn't been exactly . . . perfect.'

'Perfect!' He rolled his eyes.

'And I realise now I should never have gone out alone.'

'No, you shouldn't.' Jack thrust a thumb into his chest. 'Because this joker is accountable for your safety. I'm well aware that three weeks ago you made up your mind, without thought or hesitation, that the note Lewis received was sterile, but an element of danger can't be discounted.'

'Can't it?' Try as she might, she could not prevent disbelief from entering her tone.

He gave a grunt of impatience. 'I reckon the only way to get it into your thick head is to give you all the facts. When Lewis found the note, a newspaper cutting was attached—a photograph of the pair of you at some antiques fair.'

'A photograph of me?' Neille had been rubbing her backside, but now she paused. 'Why didn't someone say something?'

'Because, in his wisdom, your father insisted you weren't to be worried. He even managed to persuade the police not to interview you. How's that for irony. Your father's shredded with nerves, while you don't give a damn.'

'You think I should?' She had become subdued. This information altered the entire scenario.

'It's always common sense to be on the alert,' Jack replied, using a voice which made her wonder about the rank he had held in the SAS. Captain? It would have been a position of authority.

'But,' she began, wrinkling her nose, 'I still don't——'

'Enough!' An awesome hand chopped through the air. 'Consider the matter closed. I'm finished with you and your perpetual arguments. Why is it you always beg to differ?' Jack was at the door, wrenching it open. 'You and I will eat dinner in the restaurant downstairs at eight p.m. precisely, until which time you are to remain in this room. After dinner you return and stay put until morning. I'll collect you for breakfast at seven-thirty. And that, Neille Trenchard, is that!'

CHAPTER FOUR

AT breakfast Jack continued to treat her with concise disdain, becoming the spare-of-words, sure-of-shot hulk she had once visualised. Maybe a sweat-stained vest did lurk beneath his jersey? Maybe he did strike matches on his jeans zip as a party piece? Hoping to make amends, she tried to soften his mood with smiles and small talk, but he refused all overtures. Neille had seen friendlier faces behind riot shields.

One part of her didn't blame him. His annoyance had been a long time building and his grievances were genuine. He was entitled to keep her in the doghouse—hadn't her behaviour been that of a bitch? But another part of Neille felt vexed, betrayed even. Jack had always shown such patience and good humour, did he have to extend this'sit—don't move—stay' treatment? What must she do to merit a pat on the head? Sit up and beg? If so, Jack had picked the wrong girl. Neille stopped smiling and talking, and retreated. He had distanced himself from her and two could play at that game. Why should she concern herself with a man who had pummelled her physically, and who now seemed intent on pummelling her emotionally?

She switched her mind to other matters. He had spoken of danger, but where? She refused to panic and interpret the inclusion of her photograph as a personal threat, especially at this late stage. She

glanced around the cellar restaurant. Their fellow
guests looked stolidly normal: middle-aged French
couples, in the main, with a sprinkling of overseas
visitors. No assassins here. Danger? Phooey!
Hadn't three uneventful weeks passed by since
note and photograph had landed on Lewis's desk?
Not exactly uneventful, she decided, sneaking a
look at the man on the other side of the table. Life
with Jack could never be described as that. Neille
snapped her mind back to the note. Photograph or
not, she didn't accept threats from anyone—not
from the nasty little person who had written those
nasty little words, nor from Jack. Jack again! She
had suffered no after-effects from having her
backside thwacked—a head-over-the-shoulder peer
into the mirror had shown she was completely
unmarked—but lack of bruises did not mean she
was prepared to forgive and forget. Not now. Not
when Jack refused forgiveness for *her* past sins.

'Shall we take the Métro to André's studio?'
Neille suggested, as they walked out of the hotel.
Legs waxed, skin toned, eyes bright and shining,
she was ready to go. André possessed a formidable
reputation, and whether modelling lingerie or not
the assignment was something of a scoop. If only
that screwdiver wouldn't turn inside her whenever
she thought about removing her clothes. 'I've
worked out the route on the map,' she continued,
'and it looks easy. The studio's on the Right Bank,
almost next door to a Métro station and——' She
pointed up the hill to where a huge orange M
indicated access. '—we can board a direct line
from there.'

Jack eyed the traffic which was filling the street
with engine noise and fumes. 'I dare say the Métro

could be preferable to getting snarled up among this lot,' he acquiesced. 'Especially as it'd probably take us ages to find a taxi in the first place.'

'Then the Métro it is. Come on. I promise not to get us lost.'

They joined a band of commuters in a headlong rush down numerous flights of stone steps into the bowels of the earth.

'I'll get the tickets,' Jack offered when they reached the subterranean booking offices, and Neille was grateful. It was the morning rush hour, and bedlam. The queue—queue!—was a scrum where you were in danger of being tackled in a manner which would have guaranteed cries of ecstasy from the French Rugby Federation. When he returned, holding aloft two pieces of yellow card, he allowed her the first smile of the day. 'How's that for service?' he demanded.

Through the barriers, the pace increased. People elbowed, prodded, cursed their way along the corridors. Fall, and you'd have been trampled underfoot. Travellers barged past, clattered down steps like automatons, thrust everyone else aside. The old and infirm did not stand a chance. Keeping a sharp look out for the correct route colour, Neille acted as navigator and successfully, if breathlessly, brought them to the appropriate platform. A train was just pulling in. One gasp for oxygen, and they were stampeded inside.

'Phew!' she exclaimed, as Jack smacked up against her.

He looked around the crowded carriage where there was not an inch to spare. 'You call this easy? Next time we go difficult. We go by taxi.'

Neille managed to squeeze a hand up between their bodies to touch her brow. 'Yes, sir.'

Her humour emerged a trifle shaky. Being pressed up against Jack was disturbing. He was annoyingly *male*. All animal, as Dominic had said. This man throbbed with good red blood and muscle, energised by a discreet, yet powerful, sexuality. Not like Lewis, whose layers of urbanity often made her wonder if he was generated by nothing more than a microchip. When the train set off, Neille clung on to the strap of her tote-bag with both hands and tried to ignore the male chest, pelvis and legs which were being joggled against hers. An attempt to shift her stance resulted in being nudged back in place by surrounding commuters, so there seemed no way to avoid him. She would have expected a vapid female like Dee to turn pink and coy at this body contact, but not her. Yet her pulse-rate had accelerated, and the heat she felt rising could not be wholly attributed to the packed compartment.

When stations came and went, and the crowd began to thin, she was grateful. No longer pressed up against him, Neille felt sturdier. At a mainline station there was a decided exit, and she was able to sit down. When another seat came free further down the carriage, Jack walked off to make claim.

'Give me the nod when we're due to exit,' he instructed.

Taking out her guidebook, Neille rechecked the route. In actual fact, the photographer's studio was positioned half-way between two stations. She had given Jack the name of the second, but there was no reason why they shouldn't surface at the first. The stations were close together, there would be nothing in the distance. A slow grin built on her mouth. Yesterday's assurance that she would behave had been extracted under duress, which rendered it null and void. And as long as he continued to treat her like a disobedient mutt which he was attempting to train, there was the temptation to behave that way. Neille mulled over the idea. It might work. She would make it work.

Ten yards away, her companion was growing restless. He had guessed they must be nearing their destination, and when they pulled into the next stop he looked up expectantly. She shook her head. The carriage doors slid open to allow passengers to depart, passengers to file on. She saw Jack stretch, yawn, lean back his head and rub his eyes. As the doors started to close, Neille leapt up. She whistled through the gap and landed with a thump on the platform. There was only time to glimpse an astonished Jack rising from his seat in the departing train, before she turned and ran. Tote-bag banging against her hip, Neille pounded up the stairs. It was impossible to contain her glee, and her burst of laughter had other commuters turning around to gape. She ran along the corridors, not knowing why running mattered when he wouldn't, couldn't follow, only knowing that running comprised a vital ingredient. Her escape was like something out of *Boy's Own*. Trenchard strikes again! Hee, hee!

It was only when she reached the final flight of steps that she slowed to walking pace; then she was free to step out on to the busy Paris street. Cold air slapped her face, but the zing of blood in her veins meant Neille did not notice. Her evasion of Jack might only be temporary, yet it was

enough. She had proved her superiority. Hee, hee
again! It could well take him two hours or more to
trace her because, even if he had memorised
André's address, his inadequate French guaranteed
he'd hit a few snags. Great! And if he punished her
again—well, this freedom gesture was worth it.
Consulting the guidebook, Neille worked out the
path to the studio and set off, hips swinging in
delight. She turned a corner. Hee, hee! How clever
she was. She turned another, passing flower shops
where roses and carnations were arranged with
a natural flair for colour. Not merely clever—
brilliant!

'Gotcha!'

A heavy hand landed on her shoulder and Neille
almost jumped out of her skin. When she jerked
her head around, her blue eyes grew to the size of
saucers. Clever? Brilliant? Here was Jack. He was
panting, his broad chest rising and falling beneath
the leather jacket.

'How—how have you found me?' she asked,
uncertain whether she should be furious or lost in
admiration. When he remained silent, catching his
breath, her imagination took over. 'Did you pull
the emergency cord and stop the train?'

'No,' he gasped. 'I jumped off at the next station
and ran back.'

'Ran back? Along the line? Through the tunnel?'
He nodded, and she gazed at him in horror.
Images flashed through her mind. A train mowing
him down. Jack being flung into the air or sliced
limb from torso. Going up in a puff of smoke if
he'd stumbled against a live electric cable. And she
had made him take these chances! Her escape
attempt now seemed frivolous and shallow, ill-

considered in the extreme. 'But only an idiot would run along a railway line,' she protested feebly.

'Only an idiot did.'

Neille felt dreadful. 'You could have been maimed or——' Her voice trailed into silence as her thoughts preoccupied her. 'How did you know which way I'd gone when you came up on to the street?'

'I——' He spoke on an outgoing breath. 'I bugged you.'

'Bugged me?' After a moment it sank in. 'Bugged me!' she shrieked.

'In there.' He nodded at the tote-bag on her shoulder. 'Don't worry about it now,' Jack said, when she ripped open the drawstring and began scrabbling her hands through a conglomeration of lipsticks and blushers, scarves, tights and brushes. 'I'll remove the bug this evening, when we're back at the hotel.'

'But I *do* worry.' Her look scorched him. Maybe she wasn't to blame for him living dangerously. Hadn't the do-or-die response been all his own? 'How dare you bug me?'

'How dare you continually challenge my credibility?' enquired Jack, lobbing home an equaliser.

With compressed lips, Neille fastened her tote-bag. She had not found the bug, did not even have much idea what she was supposed to be looking for, and now there seemed nothing else to do except continue on her way.

'So, what happens?' she asked, as he walked alongside, yet again. 'Another assault on my posterior?'

He produced a curt laugh. 'Physical contact's too risky.'

'Is it?' she asked, dry mouthed, as she jumped to the conclusion that Jack, too, had been aware of that sexual buzz. But he hadn't, his next words proved it.

'Yeah. I said if you'd been a man I'd have knocked you out cold and, believe me, only by exercising the greatest restraint did I manage to keep from throwing a left hook yesterday. If I lay my hands on you a second time it might well result in murder, and I've no intention of growing old in a French jail on your behalf.' She received a strafing glance. 'This time your punishment will be—subtle.'

'How—subtle?' Neille enquired, feeling itchy. She might have outwitted him just now, but for no more than a few minutes. And her success, if it could be counted as a success, was only the second in three weeks of determined trying.

'Wait and see.' His eyes were mean as back streets. 'But you can be sure of one thing. Whatever it takes, you will pay.'

Minutes later he delivered her into the custody of André, a butch character in creased dungarees, and departed; though not before making certain she would not be released until late afternoon at the earliest. Whether Jack had secreted himself in a cubbyhole within shouting distance, or gone for a stroll along the Champs-Elysées, she had no idea. One thing she did know: wherever he was, he would be planning his revenge. What form would it take?

Luckily André spoke English, if heavily accented English. He introduced her to her partners, two aloof French brunetttes with short spiky hair like frozen dishmops, and then explained the programme which lay ahead. Today, shots taken would be featured as advertisements in magazines and newspapers. Tomorrow they would leave the studio and go on location around Paris, capturing publicity stills for circulation amongst women's page editors. Thursday and Friday, there would be run-of-the-mill poses for the fashion house's own catalogue.

During the two hours in which she had her hair frizzed into a fashionably shaggy style, her face painted, her body poured into sugar-pink corsets and out of silver stretch mini-slips, she constantly fretted about Jack's threatened revenge. Only when André lined her up with the brunettes before a shimmering backdrop did she abandon the subject. But she rapidly realised all she had done was swap one unease for another.

'Zee boobs oop, *chérie*,' ordered André, wind-milling wiry arms and exposing tufts of black hair in the process.

Neille had never considered herself voluptuous, but alongside the emaciated Parisiennes she became so. She felt unbelievably womanly, Rubensesque even with her clouds of copper-gold hair and her curves. She attempted to perform a balancing act between the chaste and the provoca-tive but wondered if, on this occasion, she could be accused of playing the tramp? The silk of the camiknickers she wore was fine, erring on the sheer. She told herself she was being a prude, and tried to remember topless sunbathing and sequinned girls in night-clubs, but it didn't work. Pouting at the camera in a state of undress felt *sleazy*. This wasn't a fun thing. Perhaps she would have felt different if it was? But the assignment had been undertaken as yet another attempt to solve a problem, and time was running out. Neille shivered. An added worry was the thought of her father's dismay when she appeared semi-clad in the newspapers. Poor Daddy. Here she was, distressing him again. Yet his precarious calm had to be sacrificed, what alternative was there? And short-term *malaise* was surely a small price to pay in return for the long-term survival of his peace of mind? If her ploy worked—*if*.

Her outfits were changed throughout the day, but the jitters remained a constant factor. André proved to be both perfectionist and dictator. A hair out of place created ructions, a négligé which fell awkwardly had him bellowing. A bevy of helpers scuttled around, but they never did the right thing, and as the sky darkened and the lights came on all over Paris, so pressure-cooker steam built up. Neille's head throbbed with the photographer's constant shouting, her back ached from being stretched in bizarre poses, and her smile had began to settle into a gargoyle grimace. And *still* she felt tarty. The only thing to be thankful for was that Jack had steered clear. His witnessing of her discomfort would have been too much to bear.

At last André threw up his hands in despair at having been saddled with morons, and the photo session was over. Neille hobbled off to the dressing room, but was only allowed one gesture of commiseration from the brunettes before being ignored. Chattering away in French, they never so much as glanced her way. But they glanced Jack's way when he knocked at the door fifteen minutes later.

'I want,' he said, poking his head into the room.
'I want Neille.' He found her, face creamed clean
and fully dressed, tugging on her boots.

'You wouldn't prefer either of us?' enquired one
of the brunettes, wobbling her head in a very
French way. Without warning, she could speak
English. Odd, when previously she had never
uttered a word. 'You wouldn't prefer a local girl to
introduce you to the *ooh-là-lá?*'

'Tempting, but I must refuse.' Amusement gave
him a very sexy smile. 'Neille here demands all my
attention.'

The other girl spoke up. 'You are Neille's
amant?'

Jack draped himself in the doorway. 'I guess
you could say that.'

'No, you couldn't!' Intent on objection, Neille
marched forward, but as she neared him an arm
snaked out and she found herself fitted as snugly
into his body as she had been on the Métro. 'Jack,'
she protested, '*amant* means——'

'Lover.' He bent and spoke into her ear. 'For
the remainder of our time together, sunbeam, I am
to be your *amant*, boyfriend, call it what you will.
Courtesy of Lewis.'

'Whatever are you talking about?' she enquired,
aware of the brunettes sitting up and taking notice
of what must appear to be a fond *tête-à-tête*.

'Romance.' He looked across to their audience
and winked. 'Isn't that what Paris is about? Stolen
kisses, tenderness, a hand on a naked thigh?'

As the girls giggled, Neille gazed at him in
alarm. He was implying they had been, and would
be, intimate. Didn't both brunettes have that look
of 'aha' in their eyes? Too late to claim innocence,

the damage had been done. Jack had taken her
into a hug, said a few choice words, and effectively
labelled her as his. She felt—what did she feel?
Annoyed with his trickery, she supposed, yet
contrarily pleased because the hoity-toity French
girls were so obviously impressed. Their male
counterparts had a reputation for being virile
lovers, but this tall Englishman had been placed in
the same category. And Jack was playing the role
to perfection.

'Excuse us, ladies, now we're off to find oysters
and champagne, and maybe later——' He lifted
her tote-bag on to his shoulder. '—gentle
lamplight and horizontal bliss. *Au revoir.*'

'*Au revoir,*' breathed both brunettes.

'Oysters and champagne?' Neille queried, as he
led her out of the studio, down the stairs, and on
to the street. 'Lamplight and horizontal bliss?'

Paris by night, with its glittering shops and
illuminated palaces, was the stuff of which dreams
are made, but she was too intent on questioning
Jack to notice.

'Poetic licence,' he replied.

'You're damned right!' Neille had to almost run
to keep up, for he had hold of her hand and was
taking her with him across a beautiful square
adorned with stone sculptures. Fountains rose like
silver plumes in the moonlight. They had reached
the far side of the square before it struck her how
his hand felt big and warm and *right*. It shouldn't.
Weren't they antagonists? Wasn't theirs a strictly
business and neutral relationship? She wasn't
prepared for anything else. And up until yesterday
when—her cheeks grew hot in remembrance—he
had tanned her hide, there hadn't been anything

else. Was there now? All Jack was doing was
holding her hand in a random kind of way.
Random to him, maybe, but not to her. Neille was
tempted to pull free, yet didn't, scared he might
realise how much his hand-clasp disturbed her. If
he suspected her of a weakness, especially such a
frivolous, feminine weakness, might he not exploit
it for all he was worth? 'I'd be grateful if you'd
explain,' she puffed, when he stopped outside a
red-canopied *brasserie*. 'What do you mean, you're
to be my——' She chose the lesser of the two evils.
'——boyfriend?'

She received no reply, for Jack had more
pressing matters on his mind. 'I presume you're
hungry?' he asked.

'Yes, but——'

'Then we'll eat.' He ushered her forward up
the steps and into the restaurant. Cartwheel
chandeliers hung from the ceiling, and the décor
was of rich dark wood and brass. A waiter,
officious as a penguin, marched up and led them
to a discreet booth. Menus were distributed, then
the waiter produced pencil and notepad. He
waited, regally impatient. 'We'd like time to
decide,' Jack requested, and with a sniff the man
walked away.

All that had passed Neille's lips since breakfast
were two cups of coffee, so the sight and smell of
well-cooked food instantly made her mouth water.
The menu offered a selection of *entrées, poissons,
les viandes grillées ou rôties* and *les mets
gourmands*, which required a valiant stab at
translation.

'Madame?'

The waiter had returned, thin, dark and prone to

pomposity. That they had dared to enter his shrine
had clearly caused offence.

'This, please,' said Neille, poking her finger at
the list.

He sniffed his disapproval. *'Et monsieur?'*

In an atrocious accent Jack ordered fresh
salmon with butter sauce. 'And a bottle of white
wine,' he added. 'A good one.'

'You think we serve anything else?' the waiter
demanded, and strutted off.

Jack laughed. 'How can Paris be so damned
splendid and the Parisians so damned awful?'

'They can't all be the same.' She grinned. 'Can
they?' Ready to follow on with a comment about
the behaviour of the two French models, Neille
suddenly stiffened. After a tension-packed day it
was tempting to relax and go plop, but there was a
matter of some importance to be cleared up first.
'I'm still waiting for an explanation,' she reminded
him, switching to stone-faced school ma'am.
'What's this about Lewis agreeing to you being
my—boyfriend?'

Jacket sloughed off and sweater sleeves pushed up
to reveal strong forearms, Jack was smiling. 'You
aren't the only one who was busy today,' he told her,
clasping his hands loosely behind his head and
tilting back his chair. 'I made a number of phone
calls, one of which was to Lewis. I reported how
you'd become increasingly frisky of late.'

Her chin lifted. 'You admitted you'd lost me?'

'I did.' There was a momentary hang-dog
expression before his smile returned. 'I then told
him how losing you had alerted me to the fact that
I was hampered in my role of bodyguard. That in
my opinion it was time to . . . move in.'

'Move in?' Neille didn't care for the sound of that.

There was a pause as the waiter appeared with the wine. He uncorked it between his knees and poured Jack an inch in his glass for tasting.

'It's smarter if I'm not blatantly on surveillance,' he said, nodding approval which enabled both glasses to be filled before the waiter stalked away. 'As our present arrangement stands, any villain would immediately recognise me as an outsider. That leaves you wide open.'

'How?' she enquired cagily.

'If I'm parked six feet away, I'd be unable to deflect a knife which is wielded at three.'

Neille sat up straighter. 'You want us to be glued together?'

At that moment the waiter returned and plonked down two plates. Jack's salmon, accompanied by boiled potatoes and broccoli, looked appetising, but Neille viewed her plate with wary eyes. Was this the *nouvelle cuisine* had she read about? She had never expected a fan-shaped arrangement of pale meat in a brown sauce. Chopped mushrooms sat to one side, while a heap of what could only be mashed swede was on the other.

Jack made a finger and thumb loop of excellence, and began to eat. 'Not exactly glued,' he said, once he'd filled himself up sufficiently to be able to afford a break. 'But closer in public.'

'I don't see why that's necessary, especially not after all this time,' she protested. She wished he would stop talking about moving in and getting closer. The words themselves were potent enough to send the blood rushing to her head, she dreaded to think what might happen if the words ever became actions. 'The danger—if there is danger—

hasn't increased,' Neille continued. 'Don't forget that come next Monday I'll be out in the big wide world all on my own.'

All on her own. Why did that sound like an anti-climax?

'I haven't forgotten, sunbeam, but as a response to your love of truancy I had no option but to undertake a radical rethink.' Jack broke off to make another onslaught on his salmon. 'It became clear to me that the screws must be tightened. As I explained to Lewis, any villain would be suspicious of a bodyguard, yet undeterred by a——'

'Boyfriend,' Neille provided, when he paused.

His grey eyes crinkled. 'You got it in one. More wine?'

'Please,' she said, surprised to discover her glass was empty.

'Allowed perfection, our villain would leap in believing I'm no threat at all and then be overpowered.' He noticed how she had not yet begun to eat. 'I thought you were hungry.'

'I am.' She filled her fork. The meat tasted like solid chicken, and required to be washed down with a mouthful of wine. 'All this talk of villains leaping and you overpowering makes me wonder if you've seen too many episodes of Batman and Robin,' she said drily.

'Could be.' His smile was ingenuous. 'Whatever, until we go our separate ways I am officially——' The way he paused made her scowl, '—your boyfriend.'

'And Lewis agreed to this?'

'Gave me *carte blanche*. Please feel free to ring him and verify.'

'No thanks.' Neille abandoned the meat to make a start on the mushrooms. Thankfully they were normal. 'Verification's the last thing I need. It doesn't surprise me in the least that the two of you have gone behind my back and fixed things, once again.'

'For your own safety, sunbeam, for your own safety,' he assured her solemnly, but there was a gleam in his eye.

'I bet! This radical rethink is just you getting even.' She glowered for a moment, then asked haughtily, 'Aren't you forgetting something? It takes two to be——' The word needed to be pushed out, '—lovers. And I have not the slightest intention of pretending to be in love with you.'

'Maybe you'll discover you like it?'

'Maybe I won't. A bodyguard you are, and a bodyguard you'll stay.'

Jack shrugged amiably. 'Aren't you going to eat that meat?' Neille shook her head. 'Then shall I?'

'Make yourself at home,' she muttered.

He grinned as he leant forward to help himself from her plate. 'Don't worry, I intend to.'

A double-edged comment if she had ever heard one! In threatening to move in closer, Jack had located her weak spot with dispiriting ease. For two years she had lived in an uncomplicated emotional vacuum which suited her fine, but now this carnivorous cowboy was galloping in, pennant fluttering in the breeze. Her nerves jangled. Had he guessed she did not find him entirely unattractive and intended to take a ride at her expense? Well, think again, Jack!

'A public charade is pointless, and especially

here in Paris,' she insisted. 'Any villain will have stayed at h0me. He'd never have bothered to cross the Channel.'

'So spake the oracle.' He laid down his knife and fork. 'Neille, the way in which I make my living is security, and right now I happen to be looking out for you. If I consider I can be more effective closer, then closer I will be.'

Jack started to eat again, leaving her to accept she had been out-classed, out-pointed, and only had herself to blame. If she had behaved, the bodyguard relationship would have been maintained. Now anything might happen. 'Moving in' sounded nail-bitingly ambiguous. What did Jack intend to do? There was no point asking him to spell it out; keeping her guessing would be an integral part of his game. And to him it *was* a game. From the occasional comments he had made about his past, it was obvious he had never been troubled by a shortage of feminine company. Kissing and cuddling would be second nature. Suppose he decided to kiss and cuddle her? Jack's sexual fire-power promised to be impressive. Once intimacy had been no problem, but ever since Simon's death she had shied away. When she did fall in love again she had promised herself it would be the real thing, devout and lifelong, not just a brief dizzy spurt. Love? Where did love fit into this? She was not making sense. At most Jack would kiss her. A kiss wasn't much. She was panicking without reason.

'Enjoy my meat?' she enquired sweetly. 'And my swede?'

'Very tasty,' he grinned, wiping his mouth on a napkin. 'I presume that was the *Cul de Lapin?*'

'I'm afraid so. I didn't mean to order it, I thought I'd asked for fillet steak.'

'Desserts?' barked the waiter, bending over them.

Neille chose a calorific Bombe Alaska, followed by coffee. Jack just had coffee.

'There's really no need for you to hang around and watch me in action with André tomorrow,' she said, spooning in meringue. She had attempted a flippant tone, but heard it fall flat. 'Your dash along the Métro this morning has put me clean off escape attempts. But that apart, I'm not going to do a bunk mid-session, am I?'

Jack looked her straight in the eye. 'What's the matter?' he enquired. 'Don't you want me to see you in your underwear?'

'Um, no—no, it's not that,' she stammered. On the first evening they had met he had said something about climbing into people's minds and now, to her confusion, he had climbed right into hers! He could never have guessed how much today's modelling had upset her, could he? 'It— standing by all day seems a waste of your time,' Neille finished weakly.

'Haven't you been listening, sunbeam? I'm moving in. Which means I shall be there tomorrow, watching you every minute of the day.' His grin was mischievous. 'Shouldn't be too onerous. You have a great body and an especially tantalising backside.'

'Thanks,' she smiled, then straight away cursed herself for responding. She must remember that from now on every single thing Jack said or did was suspect.

'By the way,' he said. 'Can you translate *lapin*?'

'Rabbit.'

'What!' He had been drinking coffee, but now he slammed down his cup, setting the saucer awash. He stared at her aghast. 'Rabbit? But I thought it was beef or veal or something. Rabbit? I've eaten rabbit? But I had a pet rabbit when I was a kid. He was called Snowy, and was big and white and cuddly. I used to rub my cheek up against his fur. And now—oh, God! I've eaten one.'

His dismay restored her in an instant, and Neille giggled.

'Just goes to prove that crime—stealing off my plate—never pays.' She was on the brink of adding 'zonko', but decided it was wiser to refrain. From now on she must tread carefully. 'May I ask the waiter to bring you another dish?' she enquired. 'Why not try a few frogs' legs or a plate of snails?'

Jack held his stomach. 'Don't,' he groaned.

Looking pained, he settled the bill and led Neille out into the night. When he reached for her hand, she made no protest. Although the gesture had appeared automatic, she was not fooled. Holding her hand was a part of Jack's plan. Well, she would show him she didn't care. Maybe if he felt 'moving in' was having little effect, he would 'move out'? Besides, his hand was warm and comforting, and if passers-by were glancing at them, marking them down as yet another pair of lovers, being coupled in public with Jack was by far preferable to being coupled with Lewis.

By the time they reached the hotel he had recovered.

'How about a nightcap?' he suggested. 'It would make a pleasant end to the——'

'No thanks.' Cutting him off in mid-sentence, Neille darted for the lift. There was something in his grin which she didn't trust. In addition to a nightcap, was he lining up a kiss as another pleasant end to the evening? Did he intend to enfold her in an embrace? It was the indecision which killed, not knowing which way he'd jump. 'Alcohol makes wrinkles,' she said pretentiously, 'and I need an early night. But you go ahead. See you tomorrow.'

'Until tomorrow,' he agreed, smiling as she rose slowly skywards.

Tomorrow will be different, Neille told herself as she undressed. By tomorrow she would have grown a second skin and become blasée. She would. She would! Eight hours' sleep was necessary to maintain her dewy look, but sleep refused to come. Later, when the door to Room 42 was unlocked, her ears pricked up of their own accord. Jack was moving around, and then he began to whistle. The tune sounded vaguely familiar. What was it? A children's song? Then she recognised the lilt. He was whistling 'Nellie the Elephant'!

CHAPTER FIVE

THE two great stone towers of Notre Dame stood high and proud against a clear blue sky. Built many centuries ago, the Gothic cathedral continued to inspire awe in the visitors who travelled from all parts of the world to pay homage, but this morning there was an added attraction. A mobile caravan had been parked alongside the Place du Parvis, the large square in front of the cathedral, and it was apparent from the frenzied comings and goings that this did duty as an operations centre. A portion of the square had been cordoned off, and here tripods and arc lamps were being assembled. Long lengths of cable appeared. André, as domineering as ever, shouted instructions, countermanded them, regurgitated the original request. Tourists began to gather in knots, discussing among themselves what all the fuss could be about.

When Neille stepped down from the caravan, there was a sudden hush. The tourists gaped. Tall and willowy, she made a seductive figure in a diaphanous silk chiffon robe worn over matching wide-legged trousers. The robe was wisteria-mauve, trimmed with marabou. Behind her came the French brunettes, wearing identical outfits: one almond-blossom, the other pale blue. A murmur of appreciation ran around the crowd. A dapper Chinese switched from snapping the Great Rose Window and instead began to snap the three girls.

Other tourists followed suit. Even the man peddling
souvenirs at the cathedral end of the square
paused mid-sale to take note. A member of
André's corps unlinked the rope and led the girls
into the arena. The crowd swelled.

'Zere.' André indicated a narrow knee-high
stone wall. 'You stand zere.'

'On it?' Neille asked in dismay, for her shoes
were marabou trimmed mules, inappropriate for
rock climbing.

'On it.'

A helper lent a hand and above the ground she
teetered, while the photographer directed his
attention to the other models.

Feeling the warmth of the sun on the back of
her neck, Neille sent up a silent thank you for
small mercies. Goosebumps never photographed
well, but after a chilly start to the final season of
the year the weather had skipped capriciously back
a notch to provide an Indian summer. Another
mercy was that the outfits organised for today did
not—so far as she could ascertain—appear to be
too sheer. Mutely Neille urged André to hurry.
This pose could not be held for long. Not that she
was posing, more standing like a prune on a knife
edge, trusting to luck she would not fall.

She took care to keep her gaze well above the
heads of the crowd. A single day in France had
taught her how every male between six and a
hundred-and-six believed it his bounden duty to
catch your eye, but exchanging steamy glances
with strangers was not her style. What *was* her
style, she wondered? Neille did not know any
more. At the start of her love affair with Simon
she had been carefree and passionate. With Lewis

she was reticent. With Jack—she nearly overbalanced. Jack was a special case, transitory and spurious. He was a 'here today and gone tomorrow' man. She steadied herself. That sly whistling of 'Nellie the Elephant' had been a red-rag challenge. Yesterday's uncertainty had vanished. Neille was on the attack. Now she knew exactly how to spike Mr Rea's guns.

'Arms out,' ordered André, flapping his around as though guiding Concorde into a safe bay.

Gingerly Neille stretched out her arms. Below, on solid ground, the French models spread out their arms, too. A command from André, and six corps members appeared, each with a small bundle cupped in his hands. Two went to each brunette, two came to Neille, climbing awkwardly on to the wall either side of her.

'Good grief!' she gasped, when they shed their cargo. A plump grey pigeon now stood on each outstretched arm.

Her skin crawled. She was not enamoured of birds at the best of times and to have clawed feet tightening and slackening, tightening and slackening, just inches away from her face, made Neille feel slightly sick. Whether the pigeons were drugged, had had their wings clipped, or simply derived a kick from standing on what had become petrified flesh, she did not know, but they made no attempt to fly away. If only they had. After a minute's more shuffling they sat, warm and feathery and horrible, and began to croon. Actually croon!

'You all right, sunbeam?'

'I don't know.' Terrified to move her head, Neille swivelled her eyes to right and left, but could not find Jack. The Chinese man continued to take snapshots and André was yelling at one of the brunettes who was threatening to have hysterics, but no Jack. 'Where are you?' she hissed from the corner of her mouth.

'Behind, to the side. Out of camera, but near enough to catch if you fall.'

'Promise?' she quaked.

'Promise.'

Jack's company had been the last thing she wanted—as Neille had insisted all through breakfast—but now she was grateful. His support wasn't *vital*, of course, but she admitted there was reassurance in having him near. The photographer took his place at the tripod and gave orders, and she managed to raise her head to stare haughtily into the sky. Click went the camera.

'Profile à gauche,' commanded André.

Neck sinews moving like rusty steel rods, she inched her head around, giving an involuntary shudder when she discovered the left arm pigeon regarding her from close unblinking range. The other pigeon had begun to fidget.

'Hold on in there, sunbeam.'

'Smile,' commanded André.

She smiled. Inches away the pigeon refused to respond. The camera clicked again. Next Neille was instructed to look right. In tortured slow motion, she obeyed. The right arm pigeon had discovered something among its feathers. A flea? If her arms didn't drop off with exhaustion, if she didn't plummet from the wall in a tailspin, was she then destined to contract some rare ornithological disease? Let it end, she prayed. Let it end. If only that pigeon would stop ferreting around. Then she saw Jack, just a glimpse of his dark head beyond the flea-ridden bird, and felt a totally inappropriate rush of relief, affection almost. He was nodding encouragement and mouthing, 'You're doing fine.' Was she? Really?

'Smile,' urged André. 'Chin higher Oop, oop, *chérie*.'

Everything ended in confusion. After taking a rapid series of shots, the photographer grinned. *'Merveilleux!'* he cried with uncharacteristic satisfaction, and clapped his hands. At the noise the pigeons took fright. They pinned her arms with needle claws and, in reflex, Neille jerked. The birds took off to soar, she joggled back and forth, and was capsizing when strong arms plucked her from the wall.

'Oh, Jack,' she whimpered, held close and safe against a solid chest. 'Oh, Jack, thank you, thank you.' She nestled her head into the hollow of his shoulder. 'Oh, Jack. You're a lovely man.'

He grinned down. 'I bet you say that to all the guys.'

'I don't!' Neille objected, then saw he was tongue in cheek. 'No, I don't,' she repeated, smiling now.

He *was* lovely. She knew exactly what Dee and the brunettes saw in him. He had lovely grey eyes with lovely thick black lashes. His straight nose was lovely, too. And his mouth, especially his mouth. Why had she never taken time off to study it before? He had full lips with an impudent little crease at each corner. Lost in his nearness, she decided he was the loveliest man she had ever seen. Not as film-star handsome as Simon who, with his silver-blond hair and green eyes, had only needed to take one step into a room to set female eyes popping out on stalks, but more solidly attractive. Jack wasn't a pretty boy, he was a man who had been and seen and done, and his character was etched in his face. Such a lovely face. Neille's hand slid up to curl around the back of his neck where the dark hair waved thickly, and applied pressure. As his head came down, so she reached up and kissed him.

'Hey,' Jack murmured, the creases at the corners of his mouth deepening. 'Hey, what's all this about?'

A second time her hand applied pressure and a second time she kissed him, but this time his lips parted fractionally ahead of hers and the kiss was transferred into a heart-racing, mind-banging, firework-popping, jazz-band-playing extravaganza. If Neille had been in danger of collapsing in a heap after playing hostess to the pigeons, now she was in graver danger of collapsing after playing hostess to the lusty Mr Rea. She may have initiated the embrace, but he had weighed in with his two pennyworth. She felt weak and breathless, and all of a sudden at cross purposes. Had she kissed him by instinct or design? Neille swooped on design. It had to be. Wasn't that her plan? Hadn't she decided that the best way to forestall his threat of moving in was to move in emphatically herself first?

Yet she had never foreseen such a deep degree of personal involvement. Could she carry through her scheme and emerge unscathed? After a kiss like that, there had to be doubts. Neille stiffened her resolve. She must not be faint-hearted. Her breathlessness was simply on account of her not having been kissed properly for ages, nothing else.

The next time she would ensure there was far less spontaneity, and much more deliberation and cool control.

Jack's response had also been spontaneous, but the moment he realised she had been making a pass, that she actively *wanted* them to be glued together, he would gallop off shrieking for solvent. Lewis might have agreed to closer surveillance, but only within understood and confined limits. All she needed to do was pretend to batter down those limits, and Jack would retreat. Integrity mattered to him. She had seen enough of his business dealings to know he was honest, fair and true. Didn't he telephone Lewis and write regular reports? Didn't he keep a close eye on expenses? The man was a professional right down to his fingertips. He might tease and taunt, but that was all. Aware of occupying a positon of trust, Jack would never do anything to put it in jeopardy. Yes, if she pushed he would retreat. Wasn't he retreating now?—firmly unwinding her arms from around his neck and standing back.

'I'm driven to contemplating what that was in aid of,' he said, eyeing her with more than a tinge of circumspection. 'Could it be I'm playing your straight man, yet again?'

'Thank you very much!' Neille chose to present herself as flip. 'I show my appreciation for being rescued and you promptly accuse me of double dealing. You just brim with Old World gallantry, don't you?'

'Sunbeam, when you get me in a clinch before a cast of thousands, it's suspicion I brim with.'

For the first time since he'd rescued her from the wall, Neille became aware of onlookers. André and the brunettes drew eyes, but she and Jack were receiving more than their fair share of interested glances. Appearing in public places in her professional capacity was something she had learned to live with, but providing a sideshow was a different matter.

'I must change,' she announced, and ran across the square and into the caravan in a flurry of silk chiffon.

The next tableau featured the brunettes perched on the wall while Neille had both feet firmly planted on the paving stones below. No pigeons, but this time a brown leather boxing glove was fitted to each fist. The gloves complemented boxer shorts worn beneath plunge-neck lounge coats. Neille was in bronze, the other girls in lemon and chartreuse.

Two hours and four changes of outfit later, André gave orders that the caravan was to roll. Jack sweet-talked himself a lift, and they set off for the Palais de Chaillot. Here their base was a wide terrace with golden statues, which overlooked formal gardens spreading down to the Seine. Beyond the river stood the metal bulk of the Eiffel Tower, and if you stretched your eyes further you could see the trees in the Champ de Mars, one of Paris's best-loved open spaces. Such grand-scale harmony of design made the terrace a favourite sight-seeing spot, though once again the tourists who gathered there were happy to transfer their interest. The Chinese man appeared—or could this be a different individual?—and worked his way through a roll of film.

André shot three different sequences and began to arrange another. His helpers ran around, tourists arrived and departed, and late lunch came in the form of spasmodic bites at salad-filled *baguettes*.

'Why not have a proper meal at that café over there?' Neille suggested, as Jack wolfed down a morsel she had smuggled out from the caravan. She had had to smuggle it, because the *baguettes* were supposed to be restricted to official personnel only. 'You could also take time off to ring your office.'

'No need. I called my secretary at home before breakfast and received an update on the current scene. I'm happy to report that, despite my absence, Rea Safeguards is ticking over nicely.'

'And I can also tick over nicely, despite your absence. Go and have lunch. I'm perfectly safe, haven't seen a bazooka or a flick knife in ages, and I won't run away. Honest.'

'You said that once before,' he reminded her, grinning at the grave face which was at odds with her appearance.

Dressed in a style André had christened 'Zee 'Ollywood Cabaret', Neille was resplendent in a tight white basque. The addition of a black top hat tipped at a rakish angle over her copper-gold tresses, a bow tie, cane and high-heeled shoes, had brought whistles from the crowd. In anyone's book she was a stunner, but right now she was too engrossed in ensuring Jack was fed to bother about any effect she might be having.

'I mean it this time,' she assured him, sombre as a witness swearing to tell the truth, the whole truth and nothing but the truth. 'Your Métro madness has changed everything. Do you think I'd risk you leaping into action like that a second time? I give you my solemn word that I'll keep to heel.'

'Funnily enough, I believe you.'

'Good.' Neille stood smiling up at him, then remembered that, although there would be no more escape attempts, she and Jack remained antagonists. Her protests had been channelled into one direction, that was all—coming on strong, *too* strong. And wasn't it time he had a second dose of his medicine? Still smiling, she raised a hand and slowly pushed the incorrigible strand of dark hair back from his brow. She had intended the gesture to appear familiar, tender and flirtatious, all at the same time, but suddenly her nerve failed her. Was she acting or was this for real? Hurriedly she withdrew her fingers before they did something ridiculous, like trembling or smoothing his cheek. 'Now, please vamoose and get yourself a decent meal,' she instructed briskly.

'What, and leave you naked and defenceless?' asked Jack, showing a remarkable capacity for copycat tactics. Her breasts were curving saucily, pushed into smooth firm globes by the boned white satin, and his eyes began to roam over them in a way which contrived to be familiar, tender and flirtatious all rolled into one. Beneath his gaze, Neille's breath seemed to stop, yet her heart was racing. 'Just a figure of speech,' he murmured. 'My God, if Brian could see you now.'

'Brian?' she asked, bemused. This attempt to make Jack uncomfortable had gone disastrously wrong. She had fallen into her own trap.

'Detective Inspector Brian Gilchrist. He was involved in the business of Lewis's nasty letter, so we meet up from time to time.'

'Oh.' That was all Neille could think of to say. Good grief, it wasn't like her to be tongue-tied. She ran back a few steps mentally, and started again. 'This Brian,' she said, leaning on her cane and determinedly throwing out one hip, 'would he think I looked . . . appealing?'

'The *crème de la crème*,' Jack said cheerfully.

'And you? What do you think?'

'Sunbeam——' He started off jauntily, but somehow lost his way. His eyes clouded, he licked his lower lip, then his eyes began to roam again. 'Sunbeam——' His voice was throaty now. 'Sunbeam, I think you are the——'

'*Vite, vite,*' yelled André. 'Neille, *chérie*, over zere. Zee big smile. Kick zee legs. Twirl zee cane.'

She could have throttled him. What had Jack been about to say? She desperately wanted to know. But the moment had gone, lost for ever. Had he been going to reveal she was the *crème de la crème* for him, too? It was possible. Hadn't his grey eyes softened? Hadn't those lovely little creases appeared at the corners of his mouth? Hadn't he been on the brink of admitting he found her immensely, overwhelmingly appealing? Neille released a breath. Who was she fooling? All she represented to Jack Rea was money, a step up the ladder for his damned company. And all he represented to her was a month of irritation, a month which was rapidly coming to an end. Next week Jack would be long gone.

Mid-afternoon they moved camp for the third and final time. Montmartre, renowned as the haunt of painters, musicians and writers, was their destination. Still in essence a hill-top village, Montmartre has a dilapidated charm which acts like a magnet for tourists. The caravan was parked in the old Place du Tertre, the hub of activity, and when Neille peeped out she saw that the cobbled square was thronged. Degas, Modigliani and Toulouse-Lautrec had once gathered here, but now their places had been taken by artists of many different persuasions. Palette knives wielded acrylics; fingers smeared on oils; charcoal and watercolours abounded. Silhouettes were being fashioned from ebony card, and likenesses reproduced—to varying degrees—in pastels. Some artists demonstrated more skill at bargaining a price than in painting a picture, but the crowds who surrounded the easels did not seem to care.

When Neille and the brunettes made an entrance, there were cries of 'Bravo' and a round of applause. Space had been cleared around a demonstrably French painter with a bushy black beard and beret, and as they made their way towards him the press of spectators miraculously multiplied. It was all the helpers could do to hold back the crowd.

'Neille, you alone for zees shot. Zee other girls no boobs. Like so,' ordered André, bending at the waist to peer into the artist's easel. 'Zee legs apart, zee *derrière* oop.'

She complied, positioning herself in a manner which sparked off a second round of applause. She was not surprised. Clad in a scarlet back-lacing corset, with bowed suspenders and black seamed stockings, Neille was uncomfortably aware of being an out-and-out sex object. By looking up she could see Jack, mere feet away in the crowd, grinning. By looking down she could see her bosom, regrettably on the point of popping out.

One deep breath and she'd be in trouble. Jack might be treating her predicament lightly, but for her the vibes were all wrong. There was too much muttering, too many elbows being nudged, too many beady eyes. Modelling always included an element of sexuality, but the proportions had gone haywire. No matter how André angled his camera, was anyone going to bother about the underwear? Or, like the men in the crowd, were they only going to see pouting round breasts and a vulnerable backside?

Too vulnerable. Suddenly a hand touched her, a hot clammy hand. With a yelp of protest Neille turned, but in one spring Jack was with her, thrusting both the hand and its owner away.

'No, no,' he chided, and she straightened to see him waggling a finger at a surly youth dressed in the leathers of a motor cyclist. The youth's face reddened and he squared up. Was there going to be a fight? Should the *gendarmes* be summoned? The crowd held its collective breath, visualising flying fists, cut lips, bruises, spilled blood. 'Not for you,' Jack said, and winked. He gave her thigh a playful tweak which made her jump. 'For me.'

The square exploded into one enormous guffaw. Everyone was laughing, the youth, André, the brunettes, the helpers, the crowd and—although it took a minute to come to terms—Neille. What could have been a nasty incident had been turned into fun and games. But Jack *had* pinched her bottom. Shouldn't she reciprocate? Wasn't this the perfect time and place to make another, supremely public, pass?

'My knight in blue jeans,' she said, smiling as she placed one hand at his waist, the other on his shoulder. Neille felt him go very still. 'What would I do without you?' she enquired, and dabbed a kiss on his mouth.

Jack did not respond. His grey eyes were watchful. What happens next? she could hear him thinking. He had accepted the kisses at Notre Dame and later her flirting, but now he was cautious. He might not be exactly running for cover, but he was definitely reassembling his thoughts. Neille grinned. She had him at her mercy. Edging her hand along his belt to his spine, she then slid it smartly down and deposited two pert patronising pats on his backside.

'Hey!' he protested, as the crowd roared. 'What the——?' All set to take her to task, he realised they were the centre of attention and changed his mind. Shrugging good-naturedly, he turned to the photographer. 'OK, André, the floor show's over. Get cracking.'

The camera session resumed, but this time with totally different vibes. Established as a woman with on-call protection, plus a healthy sense of humour, Neille was no longer up for grabs. Camaraderie and respect replaced the heavy breathing, and she was much happier. Her happiness increased when she realised Jack had become distracted, not at all his usual self. This was a morale booster, and although André kept up the pressure until darkness fell and the temperature zeroed alarmingly, she never grumbled. The brunettes might complain about the cold, but a glow of satisfaction at having outmanoeuvred Jack kept Neille warm.

Yet getting back into proper clothes was still a relief. Dressed in sweater, white slacks and parka once more, she emerged on to the Place du Tertre. The hour and the decrease in temperature had resulted in a general exodus from the square, and the few tourists who remained were far more interested in the canvases exhibited in the lamplight than in a respectably clad girl with an unmade-up face. Only Jack, waiting patiently outside the caravan, looked up as she appeared.

'We must talk,' he said, making no pretence at a greeting. His stance was stiff, his eyes wary. Was he afraid she might thrust out a hand and give him another quick pat?

'What about?' Neille asked, finding it hard not to smile.

'You know what about.'

'Do I?' She looked around. Interspersed with art shops and quaint old cottages, the square contained some interesting restaurants where menus were posted up outside. 'How about us eating in Montmartre tonight?' she suggested. 'It would make a change from the hotel.'

'Suits me, but——'

'Fine. Shall we try here?' Neille tripped over to the nearest eating place, a doll's house with white walls and green painted window shutters. She inspected the menu. 'Good selection,' she appraised, then swished her arm a joyful hundred and eighty degrees. 'Or we could try there, or there, or there.'

'This one, but later.' Jack was unimpressed by her merriment. 'First we'll have a drink *and a talk*.' He stabbed a finger at a nearby inn. 'Let's go,' he commanded, using a voice guaranteed to inspire rapid obedience.

Shabby, in a comfortable lived-in kind of way,

the inn had old horse brasses and faded paintings covering whitewashed walls. They found a table in a quiet corner, and Neille waited as he fetched a carafe of dry white wine.

'Cheers,' she smiled, raising her glass. 'I'd like to thank you for pinching my bottom. Very cleverly you rescued me and defused the situation, all in one. I never thought I'd admit freely to this, but it felt good having you around.'

'Nice to know I have my uses,' he said cryptically.

Neille placed an elbow on the table which sat between them, resting her chin on her hand. 'Want to pinch me again?' she enquired.

'And have you demanding a return bout? No, thank you.'

'Now, Jack,' she grinned. 'You're coming on like you're untouched by human hand.'

'I'm coming on like I have a sense of responsibility towards my employer, who happens to be Lewis Mitchell, *your* boyfriend. He's paying for me to be here with you, and us——' He flung her a violent glare. '—and us messing around is dishonourable.'

Neille twisted a strand of coppery hair around her finger. 'I understood Lewis had given his permission for us to . . . mess around? *Carte blanche*, you said. We could be lovers, courtesy of Lewis, you said. And maybe I'll discover I like it, you said.' Her grin was impish. 'Guess what—I have!'

'Quit acting,' he ordered grittily.

Her wholesome *ingénue* smile was trotted out. 'Who's acting?'

'You are. You know damned well that I said all that just as a device to try and make you behave.'

Her eyes seemed to grow to twice their size. 'Lewis didn't agree you could . . . move in?'

'Yes, he did,' Jack snapped. 'But on a purely businesslike footing.'

'How can lovers be businesslike?' she enquired with mock naïveté.

'Cut it out, Neille. I got carried away and painted the picture up a bit, that's all,' he growled. 'Dammit, I never intended to *do* anything. It was to be looks, words, innuendoes. I wanted to keep you guessing, wondering if. OK, it's not in the rule book, but then neither are you!' Exasperation had raised his voice, and he needed to make a conscious effort to lower it. 'Usually my charges co-operate,' he hissed. 'They ask my advice on what to do for the best, and when I make suggestions they follow them, to the letter. They most certainly don't insult me sixteen hours a day, nor leave me to rot outside public lavatories, nor——'

'Call you Jackson?'

'Damned right,' he glowered.

'How about patting your bottom?' Her eyes sparkled. 'You have such a sexy bottom.'

His jaw clenched. 'Don't push it, Neille.'

'As if I would. You were very quick on the draw where the motor cyclist was concerned. Most impressive,' she continued. 'Now I understand how you've gained such a fine reputation.'

'And now I understand you're buttering me up. But the motor cyclist was no threat.'

'He could have been my assassin.'

Jack shook his head. 'There isn't an assassin.'

'You don't know that.'

He poured out second helpings of wine. 'As this

appears to be true confessions time, I'll carry on. From the start you've insisted no one's gunning, and I may as well admit I agree.'

'But you've always maintained there was a risk,' she protested.

'There is, one which equates with being nibbled to death by a crazed hamster.'

'You said it was common sense to be on the alert,' Neille rebuked. 'On the alert for a crazed hamster?'

'I needed to justify my existence, didn't I?' he thrust back. 'I've told Lewis on numerous occasions that I consider myself superfluous, but he refuses to listen. He says he's booked me for a month, so a month it'll stay. *I* recognise I'm taking money under false pretences, but if I'd let that slip you'd have made mincemeat out of me.'

'I did think you operated in a funny way,' she confessed. 'Letting me carry on my everyday life when I was supposed to be being tracked by a killer.'

Jack drank some wine. 'Well, now you know. Even the police've advised Lewis not to take the matter to heart. Their theory, and I agree, is that putting threats down on paper was enough to satisfy whoever wrote the note. If someone really means business they make sure they're specific, not woolly. That note was beginning and end.'

'Do the police have any idea where the photograph of Lewis and me fits in?'

'Sorry, there are no theories on that score.' He threw her a glance. 'You've never jilted a guy, have you? Given someone cause to take offence? People can seek vengeance in some strange and nasty ways.'

'No,' she said, as a cold finger of fear touched her spine. Jack was referring to the past, but might he not equally be talking about the future? 'No,' Neille repeated, frightened to dwell on what might happen if the lingerie photographs did not have the required effect. 'I met Simon when I was seventeen and was faithful to him until he died.' A sadness welled in her eyes, then she shrugged and it was gone. 'Since then, apart from the occasional casual outing, I've dated Lewis.' She drained her glass. 'Shall we go and eat?'

The doll's house frontage was misleading. Once inside, the building opened out into an assortment of dining rooms linked by stone--flagged corridors.

'S'il vous plaît,' said a waiter, leading them off on what seemed a mile-long trek past kitchens and stores, stillrooms and offices. But the journey proved worthwhile, for he finally brought them to a bijou dining room where flickering candles provided a golden light, and a violinist was playing a love song. Dark blue velvet covered the tables, there was a posy of violets, and each menu was adorned with cherubs. 'Romantic, eh?' smiled the waiter.

Neille grinned at Jack. 'Soft lights, sweet music and a hefty helping of steamed rabbit, who could ask for more?'

He obliged with a theatrical groan.

The meal passed in the same light-hearted mood. They appeared to have taken a step forward and could now be friends. With a pang, Neille recognised that their relationship could have been like this from the start, if she had co-operated. But time was running out.

'Can you rustle up your coat while I settle the bill?' Jack enquired, finishing his liqueur.

'Will do.'

Earlier her parka had been whisked away, and now the waiter who knew its exact whereabouts had become involved in serving a table of ten. Rather than hang around, Neille decided to go in search herself. A wooden sign indicated the cloakrooms, and as Jack headed for the cashier's desk by the front door, she set off in the direction of the arrow. She passed two unmarked doors and came out into a square lobby. Which way now? A second sign indicated right. Right meant another long corridor, and she was making her way down it when she became aware of footsteps clip-clopping along behind. Someone else was obviously tracking down their coat, too. Neille was tempted to stop and commiserate, but the realisation that the person behind might well not speak English kept her silent. The corridor ended in a T-junction. She looked both ways. There was a faded sign further along the wall to the left. Could that indicate cloakrooms?

When she had stopped, so the steps behind had stopped, and now, as she started to walk again, so the footsteps started. How the eeriness occurred, Neille did not know. It appeared, not by degrees, but precipitately and frighteningly. She was being stalked. Since leaving the dining room there had been no signs of life, no voices, and she was aware of being marooned in a maze with a stranger. No, she was being over-sensitive. All she needed to do was turn and grin, then everything would be fine. But there was no chance to turn and grin because suddenly a hand brushed her shoulder, she felt fingers touch her hair. From behind came a soft chuckle, a soft, pleased, male chuckle. Fear hurtled her forward, but her acceleration was braked as the hand tightened, forcing back her head.

The surly youth had returned! He might have joined in the laughter this afternoon, but now he had tracked her down. He would want revenge, and that meant far more than just touching her this time. Trapped by her hair, Neille could not escape, but even so a fearful paralysis had rooted her to the spot.

'No. Please, no.'

Did she say the words out loud? The hand, once again hot and clammy, moved to caress her neck, and she squeaked in alarm—an ineffectual squeak. But standing and squeaking was the action of a mouse. She wasn't a mouse. Hadn't her years growing up with Peter, Paul and Podge ensured she possessed no hang-ups about women being useless, frail creatures? Hadn't they praised her, if grudgingly, because she could always be relied upon to fight? Why not fight now? She took a deep breath, raised her arm, clenched her fist. Wham! Neille hit the man behind her a fierce blow on the cheek.

'Oh!' If she had hit the seven-headed Beast of the Apocalypse, she would not have been more surprised for, instead of hitting the youth in leathers, as expected, she had hit a Chinese man in a navy blue suit. 'Oh!' she said again.

He was leaning against the wall, a hand to his cheek. Then, to her astonishment, he smiled. 'Pretty girl, Neille,' he said. 'Pretty girl.'

She couldn't believe it. She had walloped him

and there he stood, chanting, 'Pretty girl, Neille. Pretty girl.' He reminded her of an evil parrot, ready to swoop and peck out her eyes. In terror and confusion, she pushed past and charged headlong down the passage, instinctively heading for sound. There were no footsteps behind her now. Face scarlet, breath coming in laboured gasps, Neille burst into the front hall. Jack was talking to the lady cashier, while nearby stood the waiter, holding her parka.

'Thanks.' She plucked it from him and ran, bundling Jack with her out on to the street in an impassioned rush. 'Jack, oh Jack,' she jabbered, clutching hold of his arm. 'Jack, there's a man in there. A man—a man——' Her chest rose and fell, but fear clogged her throat and she could not say the words. 'Oh, Jack. Thank goodness you're here,' she blabbed, and collapsed against him.

'Cut it out, Neille,' he ordered. 'You've pulled this stunt once too often. I thought we'd agreed that us ... messing around was out of the question.'

She gazed at him, wide-eyed. 'What?'

'I'm not going to kiss you,' he said, holding his arms stiffly by his sides. 'Even if you don't feel you owe Lewis any loyalty, I do. Now, put on your coat and——'

'Jack, there's a man in there who——' As she flung on her parka, her voice started squeaking again. 'Who—who touched me.'

'Good for him, but I'm not going to.'

'Jack, listen!'

'No, *you* listen. I'm not going to touch you, or hold you close, or ... anything! So you can stop this act.' As he spoke, he had begun backing away down the pavement. Neille followed. 'OK, I find you attractive, very attractive. And I admit I kissed you this morning, but that was a mistake. You took me by surprise when you fell off the wall. But it won't happen twice, Neille. This time I have my priorities well and truly sorted out. I don't want to kiss you again. In other circumstances—well, there aren't any other circumstances, are there? If there were maybe it'd be different, but it's not.' He ran a hand through his hair. 'Am I making sense? Maybe I do want to kiss you. Yes, I do. Very much. In fact, if you really want to know, I'd like nothing better than to get you into bed right now, but I'm not going to because I happen to believe in the sanctity of the employer/employee relationship. Lewis is paying me, which means I don't cheat on the guy. And don't look at me like that. It doesn't matter that you're the most desirable woman I've met in years; what matters is that I refuse to tarnish a reputation which I've worked damned hard to build up over——'

'Jack!' Neille tugged at his sleeve. 'Jack, you don't understand. I've met the assassin.'

CHAPTER SIX

'THE who?'

'The assassin, the villain, the man who sent Lewis his note.'

Jack halted in his retreat. 'What the hell are you talking about?'

'The man who touched me.' Her fingers tightened on his sleeve. She was desperate for contact. Jack was big and male and protective, and she needed him. 'He knew my name. When I hit him he said, "Pretty girl, Neille".' She shuddered at the memory. 'It was weird. Perhaps he's paranoid or schizophrenic or——'

'You hit a guy?' he interrupted.

'Yes, yes.' Neille bobbed her head up and down. 'He followed me along the corridor and when I stopped, he stopped. Then he put out his hand and touched my hair. I thought it must be the motor cyclist who'd groped me this afternoon but it wasn't and—and I hit him.'

Jack was looking at her as if she was stark staring mad. 'You hit a complete stranger just because he touched your hair?'

'Yes, and I hurt him,' Neille said, with a burst of pride. It was a pity her cousins hadn't been there. They would have admired her fighting style. 'When he staggered back, there was a big red mark on his cheek.' She put both hands on Jack's arm and pulled. 'Come along, we must go and find him before he has a chance to get away. You can make a citizen's arrest or something.'

'Hang on.' Jack placed his hand over the two which were attempting to drag him towards the restaurant and held them still. 'Would you please tell me exactly what's happened?'

'But there's no time to lose,' she cried, putting on pressure. 'The man might escape. I'll fill you in on the details later. *Come on.*'

He stood firm. 'No way. You're not getting me back in there. In fact, our best bet is to exit Montmartre, and fast. The police may well be arriving at any minute. It's not a bodyguard you need, it's a bloody straitjacket. You can't go around slugging innocent bystanders for no reason at all.'

'Innocent? No reason? He touched me!'

'The guy was admiring your hair. It's an unusual colour and——'

'No, Jack. He grabbed hold and jerked back my head,' she insisted feverishly. 'I couldn't get free.'

'Isn't it more likely you stumbled and he reached out to save you?' He held up a hand to silence the protests which were bubbling from her lips and listened. 'Wasn't that a police siren?'

'I didn't hear anything, but if it was—great! When they arrive we can tell them everything. How he followed me down the corridor, how he——'

'*We* tell them? No thanks, if you don't mind I'll sit this one out,' Jack said, and began prising her fingers from his sleeve.

'You don't believe I did come face to face with the assassin, do you?' she demanded, snatching her hand away.

He moved his shoulders. 'Assassin? Frankly,

no.' When he saw how she scowled, he added, 'So sue me.'

'What a very good idea,' Neille flared. 'I was under the impression you were responsible for my safety, but am I safe? Am I hell! While you were having a great time, flashing credit cards and chatting up that cashier, I could have been raped and murdered. Or kidnapped. Yesterday you bugged me, today you didn't bother. I could have ended up bound and gagged in a car heading for Monte Carlo, and no one would've been any wiser.' Her tirade ceased without warning. 'Do you really want to go to bed with me?'

'Very much so.' Jack tilted his head. 'And that *was* a siren, so move it. If I let you get arrested by the French police, Lewis'll never forgive me.'

Employing brute force in preference to friendly persuasion, he grabbed hold of her hand and began propelling her from the Place du Tertre. Down a narrow cobbled street they went, him striding while Neille skittered alongside in her high-heeled boots. The street plunged sharply downhill and keeping pace on a steep incline was no easy task. Below them spread Paris, the lights twinkling like diamonds in the black velvet distance.

'What did this assassin of yours look like?' Jack enquired, easing up when several hundred yards had been put between them and the restaurant.

Neille frowned, attempting to assemble an Identikit picture. 'Short, skinny, with sleek black hair. A typical Chinese.'

He stopped in his tracks. 'The guy was Chinese?'

She nodded. 'Around forty, though it's hard to tell.'

'Don't say any more, let me guess,' he ordered, a

chuckle beginning to rumble. 'He was wearing a long crimson robe and one of those little black caps? With a pigtail down his back? And he said——' Jack demonstrated a low bow. 'Ah so, Missie Neille, you have velly plitty hair?' The chuckle had grown into a belly laugh, and it was fortunate they had stopped beside a street lamp because now he needed to hold on to remain upright. 'Chinese?' he gasped. 'You were locked in mortal combat with a refugee from a Hong Kong triad? Neille, you're a killer!'

'So mock,' Neille snapped, refusing to admit to any doubts. She powered off downhill alone.

'You must see the funny side,' he said, catching up. 'As an assassin, the guy sounds a great Sunday School teacher.'

She marched on. 'He grabbed hold of my hair and touched my neck. His hand felt horrible and—and I was *frightened*,' she wailed. Neille had never intended to wail, indeed she had been grinding out her tale from between gritted teeth, but something inside her crumpled. She was weary of being the fighter, of giving as good as she got. Peter, Paul and Podge might well hoot with scorn, but all she wanted was to be pampered.

'I'm sorry.' Jack's voice was low. He slid an arm around her shoulders and drew her to a halt. 'Forgive me?' He brushed a tendril of hair from her cheek. 'I shouldn't have laughed. Whatever happened, it can't have been pleasant.'

'It wasn't.' Her words emerged on a sob.

'You're trembling.' He pulled her into his arms and began patting her back, comforting her. 'Oh sunbeam, don't. You're safe. I'm here. I'll look after you.'

'Even Nellie the Elephant gets scared some-times,' she gulped, trying hard to smile. But his concern had lowered her resistance and Neille, who rarely cried, felt a tear run down her cheek.

'Sunbeam,' Jack said brokenly, and began smoothing her hair, touching her face with his fingers, murmuring reassurances.

He bent to kiss the tear away and then, somehow, his mouth moved lower until it covered hers, soft and warm and comforting. When and where the comfort stopped and the desire began was never entirely clear, but as Neille's arms slid up around his neck, so Jack's lips coaxed hers apart. Instinctively she nestled against him, drawing strength from his mouth and deep, deep pleasure. Heat began to glow, running along her limbs, radiating through her body, and with the heat came an ache, a poignant reminder of how long it was since she had been held close and loved, and how ripe she was for the taking.

'Jack,' she murmured, drawing back.

Did he read the message in her eyes? He must.

'No.' He laid a finger across her lips. 'No,' he repeated gravely and withdrew. Just one short step, but enough to break all contact. He pushed his hands into his trouser pockets and studied his shoes. 'No, the Chinese guy wasn't an assassin.'

Neille gazed at him. How could he be so calm, so rational? He had said he wanted to make love to her, kissed her as though he did, and yet . . . Had passion gripped him as it had gripped her, or had the sweet desire which had flavoured the embrace been purely her imagination?

'My guess is that he's the guy we saw taking

pictures at Notre Dame,' Jack continued, using a neutral voice. 'He must have followed us here. He meant no harm, I'm sure.'

Why this obsession with the assassin? The assassin didn't matter any more. She was beginning to have doubts about the Chinese wanting to hurt her herself. Maybe her accusations had been on the wild side? Maybe she had over-reacted? She wished Jack would let the subject drop. Other matters were far more important. This ache of hers for instance. Couldn't he guess how much she needed him? How much she wanted to——The obvious struck. She had believed his talk of wanting to make love, but it had been empty male swaggering. Akin to men in their late fifties who leered and said, 'My word, I'd be after you if I was twenty years younger.' If. The word was a barricade to hide behind, like Jack had chosen to hide behind Lewis. How very convenient! She had responded to what she had thought was genuine affection and now she was being rejected. But worse things had happened and she had survived.

Neille's chin snapped up. 'It's my guess he followed me over on the plane,' she announced, her stare advising that no one fooled around with her emotions for long, least of all some two-bit bodyguard. 'He was sat next to you.'

Not for one moment did she believe what she had said, but at least it proved she was equally adept at dismissing the embrace.

Jack laughed. 'That guy was Japanese.'

'Japanese. Chinese. They're all oriental.'

'A Japanese who had an onward flight booked to the Far East. I overheard him asking the stewardess if there was a chance he'd still make his connection.'

'Clever clogs!' she snarled, and strode off down the hill again. But as she strode along, her mood began to falter. What was she achieving by acting like a five-year-old? Not much. Why not be more mature? 'OK, I was wrong,' she admitted, throwing him a glance, half apologetic, half rebellious. 'The Chinese man didn't mean me any harm. On second thoughts, maybe I did stumble. My heels are rather high. And as far as knowing my name is concerned, I expect he overheard André giving instructions.'

'I expect he did,' Jack agreed calmly.

Gratitude at him not crowing over her repentance made Neille able to continue. 'Perhaps as a foreigner with poor English all he could say to explain touching my hair was "Pretty girl, Neille".'

'Now you're making sense.'

She looked at him sheepishly. 'I know I've always rejected the notion that someone's out to get me, but——'

'No one is, sunbeam,' he assured her.

'I accept that, but I think maybe in my subconscious there could have been a tiny bit of doubt.'

'Banish it.' Jack was firm. 'Like I said before, Lewis's note fulfilled its purpose by allowing someone to let off steam, and that's an end to it. Believe me?'

Neille nodded. 'I do.'

'That's my girl,' he grinned.

They had reached the bottom of the hill. A taxi was disgorging passengers on a corner and Jack steered her towards it. After he'd given the driver the name and location of their hotel, they both climbed in.

'I understood Dee was your girl?' she questioned, as the taxi set off. She flashed a glance through the shadows. 'The two of you always seem to be closeted together, though it beats me what you can find to talk about. I'd have thought five minutes conversation was severely stretching her powers of concentration.'

He gave a wide smile. 'I do love a woman who can disguise her jealousy.'

'Jealous! Me jealous of that cross-eyed little— little—huh!'

'As a matter of fact, we talk about you,' he revealed. 'Dee provides the lowdown on your timetable, and she does a fine job. For example, if you tell me you're due at Knightsbridge at ten-thirty, I check with her. Lo and behold, it has been known to be Chelsea at ten.'

'Trust her to snitch.' Neille huddled closer into the corner of the back seat. Not only did Jack spurn, now he was admitting to underhand tricks with a sly confederate.

'Dee's been a good friend,' he protested.

'Lucky you.' Was she jealous? How could anyone be jealous of Dee? The girl was a colourless individual, though pretty enough in a milkmaid kind of a way. He didn't really like her, did he? Jack needed someone who would meet him as an equal, not an inane yes-woman. 'What was your wife like?' she found herself asking.

He gave a surprised grunt. 'Five foot four, fair hair, brown eyes.'

'No, I mean as a person.'

'Friendly, articulate, a go-getter.'

'That doesn't sound such a bad combination.' She sat up straighter. 'Why the divorce?'

'Why the sudden interest?' he countered.

Neille shrugged. 'You've compiled a dossier on me. Isn't it time I assembled a few facts about you? Fair?' she enquired, when he hesitated.

'Fair,' he agreed, after a moment. Jack let out a breath. 'We divorced because basically I wasn't prepared to go and get what Kay wanted to go and get. Or to compromise.'

When he let out a second reflective breath, indicating that talking about his past wasn't easy for him, Neille felt sympathetic. Error-strewn memories were apparently something they had in common. She gave an encouraging smile.

'Explain, please.'

'I was in the Army at the time and——' He paused, then set off again at a sturdier rate. 'And the nature of the job meant I was posted around different bases in fairly rapid succession. The constant moving didn't prove conducive to marital bliss, because Kay was eager to put down roots. Her idea of "going" was to a stylish Thames-side village, and her idea of "getting" was a picturesque cottage in that village. Home-making was a fetish with her. She had folders full of colour schemes, room settings. She knew exactly what she wanted, down to the pattern of the bedroom curtains. The accommodation the Services provided fell far short of her requirements. They don't go a bundle on thatched cottages with mullioned windows,' Jack said pithily. 'As her dissatisfaction grew, she started to nag me to buy myself out of the Army. But I enjoyed the life and I dug in my heels. It was selfish, but I refused to sit down and talk, to see things from her point of view. My only excuse is that I was young.' He gave a rueful laugh. 'Funnily enough I want now what she wanted then.'

'Mullioned windows?'

He grinned. 'No. Roots, the settled life.'

'A nest?' Neille suggested.

He gave her an odd look. 'That's right. However, our marriage began to disintegrate. When the next posting occurred I moved, but Kay went home to her mother's. The inevitable happened. We were both lost and lonely, and for my part—well.' Jack spread his hands. 'There's something about a uniform which attracts women, and I confess I didn't put up much of a fight to protect my virtue. Then Kay telephoned one day. She'd met someone at a squash club and wanted her freedom. I know it doesn't make sense, but when she said "divorce"—phew! Up to that point I'd managed to persuade myself we were just going through a bad patch, but then I couldn't pretend any more. I had to admit to failing at the single most important relationship in anyone's life. I was shattered. In retaliation I began to sleep around. I suppose I was proving to myself that I wasn't a complete failure with the opposite sex.'

'Did it work?'

'No.' He gave a rueful grin. 'Did you think it would?'

Neille shook her head. 'But it's amazing how adept we all are at deluding ourselves. And how easy it is to analyse our actions, given hindsight.'

'You've discovered that, too?'

'I have. How long was it before you realised the futility of what you were doing?'

'Four, five years.' Jack grunted in self-disgust. 'I'm a slow learner. Since leaving the Army I've had a couple of moderately long-term relationships, but never anything which . . . clicked.'

'Perhaps something'll click with Dee?' she suggested, cloaking what suddenly seemed a turning-point question in casual garb.

'Yeah! There's as much chance of something clicking between her and me as there is of something clicking between Mr Mitchell and you.'

Relief that the secretary meant nothing was swept away by his abrupt insertion of Lewis into the conversation. Dee could be dismissed, Lewis was an entirely different matter. How much had Jack guessed about their relationship?

'And what does that mean?' she enquired, playing for time.

'That, like Dee and me, you and Lewis have nothing in common.' He threw her a look. 'And you can forget about becoming evasive. It took less than seventy-two hours for me to realise you tolerate the man—just. You never ring him, you never mention his name unless you're forced to.' Jack grinned. 'It's being generous to say you're apathetic. However did the two of you get together in the first place?'

'By—by mistake,' Neille admitted, faltering a little. How candid dare she be? There was no point fobbing Jack off with a load of lies, he wouldn't be fooled; yet equally she must not be rash. Criticisms and exposures must be tempered, because right now Lewis remained a potent factor in her life. Allowing herself the dizzy image of the freedom a week Friday might—*would*—bring, was premature.

'You met through your father?' he prompted, when she remained silent.

She nodded. 'Lewis called round one day to deliver some papers. Daddy was out, but I felt it my duty to offer a cup of tea.'

'And he liked what he saw?'

'I'm afraid so. This was two years ago when the "little girl" look was in. I was wearing a dark dress with a big white collar.' Neille's natural spark had her grinning. 'That first impression must have hit him like a sledge hammer, because no matter what I wear now Lewis still regards me as fresh out of a convent. Amazing, isn't it?'

Jack laughed. 'Like you said, we're all adept at deluding ourselves. A convent girl is obviously what Lewis requires.' He sobered. 'Two years ago makes it around the time Simon Gates died?'

'Lewis entered my life just after Simon left it,' she agreed, frowning. She accepted that her questions about Jack's past entitled him to enquire into hers, but suddenly felt threatened. Her head ruled any discussion concerning Lewis, but with Simon her heart would be involved. 'I was very down, very subdued,' she said carefully. 'There was a long period after Simon died when I felt . . . numb. Where I was, what I did, or who I was with scarcely mattered. Lewis and I had the tea, and my father arrived. In his presence Lewis asked if I'd care to join him for dinner. I must confess I was all set to refuse, but—but I saw the look on Daddy's face.'

'He didn't want you to offend the boss?'

'No. I allowed myself to be swayed.' Neille

decided to be pert. She had successfully avoided talking about Simon and now if she gave him the facts about Lewis in the form of an anecdote, maybe he'd treat them as such. Whatever happened, Jack must not be allowed to pry. 'Dinner proved to be both painless and expensive. We went to the Dorchester. Lewis talked about the wonders he was performing at Mitchells', and I obliged by contributing the odd murmur. Which suited me fine.'

Jack was watching her closely. 'I presume he commiserated over Simon's death?'

'Good heavens, no. And thank goodness.' She gave a peal of laughter. 'I couldn't have borne it if he had. Lewis was very . . . tactful.'

'You surprise me.' The comment was dry. 'From what I've heard tact isn't one of his attributes. Could it simply have been he wasn't interested? Sorry.' He held up a hand. 'Maybe *I'm* not being tactful.' They had reached the fifth *arrondissement*, and Jack leaned forward to direct the taxi driver. 'So that was the start of a beautiful friendship?' he said, sitting back. 'I presume?'

'You presume right,' Neille agreed airily. 'Though due to Lewis frequently being away on business it's a spasmodic friendship. He calls me— oh, roughly once a fortnight.'

'But you always say yes?'

'Why not?'

Jack gave her a level look. 'Shouldn't it be "why"? I thought we'd established you and Lewis aren't exactly on the same wavelength?'

'You might have established it, I haven't,' she protested, horribly aware of being shuffled into a corner. 'I agree he's a bit . . . pedestrian, but he's not all bad.'

'I didn't say he was bad. I just said——'

'We're not lovers,' Neille announced, not quite knowing why.

'I know that. Give me credit for some intelligence.' A tightening of his jaw indicated Jack was running out of patience. 'I'd just like you to explain why you continue to see him. He may be your father's boss, but that doesn't mean you're bound to him with hoops of steel. What the hell does Mitchell have to offer?'

She squirmed. 'You wouldn't understand.'

'Try me.'

'Eh, bien!' cried the taxi driver.

They had arrived at the hotel.

Neille knew she had had a close escape. She charged out of the taxi and into the lobby in double quick time. Spouting excuses about needing her sleep quota, she bade him a fast farewell, only to be disconcerted when he agreed he was also ready for bed. In the lift she refused to meet his eyes, terrified a glance might spark off his questions again, but Jack remained silent. A mumbled 'Good night,' in the corridor, and Neille achieved her goal—the solitude of her bedroom. She needed to put space between them, needed time in which to think. Had she revealed too much about her relationship with Lewis, or too little? Jack wouldn't report back, she trusted him on that, so maybe she could have afforded to have thrown more light on the odd coupling? Or maybe not. But leaving Jack dissatisfied could prove unwise.

With a troubled sigh, she began to undress. The clarinettist was well into his evening recital. If he ran true to form he would stop in a few minutes, but for now each note sounded crystal clear. Jack's movements through the wall were also crystal clear. Like her, he was undressing. Neille's movements speeded up. She didn't want to hear him, didn't want her traitorous senses going with him every step of the way. Was his chest hairy? How big was that scar on his shoulder? Did he sleep in the nude? She ripped off her clothes down to her black silk teddy, and sped into the bathroom to embark on a vigorous cleaning of her teeth. While the brush was in action she could not hear him; when she finished she could. His bed springs had twanged. Was he sitting down to remove his shoes, or lying there without a stitch on?

Neille was sorting out her clothes, determinedly paying no attention to the noises from next door, when a movement caught her eye. Hadn't the knob on the door which connected her room with room 41 twitched? Standing still, she waited. Yes, very slowly it was being turned back and forth. Because she had never heard sounds, she had automatically presumed the room to be un-occupied, but someone was in there now. A someone who seemed inordinately interested in the connecting door.

Her first thought was to knock on Jack's wall and demand he come round, but ... He would consider she was panicking again, or maybe jump to the conclusion she was pursuing him on a made up pretext. She would manage without him. The door was locked. It must be. There was no cause for alarm. The knob had stilled, so whoever stood on the other side was not about to burst in. Neille took stock. There seemed no immediate danger, but although she did not fear an assassin it would be difficult to sleep easily without the reassurance that her room was secure. The solution was to indulge in a spot of knob turning herself.

Tiptoeing over, she stretched out cautious fingers and eased the knob anti-clockwise. As the door was hinged to open into her room, she tugged. Nothing happened. Neille had relaxed when, without thinking, she gave a turn and tug in the other direction. The door gave way, swung open. With a gasp of surprise she fell back. Room 41 was in darkness. She could see nothing, no one, but she could smell peppermint.

CHAPTER SEVEN

THE porter must be on the prowl, she reasoned.
Neille was peering into the gloom, attempting to
discern a shape, when suddenly a hand shot out
from room 41, grabbed the knob and slammed
shut the door. A lock clicked and then—silence.
Looking at the closed door, she gave a startled
laugh. What did she do now? Report him, go
round to confront him, or what? Maybe it would
be wise to tell Jack what had happened? He was the
expert and he would know the best action to take.

She stepped out into the corridor and knocked
at his door. A glance along to room 41 showed no
movement. Presumably the porter was still inside?

'Jack,' she hissed. 'Can I speak to you?'

No reply. Where was he? Surely she would have
heard if he'd gone out? 'Jack!' She knocked again.
The porter, with his roving eyes, had looked a
nasty piece of work and Jack's declaration about
'How can any of us know what a twisted mind will
decide?' suddenly echoed. The porter might not
have a twisted mind, but he had been cornered and
might well retaliate. She did not intend to panic,
but all the same she cast a fearful glance at the
door of room 41. Was he ready to leap out at any
minute? 'Jack!' She pounded a fist. He couldn't be
asleep, could he? Her eyes flew back along the
corridor. What did the porter intend to do? 'Jack!
Please!'

Her fist hit empty air and Neille catapulted

forward, knocking Jack off balance. Instinctively he grabbed hold and took her with him as he buckled at the knees and collapsed back on to the bed.

'Not again,' he groaned, gasping as she lay spread-eagled on top of him. 'What's happened this time? You've found a mass murderer on the window-sill, or has Count Dracula dropped in for a quick bite?'

'No, it's the porter. He's snooping around in room 41. Oh Jack, I had an awful shock. I opened the connecting door and——'

'*You* opened it? Why?'

'Well, the handle turned and—and——' Neille broke off as an overwhelming need for comfort took precedence. Maybe she hadn't been terrified, but she had been a little bit scared. She nestled closer. His skin felt slightly damp. He smelled of soap, clean and male. His chest *was* hairy, covered in whorls of gleaming black hair. She rubbed her cheek against it and when he moved beneath her, she sighed. She was safe now. 'Oh Jack,' she murmured. 'Oh Jack!' The second time it was an exclamation, sharp and surprised. 'You're naked.'

'I thought you'd never notice,' he drawled, as Neille scrambled from him, a whirl of confusion with pink cheeks and tumbled hair.

Where did she look? What did she do? So many times she had seen Simon naked—first in the days when lovemaking had been all, and later when she had taken pity on his stupors and undressed him and put him to bed—but Jack was not Simon. Simon had been as beautiful as an alabaster statue, but never aggressively male. Jack was male. And aggressive. And aroused.

'I presume the porter wasn't naked when you paid him a call?' he asked, reaching for his jeans. He slid into them and stood up. 'I'd better go careful with my zip,' he remarked laconically.

'Yes. No.' Neille, her heart beating like a drum and her breath hard won, was unable to share this controlled amusement. 'No, the porter wasn't naked. Were you under the shower?'

'Just stepped in. I think maybe I'd better get back under and turn it to cold?' he suggested.

'Yes.' She twisted her fingers.

'Would you care to explain what you've been up to this time?' Jack asked, courteous as a duke from days of old.

'Yes.' Neille took a steadying breath. 'As I was getting ready for bed I noticed that someone appeared to be testing the knob on the connecting door,' she said, determined not to ramble. 'When the knob stopped turning, I decided to test it, too. To make certain the door was locked. I turned it one way and—zilch. But when I turned it the other way, the door came open.'

'And the porter was stood there?'

'No,' she confessed, 'but there was a strong smell of peppermints. And then, seconds later, an arm shot out and closed the door.' She glanced to check how she was doing, and saw from his frown that he was taking her seriously. 'As far as I know, no one's come out of room 41 since.'

'I'd better investigate,' Jack said, pulling a sweater on over his head.

'Shall I come, too?'

He grinned, his eyes moving down to remind her how she was wearing her teddy, a flimsy garment cut high on the thigh and low on the bosom.

'You'd better stay here. It'll be kinder on the blood pressure—mine. Keep the door shut and don't open it to anyone but me.'

The tinge of cops and robbers in his instruction proved contagious.

'Shouldn't we have a password?' Neille suggested.

He pushed his feet into his sneakers. 'How about "bodycheck"?'

'What does that mean?'

'It's an ice hockey term which describes one player's deliberate obstruction of another.' The creases at the corners of his mouth deepened. 'A rough assessment of your attitude towards me over the past weeks,' he declared, and was gone.

Neille sat on the bed and waited. She couldn't decide whether she wanted him to trap the porter or not. Proof she hadn't been letting her imagination run away with her would be agreeable, and yet . . . Alarm caused shivers. She remembered the porter's mean eyes. Should she follow in case there was a fight? Competent as Jack was, he had no immunity against a blade between the ribs. Having half risen, she sank down. She must stay put. Stop these disturbing flights of fantasy. Jack had given orders and he was in charge. Five minutes agonised into ten. Why hadn't he come? The porter had looked weedy, he wouldn't be difficult to overpower. But suppose the man in room 41 had not been the porter?

'Bodycheck,' recited a burnt-toast voice.

'What happened? Are you all right? Whatever took you so long?' As she sprang to let him in, so her hands spread themselves across his chest. He was tall and dark, and so very, very lovely that she was tempted to cry. Having reassured herself there were no knives sticking out of him, no blood stains, Neille brought her arms down to her sides. 'Did you find the porter in room 41?' she enquired, ultra sensible.

'I did, which means I owe you an apology.' Jack grinned. 'When you burst in and flattened me I must admit I had reservations, but I was wrong. Just now, as I left you, I——'

'Just now?' she objected. 'That was centuries ago.'

His grin widened. 'Centuries ago, as I went along the corridor, our mint-sucking friend stuck his head out of room 41, then popped it back in. Thanks to luck and one massive leap, I managed to get my foot in the door. After a spell of me push-you push, he decided to give in gracefully. Which meant I hurtled into the room *un*gracefully, Nellie the Elephant style.'

'Thank you!'

'Think nothing of it.' As if suddenly exhausted, Jack dropped down on to the bed. He caught hold of her hand and pulled her to sit beside him. 'The porter conveyed he was more than willing to come quietly, unlike some people who go around yelling blue murder. Don't hurt me,' he begged, when she made as if to dig him in the ribs. 'I escorted him down to reception where I spoke to the manager. Fortunately his English is good, so I was able to explain what had happened. The manager proceeded to go berserk, the porter broke down in tears and——'

Her face fell. 'He didn't? Oh, that's dreadful.'

'Don't you dare start feeling sorry for him,' Jack rebuked. 'Apparently he has a penchant for spying on young ladies, so he's no member of the League of Decency. He wasn't attempting to enter your room, just intending to peep through the keyhole. He'd been using the knob to steady himself as he crouched down and somehow disturbed the locking device. When you moved close—doubtless making all his fantasies come true,' Jack added drily, 'he backed off. Next moment you'd opened the door. He heard the racket when you came round to my room, but as he didn't know whether or not you'd realised who it was, he decided to sit tight. He was on the point of sneaking off when I cornered him.'

'I never even knew there was a keyhole,' Neille said, digesting the information. 'He can't have seen much.'

'No?' The word had a husky quality. Jack's gaze had dropped from her face to where a pulse beat in the hollow at the base of her throat. His eyes moved lower to the breasts which swelled, firm and satiny, from their nest of black lace. He tore his look upwards. 'No, I don't suppose he did,' he agreed, very matter-of-fact. 'But as this was the second time he'd been caught in the act, the manager asked if we wanted to press charges.'

'You didn't?' she burst out.

He shook his head. 'In the same breath he told me about the porter's ailing wife and five kids, so I didn't have the heart. What I did do was demand he be removed from the premises.'

'Thanks.' Satisfied with the outcome, Neille gave him a teasing glance. 'For a tyrant from the SAS you're one heck of a pushover.'

'And how about you?' He placed his hands on her shoulders and steered her firmly backwards until she lay flat on the bed, with him sitting over her. 'You might have a big mouth and be a whizz at grievous bodily harm, Nellie Trenchard, but deep down I suspect you're a pushover, too.'

'Who's got a big mouth?' she enquired, gazing up into his eyes.

'You.' He raised a finger and slowly, tantalisingly outlined her lips. 'And it's beautiful and I want to kiss it.'

Neille could feel electricity in the air, sense the throb of his heart beating in unison with hers. The world had stopped turning. They were alone together, in Paris. His fingers were moving over her face, caressing her cheek, marvelling at the smoothness of her skin, brushing wisps of copper-gold from her brow.

'Hello,' Jack whispered.

'Hello.'

Something wonderful was happening. They were meeting for the first time as lovers. Caught in the eye of an emotional hurricane, there was a stillness, a waiting, a tension. It was a crucial moment which Neille wanted to savour. She wanted to be able to say, 'That was the moment when we fell in love,' and yet also she badly wanted what came next. She wanted his kiss, to feel his hands on her body, to know the thrust and energy of his maleness. He would be a powerful lover, uninhibited and complete. She wanted all of that, all of him.

'We mustn't,' he said, answering her unspoken plea. He pushed himself upright. 'Not yet. It isn't ethical.'

'You've kissed me before,' she murmured, running her fingertips slowly down his arm.

'Yes, and that wasn't ethical either.' Jack frowned. 'But if I kiss you now it won't stop there, we both know that.' He rubbed his forehead in a gesture of frustration. 'I knew I should've arranged for Derek to accompany you to Paris. It was obvious we'd be isolated, alone together, and I thought I could handle it. But even before the damned plane took off I knew I'd made a mistake.'

'Did you?'

'Why else do you think I was keyed up? You were flirting, fluttering those long luscious lashes of yours, and all I could think about was——' Jack raked his hair with a single sweep of his hand. 'And when I slapped your backside—God! Things turned upside down and inside out. It was supposed to be a punishment for you, but instead it was sheer torture for me. How near I was to rolling you over and embedding myself in you. He flung her a fierce look. 'Like now.'

A smile played on her lips. 'Then kiss me.'

'Don't try seduction,' he warned, but it sounded like a plea.

Neille's smile widened. 'Aren't you the man who threatened to move in?'

He nodded grimly. 'And you don't need to have majored in psychiatry to analyse that as wish fulfilment, pure and simple. But I'm not moving in because I'm not changing my principles. I don't mix business with pleasure.' Rising to his feet, Jack began to pace back and forth beside the bed like a wild animal in a very small cage. 'Watching you parading around today half naked has been hell. I've been in a constant state of arousal. Neille,' his voice cracked, 'I've never felt as strongly about anyone as I feel about you. Half the time I could belt you because you're so damned sassy, the other half I'm obsessed with wanting to rip off your clothes and make love so hard and so bloody long that you're begging me for mercy.'

'Begging you to stop?' Her mood had changed. She was no longer playing the temptress. The time for playing had gone. Her love for Jack was real and serious. 'But I'm begging you to start,' she said, with no thought other than what they both wanted.

'We mustn't.' Did she know how beautiful she looked, he wondered. Lying there with her copper-gold hair dishevelled across the pillow? The black silk she wore clung to her body like a second skin. A thin strap hung off one shoulder. If he tugged that strap lower a breast would be freed, a full round breast. Already its point was pushing wantonly upwards, as her breast would push into his palm. Her skin would be warm and faintly scented, soft to his lips. He wanted to kiss her mouth, her breasts, all of her. Wanted to make a sensuous journey around her body, caressing and probing until she cried out and clung, nails gouging his flesh as he penetrated her. Jack closed his eyes. 'No,' he said, his voice harsh. 'We mustn't. It isn't fair to Lewis.'

Neille pushed herself up on to one elbow. 'But Lewis and I are . . . nothing. I don't love him and he doesn't love me. Oh, he might think he does, but he's never seen me as a real person. All I am to him is a pretty doll, one he hopes will charm his business associates and add a touch of glamour to his life.'

The grey eyes narrowed. 'Then he's asked you to marry him?'

'Not yet, though he's dropped hints. Which I've ignored,' she stressed.

Jack stopped pacing. 'I thought you reckoned your friendship was spasmodic? Sounds a darned sight more if Lewis is working up to a proposal.'

'Look, as far as I'm concerned, it's not even a friendship.'

'Yet after two years you have regular dates?'

'*Spasmodic* dates, which don't mean anything to me.'

He heaved a sigh. 'OK.'

'What you and I do together isn't going to harm Lewis,' Neille coaxed, relieved to see her statement had been accepted.

'But it'd harm me, my opinion of myself. No matter how precarious this relationship of yours is, I'm employed by the guy right now and he trusts me. He deserves my honesty. No way am I making love to you behind his back. I don't go in for deception.' His blood was cooling and Jack could be businesslike. 'Tonight we'll remain apart, but first thing tomorrow I'll put in a call to Australia and explain what's happened.'

'You mustn't do that!' she exclaimed, suddenly stricken.

'Don't worry, I'll be the soul of diplomacy.' Two steadying hands covered her shoulders and Jack smiled down. 'Even if he's hostile at first— and who can blame him?—he'll come round, the same as anyone else. He's not the first guy to be asked to step aside. Lewis has to accept——' He located the right word. '—kismet. He won't be thrilled when he hears what's happened, but it's not as though we've committed any crime. The situation's awkward, that's all.' Jack was becoming more businesslike by the minute. 'I'll arrange not to bill him for my services; that'll make me feel better even if it does nothing for him. And if his reaction is to order Rea Safeguards off his premises——' He shrugged 'Perhaps that's for the best.'

Neille chewed at her lip. 'I don't want you to tell Lewis anything.'

'Why not? You mean you'd rather break the news yourself? You'll ring him tomorrow?'

'No. Not tomorrow.'

'Then when? I feel it's important we be totally honest about this.' Jack waited, but she said nothing. 'You'd prefer to delay things and tell him to his face next week?' he hazarded. She remained mute. 'You do agree we can't cheat, that the only way is to be frank?'

'I suppose so,' she mumbled.

'Why the reluctance?' Jack caught hold of her chin, tilting her head until she was forced to meet his eyes. 'Why are you holding back?' A muscle clenched in his jaw. 'Or am I on the wrong track altogether? Maybe I'm deluding myself again? Maybe because I've fallen for you, I'm just imagining you've fallen for me?'

'I have!' she cried. 'I think you're wonderful, but——' Her gaze skidded away from the grey eyes which seemed to be whipping at her soul like the winter wind. Neille felt chilled through and through. Everything was moving too fast. If she started to explain why a confrontation with Lewis must be avoided at all costs, she would have to explain the whole story and that would involve . . .

'But what?' he demanded, his fingers tightening like a clamp. 'But wonderful as I am, I was only supposed to enter your bed for one night or maybe two, it that it? And why make ripples over something as insignificant as Parisian frolics? My God! I should have taken more notice of what was written in those gossip columns.' He snatched his hand from her jaw. ' "Game for anything" was one phrase I seem to remember. And that just about sums you up.'

'That's not true! It's just that—that my dealings with Lewis are at a delicate stage,' Neille said unsteadily. 'Now is not the right time for——'

'Yeah!' He cut her short. 'I can imagine. An educated guess says you're on pins waiting for those hints to turn into a definite proposal, one you *won't* be ignoring. Do you reckon it could be timed for his glorious homecoming?'

'Yes, as a matter of fact, I do, but—but——' She was conscious of flailing around. 'But I don't love him and——'

'What does loving matter when you're being handed riches on a plate?' Jack sneered. 'Lewis might be a crashing bore, but you can't escape the fact that he's loaded.'

'I don't care about his money.'

'Then what do you care about?' he asked coldly.

'You!'

He folded his arms and glared. 'So ring Lewis and tell him.'

'It's not that simple,' Neille muttered.

'Nothing ever is.' He was shooting out words like poisoned darts. 'But if you wanted a little excitement on the side while you waited for Mr Mitchell to pop the question, you came to the wrong man. A few years ago I regret to say I'd probably have obliged, but not now. The prospect

of a one night stand or some furtive affair leaves
me cold.' In a single stride he was at the door,
flinging it wide. 'Which means I'd be grateful if
you'd get out of my room and stay out—
permanently.'

'But Jack——' she protested.

'*Out.*'

CHAPTER EIGHT

RESERVES of acting skills needed to be dredged up in order for Neille to get through the next day. As someone who had previously turned a disparaging eye on females who whined and whimpered over broken love affairs, her instinct was to whine and whimper herself. There had been hard times in plenty with Simon, but her feelings for Jack were completely different. Simon had needed *her*, but *she* needed Jack. And now she had been trapped into alienating him. He might have journeyed with her to André's studio for the final session, and eaten meals alongside, but his presence was purely physical. Keeping conversation to a bare minimum, he refused to share whatever was going on inside his head. Not that you needed to be clairvoyant to guess the gist. In Jack's view she was the good-time girl whom the gossip columns had depicted, and he should have known better than to have been duped.

But once he heard the reasons why she could not afford to upset Lewis ahead of time, wouldn't he understand and relent? A week, just seven more days, and hopefully she would be able to give Jack a full explanation. Yet maybe a week would be too late? Neille's stomach churned. His love—it had been love, hadn't it?—was a new and fragile emotion which required cosseting, not placing on a shelf in cold storage. In a week his love might freeze to death!

Several times she came perilously close to spilling out the story, but loyalty had her rejecting the impulse. It wasn't just *her* story. The long-ago lapse which allowed Lewis his exclusive leverage over her had remained a closely guarded secret, and before she uttered a single word she was obliged to ask her father's permission. And asking premature permission was impossible. Approaching him would require certain revelations—her love for Jack, her lack of love for Lewis, and how she was currently involved in a high-wire act. At such revelations, her father would panic. The dread he had carried around for twenty years would rise again, like a spectre. She could not be so cruel as to subject him to that. So she must wait seven long days, after which, with luck, Lewis would make a voluntary exit from her life.

Saturday brought no sign of a thaw. In near silence they breakfasted, motored to Charles de Gaulle Airport, and caught the London flight. On the plane Neille brought out her blood-and-guts thriller, but received no jokey observation this time. Head down, she turned the pages at what were intended to be convincing intervals, but none of the words made sense. It was a relief when they landed and she could find solace in the activities of disembarking and collecting luggage, but in the taxi the strained silence resumed. They sat like strangers, studying the scenery through opposite windows. They scanned the countryside, the outskirts of London, and finally the suburbs.

'This is goodbye.' Jack poked out a hand as they turned the corner into her road. 'I'll drop you off and continue in the taxi to my place.'

Neille gazed at him. 'You aren't supposed to leave until tomorrow.'

'One night isn't going to make any difference,' he replied, abandoning his attempt at a formal farewell. 'I want to get home and unpack, visit the launderette, buy in food. By clearing the domestic side today, I can devote tomorrow to the office.'

'Tomorrow's Sunday.'

Despite his withdrawal, that he would wish to cut loose ahead of time had never crossed her mind, and now she felt bereft. It might only be one night—with him sleeping in the spare room and her along the landing—but at least he would be near. And while he was near she could cling to the hope, albeit a gossamer one, that his attitude might soften.

'Clever girl. And Sunday means I'll be in the office alone and free from the telephone. There's paperwork a mile high waiting for me, so tomorrow presents the perfect opportunity for tackling it. Next house,' he instructed the taxi driver, and when they stopped he reached across to open the door. 'Go along. I'll bring your case.' He joined her on the front step, holding out his hand a second time. 'Goodbye.'

'Shouldn't you check to see there aren't any mafiosi hiding under my bed?' Neille asked, pretending not to notice the gesture. Goodbye was too final, something to be avoided at all costs.

'Mafiosi?' She was allowed a glimpse of the Jack Rea grin which had the impudent creases at the corners of his mouth deepening seductively. 'Wasn't the Yellow Peril designated as Public Enemy Number One?'

'Someone *did* send those threats.'

'The taxi's waiting.'

'I'm going to ask around, make enquiries.'

His sigh was impatient. 'Nailing someone at this stage would be academic.'

'No, it would be justice. And that's apart from the satisfaction there'd be of knowing who was responsible. I don't like loose ends.' She saw he had lifted a hand to the taxi driver, indicating he'd be there. 'Jack, you can't be on guard against an assassin for a month and not even be *interested.*'

'I can. This month, for all its——' He hesitated. '—ramifications, was only a job, one of many I've undertaken over the years. Now it's done, and my only thought is to take the money and run.'

'You're a beast,' Neille ground out. She hated his coolness, his indifference, his insistence on leaving. And she hated being relegated to a mercenary consideration.

He smiled. 'I prefer pachyderm.' His smile disappeared. 'Sunbeam, it's best if we make a clean break, OK? You and I just aren't meant to be. If I should see you coming towards me in future I'll hide round a corner, and I'd appreciate it if you'd do the same.' He strode back to the taxi where he lifted a hand in a half salute. 'Goodbye.'

Neille sucked the end of her pen. 'Think hard. Who else could've gained access to the in-tray apart from——' She checked her notepad. '—Lewis's secretary, the mail clerk, any of the directors, your assistant and you?'

Mr Trenchard sighed. His daughter's detective work had begun hours earlier, immediately on her return from France. All afternoon she had been coming up with first one theory, then another.

Throughout dinner her questions about the day-to-day functioning of Mitchells' head office had come thick and fast and now, when he had been hoping to relax and watch television, she was determinedly making lists.

'The cleaners,' he said with reluctance, 'and all the people who work in the general office. Lewis's secretary acts as a buffer, but it wouldn't have been impossible for someone to sneak in.'

'How many work in the general office?'

'Ten.' He did a mental recount. 'Change that to twelve. Neille, the police have already made enquiries. I don't see that——'

'Half-hearted enquiries,' she declared. 'Jack told me they regarded the threats as very small potatoes, so it follows that all they'd do was go through the motions. And they aren't privy to inside information, like you.'

'What inside information?'

'Inter-company gossip, the comings and goings.' She adjusted her grip on her pen. 'Now, can you remember whether Lewis had any outside visitors on the day prior to discovery of the note?'

'No, I can't, though doubtless somebody would have called. He's a very busy fellow. But I don't keep a check,' Mr Trenchard protested. 'My office is way down the corridor.'

'Yet presumably some of the people who visit him will visit you at the same time?' Neille persisted.

'Well, yes.'

'And you keep a note of your visitors in your desk diary?'

'Well, yes.'

'And you're in the habit of bringing your diary

home?' He nodded. 'I'll get it.' Seconds later, it was open across her knees. 'There was an official from the VAT office—we can discount him—and Andrew Rice!' she said in surprise. 'Whatever did he want?'

Neille knew the young man personally. The son of Walter Rice, a crusty old character who had held the post of Chief Accountant at Mitchells' before her father, Andrew had taken her out a few times shortly after Simon's death. He had been a pleasant enough escort, if overly keen on promoting a man-about-town image. She well remembered how he had doused himself with sufficient cologne to asphyxiate an army. Their friendship had ended when a titled young lady had fallen into his sights. Andrew was nothing if not a social climber. Neille hadn't minded, indeed she hadn't been in a fit state to mind about anything much at the time, but she had been thrown over with mind-boggling speed.

'Andrew had other business in the building, but I can only presume it was courtesy which prompted him to call on me. He passed on the latest news about Walter,' Mr Trenchard explained. 'Poor blighter's been in and out of hospital all year with chest trouble.'

'I thought you and Walter Rice didn't get on too well?' she queried, for her father had always regarded the old man as something of an ogre.

'Walter never got on with anybody. His idea of comradeship was to give it you in the neck. But Andrew's a jovial fellow. I expect he likes to keep the social niceties alive.' Mr Trenchard gazed longingly at the television. 'You needn't put his name down on your list of suspects. He wouldn't go within miles of Lewis's office, fear of Walter would keep him away. The old man'd throw a fit if he suspected his son of fraternising with the enemy. He never could abide Lewis, always called him the whippersnapper behind his back. No, Andrew would've steered well clear. He's as much in awe of his father as anybody.'

'No Andrew.' Neille returned to her list. 'Can you give me the names of the people who inhabit the general office?'

'Now?' Her father groaned.

She took pity. 'Tomorrow will do,' she grinned, and shut her notepad.

'Thank heavens for that.' He crossed the living room to press the appointed button. 'Make it tomorrow afternoon,' he said, as the screen filled with colour. 'Mrs Dawson discovered a pocket calculator under the chest of drawers in the spare room; it obviously belongs to Jack. I thought I'd pop round to his office in the morning and hand it over.'

'I'll go,' Neille offered, a shade too quickly.

Rea Safeguards's offices were tucked away at the rear of a warehouse in an obscure little street in central London. She parked her father's saloon alongside a somewhat battered station wagon and walked across the yard. Neille actually attempted a saunter, in case Jack happened to be looking out, but a furtive glance at the building revealed no sign of life. For that she was grateful. Having set off in confident mood, the closer she came to confronting him, the more the conviction grew that she'd have done better to have stayed home. His definition of her visit would be that she was chasing him and she wasn't—was she? She had more pride than to resort to such tactics—didn't she? What she was suffering were merely withdrawal symptoms, a kind of after-the-party down. Grief, no matter who you'd been shackled to, after a month you'd miss them—wouldn't you?

Her fingers closed around the slim black calculator. She would simply post the instrument through the letter box and beat a hasty retreat. Neille sped over the final yards and thrust the calculator forward, but the door which incorporated the brass-edged slit for which she had been aiming, fell away. Her arm followed, and she was bending as a tall figure in tan cords and white sweater was revealed on the threshold. She stood up straight.

'You were waiting behind the door!'

'Naturally. I'm in security, remember? I keep my eyes and ears open, so when a car drives into my yard I sit up and take notice. I recognised the Rover as your father's.'

Beneath his grey gaze, she had become a trifle short of breath. 'Um, you left this,' she said, shoving the calculator at him.

'Thanks.'

'My pleasure.'

'Is that it?' asked Jack, as she swivelled. He rested a shoulder against the door frame. 'Where's my daily dose of abuse? Come on in and have a coffee, there're some questions I'd like to ask.'

Neille hesitated, surprised to hear he was prepared to talk. What had happened to them making a clean break? To him hiding round corners? Her spirits lifted. An invitation to coffee sounded encouraging, though she hoped his

questions didn't mean he intended to interrogate
her about Lewis again. Maybe not. Maybe they
were just an excuse to offer the hand of friendship.
Maybe he regretted his heated accusations of the
other evening and wanted to apologise?

Accepting with what was intended to be blithe
indifference, she followed him down a passageway
into a small bright office painted in toffee and
white. It was a bit spartan, but the wooden floor
was spotless. Filing cabinets lined one wall, while
another was hung with a map of the British Isles.
The paperwork which demanded his attention was
stacked in neat piles on a scrubbed pine desk.

Jack indicated she was to be seated, then
frowned. 'What on earth are you wearing?' he
asked, stripping her down and reassembling her in
a second. 'Cast-offs from a Mongolian peasant?
What is it, one size fits all?'

'This is fashion!' she retorted indignantly,
glancing down at the panels of pale fur which had
been tossed over a suede tabard, which in turn
covered leather gaucho pants. Cinnamon-brown
boots, wrinkled at the ankles, completed the outfit.
It was a November morning with a bite in the air,
and Neille believed herself appropriately dressed.

Jack walked over to a table which did duty as
kitchen, and plugged in an electric kettle. 'If that's
standard gear for sleuthing I'd better tip Brian the
wink. Poor guy's been slumming it in blue serge, but
maybe it's time he skinned himself a few skunks.
You take coffee with milk and one sugar. Right?'

'Right. Who says I'm sleuthing?' Neille
demanded, wishing she could fathom his mood.
He wasn't hostile, yet equally he did not appear to
be going all out to make amends.

'When I departed yesterday weren't you attempting to con me into believing no stone would remain unturned in your search for our old friend, the assassin?' he countered, spooning instant coffee into two mugs.

'It wasn't a con.' Neille refused to admit, even to herself, that the idea had been originally voiced as a ploy to detain him a few moments longer. 'I've already made some enquiries.'

'And what pertinent clues have resulted?' he challenged.

'Um.' She blinked. 'Um—that Andrew Rice visited Mitchells' offices the day before the note surfaced.'

Jack filled the mugs with boiling water. 'Who's Andrew Rice?' She told him. 'And how do you know he was there?' She told him that, too. 'And what was this other business which needed his attention in the building?'

There Neille came unstuck. 'I don't know,' she admitted, taking the mug he handed her.

'What line's this Rice guy in?'

'He's a partner in a snooty art gallery in Mayfair. It specialises in imported icons, that kind of thing.'

Jack's nose twitched. 'The perfect accessory for the Mongolian peasant, but hardly department store merchandise?'

'No,' she agreed, watching him sit in the chair behind the desk and stretch out his legs. Why *had* Andrew visited Mitchells'? she wondered. Hadn't his father left breathing fire and brimstone, and swearing never to set foot on the premises again, and wasn't Andrew the obsequious son? 'Maybe I should pay him a visit?' she said, thinking out loud.

'And say what? "You, Andrew Rice, are the assassin, and I, Neille Trenchard, claim my reward"?'

'Okay, Jackson Rea,' she retorted. 'What would you do?'

'Nothing. A fundamental rule in the security game is that, before you take aim and fire, you make very sure you're looking at the right target. Marching into someone's home and asking them to incriminate themselves could easily wind up with you being slung out on your ear.'

'Never!'

Jack gave an amused grunt. 'No, in your case I tend to agree. Chances are you'd flatten anyone who so much as waved an admonishing finger. But to be serious, you need much more to go on. And if you ever do have real suspicions, and not just something which has come straight off the top of your head,' he thrust, 'you must go to the police.' Jack drank a mouthful of coffee, then leant forward to frown at a folder which lay open on his desk. 'Now, question number one—was Simon Gates a drug addict?'

Neille gasped, jerking back as if he'd thrown his mug of hot coffee straight into her face. She had believed the past safely buried, six feet under, but here was Jack, ruthlessly and unexpectedly demanding exhumation. Her heart sank. Her blood ran cold. She had not been invited into his office to receive apologies. On the contrary. Having classed her as a money-grabbing minx, now he seemed intent on amassing further evidence against her! She knew enough about people's prejudices to know that if you associated with a drug user you were considered suspect yourself.

'I've been reading these press cuttings again,' he explained, calmly sorting out various pieces of paper. 'This time I read between the lines. Gates's behaviour meant he either had to be a screwball, or hyped up on coke or something stronger. And I doubt you'd associate with a screwball.'

'I've associated with *you*,' she shot back. Neille squared her shoulders. 'Does it state anywhere in those cuttings that Simon was on drugs?'

He sighed. 'You know the answer to that. No, not in black and white. But with a captain of industry for a father and a popular actress for a mother, money can't have been in short supply. Cash can buy——' Jack frowned. 'If not complete silence, at least a certain discretion.' His eyes had never left her face. 'So—was he a drug addict?'

'Yes!' She lashed the answer at him like a wounded animal. 'Yes, yes, he was! Happy now?'

'Question number two. The official version is that he died of a mystery illness, but did he commit suicide?'

Neille's head went down. Despite the covering of suede and fur, she shivered, racked with private pain. 'Does it matter?'

'Yes, it does,' Jack replied firmly.

'Why?' She tossed a rich strand of hair from her shoulder, meeting his look with burning blue eyes. There was a feeling of *déjà vu*. Once before he had asked a question, and once before she had met it point-blank by asking what she asked now. 'Why should it matter to you?'

'Shall we just say I'm interested in people, in what they do and why? Being a bodyguard can be an unenviable mix of tedium and tension, but if nothing else it provides ample opportunity for the study of human behaviour.'

The feeling of *déjà vu* persisted. This time Jack was using phrases like 'studying human behaviour' whereas last time he had mentioned 'compiling a dossier'. But weren't they part of the same syndrome—rank curiosity!

'As a self-taught psychiatrist you'd like to study Simon's case history?' Neille's tone was bitter.

'And yours.'

His cool was unnerving. Wasn't it enough to have classed her as shoddy goods without now wanting to poke around further? And to think, this was the man to whom she had been prepared to reveal her father's secret. She had imagined Jack to be—special. He wasn't special, he was one of a multitude who, under the guise of being 'interested in people', fed like vultures on the mistakes and misfortunes of others. He would set himself up as judge and jury, too. It had been done before. Neille's eyes hardened. If he wanted a juicy exposé, one for which the gutter press had offered thousands, she would provide a blow by blow account, in lurid detail. Jack had once spoken of climbing into the mind—well, catch, boyo! Here come the ropes, the cleats, a pick-axe.

'No, Simon didn't commit suicide; he died of an overdose. But, to you, that probably amounts to the same thing!'

'How did you meet?'

'Through my cousin, Paul. They were in the same house at school. Paul was a day boy, Simon boarded. When Simon was expelled—for *smoking pot*,' Neille said, with a virulent flourish, 'he came to stay with us.'

'Why?' Legs spread, Jack looked very laid back.

'Because there was nowhere else for him to go,' she blitzed, 'and Mooie took pity on him. She adopts waifs and strays, like me!' She shot him a glance to see his reaction, but he was sipping coffee. 'Simon's parents had been divorced a couple of years earlier, and as his real mother was off on a European tour and his stepmother habitually raised three cheers when he went out the door rather than in, Mooie offered a haven. Simon had got himself expelled weeks away from sitting his final exams, and she arranged for him to study at home, then return to sit the papers at school. In the event, he gained a place at university. You won't find a mention there,' she flashed, when Jack shuffled through the cuttings. 'Simon packed it in after a couple of terms. Three more years of study wasn't what he wanted.'

'What did he want?

'He didn't know.' Her chin lifted. 'But who does know at nineteen?'

'Wouldn't it be easier if you cut down on the aggro?' Jack suggested. 'I'm not holding a loaded gun at your head. Hell, I've made enough of a cock-up of my own life to hesitate before firing bullets.'

Lower lip thrust out, Neille regarded him warily. He had spoken with the voice of reason, but what did that conceal? Some of the reporters in her past had sounded reasonable, and the very next day had done a hatchet job.

'In next to no time Simon was knocking on my aunt's door again,' she continued, using a slightly less embattled tone, 'and she readopted him. His looks and charm were a formidable combination, and when he asked if he could stay for the summer, Mooie agreed. She was always ruffling his hair and telling him he looked like an angel. No one could have guessed he was destined to turn into a devil,' she added bleakly. She drew a breath, almost a sigh. Maintaining full tilt aggression had become wearisome now she had been sucked into telling her tale. 'In those days Simon was good-mannered and good fun. I'm sure he never used drugs in Sussex. If he had, Mooie would've slung him out, for all she had a soft spot. At first I was just . . . intrigued. Simon was so different from my cousins. They're sturdy types, brick walls emotionally, but he was vulnerable. He didn't wear his heart on his sleeve, it was more subtle than that, but you could sense a kind of inward cry for help. He was always so damned grateful for any kindness,' Neille added, with a sudden spark of anger. 'He found work on a nearby farm, and he and I began spending time together. We used to wander through the fields and talk and talk and talk. Nothing was held back. I suppose we were drawn together because neither of us had had what you'd call the regulation family. I mean, I know I was loved, but I wasn't Mooie's real child, was I?' She blinked. 'And Simon had never even been loved.'

'He was when you came along,' Jack pointed out softly.

'Yes.' Her throat felt hard. 'Yes. Though for a long time it was boy and girl stuff, completely innocent.'

'Where do his parents fit into this?' he asked, when she sat staring down at the mug in her hands.

'They supported him financially, period. As ambitious egotists, Mr and Mrs Gates did their own thing and to hell with everyone else, including their son. Simon had been brought up by a succession of nannies and au pairs. He'd never known a stable, loving family life.'

'And as a salve to their consciences, his parents provided sufficient cash for him to support a drug habit?'

'He was a pusher's delight.' Neille gave a laugh which sounded suspiciously like a sob. 'But that came later. Everything went fine that golden summer until his mother completed her tour and swooped down. She insisted Simon should move into her London flat. She bought him lots of new clothes, a car, and introduced him to the champagne set. Then she disappeared again. A little later I left Sussex and came to live with my father, so Simon and I took up where we'd left off. But in the city environment everything seemed ... faster. He insisted our love affair become the real thing.'

'Did you move in with him?'

'Grief, no. Despite a rapidly acquired gloss, beneath it I was gauche. And my father would've been horrified. Though I caused him enough heartache as it was,' she said regretfully.

Jack fingered the cuttings. 'These make you out as quite a girl for discos and all-night parties.'

'Initially, I was. I had no friends in London, so naturally I gravitated towards Simon's crowd. They were attention seekers—I suppose Simon was, too; smoking pot was a manifestation of that—and the idea was to project a high profile. At first I joined in. I kidded myself that acting up was the sophisticated way to behave.'

'You'd be eighteen, and adrift after being cut loose from your childhood ties?' Neille nodded. 'I imagine your father wasn't much of a disciplinarian?'

'If only he had been! But he watched on in despair while I went my own silly way.'

'Pity I wasn't around to administer a damned good spanking,' Jack remarked.

She gave a rueful smile. 'Where were you when I needed you?'

'Kicking over the traces myself, regrettably. So there you were, painting the town red with young Lochinvar?'

Neille nodded. 'That's how the gossip columns got wind of us. Simon had a taste for trendy places where a photographer's in perpetual attendance, and due to his parentage and looks he was a natural. As his companion, I also rated a line or two.'

He lifted a cutting. 'You remind me of those glamorous people in Martini ads.'

'It felt like that,' she confessed, 'until I came down to earth. Then I realised I didn't care for the people I was mixing with, and that there had to be more to life than laughing like a drain at rowdy parties. I began to back-pedal and tried to persuade Simon to do the same. He wasn't having any.' Neille heaved a sigh. 'That left me torn. I wanted to be with him, but not with his associates. I cut down on visiting "in" places, though the press never noticed. I was described as "party loving" when I'd stayed home at night for months. And Simon chugged along surrounded by sycophants.'

'Did he go out to work?'

'Off and on. His father fixed him up with a job as sales rep with one of his companies, but he never took it seriously. His lack of ambition used to drive me wild. Yet what impetus did he have when he was living the life of Reilly on handouts?'

Jack pushed the photograph back into the folder. 'Had the drug habit taken hold?'

She nodded. 'It was the usual thing, first cocaine for kicks, then the move to heroin and a multitude of other substances. I'd always been critical of those crazy enough to indulge, so for a full year or more he pretended he wasn't addicted, then——' Her eyes were stinging with tears. '——then there were needle marks on his arm. I did my best to get him to seek professional advice, to attend a drug dependence clinic, and he went along for a few times, but——' She raised and dropped her hands. '——he blew it. He always did. There were so many false hopes, so many broken promises. He was like a flame, burning himself up and scorching everyone else around him. The downs which followed his sprees left him moody, and impotent, and sometimes violent,' Neille remembered.

Jack straightened. 'Did Gates hit you?'

'No, he never laid a finger on me, though he punched other people. It was as a result of him punching a reporter that the gossip column write-ups became character assassinations. Get on the wrong side of the press, and they retaliate. I'd always been written up as a winky-pink girl, but overnight I became a tramp.' Neille looked him in the eye. 'Game for anything.'

Jack looked back steadily. 'I apologise for that. And you stuck with Gates to the end?'

'Who else did he have? Oh, I often told him it was over. That he needn't bother calling until he'd straightened himself out, but Simon only had to lift the phone and I rushed round.' The tears were stinging again. 'Your twenty-four-carat gold pushover.'

'That's what love does for you.'

The tenderness she heard in his voice almost made her sob out loud. She had never found anyone willing to listen, and though she accepted his interest as prurient, he did sound sympathetic. Her father had never sympathised, he simply preferred not to know, and Lewis had not even had the grace to acknowledge that Simon had ever walked this earth.

'There wasn't much love left at the end.' Neille gave a loud sniff. 'Love became pity. Having a rapport with a person who's either high as a kite or vomiting over the sink, is difficult.' She found a handkerchief and blew her nose, then she scoured him with a look. 'You might like to make a note in your dossier to the effect that the photograph of me swimming naked was actually taken when I was in the throes of trying to stop Simon from disgracing himself. Yet another occasion when he blew it.'

'Go on,' Jack prompted, when she stopped and glared.

'We were on holiday in Italy. I thought that if I could get him away from his cronies for a week or two, I'd be able to wean him off the drugs. Just shows how naïve I was,' she said, using a brittle voice. 'But the very first night I was awoken by the commissionaire knocking on my door. I couldn't understand him, but rapidly gathered it had

something to do with Simon causing a disturbance. I'd pulled on a robe to answer the door
and, because the man was so insistent that I hurry,
I set off with him down the staircase and out to
the fountains at the front of the hotel. There I
found Simon, fully dressed, wading around up to
his waist. He was stoned out of his mind. At
intervals around the pool were bronze fish
spouting water, and he was standing first under
one, then under another, singing at the top of
his voice. I begged him to get out and go to his
room, but he advised me to take a running
jump, or something similar.' Neille could not
prevent a small smile. 'Guests had begun to
gather, toffee-nosed and scandalised, and I grew
desperate. I tried to grab him, but couldn't get a
proper grip, and the commissionaire refused to
help because he didn't want his clothes wet, so I
climbed in. Simon thought that was great.'

'I can imagine. Communal bathtime.'

Her smile broaded. 'It was dreadful then, but
now I can see the comic aspect. Simon began to
undress, and as fast as he took something off, so I
tried to get it back on him. He kept falling over in
the water, standing up and sitting down, and in the
struggles my robe became untied. Simon realised it
before I did, and he gave one great whoop of joy
and ripped the robe clean off. I went down with a
splash!'

Jack picked out a cutting. 'And at that precise
moment someone in the crowd took a photograph.'
He grinned. 'Here you are, wearing an astonished
look and nothing else.'

'Yes, well.' The sight of his proof changed her
mood. Comic or not, that night had been

purgatory. Like the months which had followed.
Like Simon's death.

'And the press had a field day?'

She resented being nudged along. 'You've read
it all, you know their reaction,' she thrust, rising
from her chair. This interrogation must stop, she
needed to get away. 'As you've guessed, Simon's
father stepped in, terrified his son might be
labelled in public as a drug addict, and he did
manage to suppress an outright declaration. But
his dependency was an open secret. And now *you*
know that secret,' Neille said belligerently,
throwing daggers with her eyes.

Attack was vital. It held at bay tears which,
once again, were threatening to fall. She had given
Jack the truth, she would not give him anything
else. Neille Trenchard would never be so pathetic
or self-indulgent as to sob on the shoulder of an
interrogator. Flinging a fur panel across her chest,
she marched to the door. She had intended to
spear him to the spot with a challenging look, the
final gesture of defiance, but when she turned her
eyes were blurred. She rushed out into the
passageway. A dam had been breached, already
her cheeks were wet. Two long years of repressed
pain and hurt were flooding out. She needed to be
alone. To cry for Simon and herself.

'Sunbeam, wait,' she heard him call, but she
rushed blindly on.

CHAPTER NINE

THE dawning of Monday meant her life had returned to normal, or so Neille told herself. She went into the agency and, after reporting back on her Paris assignment, received details of the bookings and interviews which had been arranged for the week. Her days were jam-packed. Good. The less time available for dwelling on her relationships with both Jack and Lewis, the better. The first had already crumbled, the second soon would—given luck. But until Friday her 'good friend' needed to be kept at a distance. Neille made plans accordingly, and when the phone rang in the evening and a clipped voice announced that Lewis Mitchell had returned to home base, she was prepared.

'I hope you had a good trip,' she said pleasantly.

'Most rewarding.' He used her comment as a springboard from which to dive into a numbing résumé of what had been happening to him over the past month, and by the time he got around to asking, 'How's life been treating you?' Neille was glassy-eyed. She leapt to attention, only to discover Lewis had moved on to a lecture. 'I'm not one to point a finger, but I'd have appreciated some first-hand contact, instead of having to rely on Jack Rea's reports that you were fighting fit. However,' he sighed, relishing his martyrdom, 'I'm back, and neither of us have been bundled off by some maniac with an axe to grind.'

'All's well that ends well,' she agreed, and the prosaic comment sufficed. Lewis never required much participation, and especially not over the phone. Each call was conducted like a business meeting, with him in charge at the head of the table.

'True, true. Now, next on the agenda is us getting together.'

'I'm afraid I'm booked up tomorrow night,' Neille inserted on cue. 'The agency requested I attend an important perfume promotion, and there was no way I could wriggle out.' She crossed her fingers as she lied.

'Never worry,' he said, displaying unusual magnanimity. 'I'm tied up tomorrow myself. Actually, I'll be out of town until late Thursday. Staff from various branches appear to have ganged up, and the ringleaders need to be shown the errors of their ways.' He heaved the sigh of someone crawled over by unruly infants. 'You and I will get together on Friday,' he decreed. 'We'll make it a special occasion, so wear something long and pretty.'

Special occasion. Neille knew what that meant—his dreaded proposal. The jitters suddenly attacked. She was cutting everything very fine. Suppose the lingerie photographs didn't do the trick, what then? There was no way she could agree to marry the man. She *must* refuse him. But how could she turn him down without exciting hostility? Lewis's puffed-up opinion of himself guaranteed he would take offence—and seek revenge. The fingers gripping the receiver drained white. She wasn't the one who would stand in the firing line, her father made a natural target.

'I'll ring early evening Friday to finalise details,' Lewis continued, and made his clipped farewells.

Afterwards Neille stood, hands pressed to her cheeks, and sighed. Then her chin lifted. She would not be so defeatist as to spend each free minute between now and Friday wallowing in gloom. Not that there'd be many free minutes for her evenings, as well as her days, had been filled with painstaking care. But Lewis's absence now meant she was landed with the perfume shindig, a health shop opening and a cosmetic launch. Each promised to be dull. Should they be abandoned? On reflection, she decided to go along. The events would be a bulwark against her 'good friend' changing his mind and requesting an earlier meeting.

When the phone rang ten minutes later, she congratulated herself on her wisdom. This must be Lewis, already having second thoughts. Neille brushed off her excuses and stood them in line.

'Hello?' she said cautiously.

'Hi, it's Jack. Are you free tomorrow evening?'

Jack! Irritation mingled with dismay, yet interspliced was a hefty dose of excitement. Excitement? Only a dimwit would continue to be attracted by a man who made no bones about regarding the intimate details of her life purely as an exercise in human behaviour.

'Tomorrow?' she gasped, as if he had grabbed her by the throat.

'Yes. You see, after our talk I decided I wanted to know more about——'

He wanted to know more! He had further questions to ask! How cold-blooded and analytical and downright nosy could anyone be? Neille squeezed her eyes tight shut. Didn't he care that she had left his office shaking and shivering after facing up to her past? Her emotions heaved and bucked. Lewis displayed the sensitivity of a rhinoceros, but Jack was ten times worse.

'You can't,' she muttered. 'You can't see me tomorrow.' She snatched back her composure to speak coldly and clearly. 'I have an important engagement which I'm not in the least inclined to cancel. Good night.'

Sparing no expense, for the evening was tax deductible, the perfume company had booked a suite in a luxury hotel on Park Lane. Gold-edged invitations had been distributed like confetti, hundreds of give-away sample bottles containing two drops of their spectacular new fragrance laid on, and prayers offered up that more than three dozen stalwarts might deign to attend. By seven o'clock their staff were in place, smiles at the ready. By seven-thirty, the smiles had begun to droop. They revived at seven forty-five when a cluster of buyers wandered in, then sagged five minutes later when they departed.

At eight o'clock, Neille was walking up the hotel steps when she felt her arm being gripped from behind. She turned, then froze, frowning at her captor on the step below.

'If it isn't my favourite Mongolian,' grinned Jack, his eyes swooping up and down in swift appraisal. 'Funny, but on second inspection that outfit looks great.'

Irritably, she shook his hand away. He looked pretty great himself, camel coat over dark suit, but she had no intention of reacting to his undoubted sex appeal.

'Would you kindly stop hounding me?' she demanded. 'I'm busy. Didn't I make it clear I have a very important function to attend this evening?'

'You lied.'

'Did I?' Her eyes became glittering sapphires. 'Then let me tell you something. I'm getting very tired of——'

'You look terrific. Your creamy complexion against that fur—mmm.'

She cold-shouldered the compliment. 'See here, zonko, your little cross-eyed friend may have told you where to find me this evening, but she did you no favours because in coming here you've wasted your time.'

'Like you intend to waste yours, eating curled up canapés, drinking boxed wine, and all to the accompaniment of rhubarb-rhubarb conversation?'

'I'd rather do that than listen to you asking more of your damned questions!' she retorted, in fire-breathing style.

Jack re-established his grip. 'No questions. Answers.'

'About what?' she asked suspiciously, as he began propelling her down the steps towards his station wagon. Neille wished the doorman wasn't showing such an interest. If they hadn't been overlooked she would have given Jack a sharp kick on the shins, and marched off into the night. But such behaviour within the confines of an upmarket hotel seemed scarcely ladylike.

'About Andrew Rice and the threats.'

'You've been to see him?' she enquired, unable to keep from being intrigued.

Jack nodded. 'In view of your comments on

Sunday, I decided he was worth a visit.' He opened the passenger door. 'Hop in.'

'But you said——'

He walked to the other side of the car. 'I know what I said. Look, Neille, I'm parked on double yellow lines so you're going to have to make up your mind whether you're getting in or not.'

'Are we visiting the Rice household?'

'No, I'm taking you home. I did fix for us to visit young Mr Rice this evening, but he rang me an hour ago. Seems he got cold feet. The prospect of meeting one of the injured parties proved too embarrassing. He asked if I'd pass on the full facts, plus apologies.'

'Then he *is* involved in the threats?'

'He delivered them.'

Neille's brows lifted. Her suspicions had been embryo suspicions at best, expected to be stillborn, but here the young man's involvement was, alive and kicking.

'What's he got against Lewis?' she asked, climbing into the car.

'Nothing.' Jack accelerated away. 'The threats were contained in an envelope, which he believed contained a trade article praising Mitchells' chief competitor. That's what his father had told him when he gave instructions for the envelope to be tucked amongst papers in the in-tray. Walter also instructed Andrew that he was to sneak in between one and two when Lewis's secretary would be at lunch, and to make certain he wasn't observed. Being under his father's thumb, he agreed to act as messenger boy. Mind you, he did regard bringing the article to Lewis's attention as a bit of a jape. To paraphrase, he knew Mitchell's inflated opinion of himself and the way he runs his company, so the prospect of him throwing a tantrum was not displeasing.'

'I bet it was Andrew who threw the tantrum when he discovered he'd delivered a threatening letter!'

'But he didn't discover. His connection with Mitchells' is slight, so no news filtered through from there, and although he did come across a pencilled note last weekend which, when he showed it to me, I recognised as a facsimile, the penny didn't drop.'

'But if he'd read the threats surely he should have queried them with his father?'

'That would have been difficult.' Jack paused. 'Considering Walter Rice died ten days ago.'

'Daddy never said.'

'He didn't know until I broke the news this afternoon.' He flung her a sideways glance. 'Your father and I shared a very long and very interesting conversation. And it was he who informed me of your whereabouts, not Dee. Daddy never said that either, did he?' he mimicked, and grinned when he saw her lips had jammed together. 'Yes, not satisfied with one stool pigeon I've recruited a second—in family.'

'It was obvious from the start you hold nothing sacred,' Neille retaliated. She looked out through the windscreen. 'And you said you were taking me home, but this isn't the way.'

'Yes, it is. To *my* home. You needn't worry, I've told your father you'll be spending the evening with me and be perfectly safe.'

'Huh!' The trouble was, she did not know whether she wanted to be safe or not. 'So Andrew only realised what had happened when you arrived?'

'That's right. Bearing in mind the bad blood between his father and Lewis, he'd taken the pencil note to be wishful thinking, like sticking pins into a wax doll. He was quite perturbed when I informed him otherwise! Then he explained how his father had been so anti-Lewis that every single change made in the department stores was decried. The old man was particularly incensed when the sale of liquor was introduced, which seems to be the reference to old values being trampled underfoot.'

Neille frowned. 'Did Mr Rice ever intend to act on the threats?'

'That would've been impossible. He had such difficulty with his breathing that simply moving from one room to another wore him out. I spoke to Brian, Detective Inspector Gilchrist, this morning, and he verified that. He'd interviewed Walter, obviously when Andrew was at work, and remembered how frail the old man was. He'd eliminated him from police inquiries straight away.'

She sighed. 'So the only thing we still don't know is why that photograph accompanied the threats?'

'I think we do.' Jack turned into a tree-lined avenue. 'When I mentioned the photo it was the first Andrew knew of it and initially he was perplexed. Then, with a very red face, he confessed he might be to blame. It seems that when you and he had those few dates two years back, his father had been pleased, and——'

'But I only met him a couple of times, and on

each occasion he growled at me like an old bear,' Neille interrupted.

'Well, apparently he liked you, reckoned you had spunk.' Jack twitched his nose. 'And I confess I agree. However, Andrew met the Honourable Miss So-and-so, and—not to put too fine a point on it—dumped you. Because he knew there'd be hell to pay if his lack of chivalry was revealed, he told Walter *you'd* dumped *him*.' There was a pregnant pause. 'For Lewis. Which guaranteed you were flavour of the month.'

'And by including my photograph Mr Rice had a dig at me!'

'Seems like it,' he agreed, swinging the station wagon off the avenue and through an archway into a small courtyard. On three sides were mews houses, built of a stone which gleamed pale in the moonlight. There were balconies and flower boxes, and fir trees stood like sentries beside front doors. 'Andrew was apologetic, embarrassingly so.'

'He won't get into trouble, will he?'

'No, o lady of the soft heart, he won't.' Jack pulled to a halt beside a porch, and switched off the engine. 'Brian is to have a quiet word with Lewis to explain, and then the file'll be closed.'

'Good,' she said, as he helped her out. 'Does Andrew still go heavy on the cologne?'

'Heavy? My sinuses were cleared in thirty seconds.' He wobbled his head. 'When he was blabbering his apologies he had his arm around my shoulders, and the smell almost had me passing out. He kept saying how sorry he was it'd all happened—not that I am—and——'

'I beg your pardon?'

'I'm not.' Jack was searching in his trouser

pocket for the front door key. 'I'm not sorry it happened.'

'You're not sorry!' Neille could hardly believe her ears. How selfish could anyone be? Lifting an enraged finger, she jabbed it towards him. 'Well, I *am* sorry, zonko! In Paris I believed myself to be in danger of being hung, drawn and quartered by whoever wrote those threats, and even though it turned out I was being pursued by a fan-worshipping oriental, I was still frightened.' She began to poke her finger into his camel-coated chest. 'But *you* weren't sorry then, like *you* aren't sorry now. What concerns *you* is filthy lucre. *You* have no finer feelings. All *you* care about is taking the money and running!'

'*Wrong!*' he shot back, so fiercely that Neille jumped. His index finger was raised. 'I care about a lot of things, one of which happens to be *you*. That's why I'm not sorry, because without Walter Rice and his threats I'd never have met *you*.' Now Jack was emphasising with pokes. 'And *you* happen to be driving me crazy with unrequited lust. And *you* can damned well give me a kiss.'

Thrusting his hand to the back of her head, he grabbed her against him with such force that their mouths met in an abrupt fusion of heat, surprise and longing. Neille's eyelids fluttered closed. His fingers were gripped tight among the torrent of shiny hair, but after that first kiss imprisonment was unnecesary. Enchanted by the need in him, the taste of his mouth, the pressure of his lips, she welcomed this intrepid invasion. One kiss became two, three, four, each slightly gentler and more persuasive than the last. He was nibbling with a half-opened mouth, seducing her, taming her, letting her know who was the master. When eventually Jack raised his head, she drew in a breath which was not quite a cry, not quite a sigh. The chemistry of his kisses was potent. Neille wasn't sure how she came to be wrapped so slavishly around him, but, if she was driving him crazy, he had her completely bewitched.

'Don't stop,' she murmured.

'I'd better. Unless you want my neighbours complaining that we're causing a public disturbance.'

'I do.'

'You would.' He finally got around to unlocking the front door. 'Come inside. We'll continue our talk, have a drink and maybe . . . horizontal bliss?'

Neille went ahead of him into the living room furnished with cool blond wood and white carpets. Like his office, it was on the spartan side, but the bareness had been relieved by the deft deployment of plants. Busy Lizzies tumbled from hanging pots, ferns grew in corners, ivies fell from pine shelving.

'I thought if I wanted a little excitement I'd come to the wrong man,' she teased.

'You have.' He went into the kitchen. 'I intend to give you one hell of a lot of excitement. But all the things I said about Parisian frolics etc.,—well, I guess you must blame my hormones.' He stood in the doorway, smiling at her. 'I was so damned frustrated when you started belly-aching about keeping Lewis in the dark, that something inside of me exploded. Sunbeam, you were so bloody *insistent*.'

Neille's happiness nose-dived. How could she get involved with Jack while her 'good friend' hovered like an ominous shadow?

'I still am,' she muttered.

'But maybe everything changes on Friday?'

Her eyes opened wide. 'How do you know that?'

'I worked things out.' Jack appeared to have forgotten about organising drinks. 'Now I'm half-way to understanding about you and Lewis. Don't forget, I've spoken to your father.'

'But Daddy doesn't know about Friday, and he would never tell—' She bounced back like a wrestler off the ropes. 'You had no right to speak to him!'

'I had every right. I love you, that gives me the right. And you've been protecting him far too long.'

'Have I?' Neille was busily working through the implications. Jack had said he loved her, and that was wonderful, because she loved him. But . . . 'What did my father say?' she demanded.

'That he'd allowed you to cope with Lewis alone for far too long.'

'Cope with Lewis? He said that?' She frowned. 'But I thought——'

'You thought your father genuinely believed the pair of you were good friends, despite all the evidence to the contrary?' Jack shook his head. 'He told me he'd taken the coward's way out and paid lip service. That he preferred to pretend all was well between you and Lewis, rather than face up to the truth. And I suspect you did a little pretending of your own?'

'I did,' she admitted. 'Daddy likes life smooth. Ripples upset him, so I never said anything to rock the boat.'

'And you and Lewis drifted on?'

'I did try and swim for the shore once,' she said,

with a rueful smile. 'Remember I explained how the dates began at a time when I felt numb? That I'd sit in my private daze when he put the marketing world to rights? Well, obviously in time the numbness began to wear off and one evening, about a year ago, something went snap! I saw what I'd lumbered myself with and realised I couldn't take much more. When Lewis rang to fix the next date, I refused. He rang again, and I manufactured another excuse. And again. Then he spoke to my father at the office.'

'And he went to pieces?'

Neille nodded. 'He rushed home in a dither, demanding to know what had gone wrong. When I said that all that had happened was I'd decided to call it a day because we had nothing going for us, he pleaded with me to give it time. He refused to see any reason why the courtship shouldn't continue. Courtship!' she exclaimed. 'That was Lewis's term. But the whole thing had been so damned tepid. There'd been long gaps between dates and Lewis's idea of being ardent was the odd fumbled kiss, so I couldn't see what all the fuss was about. I told my father I wasn't interested in a courtship, that I just wanted out and no hard feelings, but—but——' Neille suddenly clammed up. She had been rambling on, explaining with no thought of discretion, and now she realised her mistake. Even if Jack *did* love her, and even if he *had* spoken to her father, by his own admission he was only half-way to understanding the situation. Was she at liberty to reveal the rest? She wanted to, very badly, but . . .

'Your father begged you to think again,' Jack told her. 'He was afraid that if you offended Lewis there might be reprisals. Yes,' he said, when she shot him a startled look, 'he didn't go into details over the phone, but he did refer to a crime he'd committed a long time ago which he felt, and still feels, Lewis might resurrect and use against him. He said you would explain.'

'Daddy gave permission?'

For years the secret had remained hidden in the dark corners of her father's mind—Neille herself had only been allowed access twelve months ago when she had tried to kick loose, and then only because Mr Trenchard had seen no alternative— yet now he had handed it to Jack as a gift.

'He did, but do you think we could leave your explanations for later?' He came forward to enfold her in his arms. 'It's time we went upstairs.'

'But you said we were going to have a talk, a drink, and——'

'You have a nasty habit of quoting what I say back to me,' he murmured, bending to kiss and then nibble at her ear lobe. 'Now I've discovered my priorities were wrong. The sequence has been changed, my darling Mongolian. Horizontal bliss come first, so will you kindly get upstairs?'

Neille did as she was told. The bedroom, like the rest of the house, was pale wood and white, and in need of a woman's touch. Not that she had much time to notice, because as she removed one of her layers of fur, so Jack decided he had better remove another. The fur, followed by the suede, and finally the leather, fell to the bedroom floor, and as each inch of exposed flesh was gilded with kisses, so her surroundings diminished into a hazy blur. A tremor rippled through her. All that mattered was this lovely man who was making the heat, such exquisite heat, begin to glow. His fingers on her skin had weighted her breasts with heavy languor, filled her blood with a throbbing urgency. No longer a glow, the heat began to smoulder as his kisses, at first gentle and seductive, became an impassioned searching which had her straining to respond.

'Oh!' Neille sucked in a breath as his lips brushed across a rose-brown nipple, stiffened with want. 'Oh!' she groaned again, as the warm moist tug of his mouth on her breast sent arrows of need shooting down. 'Oh, no!' she pleaded, as he left her. But he was quickly back, naked and muscled and eager for love.

'Hello,' Jack murmured, smiling into her eyes.

'Hello.'

'I love you,' he said, and began kissing her again, long lingering kisses.

'And I love you.'

His mouth moved to her breast again, his tongue capturing the rose-brown peak in a way which made her groan, had her back arching. From smouldering, she had burst into flame. Neille had never felt so tender, so aroused, so aware of herself as a woman designed to please a man. And such a wonderful man.

'Did you know the navel is this season's erogenous zone?' he enquired, kissing her stomach. He raised his eyes to grin. 'I read it in one of your fashion books.' Next Jack caressed her thigh. 'But how about here? And here, and——' There was a pause as his fingers slithered down. 'Here?'

'Yes, please yes.'

His mouth and his hands were shooting sparks in all directions. How could he give her so much pleasure, and how could she return it? She wanted to touch him like he was touching her, run her hands over his shoulders, his back, through his hair. Close her fingers around the proud male muscles.

'Oh, sunbeam,' he moaned, as she began her exploration.

Jack's body was lean and hard, his skin glistening with a faint sheen. He lay still while she rubbed her mouth against the curly black hair on his chest, then moved, trapping her beneath him. They kissed and fondled and whispered words of love. Neille's hips began to move, she could not stop them, and when he thrust his thigh between hers she abandoned herself to the pulsing rhythm of love. He came into her.

'Oh!' Neille was whimpering again, filled with incandescent delight.

He slid deep, then pulled back. She teetered on a trembling edge—wanting, wanting, wanting. Deeper he thrust. A pause. Another tremblingly delicious edge. Then deeper still. Her head turned wildly on the pillow. She gasped, clutching his shoulders as her desire unleashed into desperate need. Music pounded in her ears, filled her veins as Jack thrust again and again, lifting her to a climax as overwhelming and dramatic as a Sibelius symphony.

CHAPRER TEN

JACK grinned over the top of his glass of champagne. 'I suppose now I'm expected to marry you?'

'Who says I'll have you?' she enquired, her blue eyes sparkling.

'Will you?'

Neille sipped, wrinkling her nose against the ping of the bubbles. 'I might, if you ask nicely.'

'Please, my darling Nellie, will you marry me?'

She put down her champagne, to cuddle close. 'Yes, my darling Jackson, I will.' Kisses replaced Moët et Chandon. 'After all, I've grown accustomed to your face.'

'How about growing accustomed to my body?' he enquired, with a mock leer. He nuzzled her bare shoulder. 'Say the word and I'll take you on a second guided tour. Sorry, third tour.'

'The word.'

Jack laughed. 'You're insatiable, which makes two of us. Yet maybe it would be wise to have a few minutes respite and recharge the batteries?'

She made big eyes. 'But you said——'

'Bug off,' he replied, rubbing the tip of his nose against hers. He settled back on the pillow, his arm around her. 'How about explaining what it was your father did which gives Lewis his hold? And don't you dare quote back at me that I said no questions earlier. I'm not perfect.'

'Yes, you are.' Neille threw him a sidelong

glance. 'No, you're not. Did you really have to nail me to the wall over Simon in such a brutal manner?'

The arm around her tightened. 'I could see no alternative. I expect you went home and cried, but——'

'I did, for two hours.'

'Forgive me?' he pleaded. 'But as I saw it, confronting the past in one fell swoop was by far preferable to being asked picky little questions over a drawn-out period, and I needed to know. Despite my accusations, I was aware you didn't give a damn about Lewis's money so I couldn't understand what tied you to him. I thought that if you told me about your relationship with Simon I'd find the key. I didn't. There didn't seem to be any common factor. Simon was like a rocket, shooting off into space, whereas Mr Mitchell comes over as an armoured tank.' Jack handed her her champagne glass and reached for his own. 'And your father's scared of being flattened?'

She nodded and took a sip of champagne. 'You remember I told you how my mother was ill for a full year before she died, and how all that time she'd been looked after by a private nurse? Well, those were the early days in Daddy's career when he didn't earn much, and private care is expensive. My mother should've gone into hospital, but apparently she had one of those irrational fears that if she was admitted she would never come out again, so she made Daddy promise she could stay at home. Because he doted on her and could never refuse her anything, he agreed.'

Jack kissed her shoulder. 'I can understand how he felt.'

'You're nice,' she smiled, then returned to her tale. 'My mother wasn't expected to survive for very long when the nurse was initially engaged so Daddy intended to finance the care from their savings; then she established herself on a plateau. Very quickly the savings ran out. Anything which could raise a few pounds, he sold, and all other expenses were trimmed to the bone, but it wasn't enough. Next Mooie and Uncle Ken contributed, and other members of the family, but as the months went by so that money disappeared. Daddy began to panic. He decided he would have to approach old Mr Mitchell for a loan. He'd worked in the accounts section for eight years, never once been late, never had time off sick, and had contributed hours and hours of unpaid overtime, but he met with an out-of-hand dismissal.' Neille sighed. 'Lewis's father regarded himself as a benevolent boss, but in reality he was as indifferent to his employees as his son. So my father didn't know where to turn.'

'Why didn't he borrow money from a bank?'

'I don't know. Obviously he wasn't thinking straight. He's not very good at keeping a cool head under pressure.'

'Difficult for anyone if their wife's dying at home,' Jack mused.

'Yes, but—well, my father was so aggrieved by Mr Mitchell's lack of compassion that he decided to borrow the money from the company secretly.'

'You mean he cooked the books?'

'Yes, but he was only *borrowing*,' she stressed. 'An insurance policy had been taken out to cover my mother's life, so two thousand pounds was due at her death. Daddy invented a make-believe firm which was supposed to supply Mitchells' with textiles, and paid money to them which he pocketed. In turn, he doled it out in wages to the nurse. He kept strict records, only took exactly what was needed, not a penny more, and set everything against the insurance policy.'

'But that was one hell of a risk!' Jack exclaimed.

'Not so much as you'd imagine, apparently. Mitchells' accounting system at the time was a cumbersome affair and whatever my father's other failings, he's smart with figures. According to him, inventing the false company and including it in the paperwork was easy.'

'So where did he go wrong?'

'By taking too much. You see, my mother clung on and on and the nursing costs soared way above the sum of the policy. After her death Daddy received the pay out and fed it back into Mitchells', but was still left with a hefty sum outstanding. He scrimped and saved, and over the next months paid back all he possibly could from his salary. He was within less than a hundred pounds of being in the clear when——' Neille let out a breath. 'Walter Rice spotted the textile firm.'

'And all hell was let loose?'

'With a vengeance! My father was marched off to see old Mr Mitchell, who ranted on about theft and embezzlement, which to be fair it was, and said he intended to inform the police. Daddy tried to explain how he'd been out of his mind with worry, and that all he owed now was less than a measly hundred, and at length Mr Mitchell agreed to reconsider. The matter was left in abeyance for a month.'

Jack winced. 'While your father sweated it out?'

'He said that month was sheer murder,' she agreed. 'He turned pale even telling me about it. However, the upshot was that Mr Mitchell agreed no action would be taken, in view of Daddy's promise to pay back the remaining amount within weeks.'

'But I don't see the connection with Lewis. All this happened twenty years ago when he'd have been a schoolboy. He wouldn't have been involved.'

'No, but Daddy *knows* Lewis knows about him taking the money. The ledgers which include entries of the textile firm remain stored in Mitchells' basement, and he's convinced Lewis is keeping them there on purpose.' She shifted uneasily on the pillow. 'Lewis resents criticism, and there've been episodes in the past involving his staff when he's been actively vindictive as a result of someone putting him down. That's where my dilemma springs from. If I cross him by ending our relationship myself, there's the possibility he might react by resurrecting Daddy's falsification of the accounts.'

'But a court case'd be impossible after all this time,' Jack protested.

'It wouldn't need to be that. Lewis could dismiss him and spread enough rumours to ensure he couldn't find another job.'

'I don't know why your father didn't leave Mitchells' long ago.'

Neille sighed. 'Because he doesn't like change, because he was afraid to disturb the status quo. Even now his attitude towards Lewis is two-edged. He's frightened of what he might do and yet he admires him for the successes he's made at Mitchells'. But even if Daddy was sacked, it's not

so much finding another job which would matter
so much as the strain he'd be placed under. His life
would become a misery.'

'And to protect him from that, you chose to
appear in saucy underwear.' It was a statement of
fact. 'I suspected you of having qualms about
playing the *risquée* lady all along.' Jack's brow
furrowed. 'How high do you rate your chances of
goading Lewis into giving you your walking
papers?'

'They tend to fluctuate,' she confessed, feeling
her heart plunge. 'But whenever I've dared reveal
an extra bare inch in the past Lewis has done
nothing but grumble.'

'The man must be mad,' he murmured, and
lowered the sheet which had been tucked around
her in order to plant a kiss between her breasts.

'The photographs should convince him I'm not
suited to be a future Mrs Mitchell,' Neille insisted,
a little breathlessly.

'I've been convinced of that for ages. The
future Mrs Rea—yes. Mitchell?' Jack turned up
his nose. 'Out of the question. And what's
supposed to happen if this stunt of your falls
flat? The next logical step would seem to be a
centrefold in *Penthouse*, but you can scrap that,
my darling. As from this minute nude poses are
for my eyes only.'

'Yes, Jack,' Neille said obediently, her eyes
dancing. Then her expression became grave. 'But
my stunt won't fall flat. It mustn't!'

'Are you *sure* Lewis is aware of your father's . . .
lapse?' he questioned. 'It seems a long shot that
old man Mitchell would tell a schoolboy, and as
the debt was insignificant isn't there a good chance

of it having been forgotten by the time Lewis joined the business?'

'Ye-s, I suppose so.' She was doubtful. 'And no, I personally am not sure. Lewis has never hinted about the lapse to me. It's just that Daddy regards the fact he's not been made a member of the board as proof positive that he's regarded as suspect. Normally the chief accountant is offered a directorship as standard procedure,' she explained.

'But maybe he isn't a director because he's not a decisions man, or simply because he's too old?'

'It's possible,' Neille agreed, displaying little conviction. She changed course. 'What's been arranged about your company and Mitchells' security business?'

'I've given notice that we're pulling out. Pity, but—well. There'll be other chances. I'm meeting Lewis on Friday afternoon, just to square matters.'

'Friday afternoon? Perhaps by then he'll have declared me kaput?' she said hopefully.

'Perhaps. Apart from this gradual striptease, what else have you done to persuade him he's best rid of you? Picked your nose, drunk from the finger bowl, answered back?'

'Not the first two, but I confess to trying with the third. But Lewis is so thick-skinned it's unbelievable. Also I've spent hours gabbling on about how serious relationships don't interest me, how——'

'No? Just wait until I have that wedding ring on your finger, my gorgeous Nellie; you'll change your tune.'

'Yes, Jack,' she murmured, as he kissed her. '*And* how I value my freedom,' she continued, when they surfaced. 'I even vowed my intention of cycling around the world, but it went straight over his head.'

'Maybe he thought you were playing hard to get?'

'It's possible.' Neille sighed. 'I've tried being flippant, I've tried being brusque, but nothing's penetrated. But, then, I've never dared go *too* far.'

'You haven't stamped on his ego with both feet, like you've stamped on mine?' He warded off a dig in the ribs. 'And Lewis still believes he's courting you?'

''Fraid so. But he'll change his mind on Friday when he opens his morning newspaper.' She gave Jack a look, suddenly stricken. 'If the gods are with me.'

Whether or not the gods were with her, the press did their bit. On Friday, when she saw the spread she had been granted, Neille was jubilant. For once she actually *liked* the media, for there were illustrated articles on three different women's pages and four quarter-page advertisements inserted by the fashion house. Open a newspaper, and there she was. Lewis just had to sit up, take notice, and topple backwards in horror.

Modelling assignments kept her busy from nine until mid-afternoon, and then she dashed home and waited. Surely he would ring? When the phone remained silent, she submitted to the strain. She prepared a cup of coffee and let it go cold. She dashed upstairs and forgot why. Tights were washed and left in the bowl. A second cup of coffee was percolated and neglected. Neille assembled a vast salad, then remembered her father was attending an accountants' soirée and would not be home until eleven. Well, Jack would be round. He'd promised to come round. He could eat the salad. She couldn't eat anything, not until Lewis called. And interspersed with all her rushing around were quick reassuring peeks at the newspapers. Yes, she did look sexy. Yes, that was a nipple shaded beneath white lace. Yes, the Montmartre shot did have an air of 'come up and see me sometime'. But the phone remained silent.

When the doorbell buzzed at six o'clock, she flew.

'Oh Jack, thank goodness you're here,' she babbled, covering him with grateful kisses. 'Do you want some salad? Lewis hasn't rung. Maybe he hasn't seen the papers? I mean, if he had he'd have rung already, wouldn't he? Or would he? Suppose he's seen them and he doesn't care?' Neille clung on to his arm as he steered her into the living room. 'You were with him this afternoon, did he say anything?'

'Nothing. After all it *was* a business meeting. And a stuffed shirt like Lewis is hardly going to discuss his personal likes and dislikes with someone he's only met once.'

'But what did he look like—disgruntled?'

Jack shook his head. 'Cool, calm and collected.'

She groaned. 'Couldn't you have slipped a mention of my photographs into the conversation?'

'I suppose I could, but I deliberately didn't. The impetus to drop you must come totally from Lewis himself. You wouldn't want him to suspect a put-up job?'

'No, but if he hasn't even seen the photographs and he still intends to propose——' Her voice began to waver. 'What do I do?'

'You say "no"—loud and clear. Because the photographs don't matter.'

'But——'

'No buts, just listen.' Jack dropped on to the sofa and pulled her down on to his knee. 'In winding up our business, Lewis and I discussed the mayhem that Walter Rice had created, and I said I felt your father had probably suffered more than anyone. It was not a chance observation, I'd said it in the hope of drawing Lewis out, and it worked. We talked on and he revealed two things.' Jack held up a finger. 'One, hard-working and devoted to his work as your father is, Lewis doesn't consider him suitable for the cut and thrust of the board, and two——' Another finger was raised. 'That in his opinion you father could be trusted with the Crown Jewels.'

Neille smiled delightedly. 'You are clever,' she said, hugging him.

'Einstein almost, but there's more. When I gave him my résumé of the past month, I explained that certain security aspects of his stores required attention. One was the risk of fire. I suggested we should go down to the basement where I'd point out prime examples. Earlier I'd been down there with my guards,' Jack explained, 'so I was able to march straight to a store, fling wide the door and denounce it as a tinder box. I wasn't that far wrong as it happens, though maybe I did do some acting. I told Lewis that one dropped cigarette end would have the files and ledgers which were crammed in there bursting into flame.'

'And what was his reaction?' she asked, when he broke off to grin.

'To declare the entire collection obsolete. He

checked the dates, discovered they covered a period between eighteen and twenty-five years ago, and said he'd no idea why such ancient ledgers should have kept. Obviously it was an oversight. At the clap of his hands a storeman came running, and before we'd even left the basement the shelves were half empty and a bonfire was blazing in an incinerator.'

'Oh, Jack.' Weak with relief, Neille rested her head on his shoulder. 'You've solved all my problems—and Daddy's. There's only one word to describe you.'

'Pachyderm?' he suggested.

'Wonderful.'

He grinned. 'Suppose we settle for wonderful pachyderm?'

'Right.' She gave him several grateful kisses, then smiled up. 'Shall we go to bed, my wonderful pachyderm? The champagne is already on ice.'

Jack groaned. 'My God! Feminism strikes again. Aren't I supposed to do the seducing?'

'You did it on Tuesday, Wednesday, Thursday, so now it's my turn. And it's not feminism.' She dug him in the ribs. 'It's a healthy sex drive, zonko.'

'I believe you. And I'd love to go to bed, but what about eating that salad?'

She gave him her wholesome *ingénue* smile. 'What salad? I don't know anything about a salad.'

'I bet.' He tilted his head. 'Isn't that the phone?'

In the two seconds it needed to reach the receiver, Neille's mood went topsy-turvy. From being warm and happy, suddenly she was quaking. In her head she knew Jack had eradicated Lewis

Mitchell as a threat, yet in her heart she was scared. The habit of a year was hard to break.

'H-hello?' she stammered.

'Lewis here,' her caller announced, in a brisker than usual staccato. 'Sorry, but this evening's impossible. A friend's flown in from Australia, a lady friend. Should have mentioned this Monday, but I forgot. Met Fiona while I was out there and teamed up. Instant attraction. Hope you don't mind, but plenty more fish in the sea. You're a pretty girl, you'll soon find someone else. Don't fret.'

'I won't,' she inserted, grinning at Jack, who had his ear pressed against the receiver.

'Join a club or two,' Lewis stampeded on. 'Take up golf.'

'Golf?' Jack mouthed soundlessly, rolling his eyes.

'I can give you an introduction to a decent course, but then again, perhaps you want to go cycling around the world? Well, I can't wait two years to raise a family. Need heirs. Owe it to Mitchells'. Business must come first. Chin up, Neille. Your turn will come. Prince Charming might just be around the corner.'

'Possible,' she agreed, digging Prince Charming in the ribs. Prince Charming groaned.

'Well, goodbye.' Lewis had reached the end of his appointed piece.

'Goodbye.'

Down went the phone.

'What a load of unadulterated——'

'Language, Jackson,' she cut in grinning. 'And don't we make a splendid pair? You take away his left arm crutch, *I* take away the right.'

'There's only one word to describe you.'

'Brilliant?' Neille suggested, unable to keep from smiling.

'Cruel. Not to Lewis, to me,' Jack said, when she gazed at him in surprise. 'Hell, your daily production of freelance insults, all geared to crush the unsuspecting male, was bad enough, but now you constantly inflict bodily pain. I must be a mass of bruises.' He heaved a loud and theatrical sigh, and walked to the stairs. 'I wouldn't be at all surprised if your next act is to flatten me.' He grinned and held out a hand. 'What do you think, my darling Nellie?'

She joined him, face flushed with love. 'I think, my wonderful pachyderm, there's a distinct possibility you could be right.'

MILLS & BOON®

In Sultry New Orleans,
Passion and Scandal are...

Unmasked

Mills & Boon are delighted to bring you a star studded
line-up of three internationally renowned authors in one
compelling volume—

Janet Dailey
Elizabeth Gage
Jennifer Blake

Set in steamy, sexy New Orleans, this fabulous collection of
three contemporary love stories centres around one magical
night—the annual masked ball.

Disguised as legendary lovers, the elite of New Orleans are
seemingly having the times of their lives.
Guarded secrets remain hidden—until midnight...
when *everyone* must unmask...

Available: August 1997   Price: £4.99

JASMINE CRESSWELL

Internationally-acclaimed Bestselling Author

SECRET SINS

The rich are different—they're deadly!

Judge Victor Rodier is a powerful and
dangerous man. At the age of twenty-seven,
Jessica Marie Pazmany is confronted with
terrifying evidence that her real name is
Liliana Rodier. A threat on her life prompts
Jessica to seek an appointment with her
father—a meeting she may live to regret.

**AVAILABLE IN PAPERBACK
FROM JULY 1997**

ERICA SPINDLER

Bestselling Author of *Forbidden Fruit*

FORTUNE

BE CAREFUL WHAT YOU WISH FOR...
IT JUST MIGHT COME TRUE

Skye Dearborn's wishes seem to be coming true, but will Skye's new life prove to be all she's dreamed of—or a nightmare she can't escape?

"A high adventure of love's triumph over twisted obsession."

—*Publishers Weekly*

"Give yourself plenty of time, and enjoy!"

—*Romantic Times*

MIRA

**AVAILABLE IN PAPERBACK
FROM JULY 1997**

Barbara DELINSKY

THROUGH MY EYES

A Friend in Need...
is a whole lot of trouble!

Jill Moncrief had to face painful memories to
help a friend in trouble. Hot-shot attorney Peter
Hathaway was just the man she needed—but
the last man on earth she should want...

**AVAILABLE IN PAPERBACK
FROM JULY 1997**

SANDRA BROWN

ABOVE & BEYOND

Who would have believed that a man like Trevor could fall in love with a woman he'd never seen—just by reading the salvaged letters of his best friend. But how was Trevor going to tell Kyla exactly who he was?

"One of fiction's brightest stars!"
—Dallas Morning News

BARBARA BRETTON

Guilty

PLEASURES

Beauty is only skin deep.
But it holds a multitude of sins...

Lily Spaulding and Cory Prescott are two strong,
proud women with a lifetime of mistakes between
them. *Guilty Pleasures* is the story of one woman's
struggle to create a cosmetics empire and of the
daughter she was forced to leave behind—who now
seeks revenge on the mother who abandoned her.

*"Bretton's Characters are always real, and their
conflicts believable"*

—Chicago Sun Times

**AVAILABLE IN PAPERBACK
FROM JUNE 1997**

New York Times bestselling author
of *Class Reunion*

RONA
JAFFE

The COUSINS

"*Rona Jaffe's storytelling is irresistible.*"
—Los Angeles Times

"*...a page-turner all the way.*"
—Cosmopolitan

**A sweeping saga of family loyalties
and disloyalties, choices and
compromises, destruction and survival.**

MIRA®

AVAILABLE IN PAPERBACK
FROM JUNE 1997

NEW YORK TIMES
BESTSELING AUTHOR

Anne
Mather

Dangerous Temptation

He was desperate to remember... Jake wasn't sure why he'd agreed to take his twin brother's place on the flight to London. But when he awakens in hospital after the crash, he can't even remember his own name or the beautiful woman who watches him so guardedly. Caitlin. His wife.

She was desperate to forget... Her husband seems like a stranger to Caitlin—a man who assumes there is love when none exists. He is totally different—like the man she'd thought she had married. Until his memory returns. And with it, a danger that threatens them all.

"Ms. Mather has penned a wonderful romance."
—Romantic Times

MIRA

AVAILABLE IN PAPERBACK
FROM MAY 1997

Penny Jordan

New York Times bestselling author of
Power Play and *Cruel legacy*

POWER GAMES

The arrival of a mysterious woman threatens
a son's manipulative hold over his
millionaire father in PENNY JORDAN'S
latest blockbuster—a supercharged tale of
family rivalries

**AVAILABLE IN PAPERBACK
FROM APRIL 1997**